THE KASSINI DIVISION

ESA ORTEGA

Ebook ISBN: 978-1-8384424-0-8

www.esaortega.com

Cover design and typestting by Cuppatwo

Published by Sleeper Agency Books

For the space dogs

"Little though they seemed to think of it, the people of this twenty-ninth century live continually in fairyland. Surfeited as they are with marvels, they are indifferent in the presence of each new marvel."

IN THE YEAR 2889, JULES VERNE (1889)

CONTENTS

0. PROLOGUE

Light from the distant sun framed its elongated spearhead-shaped outline as the freighter adjusted its course, angling its nose towards the spin point in the outlying system of Arik-Leven, on the Empire's western fringe. A typical cargo haulier from the Aldebaran shipyards, at around 250 metres in length, the hulking freighter was a giant of the spacelanes purpose-designed for a life of long-haul multi-spin journeys between the outer and inner colony worlds of human-occupied territory.

As the ship rotated along its axis like some ponderous deep-sea leviathan and inclined towards a new bearing, its stylish, crisp white logo glinted against the backdrop of its grey armour. The 20-metre-tall lettering spelt out 'ATE', for 'Aldebaran Tentacled Exotica', along its port bow; beneath it, a smaller slogan in a stylised handwritten flourish read 'From the seas to the stars'. Beneath that, the name of the ship, the *Hildegard*, was picked out in the Empire's regulation ship-ID font.

There was nothing unusual about ATE operating a freighter out here in the shadow of ghost space, even though it was a regularly contested system on a renowned pirate route that only seemed to be getting livelier of late.

There was nothing particularly untoward, either, about the two diminutive single-person interceptors flying ahead of the *Hildegard* in a loose defensive formation. ATE had cornered their market decades ago and had long branched out beyond the merely tentacled to become one of the premium seafood brands in the Empire's sprawl. Rich, recession-proof corporations regularly sent a light fighter escort to protect their cargo. Once you got to the level of their operation, it made sense to scale back on the expense of heavily weaponising transport ships and instead entrust your security to a wing of fighters that could be redeployed across the fleet at will.

Hence the regulation two-person crew that currently occupied the freighter's bridge: no offensive shipside weaponry enabled a skeleton staff – one a pilot, one an engineer/all-rounder – and the kind of spaceports ATE shipped to were fully automated with a complement of bespoke droids to take care of unloading and reloading. The *Hildegard's* was a mindnumbingly routine run and its crews, overqualified but seduced by the excellent salary, invariably ended up desperate for a bit of adventure to escape the monotony… which was why the Federation had chosen it.

No, for something out of the ordinary about this picture, you had to zoom into the *Hildegard's* cargo hold.

"This is still spooking me, Luce," said Malfi, the *Hildegard's* pilot, as he final-checked a readout overlaid on the flight deck's display. He rubbed his eyes as he flicked the auto switch to let the ship's nav computer deal with the flight plan to the spin point. "Admit you're tense. Even a tiny bit."

Lucia Ortiz put her tablet down with an annoyed clunk, puffed out her cheeks and took a deep breath. For such a clumsy giant of a man, Malfi certainly spent a lot of his time perfecting his impression of a timid little bird. And he was a Zero-G Olympic-level catastrophiser to boot – she wondered how he'd ever convinced himself to sign up for a sensitive, classified cargo run like this in the first place.

"Gods, we've been through this," she sighed. "Whatever's in the hold, it's not our problem. You know the score, Malfi… we just stick to the script when we get to the station at Alexar. We drop the cargo, collect the Cees, disappear into the shadows for a few days, then return this crate, just like we always do."

"All fine and dandy," Malfi said, bringing up an image of the spin point on the main screen. "Except where are all the ships?"

"I dunno," Lucia said disinterestedly, glancing away from the screen and locking eyes with the pilot. He was perma-sweaty even though he'd insisted on the climate control being chillier than she'd normally like. "Given that we're carrying their top-secret shit for them, maybe the Feds have redirected the traffic in the sector? Anyway, no ships at the spin point just gets us there quicker. No queues is good news, right?"

"It's suspiciously quiet, that's what it is," said Malfi, pointedly ignoring her forced chirpiness. His dilated pupils fixed on the scope's readings of the space around them.

"Look, what's really bothering you, Malfi? We've got two interceptors as escort and three Fed marines sat in the hold, protecting their precious crate. If the worst comes to the worst, we just sit back and let the bugfuckers down there deal with it."

"Don't call them that," whispered Malfi. "The company records everything. Doesn't make us look particularly smart."

"I don't want to be smart," said Lucia. "I want to be rich."

Just as she was musing to herself about why exactly the spin point was so deserted, two dots pinged on the edges of their scope.

"There you go, Malf – ships. You feel less lonely out here now?"

They watched as the dots in the centre of the scope representing their fighter escort suddenly peeled off in the direction of the new arrivals. Malfi shifted his bodyweight in alarm to look out of the control room's starboard viewport. He was in time to see the sleek, triangular-hulled interceptors' blue engines flare as the ships arrowed into the darkness and noticed they were flying in close formation. He jabbed at the button on the console to activate the encrypted close-circuit comms channel the company had set up.

"Patrol, this is the *Hildegard*. You know, the ship you're meant to be escorting... where are you going in such a hurry?" he asked nervously. They listened to the open channel but apart from a vague burst of static that could've been background radiation, there was no response. "Are their comms down, or are they ignoring us?" asked Malfi, sweat beginning to darken the armpits of his cream-coloured ATE overalls. "Now I'm starting to shit it."

"Hmm. I think you may have a point," admitted Lucia. "Computer, who are they?"

"These ships have no transponders," the emotionless, faintly vocoded voice of the *Hildegard's* onboard computer replied. "Their origin is therefore unknown."

Lucia frowned as she manually engaged the ship's sensor arrays, probing the controls to see if she could secure anything visual. The scope blipped quietly but more insistently, to indicate that the two inbound ships were closing on them. They could see the craft were separating out to counter the defensive formation of the freighter's fighter escort, but the best image of them she could muster was from a shaky and grainy long-range feed. Hardly ideal, but she put it in a window on the main screen anyway. As they manipulated the image, they could tell the incoming ships were oval-shaped and around twice the size of the company's interceptors. The clearest of the briefly camera-locked close-ups they could secure revealed what looked like a slightly eerie writhing effect on their surface that could possibly have been down to interference on the lo-res camera. *Possibly...*

"Okay, computer, what about their drive signatures?" asked Malfi.

"Incomplete data."

"C'mon, computer, we've been through this," he snapped. "Incomplete data is not an answer. What's your best guess? Most likely origin of ships? Extrapolate from all available sources."

There was a short pause while the computer accessed and sifted through unfamiliar databanks.

"Alien," said the computer, finally, as the oval ships abruptly disappeared from the visual feed.

"Fuck," said Malfi and Lucia in unison.

The access door at the far end of the bridge swished open. They were joined on the freighter's spacious command deck by a Federation marine, evidently stirred enough by recent developments to make the short trip up from the lower section of the ship. He seated himself behind the crew, forcing them to swivel petulantly on their chairs to face him.

"Ah, Sergeant Abraxa," said Malfi, reading off of the bulky clean-shaven marine's namebadge, voice croaking as it hovered on the cusp of panic. "You're here." The pilot rubbed his face frantically with his hands.

"Someone's interested in your cargo, it seems," said Lucia. "The computer thinks they're non-human."

"Marvellous," said Abraxa, looking past them at the main screen. "How are the fighters doing?"

"They're engaging," said Malfi, eyes glued to the scope. "We've lost their comms so we can't listen in… the scope is all we've got."

They sat in silence for 30 seconds or so, watching the four rudimentary icons dance on the screen. It didn't take long before the twin fighter icons illuminated briefly, then changed from green to grey. It was over quickly, most likely missile strikes. "Shit," said sergeant Abraxa, more to himself than the room.

"Grey dots are not a good sign, I take it," Lucia said, rhetorically.

"Listen to me," said the sergeant. "Obviously this is no coincidence and they know about the cargo – gods know how. And they aren't fucking around. That means we may – *may* – have company. I've just alerted my squad, so if we need to repel boarders, we will."

"You sound pretty confident," Lucia replied.

"I would not be risking my ass on this crate protecting the likes of you if I wasn't," said the sergeant, looking at the cringing figure of Malfi dismissively. "I have two marines trained for close-quarters combat and a battle droid specifically designed for it." Looking directly at Lucia, Abraxa spat bitterly: "Us 'bugfuckers' are here to protect you, and we will. It'll all be okay."

Malfi and Lucia exchanged glances. "Sorry about that," said the engineer. "No offence, it's just…"

"None fucking taken," sighed Abraxa. "I want you two to stay here and pilot this ship to its destination. Whatever happens in the next hour, no moving from this cockpit. No bright ideas, no running round the ship waving fire extinguishers around, no heroics. Clear?"

"Clear," they both replied, backs stiffening in their seats.

"Right," Abraxa nodded, seemingly satisfied. "You can watch along on the ship's security feed. Just keep us flying in a nice smooth trajectory, and we'll deal with these assholes if we have to."

"Shouldn't we send an SOS packet to HQ?" Lucia asked.

"I already tried," the sergeant replied. "No dice. The ships are jamming our comms, even on restricted military channels, never mind your corporate ones. And when they get in range, they're likely to disable the ship's power systems and drive, at least temporarily."

"The power and drive? How?"

"If they're aliens, how am I supposed to know what tech they got? Boarding assault is always the same no matter which race is doing it – eliminate the escort, jam the FTL, disable the systems, board the ship."

"You've dealt with this before?" Malfi asked hopefully.

"Not in real life," said the sergeant. "I've read about it, run the sims."

"How did *that* go?"

"Honestly, not well. Even with a droid, we're probably outnumbered, and heavy ordnance isn't a good idea aboard a ship."

"You need to work on your bedside manner, Abraxa," said Lucia, and then more tentatively: "It's got to be the cargo that they want, like you say. Couldn't we just jettison it? At least we'd all live to fight another day."

"Not an option," said Abraxa, shutting down that avenue. "As far as the Empire's concerned, it's more valuable than we are – we aren't just hauling squid. Plus, if we surrender, there's a strong chance they'd kill us anyway, to cover their tracks. That way, none of us gets paid."

The computer's affectless voice broadcast over the bridge. "Intervention from the incoming vessels is disrupting my systems. Attempts to counteract it have failed. All drive systems including FTL are inoperable until further notice. I am re-routing remaining power to essential functions and switching to silent running."

The lights on the bridge dimmed dramatically as the *Hildegard* lost power. Its deceleration, though imperceptible to the crew's senses, was confirmed by the readouts.

Abraxa headed for the door. "Here we go," he called over his shoulder. "Do as I told you and you'll be okay."

Bad Sounds To Hear In Space, numbers #45 and #46, respectively… the resonant clunk of four heavy landing feet attaching magnetically to the outside of your hull, followed moments later by the sickening scream of mining lasers carving a crudely circular entryway through your ship's armour plating.

The security feed showed Abraxa and his two marines in cover in a defensive position. They were behind the sturdy frame of an airlock-style sealing hatch designed to prevent atmosphere escape or curtail the spread of shipboard fires. Hovering in front of them was their battle droid, a gleaming white sphere with two cannons protuding on stalks from its otherwise featureless chassis. A pinpoint blue light roved coolly from side to side across its metre-wide body.

Lucia cycled through the cameras to the other end of the corridor running between the outer hull and the ship's drive room. Around 30 metres from Abraxa's squad and the white droid's position, framed by the jagged remains of the *Hildegard's* hull, was a second battle droid. Almost the mirror image of Abraxa's unit in terms of design, this one was a giant by comparison. Around double the size, its scarred and charred chassis was as black as a starless night and its eye sensor traded the icy blue for a demonic red.

"Wait, isn't that a *Federation* droid?" Malfi pointed out.

"Definitely, it looks like one of their security units – almost the same as Abraxa's, only bigger. What the hell is going on?"

They were interrupted by the sound of Abraxa's battle droid making the first move, engaging its anti-grav with a sudden burst of thrumming resonance. Lucia switched the feed back to it just in time for them to witness a volley burst of cannon fire from the dark droid slamming into it, incinerating its white carapace. The shot was a bullseye. The white droid caroomed into the ship's reinforced steel wall before plunging to the floor with an echoing crunch, its anti-grav unit temporarily out of action. As the dark droid switched focus and began to lay down covering fire to hem Abraxa and his huddled team in their position, a third droid – humanoid this time, but with a vaguely insectile gait – seized its moment to clank down from the shadows high up on the ceiling of the corridor like some giant mechanical gecko. The new unit crouched over the damaged white battle droid and plugged some kind of appendage into it: immediately, a surge of crackling electricity spread out across the stricken sphere's front as it lolled on the ground.

"What is that thing up to?" asked Lucia, then jumped as the white droid's anti-grav unit came back online.

"I think that spindly thing just *resurrected* it," said Malfi. The white droid, now back online and rebooted into action, hovered into line behind the other two droids, apparently now somehow influenced by the humanoid unit to obey it.

"Ah fuck," said Malfi. "This isn't looking good."

The dark sphere took point and advanced up the corridor towards the soldiers' entrenched position. It soaked up the largely accurate but ineffectual fire from Abraxa and his team. Still returning fire with their beam weaponry, the three droids formed a pyramid-shaped defensive wall as they moved steadily forward, the white droid now hovering above the other two at ground level. As they did so, Lucia focused in on the makeshift airlock where two suited-up soldiers had cautiously emerged.

One was human-sized and moved with a cautious, military bearing. In contrast, the other was tall and lithe, and bounded down the corridor with an inhuman grace to catch up with the droids in only a few strides. The two crouched behind the mechs to form a phalanx, adding bursts of firepower from their sidearms to the suppression as they advanced.

The now droidless Abraxa signalled to his team to fall back, but as he did so, the lead droid fired a small grenade into their position. Detonating in a blinding flash and with a thump that reverberated throughout the ship, it sent the Fed troops sprawling messily out of their cover. With their enemies disorientated and exposed on the corridor's floor, the two soldiers now broke rank and rushed past their defensive shield of droids. In seconds, they were on their human counterparts, quickly overpowering Abraxa's colleagues and pinning them to the floor.

To Malfi and Lucia watching on from the bridge, it was all over in a blur. The incoming troops unceremoniously knocked the marines unconscious with the butts of their sidearms. They immediately began hauling their motionless bodies back along the corridor towards the *Hildegard's* cargo hold, leaving Abraxa alone. He was swiftly disarmed by the insectile unit.

The sergeant didn't struggle as he was made to kneel on the floor, hands behind his head. Instead, he looked up at the nearest security camera and flicked his head in the universal 'get the fuck out of there' gesture. One of the troops soon returned for the sergeant. This was the cue for the droids to split up and head in opposite directions – the two spheres escorting the troops back in the direction of the cargo bay and the humanoid one setting off in a bounding run towards the bridge.

That was all the encouragement Malfi and Lucia needed to cut their losses and make for the nearest shuttle, two corridors over from the flight module. But they barely made it through the door before they were confronted by the modular, insectile unit blocking their path.

Startled, the pair flinched and closed their eyes involuntarily as the droid levelled its arm-mounted cannons at their heads and scanned them. Up close, it was a weird-looking model – opening their eyes tentatively again, they glanced down to see something sprayed in red on its chest, obscured by a metal box, next to a stencilled number '.14'. "I think you two lovebirds better scuttle for the shuttle!" the droid blurted suddenly, in a strange, high-pitched old-time voice. It then stood aside to let the confused pair run past it to the safety of the emergency shuttle.

The droid tilted a sensor stalk back down the corridor and listened as the lumbering Malfi and the much more nimble Lucia dived headlong into the shuttle entrance, falling over each other in a clatter of tangled limbs.

The droid stepped over to a communications console and manipulated the controls rapidly with the fingers of one hand, opening a local channel. Its modulated voice intoned from somewhere on its chrome body. "This vessel is secured, all personnel have been restrained and no other crew detected. Krieger, suggest you transfer those marines to the secondary escape pod at the rear of the ship and launch it before they regain consciousness."

"Confirmed," came the static-laced reply.

"I'll wipe our new battle-droid friend's memory later," the droid replied, shutting off the comms link and moving over to the computer's main console. "I am just an invention of your over-active imagination," it continued quietly to nobody in particular as it shut off the communications system. Next, it plugged in a snaking cable from the unit it had used to take control of the battle droid, overriding the computer's security and restoring the ship's power and drive systems. The shuttle containing the panicking crew ejected from the *Hildegard*, a silent dart flung into the hostile void. The craft was programmed to drift to the nearest spaceport, at the mercy of the solar winds.

One of the droid's eyestalks tracked the sudden motion on the main scanner impassively, before shutting the main display down. "In space, no one can see your screen," it said to itself, persevering with the retro-movie voiceover it was falling into more and more often, lately.

Moving to the fore of the flight module, it settled its chrome, mechanical form awkwardly into the pilot's chair, and keyed to a different channel on the ship's external communication system. Switching to a more conventional voice, its invisible mouthpiece said: "Mission complete. *Hildegard* is acquired and underway for the rendezvous point. *Anomaly* is intact... see you on the flipside. This is Mak 14, signing off."

M

Specialist Sergeant Kassini, attend recall interview and psych evaluation.

Conquistador Station. 09:00-01.06.2889.

Contact = Doctor Zelinsky

1. THE SLEEPER AGENCY

Kassini Grigorivitch was pulled from deep sleep by her alarm, leaving behind a dream of an Avion child crouching in the rubble. Not ideal, given the day she had ahead of her, she thought, especially since the child had been holding a rocket launcher. She pulled off her coversheet and swung her legs onto the brushed-steel floor. Sensing her movement, her tablet shut off the alarm.

"Lights. Two," she said blearily to the darkness of the hotel room on the station, which responded by approximating her circadian rhythm and fading up a simulation of morning ambience one hour after sunrise on an Earth-like planet.

She leant her head back, closed her eyes and ran through her minute-long waking routine of mental exercises. As she calmed the psychological noise caused by her wayward combat implants, a shoal of thoughts swam lazily into her mind, which she observed dispassionately. I am in Conquistador Station, orbiting above Gatewood IIa, around the red dwarf Lalande 21185 in Ursa Minor. My psych eval is in 45 minutes. By the end of the day, I will either be reassigned or discharged. This is one of those forks in the river. I don't care either way... no, wait, I do care. Or at least, I have to care *enough*.

In the room's ergonomically efficient bathroom compartment, she swiped the sink sensor and slapped cold water on her face. She brushed her teeth and surveyed her reflection in the glow of the mirror. Standing in her military-issue underwear, she automatically swivelled to glimpse the thick scar tissue that extended from just above her coccix, up and out to her left hip. Reflexively, she pulled a clump of curls over its partner, the two-inch scar on the left-side of her forehead. As usual, the feel of her hair on her fingertips triggered the memory of the dropship crash, which hurtled briefly into her mind's eye.

'No time for that,' she admonished herself. Back in the room, she rooted in her pack for fresh underwear, pulled on her Federation Marine uniform she'd left at the foot of the bed and absentmindedly ate a protein bar to stop her stomach rumbling during the assessment. She stowed her tablet and the rest of her gear, checked her appearance one last time and thought the word 'coffee'. A faint red dot appeared on her visual overlay and she followed it out into the bustling corridor in the direction of the station's main concourse. The door of her overnight quarters swished shut behind her.

Psych-eval was on level seven, in the off-limits netherworld of the colossal orbital facility that was Conquistador Station, still the Empire's third-largest military HQ. Kassini sat in the waiting room, a windowless, white holding chamber with a row of perfunctory grey-vinyl-covered seating along one wall and a table in the opposite corner to the door. On the tabletop, a synthetic potted houseplant with two purple flowers inclined hopefully toward the harsh glare of the striplighting.

It had been years since Kassini's last psychological evaluation, she recalled. Throughout her back-to-back five-year tours as a Lieutenant, she'd grown dissatisfied with the regular Empire marine diet of atmosphere drops, crowd control and pirate suppression. Occasionally, there might be real-life ground assault if the Avions, or less often, the Elementals, ever needed kicking out of some contested turf. But this was a rarity. So to jolt herself out of the routine, she'd put in for a transfer for Specialist, which involved entering into the Federation's then-novel experimental programme of brain-augmentation designed for tactical combat situations.

Specialists were given surgical implants that enabled them to overlay models of the brain and personality patterns from other races and aggressive creatures over their own. This wetware acted as a window into the combat perspective of the enemy and was constantly updated and optimised based on data gathered from combat situations across the whole Empire's reach. She'd undergone a week-long series of tests when it was installed. These made sure the implants had taken and were working as expected. While she didn't remember too many of the details, she recalled the whole experience was pretty gruelling. This would – should – be a cakewalk by comparison.

The door slid open with a ping and a tall, prison-tattooed marine stepped out. He glanced at Kassini and instinctively noticed her rank, prompting a well-executed salute. She returned it from her cross-legged position, noting the beads of sweat on his brow and his slightly faraway expression as he crossed the room to leave and return to the station.

She was musing on this when the houseplant turned its flower towards her and spoke in a soft, robotic female voice. "Specialist Sergeant Kassini Grigorivitch?" it enquired. She nodded back to it, awkwardly. The plant's flower drooped down and back up again, as though checking its paperwork. "Proceed inside for your appointment with Doctor Zelinsky and Professor Epsilon."

"Thanks," said Kassini as she gathered her pack.

"My pleasure," the plant said and tilted its flower back towards the ceiling.

Kassini entered the office and sat in the single plastic chair opposite Doctor Zelinsky and Professor Epsilon, who were seated behind a standard wooden desk. The former was a young and broad-shouldered innerworlder with a fresh complexion hinting at what Kassini guessed was distant Mediterranean ancestry; the latter was a transparent perspex cube housing a mess of circuits and lights.

"You're late," the professor said, in a detached, but accusatory machine tone.

Kassini checked her appointment notification on her tablet. "I was told to report at 9:00… has there been a miscommunication?"

Doctor Zelinsky took a break from squinting at the transparent screen in front of him and looked her in the eye. "You're right on time, don't worry about the professor here. He's in a difficult mood today… much testier than usual."

Kassini glanced briefly at the cube. Its internal lights pulsed in a steady rhythm, but other than this, it was giving nothing away.

"Specialist Grigorivitch, thank you for attending your appointment with us," Doctor Zelinsky began, taking off his circular-lensed reading glasses. He cleaned them with a microfibre cloth as he spoke. "The purpose of our meeting today is to assess your psychological readiness for alternatives to combat duty in the Federation's armed forces, after your recent period of rehabilitation. As part of the assessment, myself and Professor Epsilon will ask a series of open-ended questions in a projected test. We want you to answer them as honestly and naturally as possible. We will evaluate your suitability as we go and adapt the test according to the answers you give us. Understood?"

"Understood, Doctor," Kassini replied.

"For security purposes and to monitor your physiological reactions, we will be using a medidroid," the doctor continued. "Caspian?"

A spherical silver droid activated in the corner of the room and hovered over beside Kassini's seat. It was around a metre in diameter and had no facial features. Instead, it had deployed a mechanical arm culminating in a scanning unit from its body, which it proceeded to position uncomfortably close to Kassini's eyes, level with her left temple.

"Is this your first time on Conquistador Station?" the doctor asked, convivially.

"On the station itself? Yes. But I've been in orbit around it a few times. The last time was when I served on the *USS Vesuvius*. Before that, the *Adamantine*," Kassini replied. As she spoke, she became aware of a slight variation in the hum emitting from Caspian. The medidroid hovered motionlessly, glinting in her peripheral vision.

"You were a lieutenant before your promotion," the doctor continued, looking back at his onscreen notes. "Why did you request the transfer?"

"I felt as though I was repeating myself, ad infinitum. I loved the crew and my squad, obviously, but after two tours of duty, it was time to change."

"Miss Daisy is old. She drives her car into a ditch but refuses to accept it's her fault. Why do you think that is?" asked the professor, out of the blue.

Kassini deflected the curveball with a straight bat. "It could be for any number of reasons. Mechanical failure? Perhaps she's too proud to admit responsibility?" Caspian made minor adjustments to his scanner position, causing Kassini to shift her weight slightly in her seat.

"You're paddling in a stream," Epsilon continued. "A crocodile appears on the river bank. You have your firearm. Do you kill it?"

"No. Not unless I assess it as an immediate threat."

"Does the alligator scare you?"

"It was a crocodile, wasn't it?" Kassini queried.

"Same thing. Denial," Epsilon answered, evenly. "It's okay to be afraid, sometimes, isn't it?"

"'Afraid' is the wrong word. It's a potentially deadly animal. It concerns me."

"Of all the locations you've visited in the marines," Doctor Zelinsky asked, "where have you seen that you'd most like to settle down?"

"Erm... well, I like ocean moons. Houses on the endless water. My partner, Octavia, when she was here, always wanted one of those." The intensity of Caspian's whirring increased; Kassini did her best to ignore it.

"Your Zyg reports that your eggs have failed," said Epsilon. "It is your fourth term, still no hatchling. Your feelings?"

"Devastated... angry. Disappointed," said Kassini automatically. She kicked herself. "I imagine, anyway. I have no children of my own."

"No children," said the doctor, leaning forward as though to study her more closely. "A necessary sacrifice for the Marine Corps?"

"Not 'necessary', in my case. I'm a cold fish around kids. Always was."

"Good of the whole. Personal incentivisation," Epsilon chattered. "Are children an unnecessary luxury for society?"

The disturbing Avion child from her dream popped into her head for a moment. "I don't think about them in those terms."

"Your records show you have a talent for survival," said Doctor Zelinsky, in a calm tone. "What do you personally put that down to, in two words?"

Kassini paused. Caspian's constant instrument adjustments next to her face were unnerving and she fought the urge to swat its arm away. "Honed instinct," she replied.

"At what cost?" said Zelinksy. "In two words?"

"Deeper connection."

"Elemental armour on the hills to the east," Epsilon said, more urgently than before. "Three targets. Two squads of ground troops and a forest between them and your unit. You have 10 marines plus air support. Strategy?"

"Divide the squad into four teams. Establish two sniper positions on the flanks at the edge of the forest. One team takes heavy weapons and occupies the armour. The other cycles through cover and attracts their fire. Airstrike on the armour when anti-tank team is in position."

"How did the operation turn out?" asked Zelinsky.

"All Elemental units destroyed, two marine casualties."

"Extreme coping mechanism. Did you ever forgive yourself?" said Epsilon. Kassini noticed the professor's lights were pulsing more rapidly.

"Not my fault. I made a call. She died as she lived," Kassini shot back. She cursed herself and monitored her heartrate, slowing it down. Caspian's sensors flickered slightly.

"Operations could have provided droids. If they had, she would have survived. Why didn't you make *that* call?" said Zelinsky.

"I was unaware of the backup."

"You didn't ask for it. Why not?" he pressed.

"Time pressure. The Elementals were closing on our position and we were outnumbered."

"Functional fixedness. *Einstellung*. Did you know you suffer from it?" asked Epsilon, accusingly.

"I do not."

"Name three things you can do with a wasp, Specialist Sergeant Kassini," said Zelinsky.

"Swat it. Sting someone. Erm..."

"Add 16,153 and 751. Divide by four. Do it now," urged Epsilon, angrily.

Kassini paused. "Come on!" he shouted, lights pulsing quickly and more colourfully.

"4,662. No, 4,226," Kassini blurted.

"Average Empire forces casualties during last four major conflicts is 4,226," Epsilon moved on rapidly. "An Elemental kills a wasp in cold blood. How do you react?"

"I'd be shocked."

"Ambiguous stimuli. An Avion kills an Elemental in cold blood. How do you react?" Epsilon countered.

"I train my weapon on the Avion. I take revenge..."

There was cold silence in the room. Caspian withdrew his sensor unit and finally hovered out of her personal space, back to his corner. Kassini was aware of sweat forming on her brow despite the climate control in the office. Her heartrate was way up on where she'd started from.

"Thank you, you will pleased to know that Caspian and Epsilon have collected enough data and will not be required for the remainder of the interview," the doctor said, equal parts command and explanation. Even he seemed to relax somewhat at the prospect of a simple one on one, which in turn caused some of the tension in Kassini's shoulders to subside.

"To conclude the assessment, I'd like to ask you about your combat implants. I know these were damaged in the unfortunate incident that put you in Barnard's medical hub. This meant the standard practice of removing the wetware installation in your brain could not be carried out as a consequence. This leaves you with a highly specialised piece of military hardware in your head, and is something you've been living with for a while now. Has it caused you any psychological ill effects?"

Kassini willed herself off the defensive before replying, pleased to be able to have a normal conversation with the human now the droids were done with her.

"Nothing that hasn't already been diagnosed, or that wouldn't be in my files from Barnard's," she said. "The main purpose of the implant is to give access to simulated personalities programmed from study of our alien friends' combat troops. The damage to it meant it wasn't medically removable without risk of significant injury so, having lived with it for a long time anyway, I chose to keep it."

She stopped for a moment, almost expecting an accusatory interjection from one of the droids. Epsilon's glow continued to cycle inscrutably in her eyeline, but no questions came, so she continued.

"In technical terms, I've lost part of the control interface that separates its functions from my own personality. It manifests as occasional periods of slow and confused thinking, weird dreams and some intrusive thoughts which don't feel like my own. Because, literally, they're not."

She smiled briefly, and the doctor nodded.

"Go on," he said. "How badly do these affect you?"

"Oh, even early on while I was recuperating, the issues were infrequent and didn't interfere with my functioning, and I'm careful to always observe the therapeutic coping mechanisms I was taught – they're a daily process, like a meditation, and several other mental activities designed for particularly bad episodes, should I experience any. Frankly, it's the same as the physical injuries to me… keep fit, keep on top of it."

"Indeed," said Zelinski, tapping his keyboard. "According to your medical report, you've avoided drug therapy for that particular injustice altogether. A good outcome. Thank you for your patience Specialist Kassini, that will be all for now."

The doctor squinted again at his monitor and swiped a couple of boxes on the screen. "You will be summoned for our verdict within a few hours."

Kassini left the office vaguely pissed off. She remained that way as she sat in the antechamber for over an hour with nothing but the synthetic houseplant and her thoughts for company, unsure if the wait was an ongoing part of the tests that would determine her near-future.

The interrogation had seemed unnecessary to her. She'd been a soldier on the team for most of her adult life and, as far as she was aware, the Federation knew just about everything she'd ever done up until the last year – the 12 months after she'd gotten out of the medical facility that had patched her body up. As she calmed herself and settled in for a wait, she decided she was ready for whichever way the day may go.

If it came to an honourable discharge from the corps, she'd continue to push the interests she'd been building in the burgeoning black markets. She'd carry on until she had enough Cee-bills – the Federation's main form of currency – to strike out for an established planet and set up a legal business she could call her own. She wasn't getting any younger, she reflected, and the stint in the hospital had been enough to make her grateful that the injuries she'd sustained in service were largely manageable. There were plenty of other less fortunate souls still lying in those med-cubes back on Barnard Station, she knew.

On the other hand, she was also grateful this wasn't wartime – the last major war between the Human Federation of Inhabited Worlds and the Taa-Ruu Lineage-led Avion Coalitions had officially ended some 30 years previously, even if skirmishes had continued for many years after.

The war support for the military among the population of humanity's powerful inner planets had long waned. Its military preparedness had gone the same way and so, consequently, had its demands on invalided service people like Kassini. In the event of the day's outcome going the other way, her injuries would preclude even a routine non-combat shipboard role. She imagined she'd be reassigned to either the training division or a planetside tech-support role.

This would also be an acceptable holding pattern for her, she thought, which was handy, because there was nothing she could do about the latter outcome if it wasn't. The Federation did still own the life of a marine who chose to re-enlist, as Kassini had done three years ago, until the five-year contract was up or until such time as the firm chose to let them have it back. She'd lived that way for so long that working out the term really didn't matter to her – she'd take it as it came.

The pot plant had been silent as Kassini waited, occasionally drooping its flower as though surveying the room. It repeated this action again now, but continued the arc until it faced her.

"Specialist, please proceed inside again to discuss the outcome of your appointment," it said cheerily, pointing a short leaf gracefully in the direction of the office.

For a second time, Kassini opened the door to the office and stepped inside. The robots and the doctor had cleared out, taking their equipment with them, and had been replaced with an older man in military uniform bearing a ranking insignia, who returned Kassini's automatic salute and motioned for her to sit. He was a nondescript sort, Kassini noted; his receding, dark hair turning gently to grey and dark eyes framing a solid jaw. He wore the entitled expression of the kind she'd seen walking out of the officer's club many times.

"Specialist Grigorivitch, welcome. I'm Rear Admiral Drexler. There should be no further formality, I expect you to speak openly today," he said, in a boomy bassnote clearly intended to put her at her ease.

"Thank you, Admiral," she replied, taking the seat opposite the man.

"First up, and I want to get this out of the way, I'm happy to see from the evaluation that you have recovered well from your injuries and I need to inform you that the Federal military has continued need of your service. You will not be discharged from the fleet arm today."

"Again, thank you Admiral, I appreciate you getting to the point."

"That's good. There is the matter of a new assignment, however. It is quite unusual by the standards of your past record with the marines, but not that unusual, considering your more recent activity."

"Which activity would that be, Admiral?"

Drexler leaned back, his chair creaking against the size of his frame. He smiled a practised smile that reminded Kassini of a reptile.

"As you said, we should get to the point. We're aware of the contacts you've been making since you left the medical facility at Barnard's Star, and where the credits you've been earning have been coming from."

He scrolled a tablet on the desk in front of him briefly, appearing to read off it as he continued.

"You contacted an ex-Marine Corps armourer with whom you served for some years aboard the *Hydrae Bee* not long after your discharge, who introduced you to key contacts in the grey market in weapons and equipment. No doubt this was prompted by those connected to the staff at the medical facility in the first instance, and you have since facilitated the exchange of numerous lost Federal properties... small arms and small ship weapons, mostly... to a number of mercenary groups in the midway belt systems."

"I thought of it as the black market myself," said Kassini, levelly. All the information Drexler had relayed to her was true.

"Well, that's an interesting point. Obviously, the Federation keeps an eye on the movement of goods originating with us wherever we can – it's not a good idea to genuinely 'lose' the kind of equipment that you can find on these markets, and it seems you weren't moving these items to just anybody. You do your homework, and have already established a smart preference for dealing with smaller outfits who are closely linked to some of the larger mercenary firms."

Drexler looked up and leaned forward to fix Kassini with a colder, more incisive look.

"If I didn't know better, I'd say that's a good start to make yourself a tidy sum should we have chosen to muster you out. As you are no doubt aware, those firms provide services to the Federal military when we need them and give our ex-service people valuable employment opportunities. Hence, to us, a 'grey' market – neither regulated, nor entirely unregulated."

Kassini smiled at this, but said nothing. She wasn't unduly bothered by any of Drexler's revelations – after all, every Federal citizen knew that managing the conflicts and intrigues of hundreds of worlds in a galaxy populated by three distinct races was impossible for any single government to manage centrally. The fundamental freedoms enjoyed by Federation citizens during the Great Expansion had actively encouraged them to form militia to protect the interests of the worlds they and their ancestors had built.

The mercenary or bounty hunter was a recognised occupation in human space in an age where almost anybody could own a spaceship capable of faster-than-light travel. Such individuals operated routinely both as freelancers and in the employ of businesses, corporations or governmental organisations.

The weaponry and expertise these professions relied on had to come from somewhere. All this meant Kassini's more recent activities were straight out of a well-thumbed playbook every Federal soldier knew well after a few years of service. No matter what they wanted to do upon getting out, there would always be work around. Most of it was with the expansive quasi-military organisations that were the natural evolution of every planet's homegrown defence forces. These had grown increasingly intertwined with the operation of the vast centralised Federation military machine proper over the many centuries of the human Empire's existence.

"And so," continued Drexler. "Whilst you will remain in Federation service, we want you to do so incognito. We would like you to continue your civilian life and to exploit your newfound interest to a specific end of benefit to us – as an agent."

"I knew it. You're no fleet Admiral. You're with Service Intelligence, aren't you?" Kassini said, directly.

"Correct, though I served my time aboard ship, as you did. Comms and ships systems by background, moved gradually into more classified work, joined Naval Service Intelligence formally 10 years ago – we're requesting you take your first step on your own similar trajectory today, Kassini."

Now she had a better handle on her situation, some of Kassini's usual confidence had returned. She had to resist the temptation to be insubordinate with a jibe about Drexler's former profession. Shipboard comm-techs had been a regular point of contact for a coordinating combat officer like her in the field, and the relationship between the two professions was as fractious and laced with opportunities for exaggerated banter as any in the military.

But Service Intelligence was a largely unknown quantity to her, a shadow occasionally revealed to be behind some of the worst and best of the Federation's past by clever journalists or whistleblowers over the years. The organisation had formal connections to all of the arms of the military, and indeed was an official centrally funded arm of the services and an individual career choice in its own right. It also operated a vast apparatus of just about everything clandestine a person could think of.

The rumours ranged from the nondescript and obvious – counter-insurgency, military and alien intelligence and special forces black ops – all the way up to directing coups and war crimes, ghost fleets… there was even talk of it operating as a shadowy governmental organisation manipulating the rickety democratic structures of the Federation itself.

"Why me?" she said breezily. "I was all about shooting and booting with the troops in a warzone, not intelligence-gathering or knocking over tinpot pirate despots in the outer rim."

"That would require I explain the mission – we have a somewhat unusual problem."

"Go on, then. Not only do I not have a choice, I'm genuinely interested."

"Your profile suggested you would be, of course. The problem is one Vincent Krieger, formerly Commander Krieger. I don't think you'd have heard of him?"

"Nope, didn't really move in those circles."

"Navy lifer, he was picked out at college age with the standardised personality tests as top-percentile officer material at the backend of the Avion conflict, and the tests were right. Very good results at Centre Academy, became something of a specialist in boarding operations and shipboard defensive strategy based on the models of mid-sized capital ships in service in those days. Take a look: a picture says a lot words can't, in my experience."

Drexler tapped the tablet in front of him and spun it across the desk to Kassini. It showed the standard naval ID shot of a young man with close-cropped blonde hair and light brown eyes. He was generically handsome, with the kind of chiselled face that could have adorned a military recruitment poster, though his expression retained a hint of defiant self-confidence. The image morphed as she looked, ageing the man in the picture through the updates to the photo to add a variety of hair changes, spraying stubble across the face then removing it, all the while gradually adding the lines and scars of age and a life in service.

It stopped in roughly his early 50s, Kassini guessed, now considerably weathered and having added a particularly nasty hard-looking wound to the middle of his chin that ran down into the man's neckline a few images previously. This disappeared in the very final image, apparently the result of corrective cosmetic surgery.

"Lived the life, by the look of him."

"He did," the Admiral continued. "Krieger was out of training and in service as a junior officer by the time the Avion war was finally settling down, and saw plenty of action in the final skirmishes. Captured more than a few of their ships, gathered a fair few awards for valorous actions and good conduct. A leader, by all accounts, if you discount the somewhat grandiose tendencies detailed in his psych-evals. He became a captain in his own right by the time the Elementals started their aggressive – if you can call it that with them – expansion in the Coalstar Nebula."

"Some of my earliest postings were in that conflict, Admiral. It wasn't a good fight for a rookie early on. Our training on Elemental warfare was, frankly, completely inaccurate," Kassini said, pushing the tablet back across the table.

"I'm aware, I was there, too. The *USS Coriolis*, mostly."

"I remember the *Coriolis*, your planes pulled us out of the shit on one of the moons in Corcoron."

Drexler smiled at the reminiscence.

"Fleet Arm were always ready when you grunts overreached yourselves," he said, and Kassini laughed as he continued. "Fact was, we pushed back at the Elementals too hard, too quickly and with too little intelligence. Some of us saw that coming. The Elementals were more of an unknown quantity then than they are now, and it was as a consequence of it all I moved over to SI, in the end."

He stopped himself, and checked the tablet again briefly as though regaining his place in an old printed book.

"Now Krieger, he was in command of the frigate *USS Elvira* for much of it, and acquitted himself well. We learnt a lot about Elemental ships and tactics from some of his raids – right until it was just about over, that is. When we had finally managed to get the Ellies to the negotiating table and were working on the ceasefire, he was assigned to patrol a colony sector away from the frontline back towards Centre – should have been quiet, but some enterprising Elemental captain made it a target. Krieger dealt with the incursion and captured some of their crew."

Kassini's face suddenly lit up with recognition.

"*Elvira*! I remember the scuttlebutt about it. He wasted a load of the prisoners, right?"

"That's the short version. Krieger was summarily court-martialled. He maintained the prisoners escaped and he was protecting his crew and ship, which he most likely was – but that didn't matter, the timing was the problem. The incident had nearly scuppered the negotiations, which were fraught enough with the Elementals being so aggressive with us at the best of times. They demanded he be turned over to them as a war criminal to satisfy one of their quasi-religious wartime commandments."

Drexler's face turned grave and he fixed Kassini with his commanding stare again.

"To our shame, the negotiators agreed, frankly judging one of our people by the enemy's standards – one mid-ranking commander to avoid the hostilities hotting up again was a no-brainer, diplomatically. He was relieved of command, shipped to the Elementals... and assumed executed."

"Assumed?"

"Yes, no other outcome made sense with the Elementals at the time. You have first-hand experience of their ruthlessness on the battlefield. And so we come to today..."

"I'm guessing somebody assumed wrong?" said Kassini, with an amused grin.

"Correct. One of our experimental vessels out of the Aldebaran yards was hijacked during a routine, and entirely secret, transfer a week ago. From what we know – which, I should add, isn't very much – Krieger now has the ship."

Kassini laughed out loud.

"So, did you want me to go waste this guy and get the ship back for you? There's better people for that, Admiral."

Drexler sat back and spread his hands in front of him.

"That's not what I had in mind – though significant violence was involved in the hijacking, so other agencies have already moved to issue relevant warrants. First, Kassini, it's important to understand we want that ship back. It represents a significant investment of funds and R&D and it's at a vital stage of the project's development."

The man examined his hands for a moment, considering his words.

"Of more importance to SI, however, is how the hell Krieger has made this sudden return in good enough shape to steal a secret Federation prototype vessel. We suspect he's working with somebody with clout – and we would very much like to know who that somebody is, which is where you come in."

Kassini nodded for the admiral to continue.

"The ship is small-freighter size, and recently completed core systems testing. It's intended for search and rescue but was stolen before it was properly kitted out for field tests for those ops. Krieger has already made contact with the market for ammunition and equipment near your patch of space – I told you we keep an eye on these things – and we need you to take on the job of fulfilling that contract, then try and get aboard the ship and learn everything you can about the captain's plans. This is the only chance we'll have to get at him before he disappears with the ship – it's a stealth model, too, so once he figures out how to use it, he'll be gone."

"I'm an out-of-the-loop marine, Admiral. Don't you have people trained for this sort of thing? Why me?"

"A case of right place, right time. Using other agents is problematic, as we have no idea who he's working with or what access he may have. Obviously, somebody on the inside helped set this up, given the timing and the fact he knew which of a thousand freighters in the sector was hauling the ship. Counter-espionage is a persistent problem in my line of work, but your story up until today is genuine and so suits the operation perfectly, as does your background when it comes to the man himself – both of you are navy at heart."

Kassini wasn't so sure about that, but let it pass without challenge. Drexler paused for a moment.

"Plus, you're already kitted out with some extremely relevant tactical equipment. I mean your implants, of course – the more mundane aspects of that system are very similar to those we use to communicate with our field agents, and you are very well trained in their use."

"Wireless data link for comms, mapping, tracking," Kassini intoned. "I see your point."

"And it's surprisingly hard to find somebody with a convincing reason to have retained that kind of equipment, should it be noticed, in civilian life. We'd need to update the software a little, but that's easily done," Drexler concluded.

Kassini sat for a moment to let the import of the discussion sink in. Drexler gave her the time, looking away.

"You say there's a price on the captain's head already?" she asked, finally. "How am I supposed to keep him out of the hands of the bounty hunters?"

"We're running this quietly, to one side of the main operation to retrieve the ship, so to speak. So I can't influence the normal order of things in that regard very far at all. But suffice to say, nobody gets paid if the ship is destroyed and nothing has been issued with regards to those found to be connected to Krieger – we have no real idea who they may be, so consider any information on them to be worth your time, too. But ultimately just stick with him, find out everything you can and keep yourself alive until we can intervene," the admiral replied.

Kassini considered all of this – she was telling the truth about being intrigued, but could imagine that nothing involving SI was quite what it seemed. Her instincts told her that infiltrating the crew of a loose-cannon ex-commander in a stolen secret ship was likely to be way more exciting than whipping some no-mark conscripts into shape, or punching her card on some dull Empire military helpline for the rest of her days.

"Okay, I'm ready," she said. "How long do I have?"

"Good. Two days to prepare, we've already arranged the equipment the captain is trying to purchase via a cutout and we're in the process of setting up a meeting. You will be the contact and I'll be your handler for the duration, so consider what gear you'll need and I'll see you get it. You should report to the medical sector next today. I'll arrange for your implant to be upgraded, which will put you in touch with me as required. You know where that is?"

"Understood, and I'll be able to find it," she said, tapping her skull as she stood up, before saluting the man in front of her and heading for the door of the office for the second time.

"Kassini," Drexler called after her as her hand reached for the door control. "Krieger was a decent officer who always kept the best interests of his crew at heart. Keep that in mind."

"Will do, sir," said Kassini and left, closing the door on Drexler as he began clearing the desk.

As she swept through the ante-room the plant raised its flower one last time as it opened the outer door for her, allowing the distant sound of the huge, bustling station to reach her again for the first time in a few hours.

"Goodbye, Kassini Grigorivitch," it said. "And safe travels!"

M

Drexler: proceed to meeting point,
Warren City at Reece-Kolarov in Cerapholon.

Sell the weapons in your pilot's hold. Infiltrate
the crew of *Anomaly*, confirm success.

Reece-Kolarov in Cerapholon -46.78978 76.7890.
Contact = Avion, Vonya of Ok'cuu.

Drexler out.

2. STUCK IN THE MIDDLE

Out on the level-four station concourse, Kassini wove through the bustle of military staff that moved like a rush-hour crowd at a transit hub, blurring the outlines of the scene around her. She stowed her luggage cases by a table at the cafe and ordered a black coffee from the crew hatch. The hubbub of gliding droids, off-duty marines, blaring announcements and passing conversations soon resolved into background noise. Repositioning her chair to spectate on the incoming and outbound ships through the colossal window of the station's viewing gallery, she sipped the reassuringly burnt-tasting Federal Navy brew for what, it occured to her, could be the last time for a while.

The base she was on, Conquistador, was a recent creation. One of a quartet of new strongholds unveiled to much fanfare by the FedCor, it nestled in the comparative safety of the inner Empire to bolster the Federation war machine. And for once, those proud PR reports weren't kidding – it really was a jewel in the Empire's military crown, capable of servicing and support for entire exploratory, colonisation and task-force fleets.

Though the navy was spread out far and wide nowadays, this was still a stronghold to rival some of those of the Great Expansion times. Although because it was technically peacetime, more progressive factions in the Empire's debating chambers had questioned the need for such defences at all. They would have happily diverted the funding to any number of other pressing Empire-wide concerns, since resources were spread ever-more thinly across the Federation's sprawl of colony worlds. Everyone needed more of everything, from ship parts to farming machinery to comms networks, to luxury goods… the list of citizen demands was endless. In the end, though, the wars may have been an increasingly distant memory, but they were a painful one; the votes were passed, the bases were constructed and here Kassini stood.

Her pilot messaged her to say she was refuelling and boarding would be a further half an hour, which was still within their schedule. Kassini idly flicked through her tablet feed and sent a few check-in messages to her friends – mostly still in the forces – saying she'd be off-grid for a while… they were fellow spacers and knew the drill all too well. Aside from them, her only surviving family was her younger sister, Martina, who was perma-busy raising her kids on a colony near Proxima. She was used to Kassini disappearing into the void for months at a time.

She was just about to order another coffee and check their replies when a rumbling resonance thrummed through the concourse. Activity paused on the deck and all eyes turned to the gallery window to watch as one of the navy's new-design capital ships powered into view out of the station's main dock below them. This was the *USS Matador*, a Constellation-class battleship and a trainspotter's dream: 2,000-plus experienced crew on a quarter of a mile of silvery hardware glinting menacingly in the light of the distant sun.

The colossal ship's bulky triangular hull elongated to a sensor-filled arrowtip at the bow and inbetween these two points sat a bristling array of heavy-weapon hardpoints, ECM turrets and an entire squadron of hull-mounted raiders. All of the navy's capital ships could be repurposed depending on their mission imperatives, but the *Matador* – the latest in a long line – was, according to despatches, the recipient of the Navy's latest developments in shielding tech. Energy-hungry shield systems were the preserve of bigger vessels, and like the Avions, the Federation was forever playing catch-up with the Elementals on this technological front of the cold war between the three Empires. The extra investment in them was a clear indicator that the *Matador* had been specc'd out for fight-to-the-death fleet combat, if it ever came to that.

As the battleship scrolled past hypnotically out of the station flightpath to begin its approach to the system's spin point, Kassini watched its powerful engines glow blue and recede, sidelighting the retinue of frigates, destroyers and support ships that accompanied her in close formation. She picked out the complement of streamlined troop ships and reminded herself that those days were over – Specialist Sergeant Kassini Grigorivitch had a new mission. Her tablet sensed her mood and moderated its alarm down to a gentle prompt that it was time to go. She shouldered her bags and made her way to the station's shipyard to meet her pilot. Time to get the Captain Krieger show on the road...

The lift door swished open onto Hangar Bay 17 and Kassini hauled her bags out and set them down in front of her. The large atmospherically sealed chamber had eight bays for small-to-medium-sized ships, five of which were currently occupied. To her left, a trio of haulage freighters with Federation markings were being unloaded by a team of droids, while next to those, a small police Hornet was undergoing repairs. In the next bay but one sat the odd-one-out – a squat yet sleek Avion-designed twin-engine interceptor with black-and-silver-striped livery. Its cargo-bay ramp was lowered between the two rear hydraulic landing struts, which poked out diagonally beneath a two-seater cockpit positioned just behind its small wings.

An Avion ship on a Federation base was a rare sight, and a pair of bearded mechanics on their break were eyeing the fighter with some interest. One wiped his oily hands down his overalls as the other gesticulated, pointing in the vague vicinity of the craft's custom weapons mounts, encouraging his colleague to go and take a closer look.

As they wandered over, the Avion pilot appeared from inside the cargo bay, stormed down the ramp and stomped over to confront them. Dressed in a stylish and pristine grey flightsuit, her unmistakably alien, yet vaguely bird-like form was tall and fine-boned, even for an Avion. She had sharp, aquiline features and small and piercing eyes. When the pilot fanned out her wings in a display of annoyance, Kassini could see that the tips of her dark feathers had a purple tint, a beautiful pattern that was a rarity in the Avion genome. Hands on hips to display the sidearm she was carrying in her belt, the alien pilot squawked at the mechanics in her high, melodic voice and they scuttled back to the other side of the hangar, heads down.

The Avion watched them go, then spotted Kassini at the lift entrance and came over, regaining her poise by retracting her wings and smoothing her facial feathers with a long, slender talon as she walked.

"You are Kassini Grigori-veetch?" she said, her harmonious twin larynxes struggling with the pronunciation. "I am Vonya of Ok'cuu. Your pilot and protec-tor. Sorry," she said and nodded behind her to indicate the two mechanics. "They stick their beaks too close to my bird." The Avion held out her slim hand with its three talons in greeting.

Kassini laughed and shook it. "So, Vonya of Ok'cuu," she replied. "The Ok'cuu line is practically Avion royalty. How come we meet here in Federation space?"

The Avion paused, interpreting her speech with some difficulty. "Not 'royalty', exactly," she said. "Avion word for it probably not quite the same thing."

In her head, Kassini summoned her implants. As much as she resented the Federation for leaving her with tech that was effectively at war with her psyche, a happier side-effect of this malfunctioning battlefield system was instant recall and near-fluency in a number of languages, Avion included. She repeated what she'd said in a dialect of Avion that was necessarily adjusted to suit her human voicebox.

Vonya let out a loud musical laugh at this and the tension visibly released from her shoulders. "You speak my language? So few of you do – thank you," she replied in her native tongue, her voices harmonising warmly. "Honestly, I'm better at shooting humes down than talking to them… no offence, Miss Kassini."

"None taken. Call me Kass."

"And you are right, my family gene-line is prized among the Avions… it's sometimes a blessing, sometimes a curse," Vonya sighed. "A long story which no hume should really be forced to listen to. The short version is I am here because I want to spread my wings as a star pilot and once I was made 'Gunstar', I had learned all I could in the navy, so I 'borrowed' this ship and took off on my own."

"You're a Gunstar? So you were top gun in your squadron?"

"In the fleet," Vonya corrected her, narrow eyes sparkling with a sheen of pride.

Kassini was genuinely impressed, given that Avion pilots were feared throughout the Fed navy and Gunstars were the cream of the crop. "Those are pretty impressive credentials," she replied. "But you look too young."

"We don't live as long as you humes, so we need to get a move on," Vonya shrugged, matter-of-factly. She looked back at the mechanics to check they were still firmly in their place. "Talking of which… my bird is ready to fly. We should load up and you can check the cargo before takeoff."

Vonya picked up one of Kassini's bags and led the way. They clanked up the ramp into the fighter's small hold and as they ducked inside, automatic lights flickered on, revealing supplies in neatly organised wall-mounted units and tools arranged on flight-proof racking. Beneath these, a cargo of reinforced munitions crates lined the floor, taking up most of the available space.

"Here they are," said Vonya. "I was given coordinates for an anonymous pickup in a nearby system, a droid loaded the crates, I didn't ask any questions. I have no idea what's in them, but they're clearly Federation military in origin, never mind the independent markings."

"It's okay, I know what they are," said Kassini, entering a code to open a crate and reveal complex-looking, individually wrapped equipment. "Those two crates are flak ammunition and these three are ignition systems for some hefty ship-to-ship railguns… standard-mount, but enhanced spec, of course."

"Sweet," said Vonya, approvingly. Kassini peered behind the stack. "And that smaller crate is a set of Empire military battlefield suits. Okay, it's all here. I'm ready when you are."

Vonya nodded and asked: "So you're a weapons dealer?"

"Like yours, it's a long story," sighed Kassini as they climbed down the ramp and sealed the cargo bay. "I used to be a Specialist Sergeant in the marines, but they discharged me and I ended up using my Fed contacts to make some deals on the black market. It's easy work for the most part… until all of a sudden, it isn't."

Vonya paused and nodded, her piercing eyes filled with a knowing look. "Don't I know it, Kass. So what's the mission plan?"

"A long spin to Cerapholon to the rendezvous point with the buyer. They're at some kind of pirate hellhole."

Vonya's expression flickered in recognition. "Cerapholon? That's an Empire-run system, or at least it was once upon a time. From what I've heard lately, I think you'd best wear one of those suits."

Kassini was surprised. "Why? Do they have an atmosphere problem?"

"No," said Vonya, rolling her talon over a sensor to open the cockpit hatch. "It's just a really grimy place."

They climbed into the fighter and Kassini strapped herself in, adapting the Avion buckles and belts to her slightly shorter, much less feathery form. The interior clearly took some alteration to accommodate a passenger: it looked like

Kassini's chair was a temporary fixture at the back of the cramped space, with a second added in front of it within reach of the banks, controls and viewscreens for the pilot.

"You fly the ship from a chair?" said Kassini, as Vonya took her own seat and began to fiddle with a set of wing trodes, clip-on electronics which interpreted the movements of Avion wing muscles into finer control of their vessels. Avion ships were known to interface perfectly with the race's physiology, with the inclusion of their innate ability to fly on the species' strong, agile wings.

Kassini knew this meant they usually piloted their ships in a suspended horizontal position, but was hazy on the details. The Avion replied to her question without looking back at her.

"Not as standard, just when I have a passenger. We train both ways to account for the possibility of injuries and system failure, also in case we have to fly your ships from time to time. The flight module's..." she searched for an alternative to a word that wouldn't have been readily understood for Kassini, even in Avion, "...control suit? It stows above us if not required, and I can still simulate multi-limb control with the trodes, to a lesser degree."

Vonya clicked a switch and requested clearance to leave the station, and they were soon following the earlier flightpath of the *Matador* battleship away from the gravitational effects of the nearby planet. Interstellar travel using the Henslow-Dolan-Clarks Spin effect – known to the Avion pilot as Kreeen-Toriks Rotational effect after her species' parallel discoverers – was a complex, if routinely automatable affair. Every ship and pilot in the galaxy worthy of their title familiarised themselves with the rough map of the spin routes in the area they were working, even if few understood the complex mathematics used to calculate the intersection of stellar forces at a particular point in space which decided the relative likelihood of completing a spin from one system to another. The journeys were a generally reliable brand of miracle, but as with any long-distance travel, when the countdown began, stories about exceptions to the rule invariably sprang to mind.

On the way to the spin point, Vonya called back over her shoulder, enthusiastically chattering about the modifications she'd made to her ship and pre-warning Kassini about some of its eccentricities. It transpired that her interceptor was one of the Avion navy's latest prototype models, an experiment into dogfighting supremacy – lightly armoured but fast, insanely manoeuvrable and relatively well armed for its size. Vonya had fallen in love with it while working as a test pilot and, as she put it, 'borrowed' it for good.

The Avion explained that in the last few months before this job, she'd been trading up its components. She'd then tested it in the field, spoiling for fights at spin points but just "ruffling feathers" rather than going in for the kill.

As they approached their spin point and waited patiently in a queue of traffic for their slot, Kassini felt strangely reassured. Even though her pilot was a renegade with a price on her head in Avion space, so long as they stayed on the fringes or on the human side of the border, there was probably no one out here who could match her in space combat. The more suspicious, questioning portion of Kassini's mind – lately preoccupied with assessing the seriousness of potential clients or the dicier aspects of deals – did quietly wonder at the wisdom of allocating her a known fugitive for a taxi driver.

Shortly after the fighter had resynced with normal space at the incoming spin point in the system of Ceraphölon, Vonya checked her scanner's scope and her ship's readouts for anything anomalous. She was satisfied with what the instruments told her – they were where they were supposed to be. She altered course smoothly and engaged her ship's afterburners with a practised series of motions to put some space between her interceptor and whatever was going to be next to emerge from the busy traffic hub.

Kassini blinked as the eerie, misty dissociation of spin-drive travel gradually lifted from her vision and her body began to slowly readjust. She knew from military training that Avion recovery from the disorientation of spin flight was far more rapid than that of humans, but witnessing her companion's swift and decisive return to normality up close was humbling. It was another of those instances where you realised how divergent yours and another species' paths through evolution had been.

In comparison to humans, Avion reflexes and speed of thought were mercurial; in so many ways, while they soared in the skies like eagle-eyed predators, humans flailed around in the mud, like fattened-up, slow-witted prey. An image of the *Matador* and its bristling weapons swam into her mind's eye. 'Thank the gods for technology,' she thought to herself idly.

Kassini powered up her tablet and shared the coordinates with Vonya for Warren City, a naval port on Ceraphölon's only inhabited planet – a partially terraformed dirtball called Reece-Kolarov, named in honour of the ill-starred rock's original settlers.

Reece-Kolarov was typical of the colonies out in the Empire backwaters. A Federation station orbited the planet serenely, monitoring the traffic flow, while the occasional police Hornet buzzed back and forth intercepting the easiest targets among the pirate infidels who were hoping to make a quick buck for their ill-gotten cargoes. It was an open secret that, in systems like this, the Feds confiscated the most profitable wares and skimmed an ever-greater cut to sell on the black market for a tidy profit. 'Figures,' Kassini mused. Fed trooper is a bad enough job as it is. Why else would you work a properly dangerous pirate system day-in, day-out otherwise?

The map of Warren City's urban sprawl on Kassini's tablet pinged with safety warnings and the latest news bulletin on her feed read like despatches from some galactic-atrocities court. This prompted her to check her weaponry and ammo for the third or fourth time in the last 24 hours as she ran through the plan in more detail with Vonya on her approach. This was more for her benefit than the pilot's, since Vonya had already been careful to mention that she was contracted to wait with the ship while Kassini met the crew.

The pilot listened patiently, before piping up. "So, do I want to know who it is you're meeting?"

"Standard-issue pirate badasses, but the captain is interesting," Kassini replied, opting to trust her pilot with the outline of her mission. "He's an ex-Fed commander who's a new entry in the Empire's Most Wanted list for somehow stealing an experimental ship. Sounds like a loose cannon."

Vonya perked up at this. "Hmm. An experimental ship? Now I'm intrigued. Bet they can't fly it. Maybe I should stick around after the deal goes down, I could earn a few more Cees for escorting them to the spin point, maybe..." She paused. "But do you think they'll be trouble?"

Kassini shook her head. "I think they'll be *in* trouble. Judging by this cargo we're selling them, they won't have all their defence and combat systems online for a start... no idea about the rest of the crew."

"Interesting..." said Vonya, and a communicator screen lit up on her instrument panel. "Okay, we have clearance. Starting my descent, destination in five minutes."

It was late evening on Reece-Kolarov. Although it was currently being drenched by a continuous heavy downpour – the colony was decades and a few billion credits away from climate control – they could snatch glimpses of Warren City in the diffuse streetlights. Shards of neon and the searchlights of Federation patrols passed beneath them. The edge of the city was neatly divided into two zones; the outermost was the starport, with large gantries and hangars equipped with built-in cranes for moving merch to transports, surrounded by a maze of narrow alleys. Over the other side, the second district was a mongrelised assembly of buildings ranging from pre-fab temp stalls and run-down tenement apartment blocks, graduating to multi-storey skyscrapers that marked the beginning of the city's suburbs. The two zones were separated by a single continuous street that was the district's main strip.

Security protocols were lax – the Fed orbital station hadn't bothered them beyond the standard hail-and-scan. Vonya coasted the interceptor into a hover above the wide, cone-shaped entry port for the nearest free hangar. She cursed as she narrowly avoided colliding with a wayward fuel tanker that swayed unsteadily as it cleared the structure during vertical takeoff and the atmospheric wind took hold.

The hangar building spread out beneath them was a massive structure, but perfunctory and disorganised by the standards of a higher tech spaceport. Unlike the one they'd just left on the state-of-the-art Conquistador Station, there was no automated landing control and no isolated landing bays. Manual loading and unloading caused inevitable delays for pilots and provided a constant menace for the dock workers, adding up to a very dangerous place to both fly and work.

Vonya selected a landing zone and gently dropped the ship into the cone nose-first, using reverse thrust and fine control of manoeuvring thrusters.

This allowed Kassini to see the chessboard of widely spaced landing squares demarcated with bright perimeter markers directly underneath the open entry port. The bays were surrounded by racking for cargo and shipping containers, loading machinery and modular buildings, all under the cover of the roof which sloped up to support the entry way.

The Avion righted her ship 10 metres above a smaller bay towards the edge of the chessboard close to the sheet of rain running down from the edge of the roof above them, and then touched down. She powered down everything except the interceptor's weapons systems while Kassini prepped her kit.

"Here if you need me, here if you don't," the Avion pilot said to her, triggering the flight module hatch release. "Watch yourself out there."

Kassini nodded her thanks and descended the ladder. For a moment, she enjoyed the sensation of rain hitting her and the sound of it running down the ship's slick sides before it sluiced into the drainage system beneath it. The pilot stuck some dance music on her headphones and began scrolling through the options she could have delivered from Warren City's Avion fast-food outlets while she waited.

Kassini ventured out into the humidity of the city's rainy streets and pulled the hood of her nondescript black top over her head. She summoned the map of the sector on her behind-the-eyes overlay and began to follow the faint lines in her peripheral vision towards the pale red dot of her destination, where she was set to rendezvous with Krieger's merc crew.

He'd chosen their meeting point and for some reason, had specified the showroom for an Avion-run business called Yu-Fo's. The outfit specialised in custom-graphic ship decals, but was no doubt a front for some other, more sinister operation. It was some five minutes away in the backstreets of the port, just off the main strip of the warehouse district.

Kassini splashed down the main drag, the commercial no man's land sandwiched between the warehouses and industrial sprawl of the port district to her left and the city's tall buildings to her right. The strip was largely deserted save for the shuffling figures of saturated citizens in a hurry to get somewhere, or small groups ducking past security into bars to get out of the polluted rain. She paused in a doorway for a few minutes as the rain intensified. A maze of dimly lit alleys snaked off into the darkness around her.

As the storm eased and she resumed walking, she unconsciously took in the layers of graffiti covering virtually every visible wall of the buildings on the city side. They were gangland tags mostly, she figured: territorial daubings in a range of languages, glyphs of human and alien origin. The faded flourescence of the occasional artistic creation poked out from beneath the smeary patina of rain and smog.

High above her head in the gaps between the buildings, giant digital billboards the size of freighters lit up smoky vistas that led deeper into the city proper. In between the relentless promotional blaring of ads from Quick Cash loan companies and perfunctory Federal civic messaging, slick commercials for inner-world colony living were broadcast through the drizzle. Their cinematic drone shots and swirling orchestras punctuated the night.

Kassini couldn't help but be mesmerised by the way the tantalising soft-focus glow of white sandy beaches and splashes of infinite blue surf contrasted with the saturnalia of sex clubs, casinos, tattoo parlours and half-heartedly disguised drug dens crowding her peripheral vision. Back at ground level, the more established businesses she passed along the port strip sported eyecatching holographic animations in place of signs. But for the most part, the city was a blur of cheap lasers and the A/B frames of old-school neon signage, crackling in the rain.

She heard light footsteps in front of her. Two unknown figures retreated into the shadows of the alleyway ahead of her to the left. Lurching back into combat mode, she kicked herself for being so easily distracted and instinctively unholstered her sidearm.

'Wake up, Sergeant,' she chided herself angrily as the street in front of her was suddenly bathed in the suffuse yellow radiance from the searchlights of a pair of Federation police drones. Their engines hummed as their glistening, streamlined hulls passed around 20 metres overhead and sent the two figures scuttling away, back down the alley. She tracked the retreating patrol as it shrunk to a surreal silhouette against the gigantic palm-tree vistas shimmering on the digital billboard, holstered her weapon and broke into a jog across the strip's slippery surface.

Yu-Fo's turned out to be more of an impromptu bar than a business at this time of night. As Kassini was moodily ushered into the dry through the tall, canopied doorway by a scarfaced Avion bouncer, her eyes adjusted to the low light that suited the clientele. The walls were covered floor to ceiling in ship decals. In among the hackneyed selection of snakes and pirate skulls, kill-count icons and go-faster swooshes was a section of bespoke pieces that were the spit of some of the imaginative artistic graffiti she'd spotted buried beneath the tags on the way over.

The room was filled with lively chatter from its eight occupied tables. Its back wall was devoted to an impressively stocked bar beneath a giant fresco of a tropical planetary scene, dominated by bands of azure sky. She glimpsed the edge of a snooker table in the back room: it was one of the few human bar sports that had translated to the stars and remained universally popular, since its focus on unerring precision didn't confer any advantage for the physiology of any particular species.

Kassini half-turned and took her outer layers off, surreptitiously unlatching the safety on her sidearm while she surveyed the room in profile. At a corner table in her peripheral vision, sat either side of a bottle of local spirits with three glasses, were the two faces she recognised from her briefing. Aside from her, they were the only non-Avions in the place. She rinsed some of the rain out of her fringe then strode over to them. Pulling up a stool at the end of the table, she introduced herself.

"Kassini Grigorivitch... tell me I'm in the right place," she said. The shorter of the two, all impeccable grooming, stood up with a reflex of mannered politeness and offered a manicured hand to match his businesslike attire. Kassini noticed the look was slightly offset by a sly smile. "Nice to meet you... thank you for agreeing to meet us at short notice," he said in his rapid, well-educated diction. "I'm Taro Watanabe and this is Vincent Krieger."

The latter remained sat down and grunted a curt greeting, offering her a piercing stare rather than a handshake. Krieger was older than Taro by close to a couple of decades – Kassini was somewhere inbetween – but aside from weathered lines around his eyes, streaks of grey in his week-old stubble and his thinning strands of neck-length silvery blonde hair, he was still in good shape. He wore faded dark overalls over a white tee and Kassini glimpsed Federation Navy-issue dogtags with an out-of-date logo on the chain round his neck. He surveyed her with a stare she guessed was pitched somewhere between mild curiosity and open hostility for an uncomfortable few seconds, then turned his attention to uncapping the bottle and pouring out three measures of hooch.

"Interesting meeting place," Kassini ventured, expertly intercepting the glass Krieger pushed across the table at her, noting his flair for the dramatic.

"Well, you can't be too careful... and we weren't about to do business in the landing bay," said Krieger, eyeing his shot glass disinterestedly. "Firstly – for all we know, you could've arrived with a team of merc security. Here, we know the quick way out, and the owner, and you don't. Secondly –" he paused for effect and to drain his glass, then gestured around the bar, "these Avions don't give a shit what we discuss with each other, unlike the human scum in a Fed backwater like this. Hell, those paramilitary Feds running the show are jacked up on the same shit they're supposedly trying to intercept. They didn't even question us on the way in, once they realised we don't have a cargo they can sell on. And finally – the moonshine they distil out the back is much better than you'd think. Try it."

Taro took over before Kassini could reply, which was just as well, as it was pretty hard to work out what to say to that.

"So, Ms Grigorivitch..."

"Call me Kassini."

"...Kassini, I take it you've procured our order. Any difficulties?"

"None at all," she told them, sipping at her drink and enjoying the smooth coating of heat on her throat. "I've also thrown in a bonus set of the latest Empire mil-spec ground suits to sweeten our first deal."

Taro raised an eyebrow at Krieger, then turned back to her. "Much appreciated. And could I check that the weapon parts are…?"

"…Merceron Corp generics, the fast-spin version, matched to the ship spec you sent me," Kassini continued for him. "And the frag ammo is straight off the line for standard auto-reloaders as you requested. It's reassuringly heavy stuff. Hope you've got some room in your bay."

As he listened, Krieger seemed to have warmed up slightly. "Cargo space? We've got plenty. Just a couple of droids and Taro's walk-in wardrobe to haul around the galaxy at the moment."

Taro sneered. "Ah, the old smart-clothes jibes. Krieger here is just jealous because he gets dressed by rolling around the floor of his quarters and seeing what sticks."

"You *are* pretty neatly turned out, Mr Watanabe," said Kassini. "Especially for a dirty pirate city like Warren." She drained her glass and placed it down; Krieger instantly took the bottle and filled them all again.

"Taro here was a diplomat by trade," he told her. "He spends a long time each morning making sure he looks the part."

"I'm more of a medical man nowadays, really, among other things," Taro qualified.

Krieger leaned forward and fixed her with his stare. "But what about you… how come you could sort us out with this haul at such short notice?"

Kassini swiped her glass up from the table and looked around, then leaned back in her seat. "I'm sure you don't expect me to reveal my sources, Mr Krieger," she replied, holding his gaze. "But I've been around the block in these systems. And many others, come to that."

"Before or after you left the navy?" said Krieger, too quickly to be casual.

"Damn… is it really that obvious?" said Kassini, smiling and leaning closer to Krieger, adopting a slightly more challenging posture. "And I actually remembered to take my tags off for this meeting, too."

Krieger glanced down and smiled. "Guilty as charged."

Taro laughed and asked her: "So why did you leave?"

"Long story, Taro," sighed Kassini, surveilling the bar as she spoke. The Avions around them were glued to a hoverball game on the big screen, ignoring their meeting, as Krieger had predicted. "But my pilot's paid by the hour, so why don't we finish these and head back to make our exchange? I hope you've come up with a way of hauling the gear into your ship under the noses of the Feds back in the port, by the way."

"That's taken care of," said Taro. "Our ship is… let's say, a Fed-friendly model. On the way in, we transmitted our designation as a Federation Offworld Inspection team."

"Did we?" said Krieger, with surprise that was obviously genuine.

"It was Mak 14's suggestion," said Taro, flinching at the unprofessional interruption. "He told them our operation was classified and not to bother us. They couldn't care less, anyway, waved us on through."

"That droid badly needs reprogramming," Krieger said, shaking his head slowly.

"What hangar are you in?" asked Kassini.

"Hang on," Taro pulled his tablet out and checked. "12," he said.

"No way… next to a silver-and-black Avion stunt fighter?" said Kassini.

"Yep, couldn't miss it," replied Krieger. "So that's your ride?"

"It's a small universe," Kassini marvelled.

"It's an intriguing ship, too," said Krieger, eyeing her sideways. "You are full of surprises, Kassini." He raised his glass in a final toast. "To business."

Vonya had idly spectated on the night shift in Hangar 12 as she slurped her synthetic fishcakes and noodles in chilli broth. As she savoured her meal, she nodded along to a high-octane human-made dance mix in her headphones. The rain had stopped by the time she went to dispose of the carton in the bay's recycling chute, leaving the landing area wreathed in a miasma of condensation and the reek of fuel and engine burn from the departure of a couple more freighters. The loading droids had powered down and the mechanics had clocked off an hour previously, leaving her with just the still-dented Hornet and a newly arrived ship for company.

Her interceptor's rudimentary scanners revealed nothing about the craft. So she decided to wander over to a safe distance and inspect it for herself, careful not to overly vex whatever sentry units the pair of humans that crewed it had left on overwatch. Even though she couldn't make out their features as they made a hurried exit for the strip shortly after landing, she'd already guessed that the 25-metre-high craft that towered over her, taking up two bays, had to be the experimental ship belonging – at least temporarily – to Kassini's contacts.

Squatting in roughly the middle of the huge landing area, the big ship was easily recognisable from the wide chassis and thick armour plating characterising the modular template of a Federation Type 16 heavy interceptor. But that was just the starting point from which this had been further refined. The lower hull of the ship's core housed a reinforced cargo bay, big enough to be modified to accommodate a landing craft or a smaller ship – her interceptor, for example – and that was a departure from the tried-and-trusted T-16 blueprint.

Unusually, there were two anti-fighter frag-cannon turrets mounted on the underside of the ship behind a third housing a laser. She also spotted the snub, fat barrel of a forward-facing railgun in the centre of the chunky body, beneath a raised flight module. Whoever designed the ship had in mind a trade-off between ship-to-ship combat and planetside operations. This was a bird for all environments, not just a spacefaring weapons platform like a regular T-16, but with all that armour, it would be just as tough to down. Her unconscious mind plotted its likely flight characteristics, how she'd need to adjust for the extra mass in low-atmosphere flight, how she would harness the drive from its powerful engines… she felt her talons twitching.

She heard voices at the far end of the hangar. A smaller door next to two massive, reinforced cargo gates, which were replicated on each side of the cavernous building, swung open in the distance to reveal Kassini with Krieger and Taro in tow. Vonya walked back over to her fighter and opened the cargo-bay ramp, as per Kassini's painstaking instructions from earlier. She stood back as the humans approached. Krieger, intent on inspecting the merchandise, gave her a nod as he passed which was both a greeting and a rhetorical assumption of permission to board her ship. Taro, on the other hand, stopped in his tracks when he got close enough to make out the Avion's features.

"Vonya of Ok'cuu?" he said.

Vonya bristled as she replied, the ruff of feathers on her neck standing to attention. "What if I am?"

"Do you have any idea of the stir you caused?" said Taro, a slight fanboy expression lighting up his face. "A month ago, your face was all over Avion news. You're a –"

Taro was interrupted by a disorientating flash of purple-tinted wing feathers as Vonya lost her shit, taking his legs out from under him with a lightning-fast judo-style leg sweep. He landed on his back with a sickening thud and Vonya kneeled on top of him, pinning his shoulders to the floor. She pushed the muzzle of her drawn pistol in beneath the startled human's jawline and screamed into his face, in barely intelligible English: "Drekking pirates, all know my name! You want to turn me in, right? Get reward? I'll fucking roast the lot of you."

A sudden, distorted foghorn of a bass note coming from near Krieger's ship at ear-splitting volume resonated through the air and vibrated the pits of their stomachs. Vonya and Kassini jumped out of their skins at the noise, then turned to witness its source.

The intimidating spherical shape of a massive battle droid powered through the air towards them. Several heavy-duty weapons systems jutted from its black two-metre-diameter carapace. This span rapidly while a red sensor darted rapidly from left to right and back again across it, a malevolent eye that left a trailing phosphoresent afterglow on their vision. Kassini knelt down by Vonya and instinctively pointed her service pistol directly at the looming sphere.

"Back the fuck off!" she screamed at the droid. It swivelled its auto-cannon to target her and she sensed a beam tracing up her face to her forehead, to match the one that was currently fixed between Vonya's eyes.

"Avion, human, drop your weapons or die. This is your final warning," intoned the droid in a burst of bass that was near-deafening.

"Krieger," shouted Kassini in the direction of the interceptor. "Is this attack dog yours? Call the fucking thing off!"

Krieger ran back down the ramp from the hold, assessed the situation and broke into a cackling laugh. He clicked his fingers and the battle droid's weapons systems snapped back into its spherical body in an instant. The droid hovered in the air in front of them, its anti-grav unit emitting a low hum as its eye roamed from side to side.

"I see you've met Rust, then," he said, as Vonya released Taro and clambered to her feet, holstering her weapon. "Pretty scary, huh? He came with our ship, the *USS Anomaly* here. We found him in the glovebox."

"Just 'cos you know who I am, don't get any bright ideas," the pilot said, back on her feet and regaining her composure. She offered Taro her hand to help him up. "Big-ass droid or not, I am no one's easy payday."

"Everyone calm down," said Krieger, arms spread with open palms. "Vonya, is it?"

The Avion flushed again in exasperation. "Could everyone just *stop* saying my name?"

"Okay, sorry," Krieger conceded. "We are here for the cargo and we know you aren't it, so put the gun away and keep it hid. Let's all just take a look at what we've got, load up the *Anomaly*, then we can all get the fuck out of Warren. Does that work for everyone?"

There was a chorus of nods. Taro straightened out his crumpled clothes and stretched his shoulders out on his way over to the interceptor. One by one, they followed him up the ramp.

It was a tight squeeze in the interceptor's cargo bay for all of them, and Kassini had to climb across one crate to reach the next as she opened each one to allow Krieger to inspect the cargo. It also became clear from Taro's apathetic stance against the wall that he wasn't particularly interested in the technicalities, and he eventually backed out and lit a cigarette on the ramp. Vonya narrowed her eyes at him and clacked her beak as the scent of smoke made its way to her at the ship's entrance.

Krieger looked over the equipment and whistled in appreciation, but was nonplussed when Kassini talked about even the basics of the technical detail. She noted his frown as she started to explain the ins and outs of the boxed railgun slugs, stopped and said: "Look, do you have somebody familiar with your ship's systems? They should probably look this over too, right?"

Krieger looked at her taken aback for a moment, but nodded and put his hand to his ear to activate the in-ear comms system he was wearing. The captain turned his shoulder to Kassini and spoke to the air beside him.

"Mak, lay off the guard duty and come down here, I need you to check out the new ordnance. Taro, while we're waiting, get back aboard *Anomaly* and check the cargo hold has a secure place for this stuff, will you?"

Krieger dropped his arm and turned back to her, his face now masked with a polite smile.

"Our technical droid's on its way," he said, as they heard Taro grind out his cigarette and walk back across the bay.

"Is it crazy dangerous like big fuck on your ship?" asked Vonya pointedly.

"In its own way," said Krieger with a laugh. "It's a lot easier to get along with, though."

They could hear a mixture of pneumatics and clanking metal feet on the decking outside now, moving at running pace. They heard the metallic footsteps hit the ramp, and Mak appeared.

The droid was fundamentally a five-foot-tall bipedal type, a skeletal, vaguely insectile framework of chrome and grey struts around an armoured central chest. It had exposed, hydraulic arms and legs and its shoulders sprouted a nest of antennae on either side of its gunmetal grey head.

This curved to a point at the front and was without obvious eyes. Instead, two short metallic protrusions held sensing cameras, sweeping forward from the base of the head. These twisted snake-like to either side on their extendable, sectional stalks as the droid entered in order to scan the occupants.

Kassini noticed some stencilled lettering on the upper right of the unit's chest which read '.14', next to which had been sprayed the word 'Mak' in bright-red lettering, but written in reverse as though viewed in a mirror. It also sported mean-looking bolt-on oblongs on each arm, which were clearly weapon systems. A solid-structured backpack contained two other long rifle-style weapons Kassini couldn't immediately identify completed the bizarre picture.

Krieger made way for the droid, which moved from the ramp into the cargo bay proper and pronounced: "And in the red corner, weighing in at a measly 270 pounds, the veteran contender – Mmmmmmmakkkk Four-teen!"

The voice was clearly a recording replicated from an old sports broadcast, which the droid now switched in timbre to a standard synth voice, if extremely primitive-sounding by the standards of the droids of the day.

"Captain," it said, ignoring Kassini and Vonya's amused expressions. "You wish me to confirm this equipment's suitability?"

"*Yes*, Mak," replied Krieger, slight annoyance in his voice.

The droid reacted almost instantly, scuttling across to the open crates in a flurry of limbs. The sensing stalks ran across each one quickly and, upon reaching the railgun ammunition, the droid moved closer. It picked up one of the magazines – too heavy for the average human – in its hands with ease and extruded a thin manipulator arm from a port on its carapace.

"Firearms! Guns! Weaponry! My favourites!" it exclaimed in somebody else's voice. Its manipulator rapidly stripped the protective tags complete with their warning sigils from the chunky housing. Next, it expertly ejected one of the slugs, a metal-sheathed dart designed to be propelled at massive velocity across space to pierce another vessel's armour and then explode internally, with a satisfying clunk of the mechanism. The droid's eyestalks looked over it intently.

Vonya's horror at this breach of protocol overcame her and she stepped forward with a multi-tonal squawk of alarm.

"In-sec-urrre live rounds! Ideeeot! Get it away from my ship if you want to close look!"

The droid rotated an eyestalk through 180 degrees towards Vonya without pausing its inspection, before replying in another of his unusual voices: "But worry not, your safety is guar-an-teed... the warhead is primed by the firing mechanism. It presents no threat to under-armoured organics."

Even as the words floated across the cargo bay, the droid was replacing the slug in the magazine and putting the whole unit back into the crate unharmed.

The eyestalk continued to hover disconcertingly in Vonya's direction, then flicked from side to side quickly, presumably to indicate her fighter.

"Besides which," it continued, voice returning to a normal synthetic cadence, "your vessel is clearly unusual and shows signs of heavy modifications – damaging it would not aid my interest in learning more about these. I am a specialist in ships' systems."

Vonya's look of complete surprise was obvious, even to those without routine experience of Avion facial expressions. Droids didn't usually refuse the orders of a ship's captain whose vessel they were visiting, nor pronounce themselves as specialists in anything.

"Not my point – never pull live rounds on deck!" she stammered.

Kassini had clocked the strange exchange, and locked eyes with Krieger.

"What the hell is this? You have an AI droid for an engineer?" she asked, incredulous.

Mak 14 had now closed and relocked the ammunition crate. He turned back to them with a hydraulic hiss, the eyestalk remaining perfectly stationary in the air as the rest of his body rotated to align with it. His synthetic voice burbled into life again.

"My brain is a non-sentient AI, human, with a learning personality prototype based on the Gillan versions – this was considered desirable as my initial tasking was subterfuge and infiltration via large-scale data operations. I was deployed among undesirable elements during the first human expansion."

"The *first* expansion? That ended over a hundred years ago!"

"That is correct. I am now an independent contractor, much like you, I suspect."

"Come on! That's bullshit," said Kassini. "There's no such thing as an independent droid, and autonomy in AI is strictly controlled, if it even exists at all."

"Nevertheless," interjected Krieger, closing down the conversation. "Mak is here, and doesn't always do what he's told, when he's told. We took him on to help us out with the ship, turns out he's handy in a fight and we don't ask him questions about his eccentricities. Is the gear going to work?"

"Yes, Captain Krieger, the ammunition and parts are of an acceptable specification and are compatible with the *Anomaly's* systems," replied the droid, impassively.

"Then let's get them loaded," Krieger replied over his shoulder as he made his way down the ramp. Vonya and Kassini exchanged a glance and turned to help.

It took them less than half an hour to transfer the cargo, Mak 14 making short work of moving the heavier containers straight into the hold at a running pace. Krieger and Kassini worked together to haul some of the lighter crates the distance across the hangar to the base of the *Anomaly's* yawning access ramp. Kassini noted the regular pouts of annoyance on the face of Taro as he dragged them up into the hold, wheezing slightly and clearly unused to the physical work.

Kassini, Krieger and the droid then returned to the fighter to make a final sweep of the cargo hold and, having established nothing had been missed or lost, walked down the ramp to get on with concluding their deal.

Krieger, in the lead, stopped dead as his foot made contact with the deck. With a sigh, he took in the three armed agents dressed in the uniform of the local Federation port agency, who stood in a semi-circle a few metres away. He'd half-hoped Warren was such a dump that they'd turn a blind eye, but no such luck. Some distance away behind them in the direction of the nearest massive cargo doors leading into Hangar 12 were 10 other agents, dressed in the varying fatigues and body armour of hired mercenary security. They were busily taking up position in the cover of the machinery and packing crates in the area.

The closest agent, a hard-eyed human woman, stepped forward and spoke in a clipped, professional tone.

"We have reason to believe there is an unsanctioned transaction taking place here and need you to submit to a routine cargo inspection – are you the commander of this ship?"

Kassini and Vonya were already trading looks; the former mouthed a suitable expletive in Avion to the pilot stood beside her. She noticed Vonya's talons were already hovering near the small but mean-looking sidearm partially obscured by her wings at her side. Kassini motioned downward with a hand and a shake of her head.

Krieger took a step forward, the fake smile from earlier plastered across his face again.

"I'm not – that one is mine," he said, indicating the *Anomaly*. "My Avion friend here has this honour. It's a beauty, don't you think? She was just doing us the favour of a tour."

He stepped aside smoothly to indicate Vonya. Kassini clocked him tapping his ear with his hand as part of the pointing motion, then turning his head slightly to whisper something that sounded suspiciously like an order into his comms.

"We'll be needing to inspect your ship too, then, Commander," said the woman distractedly, glancing at a tablet in her hand and not appearing to notice. Vonya stepped toward her.

"I am ship's captain," said Vonya stepping forward, in her broken human speech. "You know my registration?"

Suddenly, Mak 14 stomped noisily down the ramp, striding between the human and Avion women and coming to a stop close to the lead agent, deliberately blocking her view of Vonya. Obviously well-versed in this kind of trouble, the agent backed away automatically and the other two agents at her sides raised their weapons. The one on the right was about to shout a warning when Mak loudly began to reel off lines from one of his old media tics, in a female voice.

"Look at all these agents, hanging around our cargo bay!"

"Whoever controls this droid, get it out of our way," barked the lead agent, hand on her sidearm. "We'll destroy it if it continues to impede us."

"Now, now," said Krieger with a condescending tone. "No need for that, he's just glitchy. Gets nervous around guns, don't you, Mak?"

"Don't you worry, now, they're never going to find anything untoward," said Mak. This time, he'd spoken in a male voice apparently following on the dialogue from the previous one, another one of his old-media tics. Kassini noticed Krieger had used the distraction to shuffle backwards to the side of the interceptor ramp, obviously intending to use it for cover. Kassini's combat reflexes kicked in at this. She tensed involuntarily, ready to turn and run back up into the ship behind her.

The agent shook her head and stepped aside to open the line of fire for her colleagues, who raised their weapons menacingly at the droid.

"But we're just humble traders! Why would you want to impound our stuff?" concluded Mak in a third voice complete with the inflections of a character under duress, obviously from a film Kassini couldn't identify.

Suddenly, a hail of small-calibre and roaring high-explosive rounds reverberated deafeningly around the landing bay. The battle droid Rust had opened fire on the mercenaries, having hovered silently up into the air on the other side of the *Anomaly*, towards the back of the hangar space.

Kassini watched, momentarily startled, as one of these figures flew across the hangar in a gout of blood and gore, now in several distinct pieces. She leapt back up the ramp aided by full adrenaline and hurled herself to the side onto the deck, to place the comforting bulk of the fighter's hull between her and the danger. She scrabbled with the bulky handgun holstered under her jacket.

The hangar erupted into a hellscape of small arms fire and shouting, underpinned by a much closer terrified screech of the first agent's voice. Seconds later, the winged form of Vonya with a weapon in her hand rushed into the cargo bay and rolled down awkwardly next to Kassini. A volley of automatic fire beat staccato against the hull of the fighter as the Avion checked her weapon.

"What the fuck is going on!?!" Kassini yelled in Avion, above the din.

"Drek knows!" Vonya replied in a high-pitched stream of verbiage Kassini had difficulty following. "The Mak droid threw that female inspector at the other two!"

"Can you get into the flight module and get us out of here?"

"Bad crow! They'll shoot the drek out of it as soon as I start the engines."

Another volley of incoming rounds pinged off the armour around the cargo bay, spitting sparks off the ramp and sending out a lone ricochet. They were answered with several loud reports from directly beneath them. This was Krieger, hiding beneath the ramp.

Kassini had no time to ponder how her first contact with her mission target had gone so badly awry. Her thoughts were all military survival now as her training took over. She knelt by the edge of the ramp and looked down along it, spotting Krieger lean out and fire a couple more shots from a heavy pistol. She ducked back and leaned in to speak to Vonya, who was now kneeling behind her.

"Stay in here and be ready to fly," she said. Vonya nodded. Kassini took a deep breath, then slid down the ramp and used the opening above her as a handhold to swing herself in next to the captain. A shot sizzled off the metal where she'd been moments before.

Krieger jerked around toward the sudden movement and raised his handgun awkwardly.

"It's me! It's me!" she shouted as the battle droid opened up with its explosives again on the far side of the bay.

"What's the situation? Anybody get hit?" she asked the captain.

"Only these fucking jokers!" Krieger said loudly, returning to peeking around the edge of the ramp. "Mak injured that first customs agent pretty badly I think, the other two dragged her into that storage unit over there. One of them is going to work out they can get through into that machine yard to flank us shortly."

He indicated a number of parked loaders and modular racking systems to their left rear. Kassini turned to look at the machine room: its door was smashed open. The agents were inside and one of them leant around its frame and fired a couple of shots past her side of the ramp, causing her to squeeze closer to Krieger.

"The hired guns they brought with them have their hands full with Rust," the captain continued. "Clearly hiding our ship ID didn't work... from the number of mercs they've shown up with, it looks like somebody worked out the size of our bounty."

"...and now I'm marked 'associate' too, great!" spat Kassini. "We need to get those Feds out of there. I'll reposition closer to the door. You remember your hand signals?"

He smiled and raised his fist at his side into the motion for 'hurry up'.

She smirked and crept back to the edge of the ramp for a view of the agent, who ducked his head out and then quickly back in again, checking up on his targets. In a momentary lull in the combat elsewhere in the giant hangar, filled only with the yells of the distant mercenaries and the cries of their wounded, she could hear him communicating with his partners. She spotted some containers that would cover her approach from both threats – if she could get behind them.

"Put some fire down on the door so I can get to those containers," she said, tensing herself. "In three – two – one... go!"

Kassini leapt into a full-speed run a couple of seconds after the first report from Krieger's hefty pure-projectile handgun – then heard a second shot. It passed through the door and thudded into the roof, showering sparks and plastic shards.

Krieger's covering fire continued, reverberating around the spac. She covered the distance to the containers and more-or-less crashed into the rack with her left arm extended. "So far, so good," she thought, though with no idea if she'd been seen as she crossed the view from the doorway. Weapon in hand, she worked her way to the end of the rack carefully. She could just about make out the interior of the room through an oblong window beside a second, closed door.

She turned to look back at Krieger – now 10 or so metres away – to see him duck back beneath the ramp as a spatter of return fire from the agent in the doorway clanged off the hull of the fighter above him. She gave him a quick thumbs-up, and he signalled 'Move in' in response.

Kassini now made her move to creep up on the shooter in the doorway. She quickly darted from her position into the darkness of the equipment parking area. The sound of the chaos in the hangar blurred into itself as she worked her way among the loaders to place the bulk of the building between her and Krieger. She found herself by the walkway leading up to the door a couple of metres away.

Placing herself flat against the building, she edged up to the light cast from the window, slid down the wall to a crouch and glanced inside.

Nearest to her were the terminals and water cooler of an office unit. An open door led into the second room the agents were holding, walled with component racks and storage systems and wreathed with the smoke of small-arms fire. The female agent was on the floor with a medikit strewn next to her, heavily bandaged and unconscious. She flinched as firing resumed from inside the room opposite her. Visible muzzle flash and return fire from Krieger told her that the standoff between him and the agent in the doorway was still underway.

She ducked with a start as an unaccounted-for third agent appeared in the doorway with a snub-nosed submachine gun in his hand. She shuffled back across the floor with a slithering motion into the darkness, placing the nearest load-lifter between her and the window. She saw the agent, a small man with a lean, scarred face, appear in the window. He scanned the surroundings before opening the door beside him.

Another volley of fire from his compatriot seemed to spur him to move, and he began to work his way along the wall towards Krieger's side of the building.

Kassini took her chance to silently move across the walkway behind him, closing to a few feet and raising her weapon.

"Don't move!" she said in a low voice. The man in front of her froze. "Drop the weapon, hands away, turn slowly. I'm here on Federation business."

"Fuck," spat the man in a quiet tone, as he placed his weapon by the wall and turned towards her with his hands raised. "I know who you are, what the hell do you think *we're* doing here?"

"I wish you weren't – is fucking up a Service Intelligence operation part of your brief?" she replied. Her practised hand still maintained a line of fire straight at the man's shoulder, where the body armour he wore would be weakest. The namepatch on his upper chest read 'Burg'.

"We're protecting you, you idiot! Why do you think that chancer captain is still alive?" the man replied with venom. "I'm surprised a big score like him even made it out of the city. The call went out to every mercenary crew in the sector a short time after they landed."

"Then what are you doing here, all of a sudden?" Kassini replied, and the man sighed before lowering his voice to continue.

"We do still *try* to stop a bloodbath every time a lowlife spacer crawls into town, regardless of a no-interference status from Command. We stepped in last-minute and put their mercs' bullshit vigilante kill-or-capture mission under our jurisdiction. We'd have just taken a cut as usual and cleared out, and we wouldn't have bothered at all if we'd known about that mil-spec battle droid."

Burg paused before continuing. "But your guys fired first. So you're open to all-comers now, nothing we can do. And the mercs have called in reinforcements. You've got about 10 minutes to get out of here before another crew shows up with heavy weapons – they'll blow those ships to pieces."

Kassini's face dropped at the new information. Another explosion at the other end of the hangar made Burg wince.

"Stupid to hole up in there like that," she shot back at him. "Krieger can't escape if he's under fire – now I need to take you guys out and it needs to be convincing, which means you've gotta get hurt."

"Do what you got to do, 'cause I'm getting out of here. I have stun grenades – you want one? Should take care of Candinski on the door in there... they'll probably survive," the agent pointed a finger of his raised hand downward, and Kassini nodded an affirmative. He handed her a slender, gunmetal tube with the aspect of a small cigar case.

She stepped forward and reached out as if to grab the item, but took hold of Burg's wrist instead and yanked him hard towards her. At the same moment, she raised her handgun high and swung the top face of the weighty weapon against the side of his head with a well-drilled motion, making contact with his temple just as the surprise registered on his face. The sight left his eyes and Burg collapsed like a ragdoll against the wall, sliding down it into a seated position, head lolling.

"Sorry, Burg... I said it needed to be convincing," she said to herself before retrieving the slender grenade from the ground beside the unconscious agent and striding through the door.

Krieger had lost sight of Kassini as she disappeared into the darkness five minutes earlier. He was getting nowhere with the agent in the doorway as he loaded another large clip into his gun. He could see Mak 14 defending the approach to the *Anomaly's* cargo bay access ramp only 30 metres or so away, but the ground between him and his ship was open other than for the landing struts of the bigger ship and Vonya's fighter. The mercenaries had taken casualties from the two droids' eviscerating attack and had largely been driven further back to the massive cargo doors in the wall nearest to *Anomaly*. Out of range of Rust's heaviest launcher ordnance, they were now holding next to these.

"Awaiting reinforcements," Krieger thought, and ducked against the ramp again as another shot from the agent slammed into it. The guy was clearly just trying to keep him where he was until they showed up.

He raised his pistol again and peeked out, but the agent was waiting for him. The large man's shoulder and head were visible in the doorway behind his rifle steadied against the doorframe. Instead of a shot, though, Krieger heard the familiar whump of a stun grenade going off.

He cautiously peered out again to see a pair of uniformed, unmoving legs in the doorway. Kassini stood over them, pistol in hand, signalling 'clear' with the other. Cautiously uncurling from behind the ramp, he stood up as she leant out of the doorframe and shouted to him.

"They're all down, Krieger. Tell Vonya to get the engines started and get to your ship!"

Krieger gave her a thumbs up and called the instructions up the ramp to Vonya, who was still hiding in her ship's hold. The Avion pilot's streamlined head appeared.

"No need tell a bird twice, you get away from thrusters!" she said, and gesticulated toward the *Anomaly* before disappearing back into the ship. Krieger jogged over to Kassini as the fighter's beacons activated. It rapidly began to thrum as Vonya activated the power systems.

Kassini met him most of the way back and they hunkered down by the forward landing strut of the fighter. The firing on the other side of the hangar, which had briefly died off to a few pot-shots, was now intensifying from the direction of the doors. Rust was still airborne on their side of *Anomaly's* imposing hull, routinely dropping down and repositioning behind it to reappear in different places to keep the mercenaries guessing.

More and more of the new mercs were gradually working their way back through the doors among the shattered and smoking hangar equipment. They were looking for a vantage point that would allow them to drive off the stubborn battle droid.

"Good work," Krieger said gruffly, getting Kassini's attention. "Come with me... your payday is with Taro onboard *Anomaly* and we can at least get you clear of this shithole with us."

"You want me to run that gauntlet, open ground *towards* the guns?" she exclaimed, while secretly whooping at the good fortune that would see her get aboard the captain's ship.

Krieger was already speaking to his communication mic. "Mak, we're clear over here, going to need some cover to get to *Anomaly*. Computer, get us ready for immediate dust-off."

He raised his head over the landing strut to look at the droid, which reached an arm up to its back and removed a solid-looking rotary launcher. Without turning, the chrome figure placed the weapon against its shoulder and leant backwards to fire several canisters toward them. These landed 10 metres away and erupted into a thick cloud of grey smoke: this filled a large area around them, obscuring their approach to *Anomaly*.

"Now move!" shouted Krieger, and broke into a run. She was alongside the older captain as they made it to the edge of the smoke cloud a few seconds later. The personnel entrances at the other end of the hangar nearer the fighter burst open simultaneously. The point men of another two teams of mercenaries exploded through them, weapons raised. Kassini glanced over her shoulder to see them taking aim. She clumsily spun and reached toward Krieger with arms outstretched, to drag him to the ground.

They hit the solid decking together and slid under their momentum in a tangle of arms, legs and curses, staying low as the air above them came alive with the whip-crack of projectiles. Kassini's sidearm slid across the deck out of her reach.

She had no time to make a grab for it, nor feel the pain of the fall as she began to slither like a snake through the smoke. Krieger followed her lead. A stray shot pinged off the decking beside him.

They heard rather than saw Vonya's fighter taking off. From her flight module, she had spotted the second wave of mercenaries bursting into the hangar as she powered up the ship's final takeoff systems. The volley of shots meant for Krieger and Kassini had ripped across disconcertingly close to her relatively lightly armoured canopy.

With a rising whine and perfect stability, the fighter lifted a few metres into the air on its manoeuvring jets and rotated away from the now-closing mercenary teams. The nose tipped up to a sharp angle and the main thrusters transformed the whine into a low-bellied drone. The ship now drove rapidly clear of the ingress/egress cone in front of it with a final howling boom.

The energy backwash seared the decking behind the departing craft. The expanding jet cloud set fire to several nearby objects and drove a solid wall of superheated air full of slashing grit and debris towards the advancing troops, who leapt for cover. Unfortunately, the turbulence also dissipated most of the smoke screening Kassini and Krieger who, partially deafened from the close take-off, realised the shooting had stopped. They made it to their feet to run toward *Anomaly's* cargo ramp once again.

Responding to the increasing threat from the original teams by the main doors, Mak 14 had moved into the cover of the *Anomaly* itself and was using one of its four-square landing stanchions as a shield from the ever-increasing small-arms fire. The mercenaries had wheeled a heavy laser cannon mounted on a motorised platform and were sighting the ship. The droid neatly drilled a bolt of energy from one of its wrist-mounted weapons straight through the armoured plastic surround screening its operator. He was now writhing on the floor beside the unit screaming and waving his melted hands around, his fatigues and body armour singed and smoking.

Anomaly's engines were now providing the bass note to the intermittent stabbing thunder of weapons fire. Rust had dropped into Mak 14's previous defensive position after a volley of fire from several mercs had left his carapace dented and scarred.

Mak 14's left eyestalk swivelled back over his shoulder as the fighter took off. He took in the scattering teams now threatening to overwhelm them, calculating the distance between the running humans and the *Anomaly's* access ramp. Then his hydraulics hissed as he spun in position and accelerated rapidly into a full-speed sprint towards the pair, covering the 15 metres of ground in a few seconds.

The droid skidded to a halt as they passed him and reversed his direction to fall in between the captain and the now-recovering second merc team. One arm and one eye still faced the threat, even as Mak had begun to travel back in the opposite direction.

His wrist-mounted weapon punched out several bolts of energy at the first of the mercs to recover enough to aim their weapons. As he did so, a shot thumped square into the centre of the armoured casing on his back. The droid corrected its motion for the kinetic energy of the impact with the briefest of stumbles and continued to shepherd the humans to the foot of and then up the welcoming ramp. In the process, he absorbed several more shots that would have killed the others.

Krieger and Kassini collapsed to their knees in the cargo hold. Taro rushed over to help them and the captain screamed hoarsely at the ship's computer to lift off. Rust and Mak 14 now held position at the foot of the ramp and began to expend all their remaining ammunition towards any target foolish enough to be on their sensors. Their fire converted a 20-metre arc on both sides of the *Anomaly* into a torturous barrage of screaming ricochets, flame and smoke.

The ramp beacons activated, and the spherical battle droid reacted by smoothly hovering up it into the cargo bay in one motion. Mak 14 unshipped his rotary launcher for the last time and pumped off all its remaining smoke cartridges in different directions. The smaller droid then hopped onto the closing ramp and scuttled inside as the first thrust from the gigantic engines around him drove the blanket of smoke rapidly in all directions around the ship. The ramp crunched closed and *Anomaly's* engines boomed to full power to lift its landing gear clear of the deck. The noise in the hangar was deafening.

Agent Burg came to groggily, with a sticky feeling down one side of his face and the taste of blood in his mouth. He dragged himself to the edge of the storage facility wall in time to see the ship lift off. Its bulk rose majestically out of the smoke and fire that now permeated every area of the cavernous hangar in symphonic, roaring counterpoint to the staccato stutter and rattle of shots battering its lower hull from all directions.

The squat, boxy vessel rose vertically until it reached the bottom of the launch cone high above the ground. Now out of range of most of the weaponry below, the *Anomaly* tipped slowly to face the sky above it. Gravity gradually arrested its upward motion until the four powerful thrusters at the rear of the fuselage were in a position to compensate and accelerate the ship out into the dark and humid night, trailing smoke and steam like a skyborne comet.

As the sound of the engine burn faded to be replaced by the crackle of burning insulation and the sounds of mercenaries yelling and groaning, Burg turned his dazed face to stare along the length of the landing area to the hangar door. The long stripe of twisted machinery, torn-open cargo containers, splintered storage equipment and spent shell-casings down its centre widened out as it reached the doors at the far end. The area looked more like it had been subjected to a carpet bombing by a fighter squadron than an escape attempt.

"Convincing enough…" Burg thought as he pushed himself back up against the wall and fumbled for his communicator.

M

Kassini: Onboard *Anomaly*. We're clear of Warren. We had to shoot our way out: the crew you sent sustained injuries.

My rep as a dealer has taken a hit, too.

M

Drexler: You've infiltrated the crew, Agent, that's all that matters.

Focus on staying onboard.

Drexler out.

3. DISTRESS BEACON

Anomaly tore itself free of the atmosphere above the glittering city on Reece-Kolarov, a tiny wedge of gunmetal and chrome rushing to freedom in the infinite, airless cold between stars.

During take-off, Taro had given Krieger and Kassini a quick once-over; but apart from feeling drained as their adrenaline had subsided, they were unharmed and Kassini declined his offer of painkillers. She followed the pair up a flight of steps and through a short corridor to the heavily modified ship's small Command Information Centre and bridge. This was a standard modular room to the fore which sat above the armoured bulkheads separating *Anomaly's* cargo bay and powerplant. The bridge was connected to the flight module with a sealable door and another short connecting corridor. Kassini took in the command centre's separate terminals kitted out with detachable tablets on lockable spindle arms for accessing the ship's systems. Several large viewscreens lined the walls to either side of the flight module door, each serviced by plush, movable acceleration seating.

She'd taken a few minutes to collect herself while the others were busy, and it was in one of these bulky chairs that Kassini now sat, in front of a blank console and tablet bank. She was bruised and aching from the experience on the planet below, but glad to be alive and back in a shipboard environment in which she was eminently comfortable. She expertly unclipped the harnessing system that had kept her safely locked in position during the atmospheric flight – unclip, flip, unclip and lift. She'd made so many runs in ships of this size in her service life that the motion and procedure were second nature.

Krieger sat off to her left on the other side of the cabin tapping away at his own console, with Taro seated at the one behind that. She rotated her chair to face the diplomat, whose brow had furrowed slightly. He periodically rubbed his eyes and massaged his shoulders to relieve the effects of the harsh acceleration, obviously less accustomed to the extremes of space travel than his companion.

The captain jabbed aggressively at the tablet in front of him, apparently unfamiliar with whatever function he was trying to access. He seemed unshaken by their firefight and narrow escape. If anything, Kassini thought, he seemed more energised.

"Computer, are we clear of pursuit? I can only access our close-range scans here," he said, with a note of exasperation.

A disembodied voice answered from the hidden speakers above each console.

"There are no apparent threats," said the voice, in the fundamentally sexless tone of every workhorse ship's computer Kassini had ever come across, aside from a slight inflection that was suggestive of the poshness she associated with those who grew up on the inner Empire worlds. It was also clearly simulating a very noticeable sullenness, reminding her of a child who had just been told off by their parents in a supermarket.

"Thanks," replied Krieger, sarcasm evident in his voice. "Can you manage some more detail?"

"There are three vessels within scan range," the voice continued, "...two identifying as inbound cargo ships and a single smaller vessel with no active transponder, which is closing rapidly with *Anomaly*. Visual identification confirms this is the fighter you rendezvoused with planet-side. Furthermore, with my previous clipped response I was trying to convey how annoyed I am with you for jeopardising the ship."

"That's much more informative, good. Now is a time to be professional, please," replied Krieger with a sigh, and glanced at Kassini as she laughed out loud at the exchange. "We've only just activated the personality matrix, and we don't think the ship's former owners had finished its training before we took over," he said, by way of explanation.

"So you have an ancient lunatic computer for an engineer, and the one running the ship hasn't finished school yet? Must be a bumpy ride," Kassini said, incredulously.

"Vonya made it, at least," Taro interjected from behind her, finally managing to remove his harness after much fiddling. "Not surprising, from what I've heard."

"Helped save our asses too, whether she knows it or not. That takeoff burn from a standing start in gravity was wild flying, haven't seen anything like that since combat landings when I was a young officer on the *Solzhenitsyn* – gods bless her metal soul," Krieger replied.

"Quite," his companion replied, before focusing his gaze directly on Kassini. "And... I have to ask, why didn't our dealer friend here go with her?"

Kassini held his gaze but said nothing as Krieger rotated his chair to face him and spoke pointedly.

"Because you still need to pay her for the goods, and because she *also* saved my ass down there. I figure the least we could do is give her a ride out and buy her a drink somewhere. I could definitely use one."

"We need to get to the Boneyard, Krieger!" Taro's voice, usually smooth and cool, crackled with annoyance. "I understand you're enjoying being in charge again after all this time, but do I have to remind you that we can expect the kind of treatment we just narrowly escaped in any major population centre short of the outer systems? The ship might as well have a target painted on it until we can get it worked over."

"A big target that I've just inherited," Kassini shot back at him. "My reputation just went from a *very* discreet minor player running a few weapons systems for a select clientele to a moron whose deals turn into gun battles, *and* an associate of whatever nefarious shit you've been up to in the eyes of every bounty hunter in the Federation to boot. I'm sure my former clients are deleting or selling out my contact details as we speak. Plus, you just told me where you're heading, which makes it *worth* them torturing it out of me!"

"That's not our problem. People in your line of business know the risks, and we could easily just dump you out of the airlock now we have what we need," replied Taro, coldly.

Kassini looked to Krieger. "Out of the airlock? Is this the kind of crew you're running, Captain?"

"Enough," said Krieger, steel in his voice and looking daggers at Taro for his uncharacteristically macho outburst. "The Feds down there were after a cut of our deal, not to apprehend a fugitive – just in it for the money and got much more than they bargained for. Which is exactly what I want them to start expecting when they decide to take me on with only a gang of disorganised mercs for backup. That'll be why they haven't put out a system-wide for us yet... not that anybody in a low-sec system like this would answer it."

He looked to Kassini before continuing.

"I think we can afford to risk a stop at the orbital station so your pilot can pick you up before we go our separate ways. Computer, put us on a course for that. And contact that fighter with the coordinates."

"Underway," replied the voice from the speakers, this time devoid of the simulated sullenness of the previous exchange. Kassini shortly felt the ship begin to manoeuvre; Taro sighed with annoyance.

"An unnecessary risk, Krieger. Our luck's only going to hold out so long," he said, holding the captain's gaze for a moment before standing and stalking out of the room.

"Go count her money, Taro," Krieger called after him.

The computer piped up one more time as the ship's engines began to thrum.

"The pilot of the fighter has acknowledged the coordinates. She has also informed me that your friend's safety is part of her contract and if she is hurt, she will destroy the *Anomaly* before it leaves the system. I have assured her you intend her no harm."

Krieger looked at Kassini, who smiled inside and said: "Looks like you made at least one good call today, Captain."

Reece-Kolarov's orbital station traffic serviced the spaceport they had just left in a geosynchronous orbit, so was only a short distance away and required little deviation from their flightpath. Kassini sat quietly throughout the journey, pondering the situation while Krieger was busy with the flight systems.

She'd more or less told the truth about the mark that would be on her now, regardless of her secret status as a Federation agent. The majority of mercenaries in every system had no allegiance to anything other than hard currency, and she'd be viewed as a potential source of information on Krieger now they were associated. Not that it mattered. Her mission was to ingratiate herself into this crew one way or another – and her angle was now obvious, since it looked to her a lot like Krieger would be interested in some ex-military support of her stripe in his apparently fractious relationship with Taro.

Still, she couldn't understand what the Federation wanted an eye on this rogue ex-commander for. She was sure he'd ordered Mak 14 to trigger the firefight they'd just escaped, which was suggestive of the impulsive streak Drexler had hinted at in her briefing. Plus, his allusion to taking on the Feds made him sound like every other macho piratical type she'd ever dealt with: the type that inevitably ended up as space dust after biting off more than they could chew when left to their own devices. People like him usually ceased to be a problem through natural selection, she thought. If she was going to carry out her orders, it was obvious the real trick for her would be first gaining the trust of Krieger's crew, then working out how to avoid being dragged to her death by them.

After some cursing at the tablets around him, Krieger had succeeded in activating the external cameras to output to the large screens on the bridge wall. A fixed view of the orbital station soon loomed large before them. It was a roughly plus-sign-shaped structure about a mile long on each axis, with a docking facility and cargo port built into the centre of its converging arms. As before, they were given only a cursory identification challenge upon requesting a bay. Krieger transmitted the same code over again, after stating his business as 'refuelling' to traffic control.

They saw Vonya's fighter streak in ahead of them as they approached a bay door designated active by a cordon of blinking LEDs. The dart of black and grey metal was dwarfed by the huge structure as it peeled off the approach path to pass through a smaller opening above their own.

The computer had handed over approach control to a counterpart system in the station, but had to manually adjust the approach aggressively as they entered the bay, causing alarms to blare on the console ahead of Krieger. *Anomaly* was slightly bigger than the standard model of the T-16, and the docking system apparently couldn't make the necessary adjustments quickly enough.

"Ridiculous, what's the point in an auto-dock that scrapes the paintwork?" said Krieger, obviously on edge as he silenced the alarm with his palm. He only relaxed when they felt the big ship come to rest on its cushioned landing struts with a creaking metallic sigh that passed through the hull like a shiver. He stood up, unconsciously brushing at the stains on the shoulder of his shirt like a commander about to address his troops, and spoke as he headed for the door, motioning for Kassini to follow him.

"Come on, let's find and reassure your pilot."

Taro joined them from a side corridor with a small hold-all over one shoulder as they returned to the cargo bay, his face showing nothing other than its previous practised charm as he met Kassini's gaze. The three of them passed Mak 14, now devoid of his various weapon systems. He was flitting around a small scaffolded alcove in a corner of the cargo containing the apparently deactivated form of Rust, like a buzzing insect around a hive. The battle droid was suspended in a chain and hoist device while Mak seemed to be rearming its weapon systems, removing spent casings from a protruding magazine and dropping them into a large ammunition case on the floor beside the menacing droid's dark spherical form.

Krieger punched the fat red button to open the cargo ramp and tutted at a number of dents and furrows caused by the battle as they followed it down to the deck. The onrush of air from the station replaced the faint smell of gunsmoke still lingering in the hold.

The station had the luxury of discrete landing bays, and Vonya was already waiting for them in *Anomaly's*, leaning nonchalantly against a large plexiglass window overlooking the busy shipyard and cargo dock that serviced the individual bays via a complex system of droids and automata.

Kassini walked over to the Avion, grasping her long, taloned hand in hers and putting the other to her shoulder.

"Good to see you made it," she said in Avion. "I appreciate the protection. Krieger is okay."

"Just doing what I've been paid for, usually best to be aggressive with this type of unpredictable human," the Avion replied in a quiet, lower pitched melody no louder than a whisper.

"I agree," replied Kassini, and turned back to Krieger.

"All good," she said to the captain. "Now, about the money..."

Taro stepped forward immediately and proffered the hold-all.

"All here, in old Cee-bills, as requested," he said primly.

"...you can keep it," she said straight off the back of the interruption, keeping her eyes on Krieger's. "And call it an investment in your operation, because I need protection and to keep moving more than I need money and frankly, this ship and you guys don't look like a bad option to me."

Taro laughed out loud, but Krieger looked interested. "Go on," he said curtly, allowing Kassini to make her play.

"You obviously need a crew, Captain – a ship like yours usually has a complement of around eight people, let alone the droids – and I was a tac-specialist in shipboard marine detachments for a lot of years. You said you were an officer, I'm sure you're familiar with my particular skillset."

Krieger nodded. "Battlefield squad-level command, support coordination, tactical liaison, that sort of thing, right?" he said.

"Right. And squad sharpshooter training before that," she replied. The captain whistled in admiration. "Plus, if you're in need of equipment, weapons and ammunition, which I'm guessing you will be, I know a lot of useful people all the way to the outer colonies... including knowing what and where the Boneyard is, Taro."

Taro grimaced and looked to the captain.

“Come on, Krieger,” he said incredulously, “she could be anybody, could be working for anybody – a dealer is only one step up from the mercs we were just fighting in the spaceport. And we’ve got our own contacts.”

“And I still have my tac-augs, which will also come in handy,” continued Kassini.

“Explains your facility with languages, but you can save the story of why the marines let you keep those for another time. You were clearly a lifer before, so why would I trust the loyalty of an ex-Fed marine to my crew?” Krieger asked, watching her expression carefully. “I’m not planning to become a pirate warlord in some backwater system. We’re planning to steal everything we can from the Federation, hurt them wherever we can, Kassini.”

“Then you’re definitely going to need experienced people. And I have my own score to settle, but like you said, that’s a story for another time.”

Krieger, deep in thought, didn’t respond. Taro huffed and shook his head. This allowed Vonya, who had moved to stand next to Kassini, to speak.

“If you recruiting crew, I join too,” she said, and all three of the humans looked at the tall Avion’s streamlined head with a look of genuine surprise.

“Surprise?” she continued, her voice moving to a higher register to reflect amusement. “This *Anomaly* is experimental ship, and you can’t fly it. I’d join crew for chance to fly it alone, love new ships, but also bored of picking off pirate birds at jump-points and then people-hassle-problems every time I land for fuel. Living in too small ship with no crew-friends too long also, nice to have wing space.”

Krieger recovered his voice first.

“I hear you, but I’m not sure how that could work, Vonya – you know how long I fought Avions for? Fought pilots like you?” he said.

Vonya unfurled a wing and picked at it self-consciously with a talon.

“Same for me with humes. All past,” she said haltingly and seemed to be searching for words until Taro spoke.

“Now this I *can* get behind. You know her reputation, Krieger? Because I do – defector from the Avion navy, right? There’s a big reward for bringing you and your ship in, in one piece. Ok’cuu is like a royal family in Avion society, so you must be well connected. And you’ve already made a splash with the mercenary pilots in human space, they’re terrified of you,” he said, admiration evident in his voice.

“No love for Avion society bird-shit Taro Watan, all problems to me,” she said sharply, lasering the man with her dark eyes briefly before turning them back to Krieger. “None for warmonger Federation either, Captain. Loy-al to people loy-al to me, hu-man or Avion. And know ships and systems better than crazy droid.”

“You’ve seen her fly,” said Kassini. “If you don’t take her on, I will.”

Krieger switched between the two of them, then looked at Taro for a long moment. The smaller man gave nothing away. He looked back to Kassini as he drew a breath.

“Then I think, Taro, that you keep an eye on the sergeant here and I keep an eye on Vonya of Ok’cuu. Above all, we need people who will act. And neither of you hesitated with those mercs earlier – that’s good enough for me. For now.”

Kassini nodded to him and reached out a hand, which he grasped in a firm, military shake before extending the same to Vonya. She responded by spreading her wings to half span and dipping them forward, balling the talons of one hand before smacking her shoulder with it, which only Kassini understood as the Avion military salute. She laughed at Taro's blank expression.

"Means 'okay', Taro. Avion salute."

"Good," Krieger said. "One question, though. What about the fighter? *Anomaly* has no launch capability and I'm guessing you aren't about to leave it here for somebody to find."

Vonya trilled and clacked her beak in an alien laugh.

"You think I fly all way out of Avion space? Is military bird, design for transport," she said "Mod-u-lar, as you say it I think. Have money, this station can load it to *Anomaly* cargo bay, looks big enough. Maybe work out how to launch somehow too, later."

The commander in Krieger took over quickly. "Then you'd better get to it, pilot, because we do need to spin out of the system before any authorities look into what just happened planetside. Taro, show her around and we can send Mak to help you if you like."

Vonya shook her head. "No chance, the droid is maniac. I work it out."

As Taro beckoned Vonya toward *Anomaly* and the two of them began to move off, Krieger caught Kassini's eye and said: "I'll show you your quarters and properly introduce you to the ship. Then we should have that drink I said I owe you, got some of the hooch from that dive on Warren City onboard. Been a long time since I've had the chance to shoot the shit with a fellow officer, non-comm or not – and I want to hear that story."

"Sounds good to me, Captain… I'm not as young as I used to be and I need some pain relief after that fall saving you down there – back's suddenly killing me," she answered, with a rueful smile.

Vonya had heavily customised her interceptor since liberating it from the Avion navy and had the process of dismantling it into its modular components down to an artform. A droid crew from the station was duly hired to load its four parts into the spacious cargo bay of the *Anomaly* and, satisfied they were going to pay her ship due care and attention, she came back onboard to familiarise herself with the stolen Federation ship that was to be her new home.

The galley kitchen's nutri-dispensers – like the majority of ship parts these days – were to some extent cross-species compatible. Its output wasn't going to win any culinary awards on her homeworld, but its versatile menu was something she could work with. And when the ship put in at a station, there was always takeaway… Taro showed her to a small quarters off the main corridor leading to the CiC and she set up the sleeping harness she'd retrieved from her fighter in its corner.

Kassini, meanwhile, busied herself in an alcove off the cargo bay. She prepped the new mil-tech suits she'd brought before stowing them in the ship's weaponry locker alongside an assortment of rifles, pistols, ammo and field tech that fell way short of the standard Federation equipment issue on a multipurpose ship such as the *Anomaly*.

As she ducked into the locker with an armload of ballistic resistant fabric over her shoulders, she was startled by a brief but ear-shattering outburst of electronic music exploding from the powerful comm system designed for this, the largest room on the ship. The bass-heavy music was quickly commuted down in volume to be replaced by Taro's voice saying, "Well, it's certainly loud enough," over the open comms mic. Vonya must've figured she'd be spending a lot of her time down here maintaining her fighter and was putting the most important systems through their paces first.

After these few snatched hours of R&R had passed, *Anomaly* put back into space with its new pilot at the helm, significantly more smoothly than it had made port despite the increase in weight from the four bulky sections of the smaller fighter now stashed in its hold. The ship made its way under rapid acceleration to Ceraphylon's closest spin point.

It slowed and cruised gently around a nondescript area of space busy with other ships, skirting the largest concentrations of these until the computer pronounced it had reached an optimum area for a ship of its size to spin, whereupon Vonya activated the gravity-sensitive drive system.

"Computer, watch and learn," she jabbered as she manoeuvred the ship. "When we spin, I show you an Avion trick – copy my approach to the entry point and we come out the other side ready to make evasive moves... not come out like sitting ducks, like most hume pilots do."

On the vessel's small bridge, the crew registered the nausea and gravity shifts as the spin-move proper began. Krieger saw Taro's eyes glaze a little and then close as he slipped into the trance-like state often induced in those less accustomed to the mode of travel. Kassini had bowed her head and was focused on the floor of the cabin, her habitual breathing exercises obviously a product of her training and years in space. These somehow became more audible to him as the ship bent physics to pass at impossible speed from one point to another.

He fixed on the timer in the corner of the tablet nearest him – time felt like it was passing more slowly during a spin, and clock watching was acknowledged as one of the best ways to retain a grip on the reality of the situation. His own training took over, well-worn coping mechanisms coming into play as he noted the 15-minute countdown to the de-centrifuge step that would bring them out of drive at Boneyard.

Six of those minutes had passed when an alert pinged on the tablet next to the timer – comm data processing was nothing unusual, as small data packets from comm-buoys were still accessible to a spinning vessel – but almost immediately, the sense of interference with gravity lessened, then abruptly disappeared.

It suddenly felt to Krieger like he hadn't blinked for a day as reality reasserted itself. He rubbed his eyes and forced his dumb vocal chords into action.

"Too short, why?" he asked, groggily.

"We have dropped out of spin due to a software failsafe in the drive system I am yet to deactivate," the computer replied. There was something akin to sheepishness notable in its synth-voice. "I did try to warn you before we activated that I have not yet tested all of the billions of lines of code comprising the drive-navigation protocols – I am now tracing the interruption through the system. You should think yourself lucky the drive appears mechanically sound and that *Anomaly* has not dropped out too close to a stellar body and been torn apart by gravity stress."

"For space sake, just get us to Boneyard," Taro said blearily and with evident anger.

"This is the kind of thing you should be prepared for when you steal a prototype spaceship and then ignore its advice, crewman," replied the computer.

The prim answer instantly made Krieger's temper boil, but he stopped himself being drawn into another argument with the touchy intelligence and unballed his fist.

"Where the hell are we, then?" he managed.

"The outer gravity well of Reticuli 19 – the automated system has responded to a distress call when my fundamental circuits were busy navigating the spin. I am not what a human would call 'fully conscious' during spin management, so cannot countermand the interference from a priority sub-routine like this."

"Priority? Do you run the ship or not?"

"*Anomaly* is designated as a search and rescue vessel, Captain, for operation behind enemy lines where intelligence is sparse. The ship's stealth technology and low sensor form would be wasted if I did not respond to Federation distress calls, would it not?"

"The stealth system is *also* wasted because it's something else you don't know how to use though, isn't it, you digital idiot?" said Krieger, frustration finally causing him to lose his temper.

Kassini had pulled herself together now too and stopped as she unclipped the buckle on her harness to interject. "What did the distress call say?" she asked.

"Dated a fortnight ago, the emergency comm packet reads..." the computer took on a clipped tone. "'Colonists requesting priority extraction from any Federal vessel, habitation destroyed, majority of our group wiped out, survivors in hiding.'"

"A fortnight ago? On a standard spin route for half the quadrant, 20 patrols will have looked in on these yokels by now! A farmhand probably overloaded the colony reactor and they're all afraid of the dark," Krieger said, anger still evident in his voice.

"There is an update from a week ago, Captain... 'Further – SOS all vessels, Federation priority zero assigned to rescue, any independent vessel in range SOS. Coordinates attached, xeno danger close.'"

"Priority zero! So Federation command told local fleet to ignore this," Kassini said, looking at Krieger, whose face was taking on a harder expression at the import of the words. He seemed torn.

"Seems to be the way of the Federation these days to not get involved," she ventured.

"Abandoned by the Feds," he said, clearly listening to some inner dialogue.

Taro had recovered from the spin, and put down the eyedrops he was self-administering noisily on the console in front of him. "Krieger, now's not the time for heroics. We have no idea what's going on down there, our ship is identifiable as stolen goods and, while it might be a rescue ship, we're not exactly an experienced crew," he said.

"Speak for yourself," Krieger replied immediately, and winked sidelong at Kassini. "We can't just leave them down there without a hope. You have a problem with taking a look?"

"No sir," she replied.

"Good, I think we can handle it, Taro," he punched comms for the ship's flight module and said: "Vonya, can you fly *Anomaly* in atmo?"

"Captain ask a bird if she fly?" came the musical response from the open bridge speakers, followed by the squawking clatter of the Avion's beaked laughter.

"True, a stupid question. Take us down for a visual scan, but no closer. Computer, give Vonya the survivors' coordinates and dedicate your time to clearing out anything in the ship's programming that might interrupt future spin-drive operation."

The engines were already beginning to rumble as Taro opened his mouth to protest further. He caught himself, knowing the look in Krieger's eye meant that the old Federation fleet commander in him had returned and wouldn't be swayed.

Reticuli 19 was an Earth-like planet, one of the inner few of nine orbiting the yellowest of the system's numerous suns. Stellar distance and two massive gas giants among the outer planets seemingly balanced the powerful gravitational interactions on this picturesque world with those of the paired red giants orbiting one another relentlessly at the centre of the system.

These forces of nature had seen fit to bless the planet with a higher than usual number of mountain ranges, visible as huge white and grey spines jutting from the surrounding green as *Anomaly*'s squat bulk shouldered its way into the atmosphere in a heat-shielded fireball.

They were night-side, but the colony was still visible on the long-range visual scans. It was a nest of cuboid, modular buildings nestled close to the base of one of the ranges, built in a basin of green and brown earth. The area around it was devoid of the sparse vegetation and trees of the plains that stretched away to the foothills of the peaks which overlooked it. It looked to have been cleared deliberately in a circular shape.

The distress-signal coordinates were located in the foothills between the base of the mountain and the colony. Vonya skilfully placed their heavy ship in a slow, retro-thrust glide at long range to allow them time to assess the situation.

A number of springs running from the foothills followed the lie of the land down to become streams and then a river which snaked into the distance, passing through the colony's ring of cleared land and beyond, where it was eventually lost to the vegetation.

"Something wrong with that picture," said Krieger, looking at the view on the large screen at the cockpit end of the bridge module.

"Yeah, what's that tower? Never seen one of those in an Empire colony before," replied Taro. He was pointing to a single finger of grey technology spearing up into the air from the hill forming the bowl on the far side of the colony buildings.

"Some kind of drilling rig, maybe?" Kassini said from behind them.

Mak 14's synth voice suddenly piped up from the alcove in the CiC he bolted himself into when in transit.

"Elemental terraforming technology – an impressive piece of engineering," he said, his vocal tone shifting oddly between several voices.

Krieger and Kassini rounded on him, Krieger exclaiming: "Elementals! You serious?"

"I am always serious, and I was also in service for the Federation a lot longer than either of you. I retain a lot of old intelligence reports in my databank, one of which identifies an identical piece of equipment."

"Anything useful to add?" Krieger prompted the droid.

"My data is photographic," Mak continued. "It is accompanied by only a small amount of conjecture so the capabilities are unknown to me. However, it is sensible to assume a high probability that the xenos of the colony distress call are Elementals."

"Changes the game," said Krieger, the dread he felt at the prospect of facing the galaxy's enigmatic third species evident in his expression. "And explains why they only said 'xenos' in the message. Also makes it clear that we're the only chance any survivors have, as there's no way the Federation will risk an engagement with Ellies on behalf of a few prospectors. That'll be why nobody else has, either. They're specialists in field technology, so computer, scan the energy readings around the colony and the tower."

"The tower is generating significant energy distortions in the area, making certainty difficult, but the colony does not appear to show any electrical or radio activity, or life signs," the computer intoned.

"And we've had no opposition so far, so we can assume no long-range anti-ship emplacements. Screw it, let's get in and get out quick if we're doing this. Vonya, take us down as close to the distress coordinates as possible, as low as you can."

The pilot said nothing, answering only by gunning the ship's engines so hard the hull vibration started to move anything not firmly attached to its surface in the cabin, and increasing the angle of their altitude loss. The rest of the crew leant into the banking manoeuvre which followed, swinging them onto a straight-line approach for the foothills.

Vonya picked out the specific location of the coordinates in the cockpit which relayed it to the monitors in the CiC. A graphical overlay of an oval appeared around a large clear area approaching rapidly, apparently picked out by the survivors as large and flat enough to enable a rescue landing. A short distance away from this, small dark patches on the mountainside resolved into the entrances to caves as they approached. Many were complete with the conveyors and mechanical equipment of a mining operation.

Anomaly cut main drive and manoeuvring thrusters kicked in on max in a bout of flame and noise, steadying the ship into a hover with a boom that rattled the metal of the dormant machinery nearby, before Vonya gently set it down close to the distress-call coordinates.

M

Kassini: *Anomaly* has been pulled out
of spin jump, answering a distress call.

Your Avion pilot, Vonya, has pitched
in with Krieger of her own accord.

Reticuli-19 in Cerapholon -48.13235 79.016.

M

Drexler: Interesting decision. Be aware,
other agencies have discovered your
location and are planning to intercept.

M

Kassini: What kind of ‘interception’?

M

Drexler: Mercenaries. Keep the ship in
one piece, Agent Kassini. Drexler out.

4. THE SENTINEL

On the hillside overlooking the colony, the mystery spire's outer skin began to crawl, belying its metallic appearance as something altogether more alien. It pulsed from grey to a dark, mottled green and, as the sound of *Anomaly's* engines rushed past it, answered with a vast bass tone that shook the trees and buildings closest to it. With an organic clunk akin to the footstep of a giant it rotated a fraction, then again and again until it faced *Anomaly's* landing zone.

The air around it seemed to thicken and take on the imperceptibly oily feel associated with powerful electromagnetic emissions. A previously unheard thrum rose into the just-audible bass spectrum, reverberating through the ground to rattle the boarded windows of the nearest colony building. An encoded radio frequency sprang to life, transmitting data about the *Anomaly's* projected flightpath to unknown listeners.

Krieger and Kassini were suited up in the *Anomaly's* cargo hold, pulling the equipment they needed for EVA work from the nearby lockers. They were watched impassively by Mak 14 and Rust, the bright-red LED strip across the battle droid's chassis racing back and forth to signify full system activity. Krieger had noted how keen Vonya had been about getting her talons on the controls of their experimental ship, so Taro had remained on the bridge under instruction to make sure the Avion didn't get any ideas about taking off without them.

Krieger pulled the last of the straps tight on his armour and quickly activated his rifle, a pulse-shell bullpup automatic favoured as a personal defence weapon among Federation officers, and slapped a contact to activate the ramp.

"Full scans as soon as we're on the ground, Mak," he said as warning lights flashed and the ramp by his feet began to descend, allowing the sweet, cool air of the planet to billow in around them. "Let's find these colonists before any Elementals take an interest."

Kassini hefted her own rifle – a marksman weapon, much larger than Krieger's when fully deployed, set to compact mode with the stock and sights retracted – and started down the ramp. Krieger put a hand on her shoulder.

"Rust goes first," he said, and the battle droid span down the ramp with the barest flutter of sound from his anti-grav motors. Mak 14 extruded several sensor antennae from his shoulders and followed the heavily armoured sphere, the hydraulics of his vaguely insectile frame thumping quietly.

The two humans' earpieces clicked as the droid made contact. "Local scan clear, animal life only, long range suffering interference but suggests lifeforms around the nearest mine entrance. They are now signalling with a flashlight."

Rust's booming bass tone answered: "Perimeter established, weapon systems covering colony approach vectors, humans safe to advance."

Krieger snorted a laugh as he and Kassini cleared the ramp onto the surface.

The grass muffled their boots as they made their way uphill towards the mine entrance where Mak 14 had spotted the flashlight emanating from earlier. They found two ragged men in dirty work gear waiting for them, emerging from the other side of several large vehicles which had been parked as a barricade over one of the tunnel entrances.

Both were armed with pistols and eyed them warily as Krieger marched forward to speak, with his weapon stowed.

"Captain Krieger of the *Anomaly*. We're responding to a distress call."

"Federal captain?" the larger of the two men replied, gruffly.

"Independent."

"Thank the gods, and may they smile on you for responding, Captain. We'd just about given up hope. I'm Ror Yaricks, formerly the head of this colony's security team."

"How many of you are there?"

"Six standing, six wounded – we need to get undercover and then we need to get out of here. Your ship is in danger and so are you. This way, quickly!"

They were hastily motioned down the nearest tunnel and onto a small transport car which Yaricks started up and gunned deeper into the tunnel. The droids were able to keep up as they passed a hastily erected defensive post with two more armed colonists in cover at it. Krieger said something quietly into his communicator, which caused Rust to peel off and take up a position near the two startled men, the pulsing red band of his single eye disappearing eerily into the shadows as they moved off ahead.

As the vehicle crunched over what they assumed to be a mix of gravel and bare rock, Kassini shifted her rifle awkwardly to lean forward from her seat at the rear and tapped Yaricks' companion on the shoulder.

"What's the story?" she said as the man flinched and looked at her with eyes of a startled rodent.

Yaricks raised his head to answer from behind the wheel. "That's Paulson, he doesn't talk much," he said, eyes fixed on the downhill slope of the tunnel ahead illuminated only by the weak lights of the transport car.

"We've been hiding in here for a month," he continued. "Food's low but we have electricity, most of our droids and water – there were 100 or so colonists working here on a Federal contract, as these mountains are rich in some rare element called prometheum. Fucking Elementals arrived without warning, the tower thing first. It landed overnight and sat there doing nothing, other than upsetting all the electrical equipment in the colony buildings and scrambling communications."

"We had no idea what it was, so we started evac prep of course, but our orbital lifter was already too fried to run. We did manage to move enough of the comms gear out to the mine where the interference is lighter and send a message to Centre. Then people started disappearing the first night."

Yaricks' face was grave in the light from the dashboard as Krieger leant forward, the colder air of the tunnel system whipping his breath away. "Disappearing?" he asked.

"Yeah, like literally dematerialising in front of you. You ever watch old sci-fi movies? It's like how they used to envision teleportation working – an energy field would appear around somebody and boom, they'd be gone.

"Not just people either: trees, plants, animals, anything organic. We had a small science staff, and their best guess was that it was rebalancing the energy in the local area to compensate for what we'd been using – did you see the colony on the way in? Most of the trees around it weren't there originally, it's somehow generated and force-grown them, using us as an energy source."

Krieger looked incredulous and more than a little worried. Yaricks clocked this and continued: "You can relax about that here, best we can tell it's not a targeted system. It alters things seemingly at random or at least based on some algorithm we couldn't fathom, and its range appears to be localised around the colony – drekking Elementals treating us as an imbalance in the local eco-system to be fixed. The problem is its interference with manufactured energy sources in the local area isn't so limited. Droids and other small power sources seem unaffected, but ship drives and the colony power plant started screwing up pretty quickly. We think that landing zone is far enough out, but you might be best telling your ship to get airborne and to stand off clear of the interference while we get the others."

Krieger's hand went to his ear immediately. "Rust, we're pretty deep into the mine now – if you still have ship comms, tell *Anomaly* to get airborne and get clear of the interference we picked up."

"Relayed," replied Rust a few moments later, his synth voice already modulating weirdly in Krieger's ear through the layers of rock and steel around them.

Yaricks pulled the vehicle to a halt by a massive, heavy double door lit by the first active striplights they had seen throughout the journey and climbed out. Several similar transports to theirs stood nearby, all stained and battered from hard underground work.

"This is where we set up camp, most defensible area we could think of," said Yaricks as he climbed out of the transport.

"Defensible from what? You said the tower's effects couldn't reach you out here," said Kassini.

"The tower was only the first problem. We lost 30 or 40 of the team to that, but shuttled as much kit as we could out of the colony down here and set up a link to the orbital transmitter. The Federation made it clear they weren't going to prioritise a rescue, and when we started looking for a way to try and destroy the tower, the Elemental ground troops landed."

"How many? And are they still down there?" said Krieger immediately.

"Small number, we're pretty sure. We're not soldiers, Captain, we only had one firefight with them when we tried to get back to the colony to wire the tower with our stock of mining explosives. They refused to communicate and massacred us, my entire detail of colony blue-bands included – since then, they've been picking off anybody who strays too close to the colony. But they must know we can't leave, so I guess they're just waiting for the reinforcements to show up."

"Seems there's more than a few things you didn't mention in your distress call," interjected Kassini. "The usual Elemental strategy is not to push a fight if they don't have to. It's why they're so unpredictable on the ground, no effort is ever wasted – they'll seemingly ignore your operation as long as you're not in their way for the most part, but then when you are, you'll realise they've worked out the exact measure of your force composition and all your tactical weak points as they hit you with overwhelming force."

"You seem to know a lot about them," Yaricks replied.

"I've served, as has Krieger," said Kassini and left it at that.

Yaricks shrugged and turned to swipe a keycard against a sensor, causing the heavy doors to cycle slowly open. They halted with a reverberating thud.

The room beyond was a large storage area, judging by the rows of modular racking reaching up to the vaulted ceiling. There were a number of plas-steel boxes stacked on top of each over to one side of the room. Originally the welfare facilities and office buildings for the mine, these had been augmented with several more of the temporary buildings and were clearly serving the colony refugees as a living quarters and medical centre.

A ragged group of men and women filed out from these to greet Yaricks and the newcomers. They were rough-hewn people used to hard work and their grim expressions reflected their ordeal, yet one or two were overwhelmed with emotion as Yaricks explained that rescue had finally arrived. Looking at them, it didn't surprise Kassini that they had the mettle to survive what had been thrown at them.

Krieger introduced himself and offered them the use of the ship in the time-honoured tradition of spacer rescues; the group quickly collected themselves and what was left of their belongings together. They were soon moving back up the tunnel in the transport cars – most of their wounded were walking and talking, the few with more extreme injuries were loaded into a cargo trolley hastily jury-rigged with the outpost's portable medical equipment. The sole surviving med-tech fretted around them.

Halfway back to the fortified point in the tunnel, Rust's voice crackled across the radio, surrounded by a burst of static.

"Captain Krieger, *Anomaly* reports unable to execute lift-off. Respond. Captain Krieger, *Anomaly* reports..."

"Drek," said the captain as his hand snapped up to his ear. "Krieger responding."

"Message held. Relaying," Rust's voice was replaced with a recording of Taro's. "Tell Krieger we can't lift off, as soon as we powered the engines up the local interference intensified and it's messing with the power cores. Computer says they're spiking all over the place and if we push them in takeoff, they'll fail."

"The latest in a long line of screw-ups," said Kassini with a grim smile, the message having been relayed on their shared band. Krieger answered his radio before turning to Kassini.

"Rust, tell *Anomaly* to prepare to take these survivors onboard," he clicked off his headset. "We need to take that tower out, or we're stuck here like these guys."

"With the possibility of random molecular disassembly and an Elemental ground team to get past? Those aren't good odds, Captain," Kassini said, quietly.

The lead convoy glimpsed the flashlights of the defensive post in the distance and Mak 14, who had attached himself to the side of their vehicle for the journey, rotated his chromed, eyeless head towards them disconcertingly.

"Risky business for you organics! Rust and I will deactivate the tower."

"The two of you?" Kassini said, with a note of incredulity.

"Self-preservation protocols predict humans would fail, stranding us on this planet. Besides which, I am..." the droid went silent for a moment, unsure how to communicate the conclusions drawn from its ancient, corrupted code, "... enthusiastic... about these situations."

"He means he's a fan of suicide missions," added Krieger, by way of explanation. "You think you can deal with the Ellies, Mak?"

"Data suggests they are small in number and would not expect us to attack. I am an infiltration unit, I will float like a butterfly, sting like an angry ultrawasp, and they will never even know I was there." Mak's voice suddenly changed to something akin to the melodramatic shout of the leading man in an ancient barbarian-warrior movie. "And if we have to fight, I vill enjoy the challenge of releasing zem to their gods!"

Krieger laughed at Kassini's astounded expression, while Paulson, who was now driving their vehicle, looked terrified. "What the drek kind of robot is this?" she muttered as they stopped to pick up the people stationed in the tunnel.

The convoy drove direct to the *Anomaly's* waiting cargo ramp, Krieger supervising the men and women as they stowed themselves in the ship's hold. With much of the space taken up by their ammunition stores and Vonya's fighter, 12 extra people, even without baggage, stretched the available space to breaking point. Taro was introduced to their med-tech and began helping him tend to the wounded, directing the worst injuries to the ship's medical bay.

Rust had remained outside the ship and was patrolling a perimeter some distance between it and the colony like a floating guard dog. Kassini found Mak 14 in his equipment store on the far side of the now-crowded cargo bay, tightening the bolts on a small weapon attached to his arm.

"Mak, the energy interference will present a comms problem, right?"

"Yes, it also lowers accuracy of our area scans," replied the droid, hoisting a solid pack containing several weapons onto its back and beginning to secure it in place with several chassis bolts.

"Then hadn't I better come with you and stick at a safe distance, to act as a relay back to the ship?"

"That would be tactically sound, but you will need to know the range of the tower's effect on organics."

"Your choice of weapon..." the droid continued, indicating her rifle with a flick of an eyestalk, "suggests you are skilled in long-range marksmanship. Are you able to provide us with fire support?"

"I never miss a mark," she answered automatically with the standard Marine sharpshooter slogan.

Mak nodded with a faint whine of servos and turned abruptly to walk toward the access ramp. Kassini followed, and caught Krieger's attention as he helped the last of the colony survivors into the ship.

"Krieger, is it a good idea to leave the tower job in the hands of your maintenance droid? Particularly one that's apparently nostalgic for old movies?" she said, pointedly.

The captain sighed a little and motioned her away from the colonists he was stacking into the free space of the hold.

"You've noticed Mak is a little eccentric?" he said. "Ask him about his history sometime, if you can get him to make sense – he's some kind of prototype, a personality version from before the standardisation protocols were properly implemented. He managed to avoid the recall of all the old Federation service models you'll probably just about remember."

"Come on, standardisation is as old as space!"

"I'm serious. He was some kind of autonomous agent, a specialist in manipulating other robotic systems. And everybody and everything else."

"What for? And what the hell is a robotic Federal agent doing aboard your ship?"

"I said 'was' – Taro knew about him from the grapevine, he's one of the few droids the Feds are still officially offering a bounty for, and we needed a ship's engineer – to survive as long as he has, he's developed something of a reputation for being able to keep things running. He does jobs like ours in return for access to high-grade gear he says he 'needs', and something about needing to learn more from humans, and we thought a droid would at least be predictable. Which turned out to be entirely not the case."

Krieger leaned in, speaking in a hushed tone. "We're still not entirely sure if he's a full AI or not... but as for *what* he does, besides ship and robot systems – turned out that's infiltration, subversion and a lot of quiet murder. Truth is, if he says he's going to do something, I generally just let him get on with it. *Anomaly's* computer is afraid of him too, which is a bonus."

Kassini's face made it clear she had no idea what to make of all this. She shook her head and said: "If he's unpredictable, that's all the more reason for me to go out with them – they'll need a link point for comms back to the ship, if nothing else. I need you to speak to these guys and find out what they know about the range of the tower's lethal effect."

Krieger's brow furrowed for a moment as he considered saying something about being the one in charge, but he thought better of it and turned to scan the deck for Yaricks. Kassini grabbed her rifle and followed Mak 14 down the ramp.

A few minutes later, Kassini's earpiece crackled intermittently once before Krieger's voice resolved from the interference. "Kassini, you copy?"

"Clear enough," she replied.

"The tower's radius of effect is pretty obvious – you remember the circular area without vegetation we saw as we came down? According to Yaricks that's also its handiwork, presumably to give the ground troops visibility around the colony. Keep yourself well away from the outer perimeter of that and you should be okay."

"*Should* be okay? Well, if I suddenly stop responding, you know what happened."

It was still dark as the mission to take out the tower got underway. The droids headed in a straight line downhill towards the colony buildings half a mile away, Kassini jogging to keep up.

It appeared Mak had already briefed Rust. The droid dropped into formation with them as they passed through his patrol arc, his usually smooth spherical exterior bristling with open ports that revealed a variety of weapons and sensors. It seemed oddly more cheerful than usual as it hummed along beside them, only taking the time to remark sarcastically on the obvious danger to Kassini once as they went.

Mak lifted an appendage to halt their progress. "Grigorivitch, our scanners are less effective in these conditions and we must cover the open ground. Ongoing visual scanning of the area would be advantageous. We are close enough for you to act as our link back to ship, you should find a vantage point."

"Overwatch is fine by me," she replied, and stopped to survey the thin scattering of trees around them.

The droids sped up, Mak's hydraulics pistoning noisily in contrast to the sinister hum of Rust's anti-grav mechanism. They halted in the cover of a tall thicket overlooking a set of temporary one-storey buildings of similar construction to the ones in the mine, at the very edge of the circular expanse of open ground. The grass in front of them was pockmarked with raw-edged holes where trees and vegetation had been absorbed by the mysterious tower.

"Full-spectrum scan shows anomalous readings on the closest rooftops – confirm?" Krieger said over the squad band, clearly monitoring the droid's telemetry back at the ship.

"Confirm, probable sentry position," replied Rust.

"Give me a minute, halfway up this tree," responded Kassini, audibly out of breath. A couple of minutes later, her voice returned.

"Somebody on the left building roof, wearing optical camouflage – scope thermal shows a small signature which I think is an energy-weapon power coil of some kind. The other building has several vent outlets obscuring my view, but I think there's a defensive emplacement of some kind behind one of them… yeah, confirmed, launcher platform, not camouflaged so it'll be mobile, knowing the Ellies. Nothing else visible."

"Rust, target priority launcher. Kassini, deal with the other target," Mak 14 said as he removed his own small launcher from his pack with his left arm, clicked a switch on its firing mechanism, and sprang into a run directly for the gap between the two buildings.

Kassini's explosive round split the air seconds later, targeted for the camouflaged heat signature. The Elemental soldier attached to it was laid on the roof guarding the approach, and suddenly found itself holding a ball of rapidly expanding energy instead of a weapon. The discharge interacted with its personal camouflage system in a coruscating explosion of light and bright, ethereal colour, and hurled it bodily backwards as though it had been grabbed around the neck by the talons of a passing bird of prey.

Flying through the air, it should have smashed awkwardly into the set of emergency stair handholds behind it but for a stabilising field of some kind. The metal tubes of the handholds bent before the tall alien's body hit them, seeming to slow its arc and impact in a way that defied the eye and saved it from further injury.

It still went down with a multi-tonal scream that mixed with the report from the explosion, clutching its energy-burned face and began to roll around on the roof as Rust moved out of the thicket and aimed several laser dots at the metallic surface of the vent nearest the launcher position.

Kassini's confusion was evident in her voice as she activated her radio.

"Droids – be careful, the trooper I just hit had some kind of personal shielding system. They're down, but I've never seen anything like that before."

Mak was still running inhumanly fast halfway to the buildings as Rust fired a volley of shells from a port on the top of his chassis that arced through the air. The spindly infiltrator droid rotated his upper body so his left arm could fire the launcher it held several times. Small canisters exploded on impact along the front edge of the vent unit shielding the launcher, releasing a thick cloud of smoke and metallic strips designed to cover and confuse both the eye and automated targeting systems.

A trooper-sized biomechanical pod made of a tough organic fibre which cocooned another Elemental lookout was already tracking Mak 14's approach from the roof, and fired several bolts of energy from a forward-mounted barrel as the smoke enveloped it. Its perturbed tracking system threw these behind and to the sides of the approaching droid. They burst into seething patches of electrical energy which connected together instantly to form a triangle of crackling, spitting voltage. This collapsed in on itself and intensified to bright white just behind Mak, before exploding outward into tongues of blue fire, several arcing instantaneously into the approaching droid.

Mak staggered as Rust's barrage of five high-explosive shells mortared in on the launcher, obliterating the roof around it and sending shrapnel crackling towards the resinous canopy. A repulsor shield similar to the one Kassini had seen earlier protected the operator from the worst of the danger – but not from the collapsing supports of the roof beneath it.

The Elemental visibly flailed at the controls as the unit slid through the roof and disappeared with a resounding crash to the floor beneath.

Mak 14 was still moving at maximum pace but, visibly thrown by the electrical attack, smashed straight into a door on the same building he had intended to kick open, bursting its plastic structure to splinters and upending himself. The droid skidded across the floor on its front like a skimming stone, throwing sparks as the Elemental soldier extricated itself from the crushed launcher platform.

It reacted quickly, snapping off a wide shot from a sleek sidearm which seared Mak's head as it sizzled past and blew a chunk out of the already ravaged doorframe. Mak's hydraulic arms pistoned him upright in a second, positioning him perfectly to fire his wrist-mounted blaster straight into the chest of the crouching alien. The blast spread across its shield in a blaze of colour, absorbing much of the force of the shot but still bouncing the trooper back into the ruined structure of its launcher vehicle with an audible crack of breaking bones.

The droid leapt at the soldier and drove the weapon hard into the perimeter of the shielding system, its repulsor mechanism slowing his motion down as he arrived, then fired the energy weapon again at point-blank range. This time, the shot was contained on the inside of the forcefield, instantly turning the air around the trooper's lightly armoured body into a contained nuclear furnace, which vapourised it from the legs up. As the shield mechanism itself disintegrated, the energy burst free, washing over Mak 14 in a dissipated form just strong enough to blacken his now heavily scratched outer shell.

"Target eliminated. This troop was also heavily shielded, but was vulnerable to a melee attack," he radioed, and began running an internal diagnostic as he moved to survey the long main street on the other side of the building. This was flanked by larger, more permanent structures and at its end, the alien tower loomed ominously, glowing with energy that cast a sickly light across the far end of the colony.

"So much for infiltration... I think I hit lucky with the first shot," replied Kassini, her voice crunching in the interference pattern from the building and the tower. "You've got company between you and the tower, movement towards your flanks, numbers unknown."

Rust was now moving across the open ground to the buildings. The other Elemental trooper had stopped mewling and apparently expired. A spreading pool of dark-coloured fluid dripped grotesquely down the side of the building where it lay.

"These targets deployed anti-droid weaponry," the battle droid said as it destroyed some more of the ravaged doorframe to join Mak in the room.

"Arc weapon, damage minimal," Mak replied. "The front door is open and the rest of the force must now react. You and Grigorivitch will deal with the soldiers – I will worry about the tower."

Mak again wasted no time. He smashed the window next to him with a well-placed elbow, fired a volley of smoke cartridges out of it and ran to the cover of the next building along the road. Surprised by the boldness of his advance, the flanking Elementals unleashed an unfocused hail of fully automatic fire. This threw up chunks of plascrete from the road around him and crumpled parts of the building. As he reached it, Mak smashed through another window in a crash-dive, disappearing from sight.

Rust's sinister red eye cast shadows on the wall as he moved silently to the other side of the broken window, then returned fire with the main rotary-barrelled heavy weapon mounted front and centre of his spherical body. A cloud of magnetic gauss rounds and conventional explosive shells from the alternating barrels punctured and then obliterated the walls providing cover for the Elemental troops inside. His targeting system noted the telltale sparks of colour from shielding impacts as shots, ricochets and debris peppered the targets inside.

The droid moved quickly away from the window into a corner of the building, hearing Kassini's rifle boom again as the portion of wall beside it was vapourised by a powerful single-strike laser weapon. His positional sensors told Rust Kassini's shot had passed through a window of the other building. On his other side, a number of heavy feet tramped rapidly across the hard surface on the other side of the wall. Another volley of fire from the Elementals caved part of the covering wall in beside him.

Kassini, lying along a thick branch in the low canopy of the tree, could see through her scope that Rust had been backed up against the wall. She had fired early to give the flanking troops pause and they were now scanning for her position before pushing the assault on the building containing the beleaguered battle droid.

"Surrounded in there Rust, two targets on the wall behind you with more covering them, and one in the ground-floor building in front. They'll try and hit the building from both sides. Back door only if you're planning to come out."

"Acknowledged," the droid replied and through her targeting sight, Kassini saw it extrude a number of what looked like batons from the sides of its frame, then begin to rapidly rotate. It swung wildly away from the wall towards the centre of the room, under fire from the aliens, then hurled itself straight back at the wall.

The two Elemental troops on the other side of the wall tried to leap clear as the tonne of rapidly rotating red-lit menace knocked it down around them.

Rust was suddenly in between them at a range of a couple of metres. The batons attached to the whirling droid, similar in function to the cutting torches used to weld the hull plating of spacecraft, had burst into deadly life to weaken the wall. They continued straight through the shielding and body of the nearest trooper who was struggling to get to his feet.

The tall alien was carved into pieces in an instant, seeming to liquefy from the midriff in a burst of fluid and internal organs. Imparted momentum by the rotating droid in its midst, a wave of green and brown fluid splashed up what remained of the wall and enveloped Rust. The unfortunate alien's squad-mate scrabbled across the ground away from the scene screaming, surrounded by the flying debris that had previously been its comrade. Rust moved immediately towards the source of the noise and, still rotating, opened fire with its main weapon system again.

More efficient than any conventional shotgun in the relatively confined space, the rotational storm of shot hit everything inside 10 yards and wreathed a roughly cubic area in fire and smoke, thankfully masking the aftermath of the hideous spectacle. The second Elemental trooper was battered by the impact of multiple direct hits, scudding along the ground in a multicoloured display as his shielding system struggled to protect him from both the shots and the impact.

Rust's assault was short-lived. A searing white beam sizzled from two further Elemental troopers in their covering position, striking the side of his spherical chassis and illuminating him in a blaze of energy. One of the energy batons sheared off and cracked against the wall and the droid span backwards away from the shot, seemingly out of control. His anti-grav motor failed and the heavy ball of metal clanged off the solid surface of the pathway beneath it, glowing bright red in a mist of melted armour and burnt insulation.

Kassini heard the clamour over the comms. "Rust – damage report..." she transmitted.

A long fully auto burst of conventional ammunition further battered his armour. A backup system activated and the damaged droid rolled back into cover around the corner of the ruined building, leaving the long form of the wounded Elemental soldier dragging himself towards his squad mates where he had landed.

The covering squad had been revealed to Kassini through the ravaged wall. She clearly saw the helmet of an Elemental who was lifting a large, tripod-mounted heavy weapon it had used to blast Rust. She pulled her rifle's trigger and the alien's head snapped back in a blaze of shielding, flinging it backwards into the building wall behind it. Somehow it was still alive, she noted, as she cycled another round into her weapon.

Apparently the Elemental on the other side of the building had seen her shot, because a burst of fire suddenly ripped through the branches and sprayed leaves and splinters across her position as they exploded randomly against the trunk above her. She ducked reflexively, fired another round in the approximate direction of the covering party and swung around the branch to drop out of the tree.

Hitting the ground hard winded her. Her vision tunnelled and as she fought the rising nausea in her stomach, she heard the snap and rattle of incoming fire in the brush around her. She gathered her breath for a second before shouting into her comms.

"Mak, Rust's down and I'm taking fire – tell me you're dealing with that tower!"

"I have reached the tower," came the impassive response, followed by Rust's unaffected synth voice.

"Rust still combat effective, human, battle droids do not expire as easily as fleshlings."

Mak 14 was stood at the base of the strange obelisk looking up, the bulk of the final colony building he had passed between him and the sound of the battle. Up close, the obelisk exuded a greenish light, visible between the moving organic plates that made up its exterior. It was not immediately apparent how it could be deactivated.

The droid removed an oblong box from his pack, placing it down next to what he decided was an interface built on to a flat surface extruded from the base of the tower. Mak's influence terminal was a prototype even before he had heavily modified it over the course of many years, designed to connect manually and remotely with automated systems, decode and overwhelm any software defences and allow the droid a degree of control over its host. When switched to scan, the unit hummed for a moment before it began to feed Mak overview information on the data streams nearby, linking him to the 'mind' of the tower.

The complexity of this one was intriguing and it took him a few moments to decode the information as it flowed past him. The bigger and more complex the unit, the more difficult it was to control for any length of time, and this was clearly a high-level mind capable of some autonomous action, so direct control would be very difficult to achieve. The logic and pathways were the product of Elemental semi-organic technology, but it was still just an artificial mind of the kind Mak was used to manipulating. He'd dealt with Elemental equipment before.

He offered up a standard diagnostic question.

`> System status?`

A response formed in the data before him.

`> Local area rebalancing nominal to profile`

`> Fluctuations in local energy detected`

> Probable interstellar vehicle

> Support protocol active

> Support protocol function?

> Divert local energy to colony-preparation team functions

> Non-organic intrusion detected in energy profile

> Deactivate support protocol

> Unwise. Colony-preparation team protect core functions

The answer did not surprise Mak. It seemed he'd have to take the direct, logical route with this intelligence. He stood for a moment while formulating the quickest way to explain to the alien AI just where the danger to its core functions was presently situated.

> Deactivate support protocol, or I will corrupt your logic cores

> Threat registered. How do you intend to 'corrupt logic cores'? Logic cores are well protected

High above Mak 14, a collar on the tower began to rotate, ominously deploying a mean-looking cannon towards him from a recess – a weapon not dissimilar to the one which had recently been used to great effect on Rust. He responded to this by injecting a small amount of specialised code into the system interface, and the collar suddenly jerked to a halt well before the weapon had drawn its bead.

The snub barrel dipped down to the extent of its capability, targeting a small outcrop of electronics tethered to the tower's base by several fat, snakelike cables.

> There are a number of ways. Your own defensive systems are the most efficient

> Unknown failure

> I am going to count to 10…

Elsewhere, Rust had just rolled himself along the near edge of the building, moving himself closer to the trooper still firing from the building next door.

"Anti-grav back online, scans minimal – target positions required," the droid told Kassini as he span back into the air again. Sparks flashed from the ragged hole in his exterior. He was nothing if not relentless, she thought.

"Single target nearest corner, pretty much underneath the corpse on the roof, can you hit the window?" she replied quickly.

"Coordinates understood," replied the droid before flicking around the corner, keeping the damaged armour segment to the rear, and seeming to nod its body down towards the enemy trooper. The tall alien form reacted to the movement with a burst of fire which stitched small explosions around and across the droid, but not before it had pumped several of the high-explosive mortar grenades through the shattered plexiglass of the window.

These detonated at the trooper's feet in the confined space. The combined force of multiple explosions overwhelmed its shielding in a blaze of hellish red and white and ripped the soldier to pieces. Debris skittled down onto Rust as he moved into the smoke and dust cloud to locate the remaining Elemental troops, keeping the wall of the first building he had occupied between him and them.

Kassini swung her scope back expecting to see the remaining two active troopers, but saw nothing until another shot from the heavy weapon lit the area up. Now set up on the second floor, it carved straight through the wall beside Rust, further punishing the droid with debris and setting the area around him on fire. The follow up of automatic fire from the second trooper was inaccurate, but the small explosions knocked more pits and scars out of the droid's remaining armour.

"Second floor, the heavy is on the second floor. No shot here," she shouted, and crouched up off the grass to try and resight her weapon.

Mak 14's voice now crackled across the relay. "The tower is no longer a threat. It was diverting energy to strengthen the troopers' shielding systems. These special protocols are deactivated. I am on the roof of the building in front of you – three targets on the second floor, one injured."

"Unlucky fleshbags!" exclaimed Rust loudly. "High-ex rounds are out. Closing."

Kassini heard Rust gun his anti-grav drive with a deep rumble as he rose level with the second floor. He hurled himself directly at the trooper, firing the remaining ammunition from his rotary cannon wildly in its direction. The air between them exploded with iridescence as the soldier's weakened shield collapsed. The droid smashed straight into the alien's position, collecting the heavy weapon and the soldier and barrelling all of them through a wall into the darkness of the second-storey office behind them.

Musical Elemental screams and wild automatic fire briefly ensued, silenced by a huge whumping explosion that blew out the remaining windows of the building and caused its roof to bow upwards and then collapse.

Kassini tapped her earpiece. "Rust, you read me? What the drek was that?"

Mak 14 answered after a moment. "The Elementals are destroyed, but Rust has sustained further damage – the injured one detonated a grenade while we were dealing with the others. Rust has deactivated his higher functions – I will bring him back in with me."

Vonya swept the *Anomaly* up through the sunrise-painted clouds of Reticuli 19, daubing broad brushstrokes through the atmosphere's invisible banks of thermals and turbulence. To a ground-based human observer squinting into the sun, her flightpath would've seemed elegant, graceful even... a pattern clearly guided by an intuition more akin to that of a bird of prey than their own.

It was a different story for the anxious humans who were strapping themselves hurriedly into the ship's cabin. They could feel the Avion pilot's sudden and unpredictable inertial adjustments in the pits of their stomachs and as the *Anomaly* pitched and yawed, they caught queasy glimpses of sky out of the cabin's small viewing ports. Eventually, these prismatic stripes of upper atmosphere faded from shades of blue and gave way to the reassuring blackness of space.

In the cockpit, Vonya checked her instruments and finally settled the ship on an arrowing straightline trajectory. Her scope read clear. Back in the cabin, her clipped, melodic voice projected over the crackle of the intercom. "No one follows... heading for cover of moon ahead."

Krieger unbuckled his straps and clanked towards the door, turning as he left to say: "I need to see Vonya. Taro, get back to the medibay and finish patching our guests up, will you?"

"On it, Captain," Watanabe replied and began shepherding the rescued miners to the medibay off to the ship's stern. Kassini slowly unbuckled herself while she watched Krieger disappear into the cockpit to update Vonya.

Once alone, she arched her back, asking her body how it had held up during their skirmish together. The fall from the tree had given rise to a chorus of singing pain that flared up in response to her stretching her muscles. 'Persistent wear and tear,' her debriefing had said.

'Maybe I'll ask Taro to scan me after he's cleared those miners,' she thought to herself, then decided it might be too soon to reveal any kind of weakness so openly.

In a recessed corner of the room, Mak 14 had set up a temporary maintenance station in the quieter confines of the CiC. He was already working on Rust, whom he had carefully stripped of his bulky outer exoskeleton to only his core internal modules. The rest of the battle droid's armoured exterior was now hanging in its scaffold in the hold surrounded by the refugees, and Mak had several diagnostic sensors deployed to probe the damage to his complicated innards. He carried out his movements with the gentle but methodical precision of a battlefield medic dabbing tentatively at a soldier's wounds.

As Kassini walked over for a closer look at the extent of the damage, the faint, ferrous odour of super-heated and cooled metal mingling with the ship's sterile air-con atmosphere tickled her nose. 14 paused his ministrations, rotated an eyestalk towards her, and in a cartoonish, high voice, said: "*Kinda* busy with our friend here right now, Grigorivitch..." before continuing with his work.

"I see that, Mak," Kassini said, eyeing the scorched metal around Rust's primary drive unit. "If it weren't for me providing cover, those Ellie troops would have wiped him out. Maybe they don't make them like they used to."

Mak 14 paused again. His instruments slumped almost imperceptibly, indicating to Kassini that if he could've sighed, he would have. "Rust is an experienced DefCon-series Empire assault mech and is virtually identical to the latest production-line update," the droid intoned, back in his normal synth voice.

He continued his repairs, sullenly deploying an arm with a whirring brush-like attachment to clear the carbon-scoring from a screwhead – the droid seemed strangely serious to Kassini as he continued. "You should not underestimate the combat effectiveness of this model. The Empire's synthetic battle units regularly outperform every other automated and hybrid combat-mechanoid system in field tests against those of other factions. I couldn't take a direct hit from an Elemental heavy team and continue to function. He is an Empire assault droid – taking damage on our behalf is what he does best."

"I've just seen exactly what that mech is capable of, Mak – and I've fought side-by-side with enough of them before you two came along," said Kassini, leaning in closer to the most ear-like protrusion on the skeletal droid's angular metal head and lowering her voice almost to a whisper. "And I certainly don't care if he got a 10 out of 10 in *What Battle Droid*."

"The score was 93 per cent," 14 pointed out impassively.

Kassini sighed. "*Sarcasm*, Mak. Look, all I care about is whether or not he's going to be fully on-point when he's back online. Because if we send him out to protect us, we need to know we can rely on him."

"Rust is infinitely repairable. He will only require several off-the-shelf components to ensure he is restored to full operational capacity," Mak replied. He scanned her from head-to-toe with an eyestalk as he spoke. "Once we have acquired the parts, he will be there to save you from sustaining serious injuries. Additional ones."

At this, Kassini became aware of the throb in her leg and side again. "Someone's a pretty smart robot," she said, patronisingly. "And if you are indeed so smart, and he is indeed so effective in combat, I ask again: how come that small squad of Elementals was able to take him out?"

"I was as surprised at this outcome as you," 14 conceded.

"Sorry, is this the bridge? Am I allowed to come in?" Yaricks asked, looking furtive in the frame of the open door.

Kassini nodded and he entered the cabin, quickly sensing her tension. "Your robot's right about one thing," he offered. "We underestimate at our peril, they wiped out my team in minutes... those soldiers down there, who did this to your battle droid, were some kind of advance Special Forces team. They're not just your regular Elemental grunts."

"Again, that much is obvious," said Kassini, impatiently. "So how come they were shielded? I've never seen personal shields on the battlefield before."

"The tower was both a defensive and a utility device, it seems. It was the source of the personal shielding deployed by those troops – a mechanism I do not understand," 14 offered.

"Something you don't understand, Mak? That's new," said Krieger from the doorway. He re-entered the cabin with Vonya in tow and Yaricks flashed a momentary look of surprise at the Avion pilot.

"We were trying to get to the bottom of how the Elemental troops were able to take so much of a beating and still fight on," said Kassini. "Mak discovered they were protected by personal shielding systems from their tower of power."

"Wait, I thought the tower was a terraforming device, not a weapon?" Krieger said.

"It's a battlefield support system, too. And probably more besides. Hence why they sent those specialist troops to protect it," replied Kassini.

"Right, Yaricks, you gave me the skinny version of what happened down there, but we need to figure out what you're doing next," said Krieger. "What were your mission parameters?"

"It was just a regulation shitshow – to begin with, anyway," said Yaricks. "You know, send out a prospector ship to some likely planet, in our case the *Pali Gap*. Seeing as she's no longer in orbit I'm guessing the Elementals stole or destroyed her when they dropped the team off. Anyway, job was to deep-survey the planet and report back to HQ… hopefully, you strike gold and get the green light to expand further. That's when the commission really kicks in."

"How far through the surveying were you when the Ellies turned up?" asked Kassini.

"Months. But it wasn't really the length of time, so much as what we found that attracted them. See, that rock down there, Reticuli 19, is bristling with rare minerals and our AIs uncovered some volatile chemical deposits in the rock. The Elementals can't get enough of that shit… so we reported back to our HQ, saying we're sat on a nest egg –" he glanced apologetically over at Vonya, before continuing – "and not much else. Then within a day or two, whoosh… the tower appeared near the base. We thought it was pirate attack or a meteor strike at first."

"The Elementals intercepted your transmission?" Krieger asked.

"They must have. This system is way off-beam for them, hence the Feds sending the *Pali* out there with no escort whatsoever." Yaricks paused to raise an imaginary glass in a gesture of sarcasm. "Thanks again, guys."

"So the tower springs up…" Kassini prompted.

"…the tower springs up and our power more or less goes down. We send them the usual diplomatic hailing protocols and, well, you already heard the rest. I've been in the colony game a while and never heard of anything like this. We all know the Ellies rely on harnessing natural forces and they've certainly picked off our operations before, but you'd think a completely unheard-of method of attack would have pricked up enough ears at Centre to warrant *some* interest, right?"

"You heard nothing from the Empire in all of this?" Krieger asked.

"Not a word, other than the zero-priority acknowledgement, and we asked more than once while we were hid away in that dank cave you found us in, believe me."

Kassini interrupted. "Elementals are normally ruthless in battle, but they don't tend to bother civilians. Is it possible there could still be prisoners down there?"

"No idea," Yaricks said, staring down at his feet. "We lost track of people when we figured out the disappearances and abandoned the colony for the mine in a real hurry – shit, for all I know the tower was teleporting those people away, not killing them."

"Scanner pinged orbital debris on way down, guess that was remains of your mothership?" Vonya added. "Looks like civilian humes are fair prey for the Ellies."

"Must be. What went on seemed pretty damned cold-blooded to me," replied Yaricks, looking Vonya in the eye, but with a hint of nervousness. "In any case, we're out of there now. Plus, the tower is still there and your battle droid is damaged, so going back and rescuing anyone else ain't really an option."

Krieger shook his head in disbelief. "Things have definitely gone to the dogs since I've been out of the action. The Feds just leaving a prospecting crew to fend for themselves like that... those scaly dreks stealing colonies in broad daylight with their elite troops armed with new tech we've never seen before, these sentinel towers... this is all the universe needs. So what's next for your crew?"

"The only upside to all of this is that we're covered. We just need to report back to the Federation and let them decide on the next step," said Yaricks, leaning back into his chair. "Our contracts have built-in danger-money clauses in the event of an attack like that. The corporation left us for dead, too, so they won't argue with any extra demands we make."

Vonya flexed her wings outward – an excellent way to command the attention of groups of humans, she'd found – and brought up a map of the system on the cabin screen. She walked over to the display and tapped the icons with a slender talon as she spoke, zooming in on each world in turn. "We just left here. All moons... here to here... are empty nests... no good. Near the spin point, this one – it's a 'dice' world. Active starports, low security. Easy in-out."

A photorealistic representation of a relatively small moon rotated before them, boasting a hazy turquoise atmosphere, seas and weather. The accompanying readouts described it as Mareas de la Luna, an elite tourist hotspot of stylish casinos, elite resorts and specialised low-gravity watersports once frequented by the bejewelled inner-world set, but now all-but deserted.

Krieger addressed the ceiling, for want of a focal point for the ship's intelligence. "Computer? Give us the latest travel advice for this moon."

"Advisory warnings are currently in place for the resort world of Mareas de la Luna and the Empire no longer guarantees safe passage between colonies in the system," the computer's vocoded voice reported back. "These measures follow a series of pirate infractions against the moon's tourist trade, culminating 18 months ago in the destruction of the *Diamante Dream*, a luxury Infinity-class starliner operated by the Everglade Corporation."

A gleaming white corporate pleasure liner flashed up on screen, its elegant curvature punctuated by transparent domed terrace areas housing luxury pools and bars with a view of the stars. Krieger winced, his mind's eye conjuring up an image of missiles tearing into the defenceless civilian ship and smashing it to atoms. "Ouch. What's the latest traffic report?"

"Official reports are discontinued. Orbital engine signatures reveal a total of 15 ships in the last two days, all small-to-medium-size vessels of unknown designation."

"A moon full of dilapidated casinos in a resort that's gone feral," said Krieger. "Sounds like you'd be able to catch a ride from there, or at least be able to charter spin-pods back to your HQ... what do you think?"

"Sounds great to me," said Yaricks, looking a little relieved. "It's definitely an upgrade on living in a cave. We can let our hair down, too, spend some of the Cees we've got coming to us. Hey, do you fancy joining us? You'd be our guests – we can pay you back some, for rescuing us."

"Could be fun," said Krieger. "But our priority is to fix this ship up, that's where we were headed before we picked up your beacon. Computer, set a course for the moon... and make us all something to eat on the way."

Back in orbit after the drop-off, the *Anomaly* headed for the jump point to resume its interrupted mission to the Boneyard. The crew took the opportunity to lie low for a few hours and catch up on their sleep after the exertions of the rescue.

After they'd rested, they drifted back to the CiC, one by one. Taro sipped a coffee in between brushing absentmindedly at his suit jacket, staring out of the portal as the rapidly receding turquoise gleam of Mareas de la Luna diminished to a pinpoint.

"The Feds have basically abandoned this entire system," he said to Krieger. "Mining colonies, their mini Las Vegas back there... things must be worse than we thought."

Krieger was running the *Anomaly's* weapons inventory onscreen for the fifth time and didn't look away from the readouts. "No doubt about it. These worlds are right on the Empire fringe, security must be stretched. Systems like this are the first to be neglected."

"But that strip, those hotels, casinos... billions of Cees of real estate, right there. And now it's a free-for-all for the Elementals, pirates, anyone."

Krieger looked across from the inventory data. "And you think the 'anyone' could be us?"

"Consider it, Krieger. Those casinos have working starports and repair shops. There's enough fuel for months, years, even, just waiting to be plundered. We could run our missions out of there, trade what we find on the markets, resupply and go again. Plus, we get to live in a luxury resort..."

"Ha ha, *now* we get to it," said Krieger. "Hey Kassini, Taro reckons we should hole up in one of the resorts back there on the strip and sip cocktails in between missions. What do you think?"

Kassini put down her tablet and leant her head on her arm, deciding to risk a mischievous taunt. "Well, I can see how that would appeal to you, Mr Watanabe."

Taro took the bait. "And what do you mean by that, exactly, Sergeant Grigorivitch?"

"What she means is, you're clearly no stranger to the finer things in life," smiled Krieger.

"Oh, come on," Taro protested, glowering back at the pair, in turn. "Just because I don't wear worn-out Fed overalls and wallow in my own filth, doesn't mean I can't rough it when I have to."

"Put it this way," Kassini teased. "You're the first space pirate I've ever met who has a lint roller."

Taro looked down at the roller in his hand and pointed it at her, accusingly. "I'm a diplomat – appearances are..."

Vonya interrupted him over the comms. "Craft in range."

"Computer, is 14 active? Get him up here," said Krieger, and made his way through to the flight module. He was greeted by an arrowhead icon blinking on the *Anomaly's* HUD, tracking a vessel sequestered by the upper atmosphere of a moon orbiting a gas giant near the jump point.

"Vonya, hold us here," ordered Krieger.

"You sure, Kree-gar?"

"I'm sure," he confirmed. The pilot began decelerating the *Anomaly*, bringing her to a virtual standstill.

"What do we know?" Krieger asked.

"The bird has navy transponder. Infiltrator model, Federation cargo onboard. Crew max 10 humes."

As Vonya spoke, Kassini realised this was the play she'd been warned about by Drexler. "Could they be the rescue team?" she called through from the CiC.

"Haven't they got the wrong moon, then?" Taro asked.

"Could be part of the protocol, waiting for backup, maybe," Krieger speculated. "More importantly, can we take 'em?"

The computer chipped in. "This area is rife with piracy, Captain Krieger... until we fit the new parts, the *Anomaly* is currently extremely vulnerable to any offensive weaponry more powerful than laser fire."

"They're a rescue team. They won't have missiles onboard," said Krieger. "Plus, we do have the element of surprise."

"Drek!" shrieked Vonya suddenly. "Missile lock!"

"Wrong on all counts, there, Captain," Taro scalded.

"Drek... evasive action?" Krieger barked.

"Missile's too close... this bird is too slow!" Vonya squawked and whacked the *Anomaly's* controls in frustration. She squinted at the readouts, talons a blur as she desperately tried to wring some acceleration out of the ship. "Strap in, crew. Prepare for impact."

The crew held onto the walls of the CiC as Vonya swerved violently to buy them some time. Krieger paused on his way out to summon a close-up of the enemy ship onto the scanner screen; the custom shipkit and decals told him it was a Fed vessel in fake transponder only. It was accelerating out of cover of the banded moon's upper atmosphere and heading towards them on an elliptical course, following up on the missile rapidly eating up the space between them.

"Drekking pirates!" Krieger cussed, and ran through into the cabin to strap in.

M

Kassini: Gods, Drexler! Elementals on Reticuli with unforeseen shield tech?

Mercenary ambush has downed *Anomaly.* Are you trying to kill me?

M

Drexler: You're clearly still in one piece, Agent.

Orders remain = Make sure the *Anomaly* survives this intervention intact.

Drexler out.

5. HUNTER'S MOON

The moment the airlocks slammed shut and auto-purged the sleeping quarters where the missile – actually a proximity warhead – had detonated and punctured the hull, Krieger realised the game had changed. He gave the order and Vonya dived for the cover of the nearest moon, flightpath crisscrossing the thermals to ensure their descent outpaced that of the pirate interceptor, which cautiously followed them in.

Burning through the bands of cloud in the atmosphere, she levelled out and brought the *Anomaly* in for a controlled emergency landing in a small clearing encircled by miles of dense jungle foliage. She clipped a few trees before skidding across the grass and sliding to a halt in a cloud of steam. Vibrations groaned through the metal of the hull as its temperature equalised. The engines powered down, their low-level thrum replaced by the faint drumming of rain on the fuselage.

Taro shook his head to clear it, unstrapped and checked the crew. Everyone had buckled up and was unharmed, except for Vonya, who lolled in her seat, still in her flight harness but knocked out by the rough impact. He tended to her and was joined in the flight module a minute later by Krieger, who was pressing a towel to a cut on his temple.

"Her shoulder and side are injured," said Taro, without looking round. "Badly bruised ribs, or whatever it is she has *here*," he said, waving his hand over his flank. "She came round briefly; she seemed annoyed about the Federation putting the cockpits up front on their ships."

Krieger placed his hand briefly on Taro's shoulder and ducked back into the cabin. "Computer – immediate threat update," he said. "Where are those pirates?"

"Their craft has landed 0.5 klicks north-north east of our current position in relation to this system's sun," the computer's vocoder voice reported. "Multiple smaller lifeforms in immediate surroundings. No threats identified."

"Send the drone out. Recon patrol, altitude outside of weapons range," Krieger ordered. They heard a small hatch on the *Anomaly* open above them and the drone silently took to the air. The cabin screen transmitted a high-resolution feed from its perspective above the endless ranks of wide-palmed trees.

"That cover is thick, so we have at least 10 minutes before they're on us," said Krieger. "Mak, I need a damage report. Go outside, check the hull. Report back with what we'll need to make the *Anomaly* spaceworthy."

Mak 14 unbolted from his wall mount and clunked past Kassini towards the ramp in the rear.

"Computer, environment report," Kassini requested from behind her hands.

"Moon designation: Alphoron Six, orbiting gas giant Beta Alphoron. Terraformed, Earth-equivalent gravity. The current daylight cycle will last for six more hours, measured in Universal Standard Time. Rain will remain constant, humidity is 88 per cent. Atmosphere is breathable, but contains dangerous levels of toxic background radiation. Probable cause: reactor meltdown. FedNet archives confirm an incident matching the description took place one solar year ago. The report reveals the colony was subject to emergency evacuation."

"What was this place before this accident?" Krieger asked.

"Playing archive material," said the computer, and saccharin strings began to swell behind a lilting, softly spoken narrative. "Welcome to the Nido de Sombras Game Reserve, a deep-space safari hideaway brought to you by The Sears Corporation. Regularly voted one of the Empire's top-three elite hunting destinations, the tropical moon you now stand upon is a miracle of modern climate science – a showcase of cutting-edge Empire terraforming know-how. With over 200 luxury enclaves, you're sure to find..."

"*Pause*," said Krieger. "Where are you getting this info?"

"From commercial material," the computer replied.

"A holiday brochure?"

"The information is the most accurate currently available."

"Look, computer, I don't need to know how many pools the hotel has. Flick through your 'brochure' for something we can use... this was a tourist hotspot, so they must have shipyards for repairs and a hospital of some kind, to deal with bites from the local fauna."

"Hotels will be our best bet, though," Kassini said, scrolling through the blueprints of the nearest sector the computer had sent to her tablet. "This place has only been abandoned for a year and they must have left in a hurry after the radiation incident. They'll still have backup power and working facilities for minor repairs. That's all we need until we get to the Boneyard."

"Quite a leap of faith," Krieger countered. "The shipyards could've just as easily been based around the perimeter of the tourist settlements."

A dripping wet Mak 14 had re-entered the cabin, a layer of steam rising from his shiny metal form. "There are seven locations with residual traces of starship signatures, large and small, in this three-click-square quadrant," he announced. "Radiation levels are hot-hot-hot for humans, but only in places. With the Federation-issue blockers we have onboard, you should be able to survive out there for a limited time without permanent damage to your systems."

"How long will we have?" Kassini asked the droid.

"Two hours, maximum," 14 replied. "Any longer and symptoms will rapidly manifest. These will begin with nausea, vomiting, internal bleeding, blackening patches of skin, sensory disorientation and soon after..."

"*Okay, okay*," Krieger shouted over the droid. "We get the picture, Mak."

"...extremely painful death," the droid trailed off. "Sorry, Captain."

"What's the damage report?"

"Good news for a change," said the droid. "I can repair the hull itself with portable welding equipment, but we will need more internal sealant than we have aboard to mitigate against the possibility of the welds failing during lift-off."

The computer interrupted them. "Drone stream of threats on main screen," it said. The cabin display showed the vantage point of the drone, hovering above the pirate interceptor in the nearby clearing. Fat, grimy raindrops clung to the camera lens, cleared periodically by a small wiper blade.

The interceptor had an expert rendering of a death's-head moth across its roof, which Krieger secretly quite liked the look of, despite cynically noting the lack of originality. Its ramp lowered and three figures stepped out. "Taro, come and see this," Krieger shouted to the cockpit. "We've got visuals on the enemy."

Taro joined them in the cabin. "How many?"

"Three so far," replied Kassini, eyes fixed on the band of scruffy barbarians, still clad in their outlaw uniform of battered leather and animal skins rather than the more sensible option of atmosphere-filtering suits. "Human pirates. Two rifles, one heavier weapon, looks like some kind of belt-fed machine gun... more for show than anything else." She watched them move out to around 15 metres of their ship's ramp. "No recognisable sweep formation – no one's been to military school, by the looks of it." She turned to Krieger. "Shall we attack them, or wait for them to come to us?"

"I can take 'em," said Mak 14, eagerly.

"Cool your metal boots," said Krieger. "There's half a click of potentially deadly jungle between them and us. Let them take the risks... we'll track them and deal with them when they're within range."

There was a flash of light and movement on the screen. They turned to see the lead pirate rolling around on the floor, wrestling with a dark-furred, heavy-set creature with a sleek and powerful low-lying outline and an oversized skull. The drone's camera zoomed out to show the other pirates stumbling backwards to the ship's ramp, where the machine-gunner opened fire, aiming a sweep of panicky, stuttering bursts at the perimeter of the clearing.

The wiper cleared the camera and focused back in to reveal slavering jaws snapping at the lead pirate's screaming face; his arms extended out to jab at the creature's eyes but quickly fell limp. A jet of blood arced out of his neck and squirted all over the predator's ravening face.

"Bad dog," said Krieger, screwing up his face in disgust.

"Technically, more a cat than a dog, Captain," said Mak 14. "The species is likely a variant of *hyaena stellaris*, genetically engineered for this lunar ecosystem. Probably severely irradiated and extremely sick."

"It's definitely not a vegan, whatever it is," Kassini added, watching strips of skin being torn off the pirate's face.

The surviving pirates had disappeared back into their ship and slammed the ramp shut. Four or five other creatures had taken this as their cue to emerge from the undergrowth: a blur of teeth and claws signalled a vicious fight had broken out over the pirate's lacerated corpse.

"Guess we got lucky, then," said Kassini, watching the interceptor's engines fire and glow blue, readying for take-off. "They clearly didn't fancy their chances with the hyenas and they must've worked out from the presence of our drone that we're not as easy to pick off as they thought. Plus, they don't look like the types to stockpile radiation meds."

"Quitting without a fight," said Krieger. "Computer, make sure they leave in an orderly fashion and lock the autocannon on them if they come within range."

Onscreen, the pirate interceptor lifted off, hovered briefly, then began a full-thrust ascent.

"Doesn't look like they're even going to give us the courtesy of a flyby," said Krieger, puffing out his cheeks. "Okay, computer. Send the drone to the settlement. We need eyeballs on the facilities."

Taro thumbed towards the cockpit. "Vonya's going to be fine, Captain, but she needs different medication than we have here if she's going to heal enough to fly the ship. I promised we'd make it a mission objective."

"Right, you'll be with us, then. Let's suit up," said Krieger, springing into action. "Taro, Mak – Kassini has identified the Bellevue Range one click away on top of that ridge to the south east as the nearest hangar-equipped hotel facility. It should also have a hospital section. Check the drone stream for your most likely way in.

"While you're doing that, Kassini and I will recon the lodges in the quadrant. The objectives are Vonya's meds and sealant patches for the hull, nothing else. Understood?"

Taro nodded. "We need a dose of radiation meds now and a second ration in case we get delayed," he said, over the sounds of Mak 14 noisily assembling into a form suitable for hacking the jungle foliage back.

"Remember, we don't know what's out there. All we know is we're very much the hunted and not the hunters," Krieger said, pulling his favoured rifle and several spare magazines from the munitions cabinet. "So keep your eyes peeled and comms chatter to a minimum."

The computer live-streamed the drone footage from its approach to the resortonto the cabin screen. As they climbed into their suits and checked their weapons, the crew watched intently. Nido de Sombras was a ghost town, its streets eerily deserted apart from lines of rusting motor transports: luxury streamlined status symbols, abandoned in haste. The elegant but weather-beaten building façades were gradually becoming overgrown, too, with no one left to manicure the aggressive foliage of the safari areas surrounding them.

"Are those plants following us?" Kassini asked, glancing back over her shoulder at some thick-stalked sunflower-height monstrosities, suddenly minding their own business against the tangled jungle backdrop as they sensed her scrutiny. "Those things with the purple-and-pink tops... I could've sworn they were back there when I looked around a few minutes ago."

"Probably a mobile carnivorous species," said Krieger.

"Like triffids?" asked Kassini.

Krieger was nonplussed. "Triffids... is that the genome or something? These guys are probably semi intelligent. I think I bought some seeds for something like them, back when I was a kid. Somebody engineered them from an idea in an ancient film."

"That's them. They're freaking me out," Kassini shivered involuntarily, despite the syrupy humidity of the atmosphere. "Let's keep our eyes on them."

They made their way slowly and deliberately through the thick fronds, protected from the relentless downpour by the canopy of leaves overhead. Kassini glanced down through her visor at the route on her tablet from time to time; Krieger realised he was gripping his snub rifle too tightly as he swept the scene ahead of them, trying to filter out the distant animal calls.

After a few minutes, Krieger held his hand up in the 'halt' signal. Kassini checked her tablet. "It's the beginning of the trail to the cabin."

Krieger clicked a button on the wrist of his new suit. Nothing happened; Kassini pointed to the correct button on her own wrist that activated his comms. "Taro... we're at the first cabin. Sit rep," he transmitted.

The pair waited 10 seconds or so, scanning the undergrowth. "We're along the main street. No contacts," came the ring-modulated sound of Taro's radio reply. "Approaching the Bellevue Terminal."

"Look sharp," Kassini shouted, pointing at the bushes to the side of the pebbled path. Krieger followed her finger to some shaking leaves and saw a striped tail vanish into the undergrowth.

Krieger began to jog up the path, rifle raised. Kassini turned round and jogged backwards, covering their rear. "We've got company," she yelled to Krieger, as a snapping branch alerted her to darting movements in the taller trees. 30 metres or so away, at the entrance to the path, the slinking shape of a big cat prowled into view. "Firing a warning shot," she said breathlessly. Her rifle crackled into life, its echoes quickly deadened by the banks of vines and foliage. Startled, the cat sprang on all four paws at once and leapt into the safety of the leaves.

"Let's move!"

They half-jogged, half-ran to the cabin, where the tinted glass of its floor-to-ceiling windows glowed coolly, diffusing the rays of sunlight. The design was that of a high-spec single-level hunting lodge, an opulent vision of wood, reinforced glass and spotless white metal spacious enough to comfortably house a family.

They clumped up onto the porch and Kassini crouched down behind the railings, tracking multiple movements in the undergrowth with the barrel of her rifle. Krieger ran up to the door and leant his elbow on its old-style handle. To his relief, the mechanism turned and the door swung open.

"We're in!" he shouted through his visor.

Built with the security of its high-profile clients in mind, the lodge still had emergency power. They part-closed the blinds and quickly conducted a brief recon of its minimally decorated rooms, Krieger pausing only to order the drone to fly over their location and lock onto the wildlife surrounding them.

"Krieger," shouted Kassini from the main bedroom. "There's a First Aid unit in here. Looks pretty heavy duty."

"What's our play?" she asked as she joined Krieger in the open-plan living area. She fired up the medikit and scrolled through its menus before turning it off to conserve the battery.

"You're a sharp-shooter, right? So let's take the critters out one by one from the highest vantange point – in our case, the roof, through that skylight," Krieger replied.

"Standard Federation field-combat protocol," Kassini teased.

"Old habits die hard," said Krieger, opening each of the cabinets in the adjoining kitchen area in turn. "That stuff is hard-wired into me."

"And me," said Kassini. "Quite literally, when it comes to my ATOs."

Krieger halted his rummaging and walked back over to stand in front of her, toying with a kitchen knife he'd found. "Alien tactical overlays? That's what those implants they gave you are? They were classified to the hilt when I still had the clearance."

"Well, I have them," Kassini sighed. "Problem is, when I got smashed up – dropship accident, long story – part of the damage meant that they couldn't find a way to remove them because of my head injuries. They tried... it was horrible."

Krieger sat down on the mock-colonial armchair by his side. "So what's the upshot of that for you?"

"It's a mixed bag, I can tell you," Kassini said, glancing away towards the window. "On the plus side, I have access to archives of tactical combat intel for the Empire, the Avions, the Elementals and loads of other minor species, too."

"The downside?"

"I have episodes," she said, breaking off from scouting the window and fixing him with her stare. "Conflicting voices... urges, almost. They're some kind of manifestation of the alien mindsets that I adopt to understand their combat motivations. I have some exercises I do, y'know, to stay in control."

"And they couldn't do anything about it?" Krieger asked. This was the first time he'd studied Kassini's face, he realised, registering the unusual grey-green of her eyes through the helmet visors they both still wore. "How hard did they try?"

She let out a sarcastic laugh. "They did as much as the Federation ever does for troops who've been through the machine and are spat out the other side," she enunciated with resignation, a note of emotion in her voice. "De fucking nada."

"So you left?" Krieger asked, tentatively.

"They let me go. Honorable discharge for damaged goods. Anyway," she said, deliberately shifting the focus. "What's your Federation hard-luck story?"

"Oh, they put me in prison," said Krieger casually, allowing himself a bitter half-smile. "Well, a penal colony somewhere in Lyra, to be precise. Elemental."

"An Elemental prison?" said Kassini, reminding herself that this was supposedly the first she'd heard of this. She summoned the details of Krieger's backstory from the briefing to mind. "What did you do?"

"10 years ago, I was a naval commander, out on the rim," said Krieger. "A Sirius-class frigate… the *Elvira*. We were engaged by Elementals, captured some prisoners, who then escaped. They were running around on the lower decks somewhere – same deck as our armoury – so I had them shot."

"To protect your crew?"

"That's exactly what I said in my court martial," Krieger replied. "But they didn't see it that way. Instead, they sold me out – handed me over to the Elementals as reparation. So I followed protocol to the letter and all the thanks I got was to be handed over to the enemy. From wartime Commander to terrorist, in the blink of a judge's eye."

"Holy shit," said Kassini, careful not to overdo her mock-shock. "How did you make it out of that?"

Krieger's tablet glowed. "I'll tell you the rest of the story some other time… we've got about an hour and a half of radiation protection left," said Krieger. "Drone's overhead. Ready for some target practice?"

"Sure am. Let's put these radioactive furballs to sleep," said Kassini, flicking a switch on her rifle to deploy the mid-range scope and reflexively checking its magazine.

A distant shot rang out, causing Taro to start as he peered cautiously over the top of the dense thicket that had begun to encroach onto a large expanse of flat asphalt overlooked by the plexiglass façade of a large public building. Rain had begun to fall gently again, pattering on the skins of the hastily abandoned ground vehicles which were strewn all over the approach. Several armed military vehicles formed an approximate cordon around what appeared to be the main entrance.

"Terminal car park," Taro noted. "The last of the population clearly left in a hurry."

"Unsuccessfully, in this case," Mak 14's reply modulated at low volume in his earpiece. The droid was standing next to the nearest vehicle ahead of Taro, which was sporting smashed glass, talon marks and a faded trail of organic detritus leading into the undergrowth.

"This facility housed the administrative functions of the settlement. There is an entrance for a hospital marked on the local map on the other side of the building, fastest route is directly through it. I will open those doors."

Mak raised the bulky autocannon he was holding and began to sight a mortar-style trajectory.

"Hold up, Mak!" Taro said quickly. "Explosives are probably going to draw a crowd. Do you have any lifeforms showing on your local sensors?"

Mak lowered the weapon and said: "Six to eight thermal blips have been tracking you since we left the ship. They are currently spread out between 75 and 100 metres to your rear. It is probable none of them wishes to be the first to close."

Taro visibly went a whiter shade and quickly fumbled with the holster at his side, pulling free a slender combat pistol. He checked the ammo counter and flicked the safety to off before repositioning himself quickly next to Mak.

"Right. It would be useful to mention that sort of thing when you find out about it. Humans don't have thermal sensors," he said.

"Understood. Shall we move into the target building now?" replied Mak. Taro nodded and the droid led the way across the open ground which was scarred and pitted from the impact of small-arms fire and explosives. Several unidentified bones crunched under Mak's armoured feet.

More shots cracked in the distance as they approached, followed by the distant thunderclap of an explosive. The echo dissipated, melting eerily into the sound of the rain on the solid surfaces around them.

"Those signatures match Krieger and Grigorivitch's weapons," said Mak, as they passed between two of the military vehicles into the rough cordon. A large side door of one of them had been left open, and Mak stuck his head in to examine the interior.

"Some explosives damage. Probably the departing military force quickly rendering the vehicle inoperable. Its onboard systems may still be of some use," he said and reached inside, an interface cable snaking from the pack on his back to his manipulator.

"You check that out, I'll see about this door," replied Taro. He walked the few steps to the sliding double-doors, through which he could see a hastily erected zombie-movie-style furniture barricade. The fight clearly hadn't reached the interior and the glass of the door was undamaged, except for a light frosting from the smoke of the exterior battle.

The lock wasn't active, according to a blinking green light on a small access panel, which had clearly been tampered with since the original owners left. He flipped the cover on this and pushed a button marked 'open'. The doors obliged after emitting the short whine of unused servos powering up and Taro followed his weapon into the vaulted room beyond, scanning the two wide corridors either side of the door and the concourse balconies overlooking it.

He thumbed his comms over to the team frequency. "Krieger, we're into the hotel. Some of those things followed us here, but haven't attacked yet."

A burst of automatic fire sounded in the distance, but suddenly cut into the live circuit of his earpiece. It subsided and was replaced with Krieger's voice, the tightness of combat evident even through the harsh low-bandwidth tone.

"That's good, all of them seem to be over here. We've shot a few, but killing them seems to bring more of them and make them mad. We've got some meds but we're going to have to shoot our way back to the ship. Krieger out."

Mak had removed himself from the armoured vehicle's innards and strode straight past Taro into the building.

"I have activated a feed from the vehicle's remaining sensors. If anything follows us, we will know," Mak said, as Taro thumbed an identical panel causing the doors to slide shut again and took a last look out at the expanse of vehicles. He noted a gentle movement in the undergrowth they'd vacated earlier.

"The medical facility is directly ahead along the large corridor, no lifeforms are evident inside the building according to sensors," Mak said, allowing Taro to get a head-start. He seemed to have been able to curb his usual frenetic pace for the moment, though Taro couldn't know how long his counsel would hold with the droid, which was still under Krieger's command.

"We will also need to check the engineering stores," Mak added.

They began to move down the corridor, caution still stiffening Taro's posture as they passed from the daylight into a space lit only by their own lights and emergency sodiums. He clicked off his communicator system and spoke into the gloom.

"Krieger and Kassini sound like they're in a spot over there."

"Yes. We lack solid intel on the creatures of this planet, we should not have split our combat potential into two teams," Mak replied immediately.

"True… another smart decision from the master and commander. He's not thinking things through properly more and more often since we acquired *Anomaly*."

They reached a heavy solid door with the classic marking of a medical unit above it, a manual unit designed to be accessible in emergency situations. Taro stepped aside as Mak moved past him and swung it open with a single movement. He followed its arc with the barrel of his weapon, but nothing materialised to challenge him.

"Errors have been made," acknowledged Mak. "Krieger is not inept; circumstances have proved complicated."

Taro, surprised to conjure such a considered response out of the usually mysterious droid, holstered his weapon as he followed him in. He surveyed the room, a standard medical facility with capacity for treating run of the mill injuries of a kind he was familiar with. He quickly began rifling storage units and scanning the foil and plastic packages and bottles they contained with a hand-held unit from his backpack.

"Perhaps. It just occurs to me that his fixation on the Federation is making him rash and that's a risk. There are simpler ways for us to carry on. The *Anomaly* is worth plenty if somebody decided to turn it back over to the Feds for example, and at this rate Krieger is going to get us all killed," he replied.

Mak 14 kept quiet for a moment – monetary gain was of little interest to the droid – as the scanner flashed green on the contents of a storage packet Taro was now holding.

"Avion-safe meds. Standard issue in the territories close to the border." Taro pulled some more packets out of the wrapper and squinted at the bright readout in the dim light. "Painkillers, and an equivalent of antibiotics and anti-virals in human medicine, apparently."

He quickly loaded the whole package into the backpack along with the scanner, then turned his attention to a nearby wall-mounted container clearly marked 'Synth mats' with a number of chemical warning symbols plastered across it. Taro yanked at the doors.

"Organic causes and loyalties always seem important to them until they are not," said Mak suddenly, still facing the dark doorway behind Taro. "This is not a weakness I share. You are all equally dead in the end. Krieger is in charge, and I am here solely for what you would call the 'experience'. Whether a course of action brings you closer to your demise is of no great consequence to me."

"Reassuring as ever, Mak. You ever considered being a counselling unit?" said Taro, finally forcing one of the doors open with a crunch. A second layer of mesh inside screened off a number of plastic bladders containing the liquid building blocks used by his equipment for medical synthesis. Taro smacked the locking mechanism with the butt of his pistol and one side of the screen sprang open, allowing him to rapidly clear out the cabinet.

"That's all I need, let's move on," he said.

"My sensor link indicates the creatures are now at the entrance we used to enter this building, and their numbers have increased. The fact that they are not currently trying to tear your limbs off also suggests none of them have found a way to access the building on that side. It is safe to assume they are waiting for us to come out."

"Any other way out that would let you take a look at the starport stores?"

"Probable. Follow me."

Mak moved back out into the corridor and led them deeper into the complex.

"That last grenade drove them back a bit, let's move!" yelled Kassini, and turned on her heel to run back down the main street towards Krieger, who was 20 metres ahead of her. Seeing the prey in flight again quickly restored the confidence of the jostling mass of 15 or more of the creatures at the far end, which screamed guttural cries as they leapt into pursuit, claws clattering onto the hard surface beneath them.

Krieger backed up a further five metres as Kassini approached at full tilt, then steadied his rifle atop a metal post and squeezed the trigger. A short burst of automatic fire scuttered out, heavy shells ripping through the three leading creatures and dropping them to the paved ground mid-bound amidst a bout of unearthly shrieking. The result was a yowling ball of blood, fur and teeth in the middle of the road as the wave behind them barrelled into the sudden obstruction.

He allowed himself a macabre grin as he clicked over to single fire and sighted the only creature which had managed to flank around the fallen mass of its fellows. It was only a couple of metres from him as Kassini flashed past to his right. He carefully placed three rounds into the oncoming beast, showering gore across the paved road behind it. The twitching corpse slid to rest near his feet like an exploded bear.

"In position, clear the range!" shouted Kassini from behind him, and it was Krieger's turn to run as the other creatures recovered themselves once more. Kassini took up the covering fire, mercilessly dropping the creatures until he reached her, but instead of continuing on he took up position next to her. Together, they laid down a punishing volley of shots, withering what was left of the oncoming pack.

"We can keep them back while we're in the open like this," he said between shots, "...but we're going to hit the jungle around the ship again soon. Need something decisive to put them off the scent!"

Kassini hit their final pursuer square in the chest and it collapsed sideways, tried to raise itself once, and flopped to the ground with a final thump as her second shot removed its jaw. She checked to her sides and rear quickly before dumping the mag from her weapon and grabbing a replacement from her suit waistband.

Krieger checked his angles and did likewise. Already, they could hear the shrill bawling yells of another group somewhere on the other side of a building across the road to their right. Kassini surveyed the tangled vegetation on their route, noting the heads of several of the pink and purple plants they'd noticed on the way in swaying between the foliage and the bottom of the trees.

"Let's see how this stuff burns. The drone will need to guide us in there anyway," she replied, slinging her weapon to her shoulder again and heading for the green expanse.

Krieger followed, walking backwards and sweeping his weapon from side to side as he activated his comms. He issued some orders to the drone before switching over to their inter-group frequency.

"Taro, Mak, we're a half-click from the ship on the edge of the jungle settlement side. What's your status?"

"We're almost back and found what we needed, though Mak blew a wall down getting us out. Watch the plant life on the way in, it seemed to converge ahead of us and try to slow us down," came the reply from Taro a few moments later. He sounded out of breath.

"Okay, the computer is instructed to let you onboard when you arrive, and you have authority over systems to get *Anomaly* ready for take-off. Tell Mak to get the hull repairs out of the way as quickly as possible, and to man the ramparts when we get close," replied Krieger.

"Understood," Mak 14's synth voice cut across the comm channel.

They had reached the beginnings of the belt of vegetation, creepers and small shrubs rising to knee-height around them. Krieger cut the link as the other pack of creatures bounded into view a hundred metres away, even larger than the previous one. He looked over to warn Kassini.

"Got about 30 seconds here," he said. She was holding several small grenades expertly between her fingers, tapping away at a small digital readout on the front of one.

"Get ready to move, you lead, I follow, on a count of three," she said. "The drone has marked the easiest route it could see for us, follow your comm signal."

A repetitive pipping began in his earpiece, which would guide him along the route the drone had marked leading to the *Anomaly*.

"Three – two," Kassini passed under the perimeter of the canopy of undergrowth, watching the approaching creatures with Krieger jogging on ahead. She armed the grenades.

"One, MOVE!" she yelled, and hurled them to the ground 10 metres in front of her in the path of the approaching pack. The pair ran full tilt into the jungle, relying on the weight of their armour to crash through the vegetation.

The grenades were set to incendiary and went off a few seconds later. They sprayed a thick flammable mist several metres to either side of them before exploding as one in a roiling slew of dirt, greenery and smoke. Kassini had been a little early and the concussion did more damage to the pack than the flame, throwing several of them to the ground. But all of them panicked at the ensuing sheets of bright white flame which caught the undergrowth and canopy and rapidly spread toward them. The pack skidded to a halt in an angry barrage of howling as the two humans made their escape.

Anomaly towered over Mak 14 and Taro like a huge, brooding toad as they approached. Several rotational beacons lit as an access ramp to the hold began to descend, and they boarded rapidly. Mak stayed below and immediately began to strap portable welding equipment to his frame as Taro climbed a ladder to the main deck.

"Welcome back," the computer chirped as Taro headed straight to the medical bay and began ministering to the machinery hooked up to Vonya.

"Vonya is still incoherent but has self-medicated while you were gone," the computer updated him. "She said you'd better find some more meds for her, because she's 'all out'. The drone indicates the others are incoming with a large number of hostiles in pursuit, and my prox scans show movement from all sides of the ship, indicating many more hostiles in our vicinity."

Taro selected the drugs he'd identified as Avion from his backpack and laid them on a trolley next to Vonya, who was face down on a couch with her wings hanging over either side of her, touching the floor.

"Let me know if she wakes up, I'll need to check with her what the hell I'm to give her before I do, and give me full manual control of the ship's access ramps," he said.

"The captain is off-ship. You have temporary authority. This is done," replied the computer.

Taro clicked his communicator on and said: "Mak, are you making the repairs?"

"I will complete the necessary external welds shortly and move on to the internal reinforcement required to make *Anomaly* space-worthy," the droid replied, radio reception crackling through the hull.

"Computer, can any of the ship's weaponry be used to cover the retreat?"

"Most of *Anomaly's* weapons are turret mounted. Our lower hull, front and rear weaponry can be tasked to provide fire support, but this is risky. It is ship-to-ship and anti-fighter weaponry largely designed for use outside the atmosphere. It may be somewhat unpredictable," the computer replied.

"Activate it all and target the areas away from Krieger and Kassini's approach."

"Powering up systems."

Taro made his way to the bridge and took Krieger's usual seat. He tapped a tablet and activated the main comms channel. The computer helpfully triggered a wall screen and filled it with the view from the drone and the ship's 360-degree blister cams. They showed only still, windswept jungle.

"Krieger, Taro. The ship will be ready, what's your situation?"

Seconds passed before Kreiger's fractured voice answered, clearly mid-run judging by his laboured breathing and the sound of foliage and branches whipping past his mic.

"Almost there, two or three minutes. No contacts ahead, but we can hear movement behind," his voice yelled, and the connection cut out.

An onscreen camera panned slightly, and the computer chimed in.

"A large number of the creatures are converging on the ship from the other side of this clearing. They intend to intercept the captain."

"Make sure they don't," replied Taro before barking a warning. "Mak, ship's weapons are active!"

Servos audibly whirred as two turrets on the underside of *Anomaly* rotated to face the trees on the far side of the clearing and suddenly roared into life. A screening volley of heavy shells pounded into the tree line, exploding into a mass of shrapnel that tore the tops off trees some distance away and rocked the ship with the blast wave, the super-heated shrapnel scything downwards and away from the ship from the initial velocity. This was followed by the distinctive crackle of a laser ionising the atmosphere around it as it warmed up to bathe a 20-metre horizontal line in green energy.

The vegetation vapourised and flashed into flame along the line, creating a hellscape of ash and smoke which rose high into the air. The keening of wounded and fleeing beasts could just be heard as the bassy echoes of the barrage died down.

"Holy shit!" exclaimed Taro, watching as the roiling smoke spread across the clearing towards the ship.

"Threat dispersed," the computer replied, primly.

Kassini burst from the treeline at the other end of the clearing from the devastation, visibly sagging from the exertion. She moved a few metres towards the ship, turned and dropped to one knee with her rifle raised. Taro could see her back heaving as she struggled to catch her breath, rifle weaving back and forth in a 180-degree arc like an angry snake, waiting for their pursuers to show themselves.

Krieger followed along the same path in more disorderly fashion, falling backwards out of the same bush Kassini had nimbly hurdled. His rifle fell at his side and he fumbled for it as Kassini fired a burst back past him. Three slavering creatures burst from the cover on their right and bounded towards the sound of Kassini's shots. Krieger hauled himself clumsily back to his feet and was forced to reflexively fire an automatic burst into a fourth beast that hurled itself from the darkness he'd just vacated.

With no time to reload, he let the rifle swing from its harness to his back and drew his heavy sidearm. More black shapes were spilling out of the treeline now, a rough horseshoe of squat, bounding shapes sweeping in towards the two of them. Kassini was back on her feet and moving backwards firing shot after shot, cracks of the rifle felling the closest threats one by one.

"Krieger, low ammo! MOVE!" she yelled, distorting the comms channel with the intensity of her voice. Krieger's handgun boomed a single shot which destroyed the face of a creature approaching from his side, then turned and ran again.

Kassini reached the foot of the access ramp as Mak 14 appeared at the top of it. Almost immediately, the repetitive thud of his autocannon sounded, explosive shells stitching a line of small explosions among the approaching pack a couple of metres from Krieger.

"Keep them off his left!" Kassini yelled at the droid without looking, and switched her field of fire to the approaching captain's right. Mud, gore and drool sprayed in arcs around Krieger as he ran. The baying and screaming of the beasts reached a fever pitch, interspersed with the staccato crack of Kassini's last few rounds of ammunition. Krieger was now just five metres from the ramp.

An autocannon round exploded, turning a creature leaping for Krieger into a cloud of guts and fur, but staggered him at the same moment Kassini pulled her trigger to an empty click, her weapon emitting an alarmed beep. He tripped and went down awkwardly, rolling in reflex onto his front.

Kassini's target leapt into the air and landed right next to Krieger, pinning a leg. He yelled as it swept its oversize cranium down toward him and smashed his pistol barrel into its face, squeezing the trigger wildly. The beast's slavering jaws jerked away awkwardly as the blast seared its eyes, but the shot failed to connect. It planted a taloned paw squarely on his solid chest plate with a skrawk of metal, about to lunge for his exposed neck. Teeth, drool and a fleshy tongue were all Krieger could see as he tried desperately to point the gun at the creature's chest.

The air around the clearing erupted in deafening thunder for a second time as the ship's flak cannons opened up, shells ripping into the trees the two crew members had just vacated. Kassini yelled and covered her ears and the creature on top of Krieger was visibly startled, swinging its head to look back for a crucial second – just long enough to spy the *Anomaly's* drone as it smacked at full speed into its side.

The whirring chunk of metal and glass lifted the animal clear of Krieger in a spray of blood and cracking bones, projectile-vomiting blood and saliva across his face visor. He recovered for a moment, amazed, as the broken beast landed nearby in a wheezing, groaning heap with the drone still embedded in its body. He began to struggle backwards in the momentary lull as the blast wave rolled across the field – this and the initial barrage had confused the other creatures totally, slowing their advance as some panicked and others ran into them.

The combined noise and shock meant only an incredulous Taro heard the computer say: "Threat dispersed," with an added hint of smugness.

At the foot of the ramp, Kassini recovered enough to draw her own sidearm and run to Krieger, helping him to his feet. She man-handled the stunned captain to the ramp and drove him up it in front of her, so Mak 14 could grasp his harness and hurl him inside. The same manipulator arm then punched the bright-red manual 'close' control for the ramp and it began to roll in; he heard a clunk as the heroic drone recoupled itself to the ship in the nick of time. All the while, Mak maintained a steady single-armed grip on the autocannon, its muzzle trained on the confused creatures as the large ramp gradually sealed the crew off from the smoke and noise of the battlefield.

The ship's lift-engines fired the second the hatch lights went green, wild energy carbonising what was left of the clearing to drive the ship up against the planet's gravity. This was the final straw for the beleaguered inhabitants, who scattered as the wind and flame whipped around them.

Anomaly pulled away from the smoking scar beneath it, nosed up and cut in main thrust, pinning the occupants of the loading bay where they had collapsed. Kassini was on her back yelling into the sound of the engine burst, the stress of the last half hour dissipating in a burst of self-congratulation straight from an earlier life.

"Wooohoooo, best drekkin' shot on this or any planet!" she lapsed briefly into a pidgin version of Avion language, clearly tangled up by her implants, before eventually getting a grip as the acceleration began to ease.

Krieger managed to look wearily over, noting her carping mouth, his face streaked with dirt and blood, suit ripped and armour dented.

"The barrage! I can't hear a fucking thing!" he yelled, pointing to his ears.

Mak 14's repair work held solid, and *Anomaly* ripped clear of the atmosphere of the ill-fated safari moon of Alphoron Six.

Taro found Krieger a few hours later, having checked him over with the medibay instrumentation and left the captain passed out there from his exertions. He was now awake and dressed, the computer had informed him.

The door slid open as he arrived and Krieger walked out, notably rumpled and moving stiffly.

"Body's too old for running like that these days," he said, noting Taro's slightly furrowed brow.

"It'll pass – take the painkillers. Hearing okay yet?" replied Taro.

"More or less, but it's still ringing. Haven't been blown up like that for a long time," he tapped the side of his head. "We should leave Vonya in peace, let's head for the bridge."

Kassini nodded from one of the acceleration chairs as they entered the small command centre.

"Glad to see you're up, bet you'll never want to see another dog as long you live," she said to Krieger, smiling.

"Thanks, fine work back there, Kassini. Falling back under fire hasn't changed much since my day. You uninjured?" he replied, returning the smile.

"Shoulders wrenched, hands are numb, still can't hear on one side – easy one at the office, back in the day."

"Good, we need to get moving for the Boneyard. I didn't intend for them to repair the ship as well as upgrading it for us, but looks like that's what we'll be asking for."

"About that, Krieger..." Taro said, exchanging a glance with Kassini which Krieger clocked. Krieger looked at him blankly.

"We keep getting into these scrapes, Captain. Half the crew is injured, Rust is out of action, *Anomaly* is battered. I wouldn't say it's been the quietest journey so far."

"So you don't want to set up shop around here after all, then? Get to the point."

"Your *motivation* is my point. We would never have rescued those miners if you hadn't been so incensed at the Federation ignoring them, and we'd never have gone anywhere near the pirate ship that promptly blew us out of space if you hadn't fallen for the 'Federal cargo onboard' line." Taro let this sink in for a moment, before continuing. "And if you'd have ended up dead on that rock just now, we'd have had to do gods' knows what to get the computer to give us full control of *Anomaly*."

Kassini's eyes were flicking between the two men, trying to read what was behind their words. Krieger seemed to understand the subtext well enough. He laughed.

"I give you temporary responsibility for five minutes Taro, and you want a promotion?" he said, before his voice cooled. "You think you could run a ship? I did this for years with a bigger crew than this, and you can't have two votes in a command chain."

"Your past is the reason I think you need a second opinion with some actual weight behind it, and this last episode shows we need an official second in command. I don't carry the same baggage you do, and I'm the only one you can trust... no offence, Kassini," Taro looked over to her with a meek smile.

"None taken," she said, face in neutral. "I just covered his ass all the way home, after all. For what it's worth, too, the *Anomaly's* computer saved you with the drone and the ship's guns, despite risk to the rest of us. That's standard Federation programming at work, nobody gets left behind. So I guess we aren't the only ones with some useful reflexes hardwired in."

Krieger thought about this for a moment before responding.

"You're right on the need for a backup plan in case things go south. I'll tell the computer to consider you acting Executive Officer from here on, Taro, so it'll seek your input on major decisions under normal circumstances. It'll also give you control over Rust, such as it is."

Taro nodded and stood up to leave. Krieger reached over and stopped him. "Don't forget," he said. "There's still only one captain on my ship."

Kassini managed to keep her face straight. It took some effort.

M

Kassini: The mercs failed, Drexler... the ship has been patched up and we're heading to Boneyard for repairs.

What's my next move?

M

Drexler: We can't intervene there, we'll have to wait until Krieger is back in civilised space.

Orders = Gather intelligence, send updates.

Drexler out.

6. THE BONEYARD

The *Anomaly* slowed in its straight-line trajectory and began making the familiar series of subtle rotational adjustments to its aspect that preceded an FTL jump. The cockpit comms crackled into life.

"Approaching spin point," said Vonya, her voices lower and slightly less melodic than usual. "Strap in for the spin. Boneyard system travel time seven minutes."

Kassini and Krieger were already nestled against the still-shiny synthetic leather of the *Anomaly's* travel seats. Their buckles were unconsciously placed over their laps – less a product of the pre-flight nerves of passengers throughout the ages of aviation, more the result of conditioning from hundreds of combat jumps.

Taro hurried in to join them in the main deck area from his quarters off to the side. "Is she alright to fly?" he asked, as he fumbled to free his belt from under himself.

"Well, the landing beat her up," said Krieger. "But Mak patched the hull and the spin drive is brand new, the latest Federation spec..."

Taro sighed. "I wasn't talking about the ship, I was talking about the pilot."

Krieger shrugged and turned his attention back to his tablet. "Well, you patched *her* up, didn't you?"

"Yeah, but Avion physiology... it's hard to know if the Fed meds I gave her earlier will have any effect. Avions have different receptors, different oxygenation..."

"I checked in on her 10 minutes ago," Kassini interrupted. "As soon as you left, she put some of the meds we secured from Hyaenasville into a medikit she had in her pack and choked them down that way. She said our meds had no effect on her. And that they tasted like shit."

Taro smiled to himself. "Like a dog spitting out her tablets."

"She's just humouring you," Kassini said. "Don't take it too personally."

"I won't. What did the module she used look like, out of interest?"

Kassini shrugged. "Green, glowing, weird shit on the readout, standard-issue Avion military model, I guess. You'll have to check it out yourself."

"I would advise against plugging yourself in," interrupted Mak 14. "Avion medication is toxic to humans."

Taro turned in his seat to face the droid, who had bolted himself onto the cabin wall. "I've been advising against you plugging yourself in for a while now, Mak," he said, mock-offended. "I'm trained in medicine, I'm not going to turn myself into a lab rat... and anyway, what would a tin can know about interspecies physiology?"

"Enough to know you fleshbags are weak and you leak," 14 replied.

Taro caught Kassini's gaze and rolled his eyes. Maybe the droid was cranky because of the recent shift in the pecking order, she mused to herself.

The *Anomaly's* engines hummed into life, sending a rumbling resonant frequency through the seats in the cabin. "Spin in 10, nine, eight," said Vonya over the comms, clearly back at the controls where she belonged. "Taro, try my meds later. Maybe you get nice and high – maybe you die."

Outside the window, the stars blurred and elongated. Three seconds later, they were abruptly extinguished and replaced with the familiar feeling of nausea and inner flotation that gave the spin drive its nickname, as the crew's seven-minute half-remembered dream in FTL space began.

"Spin complete," the computer announced, a touch of relief in its vocoder-like voice.

Krieger unbuckled and pushed the flight module door release. He shielded his eyes from the shimmering light reflecting off the unremarkable, grey-green colony world filling the screen ahead of them – even the minimal shine reflected by a planet this far out from its neighbouring gas giant and the system's distant binaries was squint-inducing for humans straight after a spin jump.

"Could you adjust the screen contrast?" he asked Vonya as he settled into the co-pilot seat. The Avion pilot winced a little as she shifted her weight to reach and adjust the tint control, but otherwise didn't take her focus off the scene as she updated Krieger on the sit-rep.

"Scope reading clear... no bandits, no patrols. We're at outer edges of Empire space – nothing but rocks here."

"And hopefully, Taro's magic, fully stocked shipyard on that planet," said Krieger, half to himself. "Computer, locate the Boneyard facility, take us down and dock. Vonya, join us through here. I need your help with our shopping list."

They joined the crew round the table in the cabin. Mak 14 had already started on the list on a tablet in the centre, which, in a display of mechanical loyalty, was headed by spare battle-droid parts for Rust. The next entry down read 'Fix annoying crackle on cockpit audio.'

"Okay, obviously, we need proper hull repairs. We also need them to fit the weapons so kindly provided by Kassini here, get the rest of the systems up and running," said Krieger. "What else?"

"Merchant transponders," Kassini added. "You mentioned this ship's stealth capabilities, I'm presuming they don't work, or something?"

"They *should* work," Krieger replied, mildly frustrated. "But we don't know what's wrong with them, do we, computer?"

"The system's power configuration is currently malfunctioning," the vocoded voice intoned.

"So we need to disguise this ship," Kassini continued.

"I agree. At the moment, she looks like a Fed vessel to anyone who knows how to look," added Taro. "Like the Feds themselves, for example. We could ask them for a paintjob while we're at it, I suppose."

"A paintjob? What did you have in mind? Pirate-raider skulls? Hover-racer graffiti tags?"

"No, Kassini... just something that doesn't scream 'stolen from the Empire' quite so loud."

"Agreed," said Krieger. "We'll transmit the list to them in five minutes. Think of anything else, let Mak know."

Vonya had switched on the nav computer and joined the crew in the CiC, moving slowly and painfully to position herself by the room's circular viewing port. Staring distractedly out of the window as the planet's shipyard loomed into view, she tapped on the reinforced surface and pointed a slender talon at the acreage of glinting steel shapes piled in three storeys beneath them. The crew strained to see over her shoulder; she moved her right wing out of the way, but beyond it, all they could make out were flickering silhouettes on the dim landscape.

"Look... at... that," she whispered, indicating the extent of the Boneyard's sprawl.

"Sadly, they are unable to," Mak 14 pointed out on behalf of the rest of the crew. "The space monkeys' long-distance vision is vastly inferior to yours."

"There – Avion scout raider, I used to fly one," Vonya said, her twin voices rising and falling in expressive harmony, a strange but lilting sound to human ears. "Pretty ships, fast, dream to fly – 10 years since they retired them. Bad call. And one of yours – a Federation transport... spin-drive section's long gone. Taken out by missiles, I bet," she snapped out of her reverie and turned her sparkling, pinpoint eyes directly on Taro. "This is one sweet junkyard. Where they find this stuff?"

Stunned, the crew all just blinked back at her, except for Kassini, who just smiled to herself. They were more used to hearing Avions talk in shards of melody that were short, rapid-fire and to the point, but this harmonious expression of emotion in Vonya's voices was new. She registered their stares.

"Why you all looking at me like I just hatched eggs?"

"Nothing, nothing," said Taro. "But we're not used to hearing your voice. You're usually listening to that high-energy dance racket on your headset..."

"I love human music, Watan-abe. It helps me fly," Vonya replied, recovering her composure. "I love to fly."

"No shit," said Krieger, smiling. "That we *can* see. So you're excited to get down there?"

"You kidding me?" Vonya said, turning back to the window and wincing again at the needling reminder of pain from the injuries to her side. "This is beautiful."

Vonya crested the rise first and stopped with a sharp intake of the hot and humid, almost jungle-damp air of the planetoid. She trilled gently as she took in the scene ahead.

A thousand or so battered starship carcasses stretched for miles in a vast bowl encircled by hills, rising from the grey-green soil like animal parts from a forgotten prehistory. Some still retained armour plating; others leaked arterial conduits of exposed cabling. Here and there, rusted hulls that had decayed to skeletal outlines jutted out from tangles of the vegetation which seemed to dominate the ecosystem on this part of the planet.

Several of the larger cruisers had ploughed furrows in the wake of controlled crash landings which were then filled with smaller craft. Drones and robots flitted from hulk to hulk as cutting tools flashed and sparked. The air was thick with the harsh carbon smell of spilt fuel and lubricant.

Mak 14's hydraulics thumped as he stopped alongside Vonya and deployed a scanner antenna from his shoulder.

"Boneyard," he said. "Residual isotopes indicate that the near end of the strip contains the most intact vessels, with those closer to scrap at the far end." He indicated a towering wall of twisted metal some 10 miles in the distance, dwarfing a number of bulky robotic crushing units just visible around its base. Smaller vehicles travelled between these and a mobile workshop facility – a squat, tracked oblong covered in pneumatics and conveyor pulleys – sitting in the approximate centre of the Boneyard.

"Pretty!" said Vonya, in an excitable, high-pitched tone. "You ID the ships?"

"Some. Isotope signature designates generation, visible form factors and ID numbers for models. I have also detected a droid intelligence nearby which will serve as a conveyance for equipment we require. I will acquire it."

"That probably..."

Mak was already moving down the hill in a bounding run towards a droid shaped like a flatbed truck, with tools and manipulator arms where the cab should be.

"...not a friendly idea."

By the time Vonya finished, Mak was at the tall chain-link fence barricading the closest perimeter of the Boneyard. She sighed, unfurled her wings, and preened one briefly before flicking her comms to active and taking to the air in pursuit. It was a pleasant planet for flying, she decided, gaining height and diving along her companion's path. Plus, the pain in her ribcage reminded her that flying was currently a much better option than walking.

She watched as Mak smacked an armoured manipulator through the fence and pulled a section clear. He passed through and approached the side of the flatbed droid as its crane completed loading a chunk of engine from the side of a Rat-class recon ship.

Mak's approach triggered the flatbed's proximity sensor. A camera stalk sprang out of a sensor bundle and rotated towards him, taking in the torn fence as it did so. "Droid. Authorisation?" it transmitted.

"New to the engineering team!" Mak responded, removing the influence unit from his back and deftly placing it behind the flatbed's cab.

The flatbed computed momentarily as cables from the influence terminal snaked out and probed into a small gap beneath the cab. "New droid not briefed in updates. Checking in."

A brief data burst clouded Vonya's comms. She screwed up her face at the noise as she banked gently, catching a thermal to better check out the engine section of a Granite Industries blockade runner near to the flatbed. The static disappeared abruptly just as the message was acknowledged and the flatbed's camera stalk froze in position, then clattered limply to its deck.

"Influence established – this brain has a catalogue and layout of the site in memory," Mak's synth voice said in Vonya's ear. "There are a number of Federation gunships, modules likely compatible with *Anomaly*."

Mak 14 had already mounted the truck like a tank commander and was grinding its gears. "Krieger is doing a deal here, Four-teen," Vonya sighed. "Can't just take that gear. Besides, that droid you've stolen will be missed," she replied.

"This droid is reporting as normal, it is a basic brain and can be influenced without corrupting standard operation. The requirement for cordiality in our engagement here is noted, I'm only planning to take a few things we need."

"I won't stop you. Quietly, destroy not-a-thing."

"Understood."

The flatbed began to reverse as its crane simultaneously lifted the engine block. The crane rotated to one side as the truck turned in the other, and released the engine at the zenith of the resultant arc. The slab of metal flew 10 yards and smacked into the dirt with a resounding crunch, splitting the casing and spilling components across the ground.

Vonya watched as the truck began to trundle deeper into the Boneyard. She turned to follow and landed smoothly on the flatbed behind Mak 14 as they passed an ugly, angular cruiser positioned on its side with a fin pointing skyward, like a beached mechanical whale. Vonya whistled her appreciation.

"Oram Mark 8. Fast for a ship with a big hold," she said as they passed its command module. "Transportation workhorse galaxy-wide till 20 years ago. Many expensive eggs here… would have taken a long time and a fleet of mother tugs to collect."

"This vehicle's code contained a military protection routine and the main service hub has had insignia markings removed," Mak replied. "71 per cent of the ships catalogued are military in origin, from a period roughly analogous with my own active service. It is probable this was the storage area of a navy shipyard at a previous time."

"One they abandoned? And left all the gear?"

“Unknown. This would not be the standard protocol.”

The flatbed rolled into a large clear channel among the hulks at a rapid pace, swaying on its pneumatic suspension. Vonya grabbed the crane gantry to steady herself.

“Slow it down Mak, I have injuries. And need to check some of these,” she said.

“No problem, my feathered friend,” the droid replied cheerily. The vehicle slowed and Mak assumed a voice akin to the incessant advertorial on the FedNet, which he calculated was the best mode for conveying information.

“To our left, you’ll see a number of small fighters, Beta class, by Travis Industries. Ship launchable, lightly armoured and manoeuvrable thanks to the oversized positional thrusters, but lacking firepower…”

“Waste of time. Beta class are talon bait,” Vonya cut in.

“Agreed, but the armament is lightweight and standardised. I can chassis-mount the secondary single-pulse beams.”

“What ship is beyond those?”

Vonya’s eye had picked out a smaller, alien vessel just beyond the neat row of Betas, camouflaged with silver-and-obsidian markings. Lightweight metallic fins swept gracefully forward either side of an ergonomic cockpit culminating in a row of weapon and utility mounts and rising sharply at the rear to accommodate two large engine pods.

“Low profile, big engines. Old Avion fighter,” she said.

“Probable,” said Mak as he scanned the vessel. “The ship is catalogued as an unknown design, it has been here for a long time,” he said. Vonya whistled in approval and began jabbering animatedly.

“Older Avi birds are twitchy, only advantage we had over the Fed was our pilots. Engines over armour, hit hard and fast and get gone before they could respond. Spins to switch ends in a second, thing of beauty…”

Mak 14’s metallic head with its single sensor eye stared at her impassively at 360 degrees to his body, which was busily tapping at the influence terminal. She pulled her enthusiasm up short and said: “Take us nearer.”

The flatbed picked its way through the other craft until Vonya could jump down alongside the sleek fighter. She grabbed the release handle marked in Avion lettering above the battle-glass dome of the cockpit and yanked a few times. Rust and dirt ground in the mechanism, but gave way on the third attempt. As a roof hatch crunched open, an audible hiss of compressed air released the smell of old sweat and burnt insulation.

Vonya leaned into the cockpit, checked it over and climbed into the single pilot’s seat. She was surrounded by a cocooning web of harnessing and the pair of standard wing-trodes at the rear that gave Avion pilots the option to use their wings as a more instinctive way of controlling pitch and yaw in the heat of combat. She quickly assessed the controls and punched for emergency battery power. A single display came to life above her, diagnostic information flickering across it.

She clicked her comms to active at the sound of the flatbed moving off. "Be here a while, Mak..."

"I will examine the Beta class fleet in the meantime," came the reply.

The diagnostics concluded and two further panels activated. She rested a hand on the small controls designed for long Avion talons and clicked through to the system readout. The curls and dots of Avion text appeared bright green, reflecting across Vonya's dark head feathers in the relative gloom of the cabin.

"Interesting..." she said to herself.

"I can do most of what you're asking," said the Boneyard's head mechanic, offering Krieger a powerful-looking hand with a sheen of ingrained grease coating the hardened skin of his fingers. "Let's see, we can fit the armaments no trouble, they're Federation stock... we don't have any merchant transponders, but we can ship one in overnight."

"Sounds good to me," said Krieger, following the mechanic as he walked the perimeter of the *Anomaly*, pausing every so often to run his hand over the worst of the impact scars on the hull and make shorthand notes on his tablet. "Say, what's your name?"

Reaching the aft, the mechanic leant on the cooling engine housing. He looked down at the tablet in his hand and back up at Krieger, his bright eyes narrowing almost imperceptibly.

"I'm Yonas, Yonas N'Doye. I own the Boneyard, in all its rough-ass finery. And I must say, this is an intriguing ship, Mr Krieger. Now you don't have to tell me anything you don't want to," – he shot Krieger a knowing glance – "but I can already tell from the smell of the burn detritus on these thrusters and the lack of stress marks on the hull partitions that this thing is fresh off the Empire's production line. Am I right so far?"

Krieger folded his arms and nodded.

"And it's not just any production line, either, I'll bet. It's based on a Type-16 heavy interceptor, sure, but there," said Yonas, jerking his head towards the stealth tech housing, "the similarity ends."

Krieger shifted his weight and leant against the other side of the thruster to deliberately mirror the mechanic. "I'm not particularly into games, Yonas, but as you know, we appreciate your hospitality. So you can have one more guess."

"Just one? Okay, Mr Krieger, I'll make it a three-parter. One – I'd guess from the pristine markings, the brand-new tech and the chemical streaks on that FTL that this is a prototype vessel. Hell, you might as well have plastic on the seats. Two – I'd guess from the battle damage and lack of working defensive systems that she left in a hurry."

At this point, he turned his attention from the ship and back to Krieger, more warily this time. "And finally – judging by the logo on those Federation dogtags round your neck, your Avion pilot and the lack of encryption on your comms, I'd say that you may once have been a Federation officer, but that was a long time ago; that you aren't supposed to be in possession of this ship... and that you don't know how it works."

Yonas smiled a wide smile. Krieger raised his eyebrows, looked at the ground and waited a beat before replying: "You clearly know your ships and your people, Mr N'Doye. So now it's my turn. One – in amongst the massive number of ships rusting in your Boneyard, you've got Avion stunt fighters and millions of Cees of Federation hardware. That's not your run-of-the-mill salvage, so somehow, you're operating off their scope and you won't be turning us in. Two – that military dry-dock you're using as a workshop looks very familiar to anyone who's ever brought a Fed frigate in planet-side, so as you correctly point out, I have paid my dues in the service of the Empire, but so have you.

"And finally," Krieger added, doing his best imitation of Yonas' earlier flourish, "judging by the fresh oil on your hands, you've already done a day's work before we arrived, so you must be ready for a drink. Shall we?"

"So, how long are we going to have to be on this rock?" asked Kassini, as she pulled up a chair and sat down.

The on-site bar was small, dingy and busy, with rows of plastic tables interspersed with rickety benches and cheap plastic seats. The serving area was a solid oblong along the side of the room, staffed by a line of waiting-droids managed by a solo human operative.

It was shift-change time in the shipyard. The crowd was mostly human with a few robotic companions visible here and there. The atmosphere was made up of voices, music and smoke in equal measure and the whole scene was underlaid with the scent of the illicit always present in frontier outposts.

Kassini had just threaded her way through the crowded tables to a corner Krieger and Taro had taken over. The closest knot of people were nodding appreciatively to a kind of muscular, angry folk music played by a couple of music-techs, who had set up behind a small wall of modular kit on a raised platform.

One had both hands on a plastic board covered in a kind of semi-solid jelly that could be moulded to produce different textures of sound and then trained o repeat the resultant patterns. The jelly mass at the audience side of the board was currently jumping two feet into the air to create a pulse of bass behind the stringed instrument played by the first tech, while his bandmate kneaded a second ball of the material with his fingertips to create a harmony of synthetic 'oohs' and 'aahs'.

Taro looked away from the spectacle to Kassini. "We'll be here as long as it takes... no longer. There's plenty of work to do on the *Anomaly* and Mr N'Doye has been generous so far. We can't expect him to drop everything else at a moment's notice."

Krieger was busy carving a joint of something from a platter into several bowls with a combat knife. Taro took one and offered it to Kassini. "Real meat-steak. Goes well with the beer, I'm told."

He waved a hand at several full bottles on the table by way of offering as Kassini took the bowl hungrily, and took a sip from his own small glass of something brown and potent. His face soured as she grabbed one, flicked the bottom of the cap to detach it and took a swig.

"You asked around yet, Taro? Anybody we need to keep an eye on? This isn't exactly a safe place," she said, between mouthfuls. The real meat was a rare and delicious luxury, but it hadn't stopped her noticing both Krieger's handguns were slung under his jacket.

"There's security for shipyard customers and a no-tell policy," Krieger said, settling back against the seating with his own bowl. "An op like this doesn't want Fed attention any more than we do."

"Besides which, I doubt the local population take too kindly to informants in their midst," said Taro. Most of the patrons were armed and there was at least one combat droid in evidence at the tables on the other side of the room.

A song ended and Kassini sat back with her bottle and surveyed the room. She was on edge, she realised, with Taro's increasing role in their little band. Time to get a grip on that, she thought. Krieger is the mission, the others are just complications.

"Another round?" asked Krieger, though it sounded more like an order than an offer. He tapped a small, opaque pad in the centre of the table. The music struck up again; the next song was a much more relaxed affair, the jelly on the techs' board undulating gently from left to right to create a backing of synthetic tone akin to drawn-out violins.

A small oval droid was shortly dispatched from the bar, travelling a marked path at the circumference of the room toward their table. Taro spotted it and watched as it detoured around an elderly man with a ragged beard who was slumped in a chair against the wall, an empty plastic drinks beaker dangling forlornly in his hand.

His clothes were military cut, but badly worn and faded, sporting a tear where the insignia had clearly been removed with a knife. As the droid passed, the man raised his head and attempted to strike up conversation with it. Taro spotted a glint of madness in his wide eyes as he waved the beaker towards it. The look of the loose-tongued – he knew it well.

The others were taking bets on the *Anomaly's* repair bill as Krieger unloaded drinks from the service droid's hatch. Taro interrupted them. "Excuse me both, I have some asking around to do."

He took his refreshed glass and moved over to the bar, the smell of manual labour and release from duty enveloping him as he carefully threaded through a throng of bodies. Reaching it, he leant over an edge and caught the attention of the only person behind it, a young, relatively well dressed chap. "Can I help you?" the man asked, in the local drawl characteristic of the town.

"Yes. I'm a medic, and this guy behind me looks a bit… unwell. Do you know him?" Taro replied, affecting a concerned expression.

"Boulder?" the young man peeped around Taro's shoulder. "He's often here. Doesn't cause much trouble unless he's really drunk and only then because we have to get a droid to carry him out."

"Where is he on that curve at the moment?"

"Oh, it's early for him yet."

"And what does he usually drink?"

The barman handed Taro a bottle of Clarkin Distillate, the renowned weapon of choice for those on a mission to lose a solar day to stupor.

"Thanks, charge it to our table." Taro turned away from the bar and watched Boulder. He was now placing one hand on top of the other roughly in time to the music and studying the back of each intently as he did so. He would also occasionally go rigid and slowly raise his head to the ceiling, as though watching for a ship on take-off. Taro chose one of these moments to walk over to him.

"Hello, boss," he said, causing the man to jerk out of his reverie and slowly focus on him. "You look like you could use a drink?"

"Lost in the stars. So many, so much out there," the old man laughed at an internal joke. "I've been to them, and I can show you!"

His wide blue eyes were focused somewhere just behind Taro's head. They refocused and took in the bottle Taro was proffering. The spacer grabbed it and took a long swig. "Ahhh, good!" he exclaimed loudly, causing several other patrons to look over at the interruption. "You know your rocket fuel, my man!"

"So they tell me. What are you doing here? You don't look much like a dock grinder to me," Taro smiled charmingly around the enquiry.

"I come from beyond the belt… I have touched the mystical border between this universe and next, I see the depth of it all!" Boulder swung both his arms to the sky at this, causing Taro to reflexively flinch for the bottle. The man lapsed into mumbled babbling, zoning out and following an object in front of his nose Taro couldn't see.

'Psychedelics', thought Taro, registering the disassociation as Boulder struggled to get a grip again. A sickly sweet smell rose from the man's clothes and his facial muscles spasmed whenever he lost his grip on reality. Probably Morvin Syndrome, thought Taro, noting the similarity to symptoms he'd studied in post-traumatic soldiers who'd been exposed to hallucinogenic weaponry.

"Forgive me son, the aether still takes my tongue at times. When you've passed the veil as often as I have, it's to be expected. There's a colony out in the belt, hidden. They have such riches, ships that go there never return."

He paused and took another swig from the bottle before continuing. "Old Boulder did. Just got her home with enough supplies to keep me in touch with the spirit. Of course, I can't fly now, the visions saw to that…" he trailed off into vague mumbling again, the words drowned by the music.

Taro adopted a professional air. "You need some treatment, Mr Boulder? There are stabilisers for conditions like yours."

"I know son, I know. But they cost. These bottles are easier to come by when a pilot can't work."

"That'll make it worse in the long run. I'm a medical man... perhaps there's something we can do for one another if this colony is as rich as you say it is?"

The old man inhaled the final dregs of his bottle and looked at Taro. Lucidity spread over his face, and something like a pleading edge entered his voice. "Maybe there is. Can you start with another bottle?" Taro nodded and moved in the direction of the bar.

Kassini was watching the exchange out of the corner of her eye, only half-listening to Krieger who had finished off his fourth drink and was by now explaining his grand plans for notoriety to the workers at the next table. She was in a position to see the bar door open in a blaze of outdoor ambience streaking in from the Boneyard and a tall hooded figure walk in.

Several of the drinkers closest to it did a double-take as they spotted the telltale plumes of Vonya's wings sprouting from her jacket's neckline, but quickly went back to their business. Avions were a rare sight at the Boneyard, but not unknown. Her black eyes glinted as she scanned the room and spotted them.

Kassini waved her over and she pulled up a seat, removing her hood and jacket and draping her wings over the back of the chair as she sat. She was moving much more freely than Kassini thought she had any right to: Avion healing prowess was clearly every bit as rapid as their speech. "Odd gloop," Vonya said in English, tipping her head towards the music-techs as they fiddled with their equipment between songs. "They make a good noise?"

"Redneck folkies," said Krieger. "Mostly moaning about days gone by. Where's Mak?"

"No beats no grooves get no attention," she said dismissively in her sing-song voice. "Droid gone fix up the big one, hijacked a loader, took some gear from that shipyard. Will need squaring with the boss-hu-man. That yard is something else, humes. A lot of Federal birds in there, but Avion stuff, too."

She stopped and looked at the table. "You got grain-liquid?"

"Help yourself, Krieger's buying," said Kassini, as she opened a bottle and handed it over. The long talons of Vonya's other hand reached into a pouch on her flightsuit and came up with a small flatpack canister.

This inflated at her touch and she began decanting the bottle into it. A tube built into the lid made it significantly simpler and less messy for those with beaks to drink. She trilled appreciatively as she drained the container and put it down on the table. "We here for the night, then, Kass. Seen Taro?"

"He's doing the rounds, seems to have sniffed out a crusty spacer over the other side there. He's keeping him watered... looks he'll be leaving with a lighter pocket," Kassini replied.

"Probs true. The yard agree to fix up *Anomaly*?"

"They did," replied Krieger, swinging back unsteadily from his new friends.

"We had to agree to swap the drive out for a different model, though. Only thing that would cover the work."

"What model?" Vonya sat forward as the band started up again.

"An older, dirtier one, but it's mass-rated for the *Anomaly*. They've been using it in their transport ship, so must be pretty reliable."

"Hope so. Unreliable core system in a jump ship is bad crow."

"The computer thought so, too."

"It's right, this once. Drive from old transport won't be as reliable under stress. We have to stick to green spin zones, I guess."

"I didn't give it up lightly," Krieger told her, in what he thought was a reassuring tone, but was in reality a controlled bellow. "They threw in the transponder work and a full reskin, too. Changing the drive signature will help us stay off the radar, anyway."

"Useful. Long as we stay in one piece when we jump," said Vonya, as the band struck up again.

It was now late evening and the bar had steadily been getting busier as the farmhands also knocked off for the day. The lights were lowered as the combined weight of voices and music upped the rowdiness a notch: the smoke of more exotic substances had begun to overtake the more familiar scent of vapourisers and the temperature was rising as the air conditioners strained at the load.

Kassini was weighing up her third bottle as a commotion flared up at a table opposite. A swarthy tattooed spacer picked up a chair and swung it at an oil-smeared mechanic, who made no effort to evade its telegraphed trajectory. The flimsy furniture smashed into three separate pieces as it struck his close-cropped skull and he responded with a smile before wading into his opponent, flailing punches and eventually grappling the spacer into a headlock.

A jostling crowd began to form a circle around the pair until Kassini noticed the barman gesture over to the shadows in the corner of the bar to a large chrome sphere. 'Game over,' thought Kassini to herself, tugging at Krieger's shirt to get his attention. "Look lively, Krieger," she shouted across at him, pointing. "They've got a battle droid for crowd control... older model than Rust."

They watched as a band of glowing red lights on the patched-up sphere blinked into life. The battle droid began a frenzied rotation and then used its momentum to hurl itself across the floor of the bar like a bowling ball, scattering two members of the unsuspecting crowd like pins. The mechanic barely had time to release his headlock on the spacer before the droid reached them, halted its spin in an instant and whacked them with two riot-control stun batons. The startled brawlers toppled to the floor within a second of each other, thudding against the sticky floorboards like loaded sacks of coal.

The battle droid scanned the crowd menacingly and the circle of spectators, palms up, backed off and melted into the shadows. Satisfied the threat was dispersed, it extended two mechanical claws from its centrifuge, snapped them down on the unconscious figures and dragged them out to the yard. The whole extraction lasted as long as it took Kassini to shrug, open her beer and take a couple of swigs. Krieger looked at her and raised his eyebrows. “Overkill, but effective,” he said.

“Pretty brutal. Took care of apes, but plenty more where they came from. Think we need to fight tonight?” Vonya asked, her dark eyes glancing pointedly over at the by-now quite battered Krieger.

“I think the shipyard business will keep it quiet for us,” Kassini replied. She glanced around and saw that several more-dangerous-than-usual-looking individuals had quietly taken up strategic positions around the room in the last half an hour and were keeping an eye on the louder portions of the crowd.

“Humes,” Vonya sighed, as the song reached a crescendo and the crowd swayed along with it.

The next morning, Krieger walked slowly back up the *Anomaly's* ramp and withdrew it behind him. “That was a good night,” he said to the crew, who had assembled in the cabin and were idly watching the computer verify the integrity of the upgrades as part of its prissy and exacting pre-flight check. The Boneyard's night shift had prioritised the *Anomaly's* work – Yonas's crew didn't mess around.

“Prepared for our orbital flight, departing in 10 minutes, Captain. Would you like me to procure you a sickbag?” asked Mak 14, adding a sarcastic mechanical salute.

“Where's the smugness control on this thing, Taro? We need to dial it way down,” said Krieger. “Especially since I've just been running through the receipt for the repairs and we're being charged for a replacement fence and ‘psychological repairs to a mechanical operative’. It's filed under ‘miscellaneous services’. Any idea what that might be about, Mak?”

“It was necessary. And I would prefer to focus on the fact that Rust is now fully operational again, thanks to my other ‘miscellaneous services’,” Mak 14 replied haughtily, and bolted himself to the wall. Krieger shook his head and turned to Taro.

“Hey man, give me a hair-of-the-dog shot from that medi-dispenser of yours… that's an order.”

Taro handed him a sobriety-restoring pill. “These are popular this morning. I've just donated a couple to our hosts out there in the shipyard, too.”

“Should've known better than to try and keep pace with deep spacers,” said Krieger, gulping the pill down his dry throat like a parched snake. “Even the band drank more than us.”

“*Especially* the band,” said Kassini. “Pre-flight says we're good to go, so let's get to wherever we're going.”

“Would anyone mind informing me where exactly that is?” the computer piped up. “I am the ship's computer, by the way, just to remind you. In case you had forgotten.”

“We’ll decide in orbit. Let’s hit the road,” said Krieger and slumped into his chair.

The computer flew the *Anomaly* out of the dock and ascended through the clouds and upper atmosphere of the planet, heading for the jump point with nothing on the scope except for a distant reading from a Boneyard transport ship and an escort of two heavily armed fighters. The small but radically customised craft were provided by Yonas as both a courtesy and a reminder – the Boneyard was a self-sufficient, open secret, and he intended it to stay that way.

Halfway to the spin point, the fighters swivelled, dipped their wings and turned back for the facility. As Vonya watched them recede into the distance, Mak 14 broke the fuzzy, hungover silence. “My observations reveal that the Boneyard was likely a fully operational Federal navy outpost at some time in the past,” the droid intoned.

“Funny,” said Kassini. “That’s what our observations revealed to us, too. But Yonas was an independent operator. So what’s he doing running a repair yard on an ex-Fed base?”

“I asked him about his involvement with the Empire when I spoke to him, something he would neither confirm nor deny,” said Krieger. “And he kept shtum about those Empire ships, too… I mean, tampering with military equipment on that scale is usually enough to have a colony like that nuked off the map.”

“Hey, check this out,” said Taro, holding up his tablet with the coordinates. “I had an interesting conversation last night with someone called Boulder. He was strung out on some kind of heavy hallucinogens and his mechanism was pretty far gone. But he said he was a pilot once upon a time and that he knew of a secret colony around here. He handed over these coordinates in exchange for a bag of mood meds.”

“Okay, so where do they point?” asked Krieger.

“They check out, but they’re far out beyond the asteroid belt. Boulder also said that the last few trips the Boneyard crew had made, no one has come back.”

Krieger stood up and paced up and down the CiC module. “So what you’re suggesting is we stay in the system and risk a return visit from the Boneyard’s fighter squadron, so we can check out some coordinates that you got from a drug-crazed lunatic you met in a bar? What do we think, crew?”

“I guess when you put it like that, it sounds ridiculous,” Taro conceded. “But the Boneyard’s onto something and I wouldn’t mind knowing what the connection is. We’re free to go wherever we want… there is as good as anywhere else.”

“I need to test *Anomaly’s* flight systems before we roll dice with the new drive,” added Vonya.

“That’s settled, then,” said Krieger to the floor. “Computer, here are those coordinates you asked for.”

“Finally, we’re making a move,” said Mak 14. “I’ll wake up Rust.”

M

Kassini: *Anomaly* heading to new coordinates in the Boneyard system: -44.8695 76.5901.

The diplomat Taro was given them by a mad spacer.

They clearly don't have a plan, Drexler.

Come and get them and give me a real assignment.

M

Drexler: Intriguing destination – Krieger is going to love it, anyway. Patience, Kassini.

I can see two moves ahead... I can guess where he's going to head next.

Orders = Unchanged.

Drexler out.

7. DARK CRYSTALS

"We burn fuel for this?" said Vonya to Taro, as she coasted the *Anomaly* around yet another cluster of grey asteroid fragments. "Three hours of this view... my eyes sting."

"The scope says we're right on top of it," replied Taro, staring intently at the crowded scanner that showed a cluttered debris field of rocks, none of which was a colony. He shouted back into the cabin. "Mak, what are we missing? Run the scans again."

"The last 10 scans have been identical. Running number 11," the droid replied.

Kassini had been reading for the last hour or so, engrossed in a trashy, handwavium-filled but addictive 21st-century sci-fi novel and only half-listening to the conversation. She looked up from her tablet. "When you say identical... are there any discrepancies at all, aside from position and direction of the asteroids? Because if not, we're wasting our time. I vote we cut our losses and spin to a new system."

"I have compared all sensor and operational data from the last 180 minutes and detected one anomalous factor," noted the computer. "The energy signature from the *Anomaly*'s stealth system rises exponentially in proximity to a narrow band of coordinates. Once we leave the coordinates, it falls rapidly to its normal levels."

"What does that mean, exactly?" sighed Krieger. "Is some kind of radiation interfering with the drive?"

"We have limited information on the system's capabilities and behaviour," said the computer.

"So all we know is that there's a spike in system energy when we're in a certain narrow spectrum? Then let's travel back to those coordinates and find out why," said Krieger. "Computer, send Vonya the coordinates."

Vonya accelerated to the spot, flying petulantly to give the crew a slightly rougher ride than usual to express her annoyance. She brought the ship to a deliberately abrupt halt which shook the cabin, switched to autopilot, arched her back and rubbed her eyes as the computer kept the *Anomaly* static.

"You're right," said Krieger, looking at the stealth-system readouts. "This thing's energy is practically redlining. But to the naked eye and as far as the scope's concerned, this section of the belt is the same as any other."

"I suggest we hit the big red button and see what happens," said Taro.

"Is that wise, Captain?" the computer asked. "We have limited..."

"...information on the system's capabilities, we know," Krieger parroted. "Bring the stealth online and execute the start-up sequence."

"Executing," said the computer, nervous tension in its vocoded voice.

The stealth's display flashed briefly, then was silent. "That's about all it usually does..." said Mak 14, then tailed off as he looked up out of the cockpit.

Ahead of them, a storm of intense energy beams blinked and flickered into being, leaving phosphorescent trails against the darkness of space. After a few seconds of violence, the storm stabilised to frame a starship-sized oblong of nothingness bathed in an unnatural purplish glow.

"Pretty patterns, humes," said Vonya over the comms.

"Right, of course... a stargate of some kind," said Taro. "That madman back at the Boneyard could've mentioned that, saved us some time."

"Shall I take the bird through?" Vonya asked, strapping herself in. "More fun than dodging asteroids."

"Let's do it – I *love* a stargate," said Krieger. "They never get old."

"Yeah, I'm pretty partial to a portal," added Kassini absentmindedly, eyes back to scanning the text of the novel on her tablet.

Taro scrunched his face against the circular view port, straining for a better view as though he was watching manta rays gliding by in an aquarium. As soon as they'd passed through the gateway, these glinting, indistinct forms had resolved into the impossible yet familiar shapes before their eyes – an abandoned fleet of Empire starships, lights out, tethered to a huge asteroid drifting in interstellar space.

"This is like a scene from the *Outlier* comics I read when I was a kid back on Ross 128," said Krieger, lost in the scene. As the captain watched the gleaming hulls rotating into view through the cockpit window, he listened to Mak 14 cataloguing the vessels.

"The fleet consists of one Polestar-class capital ship, a severely damaged Ariadne-class carrier, a Variable-class cruiser, three Preon-class destroyers, several frigates and corvettes and four smaller assault carriers," he told them. "These are all older models by today's standards, but they have clearly survived many historical engagements. Only one carrier has a full complement of fighters, and none are launching, by the way," he added.

"There are also several specialist weapons platforms – laser-battery ships, missile carriers and point-defence craft – plus a communications and countermeasures vessel," 14 continued. "No repair tugs or fuelling tankers are evident among the refinery craft, transports, dropships and supply vessels. Overlaying ship designations onscreen."

The text overlay scrolled, beginning with the capital ship. Krieger audibly gasped. "The *Marshall Smith*? That was Admiral Kirkwood's ship..."

"Heard the name, what are the hell are they all doing here?" said Kassini. "Computer, call up the declassified Federation mission logs for the strike force led by Admiral Kirkwood. Skip to last-known whereabouts."

"The last logged location for the *USS Marshall Smith* was in the vicinity of NGC 6543, aka the Cat's Eye Nebula, 2856."

"Over three decades ago," Krieger mused. "I presume the mission details remain classified?"

"That is correct," the computer replied. "There are no further entries relating to the strike force or its crew."

Kassini broke the silence. "Computer, all the ships are in range. Is anybody home?"

"The *USS Marshall Smith* has 123 souls onboard," the computer intoned. "There are approximately 50 other lifeforms scattered across the rest of the fleet and between five and 10 on nearby asteroids. The large asteroid the ships are secured to appears to be hollow, but sensors cannot penetrate the interior with accuracy. 90 per cent of the power detected is being consumed by the *Marshall Smith*. There are no significant drive signatures, either current or recent. No weapons systems are online across the entire fleet."

"Okay," said Taro, dragging himself away from the porthole. "Let's take stock of this. Can one of you ex-Fed navy kids tell me what it is we're looking at here?"

"Well, that's exactly it," Krieger replied. "We shouldn't be seeing this at all. It's the remnants of a legendary Federation strike force from the Great Expansion era."

"And not just any legendary fleet," said Kassini. "It was led by Admiral Kirkwood."

"Who?" asked Taro.

"Didn't you pay any attention at school?" asked Krieger, genuinely surprised.

"I studied Medicine, and Law, at Pegasi University," Taro pointed out. "I had my hands full. I definitely didn't have time for the comic-book tales they taught you at space camp."

"Impressive credentials for a wanted renegade, Taro, but you definitely missed out," said Krieger. "Especially in the case of Kirkwood. He was one of the greatest commanders the Empire's ever known."

"Are you *star-struck*?" Taro asked Krieger, who shot back his best sarcastic smile.

"The Expansion times were the absolute dog days for the Empire military," said Kassini. "Every spin was a jump into the unknown... they ran towards danger, never away from it. Men and women like Kirkwood were at the frontline, vying for planetary spoils with the Avions and pretty soon, the Elementals, too. All of the factions were operating 'in the dark', at the limits of their range, and they had the morals to match: their lives were brutal, what resources they had were stretched to the limit."

"You've heard of the Pathfinder Treaty, right?" Krieger asked Taro. "They must've taught you about that on your Law course."

"The Pathfinder Treaty was the first inter-faction agreement ever signed between the three factions," the computer piped up, helpfully. "The treaties strictly forbade interspecies conflict as part of intergalactic exploration. Pathfinder was honoured by all three races' naval forces and resulted in a ceasefire that is credited for greatly accelerating the expansion of the three territories."

"If it sounds too good to be true, that's because it was," said Krieger. "Even after the treaty was signed, when a system was contested, or even when fleets passed near to each other, skirmishes would break out. A lot of it was shadowboxing, where each faction would test the responses of its opposite number and report back their intelligence to their HQ worlds. Sometimes, though, it would descend into full-on conflict... a fight to the death."

Vonya, who was listening intently over the comms, spoke up at this. "Is that what they teach you in school, Kree-gar? Because Avions got there first, most times. Only a fight to the death when you turned up."

An awkward silence crept around the CiC.

"Didn't mean to ruffle your feathers, pilot," Krieger replied eventually. "This is all ancient history, remember? Anyway, a lot of people forget they were also expeditionary fleets, to a certain extent. They had a duty to leave beacons and rudimentary defensive bases on colonisable worlds. Their ships also had to devote a lot of valuable weapons and defence capacity to habitability over long-haul trips."

"That made them virtually self-sufficient," Kassini said, picking up the thread as Taro leaned forward, seemingly warming to the history lesson. "Strike forces like this one out here had been in battle the longest. They were the most anarchic units on the board and they marched to a different drum. After Pathfinder, one by one, they disappeared – leaving behind only holo-reports of their exploits. The navies marked their losses as 'collateral damage' in their reports... I've actually seen them, can you believe it? The admiralty thought it had bigger fish to fry, trying to work out how to defend the spacelanes of the inner worlds."

"From protecting the universe to protecting the universities," said Krieger. He took a swig from his flask of water while grinning sidelong at Taro.

"So let me guess the rest," said Taro, impatiently. "The commanders of these intrepid, no-surrender forces were romanticised by the folks tucked up safe-and-sound back on their homeworlds... and the FedCor used their myths as a tool to enlist soldiers and pilots for the navy."

"Damn right they did," said Krieger. "They were why I signed up in the first place. They were the first living and breathing superstars of the age of galactic conquest."

"It's not just you, humes," said Vonya, still listening in over the cockpit comms channel. "Avions got storybook heroes from this time. Elementals, too, I guess."

"So we have a lost fleet, tethered to an asteroid, floating in gods'-knows-where space only accessible via a stargate," Taro summarised. "They have a crew of around 200, maybe more inside the asteroid. We should presume that some of the original fleet's crew are still among them. Maybe Captain Big Balls –"

"Admiral Kirkwood," Krieger corrected.

"...or whoever is still calling the shots. Which makes you wonder: if these are indeed the Federation's grizzliest ancient space marines, why haven't we been hailed, or challenged, or blasted into tiny pieces by now?"

"Their ships are inactive. Fleet communications are virtually non-existent," said Mak 14. "Silent running. They are probably in the habit of being left well alone out here."

"Not quite alone, though," said Krieger. "Taro, you said your friend at the Boneyard told you that people had visited the fleet from the colony and never returned. So they've had *some* visitors... I think we should ring the doorbell and see who answers. Computer, hail the capital ship: use neutral callsigns."

After a five-second pause, the computer replied. "No response, captain."

"Curiouser and curiouser," said Krieger. "Vonya, dock the *Anomaly* in the landing bay of the *Marshall Smith* – and keep her ticking over, in case we need emergency evac. Computer, find out exactly what happened with the stargate and our stealth. Based on your observations, figure out why it behaved that way and from that, try and figure out how to use it in future. The rest of you – suit up for a recce. We're going in."

As the crew prepared, they watched the elongated-pyramid hull of the *Marshall Smith* loom closer on the viewscreen. As she positioned them overhead, Vonya rotated the *Anomaly* above the armoured missile batteries jutting like bastions out of the Federation capital ship's centre section. Up close, they could see areas among the white gleaming metal that had been scruffily welded, likely after the ship had soaked up bombardment from heavy projectile-weapon fire with her shields down. Capital ship or not, the *Marshall Smith* had obviously lived a charmed life and had the battlescars to prove it. Krieger's inner child desperately wanted to set foot on it and find out its stories.

As they passed through the cargo bay, Mak 14 activated Rust, whose red eyepiece flickered into life. The battle droid ran through its weapons-check protocol, quickly and silently deploying and retracting each of its systems in turn in a deathly choreography. It was intimidating to watch in close quarters, but ultimately reassuring. "Rust online. Identify targets," it boomed, in its chillingly deep mechanised voice.

"Targets unknown at present," said Mak 14. "Don't worry my friend, when we find someone to kill, you will be the first to know."

The *Anomaly's* access ramp disgorged the team into a single-berth bay with Krieger on point, face painted with wonder. He visibly got a grip on his excitement as the darkness closed around them and the ramp retracted behind them. They passed through a double-lock into the steel box of an arterial corridor, lit only by emergency lamps.

Atmosphere was stable enough to explore without helmets, but it was also cold onboard. All three humans grumblingly thumbed their suit temperatures up as their breath began to condense to mist in front of them, melding with the faint fog already present in the capital ship.

Rust's drive hum reverberated through the enclosed space, giving an eerie impression of distance. A number of recessed alcoves lined the wall opposite the access points for other landing bays, built to accommodate an older style of hulking first-gen battle droid designs that were Rust's predecessors. He paused for a moment to scan the first bay as the team passed, profiling the potential presence of the threat but saying nothing.

Kassini had unconsciously moved up next to Krieger, on point, her rifle pointing steadily into the dim grey ahead of them. She spoke quietly to him. "There's no sound of anything operating, and power's either out or off. The ship didn't look that badly damaged, but maybe they lost a major coupling or something and couldn't repair it."

"Computer didn't mention anything about power usage, other than the *Marshall Smith* was using it all. Who knows?" Krieger replied.

Mak 14's voice cut across their headsets suddenly, making Krieger wince.

"This corridor runs the length of this deck, and the ship's bridge is two decks above us. I expect most of the elevators are also deactivated and Rust is too large for personnel stairwells, so droid and loader ramps represent the optimal route. An access point for these should be amidships."

"You can vocalise Mak, it's off-putting when you're just behind me to communicate via the comms," Krieger replied, testily.

"Duly noted," Mak said aloud. "My stealth protocol is active, this requires silence wherever possible. I only communicated at all in order to alleviate the pressure on your faulty organic memory system, since it rarely remembers where you are supposed to be going."

Krieger noted 14's crankiness, but said nothing as he shouldered his weapon and moved on.

The team reached a large opening in the right-hand side of the corridor which, as predicted, led to a series of ramps that led upwards. They were wide enough for the mechanical transports used for bulk ammunition and crates, judging by the neatly parked loaders stowed underneath the nearest one. Having checked the cavernous chamber above them with their lights, they began to make their way up, Mak 14 taking the lead.

"What the hell is that?" exclaimed Taro as he played his light over an the arch that gave access from the ramps to the next deck proper. The walls around them were painted jet black, and the modification seemed to extend out into a similar corridor to the one they'd vacated below them. A field of stars and nebulae had been painstakingly added in glitter and bright colours, pinpoints of light amongst the base coat. The paintjob seemed to absorb his torchbeam, making the dark, quiet ship seem even more spectral.

Taro stuck his head through the entrance and shone his torchbeam down the corridor.

"Seems to extend out here as well. Why would anybody paint an entire deck like this?" he mumbled to himself. Something caught his eye as he pulled his head back in, the slightest indication of a movement further down.

He jumped back, adrenaline suddenly shooting up. "Saw something move down there, too," he blurted to the others, crouching under the cover of the archway. Kassini readied her rifle and moved forward to join the XO.

Rust boomed suddenly. "Active droid signatures on this level."

"Where?" Kassini asked.

"Corridor ahead right, two, closing," replied the battle droid. They could hear something distinct now as Rust's voice echoed away – a metallic pistoning, gradually coming closer.

"Use the ramps, Kassini," Krieger whispered urgently. They took shelter at a crouch on the downward slope, using its edge for cover. Mak 14 took up position by the door, while Rust simply moved directly in front of it and deployed several weapons, his red lights casting a hellish hue as they swept relentlessly from side to side.

Taro and Kassini quickly flanked Krieger as the sounds came closer. On the other side of the entrance, they suddenly stopped and were replaced by complex whirrs of gears and machinery. These gave way in turn to the sound of high-pressure spraying, which went on sporadically for half a minute as the squad exchanged puzzled glances.

Krieger flashed a hand signal to Mak 14, who clicked an affirmative in his earpiece as he stuck a sensor stalk around the corner. It panned around briefly, then retracted.

"Maintenance drones," he said and, as one, the humans exhaled. "Primitive, and unarmed. They are adding a new constellation to the wall opposite me."

"Okkaay – there's your mystery artists. Can you plug into one and find out what's happening here?" Krieger said to Mak as he and Kassini lowered their weapons.

"Yes," said the droid, and reached around the corner to drag the nearest unit into the room with a whine of servos.

It was bipedal, but the humaniform appearance ended at a torso made up of angular plates in a pyramidal shape which ended at a point, making it about five feet tall. A wig of dark hair had been glued to the top of the pyramid, and perfunctory eyes and a smiling mouth added underneath in what looked like marker pen, along with the words 'Bongo' in childish scrawl.

The drone emitted a series of alarmed noises, and rotated a small spray gun it had extruded from one face of his carapace from side to side angrily. Rust immediately targeted the movement with several red laser pointers, which danced across Mak's back as he moved around the droid to find a small hatch and plugged a cable from his influence terminal into it.

The droid fell silent, and a few seconds later, Mak said: "I am having some difficulty interpreting this unit – it has had no updates or even a maintenance reboot for several decades, and much of its memory has been flashed to make way for a complete star map of the quadrant and an archive of episodes of a FedNet show called *The Joy Of Painting The Galaxy*. It was originally part of the team managing the exterior maintenance of the *Marshall Smith*, but this one has spent the last six years perfecting the painted copy of the map you see here, in between a... variety... of other duties."

Bongo suddenly began intoning the phrase "Full of stars... full of happy stars," over and over from a speaker they couldn't see. Krieger and the others exchanged looks again, this time complete with incredulous expressions. Mak's manipulator arm whacked the unit, and the speech stopped in a blaze of static.

"It does, however, have more current schematics of the ship in memory," Mak continued. "The *Marshall Smith* has been heavily modified from its original design. The back quarter of the ship is now some kind of mining and chemical operation, and the entire top deck is human habitation and stores. This droid was instrumental in making it more 'open plan', apparently."

Mak withdrew his cabling and released the droid, which began to run a self-diagnostic routine.

"Beyond that, its logic circuits seem only to ramble about cheerful nebulae clouds and the correct amount of paint-to-thinning-agent ratios. I have instructed it to guide us to the inhabited area of the ship."

"What about Kirkwood?" asked Krieger, some of the earlier excitement returning to his voice. "Is he here?"

"The admiral is still in command of the ship and the colony," replied Mak and Krieger's smile beamed brighter than Rust's laser sights, just for a moment.

The elevator, though designed for moving men and munitions in bulk, was cramped for all five of them, as Mak had predicted. Bongo the droid accompanied them as far as its entrance before motioning them inside and wandering off to continue its cock-eyed maintenance duties.

The box moved slowly, the elderly lifting mechanism complaining as it dragged the crew upwards, and came to a gentle halt with a groan.

"Our stop," said Kassini, who was wedged into a back corner next to Rust, and the doors squeaked open. The distant sound of voices and equipment could be heard, reverberating as though from a distance. There was also an undercurrent of music, indistinct if undeniably present.

A rectangular metal room greeted them, featureless aside from a large double door at one end and a button with the words 'Door Bell' spraypainted above it. They filed out and took stock for a moment as a hot blast of fusty, recycled air hit them. The structure they stood in was clearly makeshift, the walls visibly bolted to the floor and the roof spot-welded into place in sections.

"Were they trying to keep somebody out?" Taro enquired. Krieger looked at him, shrugged and strode forward to push the button.

Nothing happened for a good 20 seconds, until a speaker somewhere above Krieger clicked to life.

"Heeeey, visitors!" it said. "You buying or selling?"

Krieger looked around for a microphone and, seeing nothing to suggest one, answered the door bell.

"Umm, this is Captain Krieger of the *Anomaly*. We might be buying, depends what you're selling."

"You Federal navy, *Captain*?" the voice responded with a sudden edge of menace.

"Long time ago I was, much like you I think."

"Well, if you got Cees or stock, we got merchandise to trade. New customers always welcome at Admiral Kirkwood's house."

The speaker clicked off and the sound of locks cycling on the door ahead of them filled the room. The double doors drew open on grinding pneumatic tracks and the sight they revealed took Krieger's breath away.

A huge chamber had been constructed covering almost the entire deck of the vessel, every wall and supporting bulkhead removed except those absolutely necessary for structural integrity. Exposed air-conditioning ducting, electrical and data cabling and fluid transport pipes were suspended from the roof in huge clumps above Krieger and his crew, who were now stepping out of a metal box welded together around the original lift shaft.

Makeshift structures had been built haphazardly from old equipment and furniture throughout the deck – a small market area hastily covered with tarpaulin, communal bars and shower areas, even a thrown-together performance venue in the style of a miniature open-air amphitheatre complete with a few rows of tiered seating around a small raised stage. All of the viewing windows from the original configuration were still visible, punctuating the sweep of ceiling and walls with points of blackness at intervals demarcating some of the original rooms, which were now largely inaccessible.

The only recognisable section of the once-military starship's top deck was the bridge area. A large set of metal stairs had been erected leading up to the original, roughly cylindrical, sealed room now bizarrely suspended at some 10 metres from what had become the roof of the hall, looking like a flying saucer from the old movies. Wiring sprouted from every side of it, rising majestically up to join the main runs along the ceiling. It seemed as though the room itself was on some kind of medical life support from the rest of the ship.

"What in the name of the gods?" exclaimed Kassini, taking it all in. The smell of wood smoke and cooking hung in the sweltering air, alongside an acrid chemical note.

"Welcome to the House!" said the voice recognisable from the speaker system, and the *Anomaly* crew turned to see an overweight man clad in olive-green cut-off fatigues and a battered officer's jacket rising unsteadily from a small terminal nearby. His red, puffy face showed every day of his advanced years as he lumbered over to the group.

"Name's Kelman Brock," he said, thrusting a hand towards Krieger. "Duty Sergeant for today. No salutes here, ranks don't mean too much aboard ship these days."

"Krieger," the captain said, shaking the outstretched hand before wiping his own on his trouser leg. He looked around before continuing.

"This is really the *Marshall Smith*? Out of Cassiopeia yards in 2354? Invented the Adams Manoeuvre during the third wave of Avion engagements?"

Kelman looked nonplussed.

"Sure is, but all that was a long time ago. We keep out of the way of politics and conflict these days. Say, you're not another journalist, are you?" he replied. Krieger's face dropped a little and he looked lost for words. Taro stepped in and offered his own hand to the sweating officer.

"We just heard there's an outpost here. We've been trading in these systems for years, but it was news to us, and we're always looking for another port. I'm Taro, this is Kassini."

Kassini gave a quick nod to the officer, and quietly said something indistinguishable to Mak 14 – she'd clocked two other older men carrying rifles who had quietly moved into position on either side of them, and was hoping Rust didn't react to them.

Kelman licked his lips and eyed the group suspiciously.

"Your droids look pretty handy for a friendly trading outfit, but it is a dangerous universe out there. We know, oh yes, we know. The Federal government has its tendrils into everything."

He stopped. "I think you should meet the admiral. Come with me, but leave the droids here."

He turned and began walking down an avenue between several makeshift workstations and some bunk houses. Krieger turned to Kassini and said: "Stay with the droids and try to keep them under control, will you?"

"No problem," she replied, and he motioned Taro to follow him as he moved to catch up to Kelman's receding bulk.

The officer led them through a maze of lanes between the haphazard structures. These were occasionally broken up by massive columns of steel and plas-fibre running floor to ceiling, which maintained the overall superstructure of the deck. They passed a number of other crew members, most of whom were practising artistry of one form or another – some were working steel or clay, others generating holographics, yet more would be painting or scribbling furiously at writing pads and tablets.

Most of the crew they saw were of Kelman's generation and often equally dishevelled, with a preponderance of gnarled grey beards on the menfolk. Almost all of them were also completely engrossed in their work to a surprising degree; not one person threw even a glance at the trio as they passed. One or two were sitting completely still, wide-eyed, staring uncomprehendingly at whatever was in front of them. The effect of a room full of quiet artists was unsettling.

Krieger, walking slightly ahead of Taro, heard the click of his comms channel.

"Starting to make more sense now," Taro's voice said quietly. "I've seen this kind of thing before in facilities treating extreme psychotics with art therapy. Either these people are all Leonardo da Vinci, or they're high on some kind of focus dope – heavily prescribed in the medical world and costly to manufacture, so where the hell they'd be getting it out here is anybody's guess."

Krieger nodded as he walked and heard Taro take a breath before continuing.

"Also likely explains our friend back at the bar. Medical-grade versions of those compounds have to be administered carefully, and side effects of prolonged usage can be mean – hallucinations, complete meltdowns, total disassociation. A long list."

The comms channel clicked off as they reached the foot of the steps up to the bridge module. Kelman turned to them and said: "Wait here."

He looked up at the steps and, sighing slightly, began to haul himself up them with the aid of a handrail. At the top, he produced a red keycard which opened the door. Krieger and Taro noticed him spread his hands in front of him as he walked through it, and he began speaking in the tone of a military subordinate as the doors slid shut.

Now out of sight of the officer, Krieger could no longer contain his excitement.

"Taro, we're actually going to meet possibly the greatest admiral in the history of the Federation! The stories about this guy were all I heard when I was a cadet, some of the old-timers had actually served with him and man, they were tough. He's from a time when the universe was wilder, before people stopped caring about anything other than what was on their doorstep. The stories he must…"

"He also quit on the Federation with one of their battlecruisers and holed up in an asteroid field for scores of years, Krieger," Taro interjected. "And now his crew are high as kites and painting their way to their graves with their stories."

Krieger refused to be deflated, and Kelman chose that moment to reappear through the door above them. "Come on up!" he said.

As they mounted the stairs and Kelman shifted his bulk to let them pass, he leant in and said quietly: "Just so you know, the Admiral hasn't left the bridge… in some decades."

He smiled meekly and thumbed the keycard against the door, and Krieger's anticipation soared as the door cycled open.

"Welcome, gentlemen!" boomed an authoritative voice, rich in timbre from years of command, as they stepped through the door and it clunked shut behind them.

They found themselves in an improvised airlock with a floor-to-ceiling plexiglass screen on the inside giving them a view of the bridge module proper. One side of it had been walled off into a small quarters, complete with folding bed and what appeared to be a tiny shower cubicle visible through a small door.

The rest of the bridge remained standard Federation-issue, a nest of viewscreens, consoles and terminals, clearly the worse for wear, but still functional. The main command table in its centre ended a metre from the screen in front of them, and seated the other side of this was the rumpled, elderly form of Admiral Tigh Kirkwood.

Krieger was struck dumb for a moment and staring through the glass with wide eyes. He stammered a formal greeting. "Thank... thank you for seeing us, Admiral."

"Always a pleasure son, my XO assures me you're not with the authorities," replied the man at the table through a small microphone on a base affixed to it. The sound of a complex air-conditioning system filled the chamber as a backing to his words. Kirkwood was still notably imposing in stature, but time had taken its toll on him, in all kinds of ways. Except, that is, for a telling detail Krieger instantly recognised: his eyes still blazed with the weird light of those long used to shouldering the responsibility of starship command, their bright blue gaze matching the rank insignia on his now-oversized uniform.

Krieger stood rigidly to attention and mouthed air, as Taro stepped forward and spoke.

"Sir, we appreciate the audience. I'm Medical Officer Watanabe of the *Anomaly*, this is Captain Krieger. We're a crew of humble traders looking for new markets, sir, and stumbled across the *Marshall Smith* when we strayed off course. We assumed this was good potential salvage until we got close enough to scan. We know the legends around your ship and just had to take a closer look."

"Well, you can be forgiven for that, Watanabe – we try not to give ourselves away, but a battlecruiser and what's left of its attendant fleet isn't always so easily hidden. If you know something of our history, I expect you're wondering where the hell we've been all these years?"

Taro nodded, on cue.

"The answer is: 'more or less right here'. When we left the Federation 30 years ago, we set up shop on these asteroids, and it took us 10 years to do it – we're a mining and pharmaceutical colony now, operationally speaking. Fortunately, they built ships to last in my day, and to operate independently of fleet-arm support for long periods. Just how long a crew might push that envelope had never really been envisioned, but we try to keep the old thing ship-shape."

"Pharmaceutical operation, sir? And what are you mining all the way out here?"

"This belt of asteroids is unusually rich in a crystalline form of methocortisone which, when processed and metabolised by the human body, grants an unnaturally high level of focus and motivation. As a medical man, I'm sure that means more to you than it does to me, but I do know it's become highly prized in some of the, shall we say, harder-working colonies in this area," he smiled at this.

"Ah, yeah, we understand," said Taro, looking across to Krieger who was now clearly itching to speak.

"So we too are in the galactic market, Watanabe, even if we don't encourage too many strangers," said the admiral, tone slightly more ingratiating. "It's impossible to be completely self-sufficient out here, of course. We trade our products for our needs with a select few trusted crews and welcome anybody who wishes to join our operation, within reason. Perhaps we can help each other. My crew has already reported that your ship has all the hallmarks of people used to working quietly and off the radar, so to speak."

"Admiral," Krieger had finally summoned his voice. "The last anybody heard of the *Marshall Smith* was just after you outmanoeuvred the Avion 4th fleet in the Cat's Eye."

"Avion 4th, 6th and remnants of their 12th Special to be precise, Captain," corrected Kirkwood. Krieger stopped himself blurting out a tactical question like a schoolboy.

"I was a raw recruit aboard the *Golgotha* under Commander Jameson back then," he said instead. "After contact was lost, every possible rumour passed the scuttlebutt – manoeuvred too close to a supermassive, ambushed behind the lines, crew mutiny – how did you all end up here?"

"It's complicated, Captain, and also unsurprising that the truth didn't make it out. I presume you saw the damage to the fleet on your way in? That was largely from that final engagement."

A change came over Kirkwood's wizened features and his voice took on a harder grade of steel as he continued.

"I had presumed you're a military man from your bearing, so I think you'll understand… we were trained to fight for humanity's right to expand in those days, to drive the birds out of the resource-rich systems the Federation had already laid claim to during the Great Expansion. Bloody battles, Captain – countless good men, women and ships lost forever. And before long, as quickly as we were taking the systems, the politicians at Centre were assigning them back and forth with the Avions in treaties."

Krieger nodded as the anger in Kirkwood's voice rose.

"It was obvious the momentum of the Great Expansion had exhausted itself. The battles in which we sacrificed so much had become no better than an exercise for the civvies, just a detail they were forced to confront and smooth over every few months," the admiral jabbed a finger into the table. "And we were still on the frontline, risking our people, because Command and the officials couldn't agree to stop the fighting and announce a formal cooperation, for fear of how it would play.

"Eventually they did, of course, when the population at Centre stopped caring and responding positively to the announcements of the mighty Federation fleet victories. After a while, all anybody really cared about was whether their precious minerals kept flowing."

The admiral spat these final words, before taking a moment to compose himself.

"We were ordered to the NGC cluster on a patrol mission, but the Avions had staged a lot more firepower there than anybody anticipated. I lost half the fleet in rearguard, and they managed to infect the *Marshall Smith* with one of their damned viral weapons. Immuno-compromising to humans, meant suddenly the most basic ailment could wipe out half the crew. It did, in fact… more than 300 people, very nearly including me. Hence this."

He gestured to the closed environment around him. "I reported to Command when we'd finally disengaged and dealt with the worst of the casualties, of course. They told me I should return to Centre with what I had left, that I would be relieved of command.

"That was enough for us. They neither knew nor cared where we were or what we were doing half of the time by then anyway," he said, with finality.

"And now here we are, waiting it out – the crew came willingly, too, in the main. We still have enough firepower left to make it costly for the Federation to do anything about it if they did find us, which they haven't yet, and I keep a few agents active on the Boneyard and a few other places to spot anybody sniffing around." He smiled again at this.

"Expediency on the part of the Federation," Krieger said with some passion. "It was no different during the Elemental engagements after your time, except they don't negotiate so readily."

"So I have heard. You fought them, Captain Krieger?" the admiral asked, pointedly.

"Sometimes, Admiral… I'm a captain now, but I was a frigate commander in the navy. The Federation were more interested in declaring their own as war criminals for protecting our people by that time. I spent years…" Krieger replied bitterly, warming up to the theme.

"…and the Federation haven't been a friend of ours ever since," Taro cut in ahead of him, smoothly. Krieger looking annoyed as his XO continued.

"You're perceptive in surmising that we have been known to operate on the wrong side of Charter rules, and we tend to consider an enemy's enemy as very much a potential friend. It would be beneficial to both of us if you were to see it the same way, no doubt."

"Indeed, Watanabe, you have a mind for business, I can tell. We can offer you trade and sanctuary if you need it, as we do for others, in return for the movement of the occasional illicit shipment between worlds. And you can consider us open for business should you find yourself in a position to supply other parties independently."

The admiral suddenly looked tired as he sighed and stood up from his chair. Taro thought he could hear his joints creaking, even through the plexiglass.

"I regret that I cannot shake on a deal," he said matter of factly. "Speak to Sergeant Brock, he'll take care of your needs."

"Admiral, there's a lot more I want to ask you about…" Krieger started to say something, but the microphone audibly clicked off as Kirkwood turned to one of the consoles behind him.

Krieger looked forlorn for a brief moment, before turning with Taro for the door.

Kelman was leaning against the handrail at the foot of the stairs. He stepped to some kind of attention as the two men reappeared. "Welcome back, gentlemen. How did that go?" he said.

"Pretty well," said Taro as he reached the bottom of the stairs. "And now we'd like some of your inventory to take away, if you please."

Negotiations were short and chits for credits from one of Taro's many private accounts changed hands before he and Kelman went to confirm the authenticity of the product. Krieger made his way back the way they had come, and came across Kassini sitting on the desk by the lift, flanked by Rust and Mak 14, who was humming an old movie theme tune in his jarring robot voice.

She had her rifle slung across her knees, magazine out, and was checking the mag well for the fourth time. Looking up, she clocked Krieger's downcast expression as he approached.

"Krieger. Did you get to meet your hero? I saw you head up the stairs to the bridge."

"We did. He's crippled, can't leave that room, and has no idea what's going on out here. They've done nothing much since they disappeared, other than set up their very own personal gear manufacturing and distribution operation."

"What d'ya mean?"

"All these old painters and carvers you see are largely the original crew – they're making some kind of focus pills out of the crystals from the local asteroids."

"Focus, like the stims they used to give us for classroom learning in military college?"

"Something like that, but judging by the state of the crew, a lot more potent. Taro has gone off to score some to trade, predictably enough."

"Figures. Seems where there's a deal, there's usually a Taro."

Krieger laughed briefly, but the encounter with the admiral had clearly left him slightly crestfallen. He met Kassini's gaze. "I'd hoped Kirkwood would still have some spirit left in him, but it looks like the years of service with the Federation crushed that right out of him – he bailed on everything when they threatened to take the ship off him and holed them all up here. The Fed is rotten to the core, Kassini, and working with that takes the fight out of even the best people after a time, I guess."

"Never meet your heroes," replied Kassini. "I can relate, but you know what they say – you fight for the person next to you, when it's all said and done."

Krieger was about to reply when his earpiece buzzed and the computer's voice, crackling through several layers of hull, reached him.

"Captain, do you read?"

Krieger turned away from Kassini, motioning his finger to his ear.

"Copy, what's up?"

"I have analysed the data from the gateway which brought us here. It is simply the weak point in a gravity-based camouflage field which is spread over this sector, blocking sensor data and spoofing ship-based navigation systems to avoid the area. The local field is generated by what is now obsolete technology, and the interactions with my stealth system suggest it is a distant prototype of that unit."

"And this is useful because?"

"We are now inside the field, and the diagnostics I have just run suggest *Anomaly's* stealth system is only malfunctioning due to a lack of available power – the overcharge caused by the field around the Marshall Smith has allowed me to activate the system several times since you have been onboard, just as we did to get here in the first place."

"So you're saying you've got the stealth to work? I'm impressed. Tell me what you need."

"Last-minute adjustments were being made to the unit prior to your taking ownership of *Anomaly*, and it seems probable this work has altered the requirements and calibration of its power system. It is also probable the *Marshall Smith* has spare power units for their similar field generators. It would now be advantageous to acquire one. I am transmitting what data I have on compatible equipment from the relevant era to your hand-held now."

The connection went dead. Krieger looked back to Kassini, who had returned to the complexities of her rifle.

"You catch any of that?" he said. She looked up distractedly.

"Hmm, no?" she replied, as an expression she'd never seen before crept into Krieger's face for a brief second, which made her add: "Vonya or the computer at a guess, though, right?"

The moment passed as Krieger smiled back at her.

"Yeah, it's just angling for some spare parts," he said lightly, as he tapped the contact to switch his headset over to Taro's channel.

Krieger paused and took a deliberate glance around the *Marshall Smith*, taking in the panorama of its open-plan deck for the last time.

"Taro, when you're done with the dope, the computer would like you to add something to the shopping list," he said, snapping out of his nostalgic reverie. "And when we've got that under control, let's get out of here."

M

Kassini: You knew about Kirkwood and his
band of hippy doomsday preppers, then.

Taro has bought cargo of hallucinogenic
crystals to sell. So I am a drug dealer now.

Orders?

M

Drexler: Krieger will shortly intercept
an offer he can't refuse.

Time for you to put your subterfuge skills to use.

Orders = Await details for rendezvous with Agent.

Gulag Mining Station in Venuri
38 -54.7204 68.0476.

Drexler out.

8. SOFT POWER

Anomaly drifted quietly, a squat block of gunmetal against the ink shades of the cosmos. The running lights around the cockpit blinked casually, red to green, red to green, informing the emptiness of its presence.

Most of the crew who needed to slept, it being late at night according to ship's time. Krieger, though, was seated in his customary chair on the small bridge, still dressed for duty in his admittedly past-their-best military overalls and staring at a tablet which interfaced with the comms array. He was scrolling through a list of short updates on a perfunctory low-tech noticeboard. The most recent caught his eye and he tapped through, reading quickly.

"Computer," he said shortly. "Are you able to find a spin to the Venuri 38 system?"

"Yes. Although I would not recommend travel to the system if it was up to me, Captain. There are many advisories against it," the synth-voice responded quickly. It had also ingested the updates Krieger was working through and didn't like the implications of what it saw.

"It isn't up to you though, is it? Plot the course and start the run to the nearest spin-safe location above 95 per cent. And tell me what you know about the place."

"Venuri 38 is in Avion-Federation shared space, Captain Krieger. It's a mining colony for rare elements where humans and Avions cohabit by treaty and share the output of the facilities. The system had diplomatic importance when this was agreed, with increased media emphasis on interspecies cooperation some time ago. It's in a state of perpetual brinkmanship now. The latest news updates theorise that the Federation administration is using the situation strategically, to test the resolve of the Avions."

The machine paused and simulated a sigh. "It is really not my kind of place."

Krieger laughed. "Well, the Feds have overstepped the mark this time," he said with venom. "Set the course, I'll tell the others when they're awake."

"Course set, but I will need Executive Officer Taro to agree a jump. Do you ever intend not to take the option with the highest likelihood of my being damaged or destroyed?"

"Not if I can help it. Head for the jump point. I'll talk to Taro."

The distant thrum of the engines began and a small, mostly unnoticed vibration increased slightly as manoeuvring thrusters spun the ship on two axes, small jets of gas spouting into the nothingness. Krieger stowed the tablet and settled down into his chair as the main engines fired crimson, propelling the ship forward.

He closed his eyes, enjoying the sensation of the ship's acceleration.

The sound of the bridge door sliding open woke him and the smell of rich, hot coffee followed a bright-eyed Taro into the room.

Drowsily, Krieger spun his seat to face him, eyes moving to the lidded container of the dark brown liquid.

"Where did you get that?" Krieger rasped, his voice cracked by the short sleep.

"One of the chemists on the Boneyard was producing beans in their hydroponic setup. With the number of comedowns those maniacs probably experience, I should think it costs more in their screwy internal market than any hallucinogenic," Taro replied cheerfully, picking up a tablet on the other side of the room.

"Yes, but how did *you* get it?" Krieger said, rubbing his face.

Taro looked pointedly at him before replying. "Let's just say the chap isn't as good a negotiator as he thinks he is."

Krieger laughed as Taro sat nearby and punched up the ship's status report. He raised an eyebrow. "I thought I felt the engines. Hard to tell out of the ports in deep space like this," he said.

Krieger opened his mouth to speak, but the computer cut him off with an impatient outburst in a tone something like that of an annoying bureaucrat.

"Captain Krieger has set a course for Venuri 38. I need your authorisation to complete the journey," it said. Krieger looked nonplussed for a moment before explaining further.

"Yeah, there's something interesting on the horizon in the borderlands."

"V38 is... unpleasant. The people working there call it 'Gulag'. What kind of 'interesting' are we talking?" Taro replied gravely.

"It's a hellhole by all accounts, but I think we can do something about that and get paid into the bargain," replied Krieger with a smile. "The Feds have garrisoned the system and the locals are paying mercs to help them get rid. We passed in range of a FedNet repeater a few hours ago, the encoded sideband held the usual local mercenary and black-market stuff, including that."

Taro took a sip from the flask as he thought for a moment. "Risky business, taking on a Federal military force," he said.

"Money's very good, which means we won't be the only ones taking the bait," Krieger said. "And it's so far out that by the time word gets back to the Centre, everybody involved would be long gone."

"Avions work there, too, so wouldn't surprise me if they're backing whatever is going down," said Taro. "Plus, it's a mining colony. No doubt this holdful of gear we've got will fetch a decent price among the oppressed citizenry. Computer, you can spin when we reach safety." He addressed this last to empty space behind Krieger.

"Are you sure?" came the disembodied reply. "This is another potentially dangerous situation waiting to happen."

"We just want to get close enough to properly assess it, computer," Taro replied patiently. "I'm sure you can use our stealth equipment to our advantage now we've fixed it."

Another simulated sigh issued from the speakers – the computer was obviously practising those – before it said: "Spin course locked."

Krieger stood up and straightened out his rumpled clothes. "Good choice. Now, how much do I have to pay you to share that coffee over breakfast?" he said, motioning towards the door.

"You'd be surprised how easily I can be bought," Taro replied, as they moved into the short corridor to the larger room between the bridge and cargo bay which served as their mess.

They found Kassini already at their single table, dressed in her usual shipboard fatigues with a ration of dried fruit and grain in a plastic bowl, hair still wet from her morning routine. Mak 14 was also active at a side bench, probing the mechanism inside one of his weapons modules with what looked like a soldering iron. Rust, however, remained bolted into the room's single charging alcove nearby, nothing stirring on his bulky black-finished frame.

"Morning Captain, Taro," she said, nodding to the latter. "We're on the move, what's new?"

Taro collected two extra cups and began pouring out his flask as Krieger took a seat opposite Kassini, whose nose was twitching as the irresistible waft of the coffee percolated through the room. "We're on mission time as of now, Sergeant. Vonya up yet?" he said, a deliberate military steel entering his voice. Kassini unconsciously stiffened a little at the tone of command, putting down her spoon and leaning forward.

"She's been working on putting her fighter into service for hours – probably simpler to patch her in from the cargo bay."

An audible buzz sounded over the comms system as the computer actioned her suggestion. It was followed a few moments later by a brief burst of Vonya's ever-present beats and her high-pitched singalong voice. A couple of Avion curse-words accompanied the sound of the music being turned off with a distant click. Kassini suppressed a smirk and shrugged at Krieger's serious expression.

"Here, Krieg-arr. What you need?" her multilayered voice purred through the speakers, a few seconds later.

"Just your attention," Krieger said. He sat back as Taro took the third seat at the cramped table, placing a cup down in front of him and Kassini.

"Coffee, courtesy of the space freaks," he said. She nodded her thanks and inhaled deeply before sipping. Krieger glanced over at Mak 14, who continued to work inside the module in front of him, but had rotated his head to face them, in deference to the human preference for attention when speaking.

"I think it's time we started to make a name for ourselves out here, crew," Krieger said bombastically, secure in his favoured position at the centre of attention. "We're heading for the Venuri 38 system on the Avion-Federation Galactic East border. A mining colony there, known as Gulag to its Avion and human inhabitants, has suffered for a long time under the yoke of the Feds, as an experiment in cooperation that ended the same way all such initiatives do – in oppression for the people and Federal military tyranny."

He paused for effect, and because 14 chose that moment to clank noisily over to Rust and open a small plate on his spherical body with a screwdriver. Krieger's face reddened as Taro and Kassini looked over.

"What the drek are you doing, Mak? This is a briefing," Krieger snapped.

"Correct, and Rust and I will no doubt be required to destroy more human and Avion opponents – I shall activate him so he can prepare accordingly. Death-dealing is one of my favourite things, but preparation is everything," Mak replied in a cheery ad-land synth tone. He pushed a contact before resealing the panel and stepped back.

The others waited for Rust's usual abusive morning greetings. Nothing happened. Mak quickly flipped the screwdriver, stepped back and telescoped a manipulator to beyond arms-length, then whacked the panel with the heavy end. The bigger droid burst into life, his body straining against the mounting plate bolts as both arms extended and swung for the smaller droid. The launcher clicked – empty.

"Gods," said Kassini angrily, who had reflexively leaped out of her seat and was halfway to the door. "What if he'd forgotten to unload that drekking thing? That would have been it for the mess and everybody in it."

"Do not worry, Kassini Grigorivitch, I always take the necessary precautions with volatile ammunition when Rust is powered down," Mak replied smoothly. Vonya was audibly clicking her beak and giggling in high pitch over the comm channel.

Rust retracted his weapons and boomed in a voice like grit and dynamite: "A good potential kill ratio predicted. Even a small malfunction can end many blood-bags. Flesh commander Krieger has the serious expression on his exoskeleton, again, so tell Rust: who needs destroying?"

Krieger sighed and sipped his coffee, Vonya's audible mirth subsiding as Kassini returned to her seat and composed herself. "Shut up and settle down. We're a working merc crew, start acting like one." The hard tone of command returned to Krieger with an edge.

"Now, we're heading for Venuri 38 for fun and profit, people. The locals are offering solid payment for any help they can get kicking out the Federal military that's occupied the system, and we have a certain amount of cargo we'd like to shift for a profit, too. A winning situation for us, and a chance to show them the new player in town on the side of the colonies they've been shitting on all these years."

"A Fed occupation this far out?" interjected Kassini. "That can't amount to much. They're spread way too thinly in the Elemental sectors as it is, and the Avions can't match anything bigger than a fleet frigate tonne-for-tonne in space."

"That's how I figure it, too, and the Avion citizenry all over the place means they can't risk extreme force. I think it'll be a small detachment of army and a fleet-arm orbital barracks, probably bored and entertaining themselves by abusing the colonists."

Kassini nodded. "How long until we spin?"

"55 minutes," the computer piped up, sounding oddly cheerless.

"So, we spin into the system with stealth active and get some more information on the op first, as well as registering our interest. If they have a battlecruiser and a spec-ops detachment, I want to know about it," Krieger said.

"Agreed," Taro replied, and Kassini nodded.

"So, get your shit together, people! We got trouble to make with the Federation!" Krieger said with a flourish. Rust pointedly loaded a magazine of grenades into his arm launcher.

"Are you done talking now, meat sack?" he rumbled as the others stood and headed for the doors.

The inhabited part of Venuri 38 consisted of a single pale star and five planetoids, two of which were little more than barren balls of rock separated by an asteroid belt. *Anomaly* was approaching the innermost of the two, the asteroid belt spreading out beneath it like spilled marbles glinting in the hard sun.

Vonya was back in the *Anomaly* cockpit, surrounded by markers on her holographic heads-up display. She cut in reverse thrusters with the nose of the ship aimed roughly between two points of light orbiting the planetoid, then flicked a switch with her thumb-talon to activate narrow-band sensing equipment. This lit up a display to her left.

"Predicted righteous Kass, big curvy frigate with minimum gunnery and plenty of surface birds," she said to her comms channel. "In geo with an orbital terminal, couple of cargo-jumpers there, too. Taking us into the belt on drift, more cover for approach."

Kassini was seated on the bridge with Krieger and Taro. She exchanged a look with Krieger and replied: "Good work Vonya, keep some distance until we can authenticate and make contact."

Krieger punched a tablet to scan the local frequencies. He homed in on one and entered a decryption key, decoding a transmission into memory.

"Scan that and play back, computer," he said.

A larger wall screen flicked into life to show a digitally distorted face, unrecognisable except for the movement of a human mouth. A similarly manipulated voice cut abruptly into the comms system.

"Greetings. I am the Coordinator here on V38 6G Colony. We still need solid labourers for the job. Dock your ship using standard Federal Epsilon codes at Hilton Terminal on the planetside, Bay D. These will identify you as on colony business and no Federal questions will be asked. Activate a transponder on arrival with this frequency and await further instructions." The screen shut down abruptly.

"Keeping it simple and face-to-face, I suppose," said Taro.

"Fine by me," Krieger replied. "Take us in with those codes, Vonya, keep approach standard and by the numbers – but let's get a decent look at that frigate on the way in."

"Firm," Vonya's disembodied voice floated for a second in response, before the dull engine throb increased to a whine as the ship began to shoulder its way clear of the asteroid field. The crew leant into the acceleration.

As she settled in for the ride, Kassini's tactical overlay ghosted green across her eyes for a moment. It left a few blinking notification pixels in the bottom of her peripheral vision. These indicated that the system had parsed a heavily encrypted low-bandwidth data channel tacked on to *Anomaly's* transceiver system and used for emergency comms only, which must have just come into range. A single 'M' – for message – now pulsed patiently in the lower right of her vision, keyed to her personal code.

Even though the others couldn't possibly see it, she couldn't help but glance furtively at Krieger, who was pointing out the general shape of the frigate as *Anomaly* approached the station.

Kassini thought a series of code phrases and the message began to scroll across her vision:

M

Drexler: Priority update.

Retrieval required, Venuri system.

Contact = Garrn. Avion.

Simple enough, she thought, and erased the message. But who and where was Garrn?

"Codes accepted," Krieger said, fiddling with his tablet. "They've just transmitted an access corridor, Vonya."

"Seen, easy glide," Vonya's voice replied, sounding bored and accompanied by a tinny burst of beats from her earbuds. She could fly an approach like this with one claw tied behind her back.

The frigate loomed large in the viewscreen now, a long, vaguely curved vessel with large blocky modules bolted top and bottom at the centre of two long arms. It was shaped like a huge boomerang covered in shipping containers, with *Anomaly* travelling beneath it some miles off its space-side bow. The hull closest to them showed a number of small and large port doors, designed to serve as launch outlets for ordnance or smaller vehicles.

Kassini switched her overlay to active and studied the resultant readouts that flashed across her vision.

"The *Major Easy*, venerable old thing," Krieger said as the stencilled ship ID rolled past the camera. "Helio class, just a support ship in my day."

"Still is," Kassini said. "Can't hold more than a few active squads without extensive refitting. If they've been here long, they'll be going out of their minds aboard ship. The expectation would be that they keep a third of the complement onboard while the rest rotate through two or three locations, to show a presence and keep whatever they're involved with here in line."

She studied the monitor as *Anomaly* completed the pass-by, camera panning automatically to the front of the bigger ship. "Standard anti-fighter barrage guns and electros, and looks like they've added some small blast artillery with the potential to thump a shielded freighter if they needed to, but they're certainly not about to take on a cruiser."

Taro nodded and said: "Nothing we can't handle, I take it?"

"Easy money, used to be a time the Feds would know better than to leave a garrison with a skeleton crew," smiled Krieger.

"We don't know that they have," Kassini replied. "Wouldn't be unusual to have another ship on patrol somewhere."

"We'll soon find out," Krieger said. The squat rectangular mass of the station had now filled the viewscreen, a huge bay door open as if to welcome them. A random assortment of cargo ships could be glimpsed inside, distorted slightly by the internal two-box of an energy shield that acted as an airlock.

The engine blocks of two larger spin-capable transports were visible, the ships moored one above the other to one side of the station above the plane of the *Anomaly's* approach. A complex network of cargo belts and machinery designed to transfer from smaller ships to the larger sat on one side of Bay D.

"On final," Vonya said, as she smoothly accelerated through the first layer of the energy vortex, their own shield buzzing at low power as the barriers interacted. She skilfully manoeuvred their ship to above a landing pad and put it down with no motion wasted, the support struts and hot metal creaking in unison as the engines powered down. Sound from outside the ship could soon be heard dimly for the first time in days, the sirens and mechanisms of loaders and forklifts processing packed canisters of ore apace nearby.

"So now we wait," said Taro and lifted his empty flask. "I'll make more coffee."

At the new-recruits briefing in the secondary hangar, the coordinator stood at a makeshift steel podium positioned at the summit of a cargo ramp. He overlooked the crews of mercs, spaced out in pockets on the deck. He counted 48 in total: perhaps one in five were Avion, the rest human… and there were a few mechs, including two battle droids, camouflaged as dock droids. 'A stroke of luck,' he thought, marvelling to himself at just how heavily armed merc crews were becoming out in this godsforsaken human-Avion sector.

The flesh-and-blood recruits were all dressed in the green overalls supplied to them as they disembarked. It was an outfit that everyone wore on their first fortnight in the station – the uniform essentially said, 'I'm a newbie, so don't entrust me with any heavy equipment.'

As far as the overwatching Fed security teams were concerned, this was just a briefing like any other. At least that's what the coordinator reassured himself with as he adjusted the height of his mic stem. The Empire's foot soldiers had long since abandoned the idea of patrolling the station this early in the morning. In fact, they were probably still hungover, thanks to the fresh cargo of unusually high-proof spirits the coordinator had allowed the garrison to discover and confiscate yesterday afternoon.

He also knew that if anyone in the control rooms did glance at the CCTV, which he was reliably informed they rarely bothered to do anymore, it wouldn't matter. The hangar's CCTV security cameras were already rigged to replay 15 minutes of unremarkable footage from yesterday's identical-looking briefing. He clicked through some menus on his tablet to activate it and verifed the feed had changed over.

"Attention, new recruits," the coordinator spoke into the mic. "This is your mission briefing. We have a window of only a few minutes, so pay attention. The occupying Feds present two main issues to us down here. Problem one is the garrison of troops; problem two is the frigate you all unsubtly eyeballed as you docked. Under ordinary circumstances, a Federation warship and a hundred of their space marines would be a major headache. Lucky for us, though, these are not ordinary circumstances.

"Most importantly, the fact that this base is a high-profile experiment in human-Avion relations – as terribly badly as that's worked out – still counts for something. It means that turning the frigate and its fighters on our station will be seen as a last resort and that buys us some time. We are going to use this time to do two things: firstly, neutralise the main garrison of troops, avoiding casualties and later reprisals – and secondly, take back and secure the command modules of this base.

"If these two parts of our plan are excuted, we will be able to turn the station's weaponry on the frigate and persuade them to spin away – and this station will finally be ours."

This caused ripples of disquiet to break out among the pockets of mercenary crews, which the coordinator continued over. "I know you're thinking that our chickenshit mining station doesn't have the firepower. And usually, you'd be right. However, over a number of months, our commercial partners out here in frontier space have kindly smuggled a complement of missiles in among our regular payloads of maintenance equipment. Plus, the Feds trust that our planetside mining lasers are offline, undergoing temporary maintenance. We've taken that opportunity to make some alterations.

"When those lasers come back online, ahead of schedule, they'll be focused with atomic accuracy on key target points on their frigate. We calculate that the double whammy of the missiles and lasers will be quick enough and decisive enough to cripple them before they can cripple us. We'll prepare the combat-ready fighters among your crews for launch, to protect us if the frigate launches its own interceptors."

With their usual military precision, Krieger and Kassini looked over at each other at this and exchanged eyebrow flashes. Taro glanced at 14 and Rust, whose processors were no doubt poring over the station layouts, calculating probability of success and combat vantage points respectively in light of the new information.

The coordinator slammed his hands down on the pulpit in front of him and the shriek of mic feedback silenced the chatter from the pirate crews.

"But before that, we have the first part of the plan to take care of. An encrypted message has been delivered to the tablets of each of your designated crew leaders. It contains our mission codes for comms and your crew's individual orders, which you need to carry out to the letter if you want to get paid. Remember that from now until you receive the green light, you're just new recruits on a mining station, so act accordingly. If the plan goes well, I'll see you in the mess afterwards for a drink. If it doesn't – I'll see bits of you floating in space."

The green-overall clad mercs looked busy as they tooled up in the hangars, doing their best impression of a set of raw recruits preparing for their first shift under the watchful eye of the station's more experienced mining crews.

Another message from her mission handler, Drexler, cycled across Kassini's vision on her private channel. Drexler gave her a room number for Garrn along with an additional order: to deliver whatever he gave her to a Fed contact, name TBC.

She erased the message and frowned. Her tactical implants unconsciously prompted her to extrapolate different scenarios and she dutifully played them out in her mind's eye. Whichever way events unfolded, this was going to be a big ask.

On the one hand, it was fortuitous that her orders for the station mission were different to Krieger's – he was to support the merc squads taking over the control room, she was to stay behind and help deal with the garrison. Their separation would easily provide enough of a window for her to go MIA and meet Garrn. This would in turn mean she could duck out of gunning down her own marines, if it came to that, and hopefully avoid getting caught in the crossfire. But smuggling what she guessed would be some form of comms device back to the *Anomaly*, then delivering it to a Fed contact... all under the noses of her crew?

"One thing at a time..." she said under her breath. Krieger sidled over to her to show her how he'd managed to obscure the outline of his rifle by attaching random mining tools to it. She feigned interest for a while, before asking him straight: "Do you think their plan's going to work?"

Krieger stopped midway through his explanation of where he'd stowed his ammo (Kassini had her suspicions) and looked thoughtful.

"I do," he said, after a few seconds' contemplation. "Mainly because when I read between the lines of that mission briefing, it's pretty obvious that those Fed marines have been here for so long with so little to do, they've virtually gone feral. They're going to be soft and slow on the uptake."

"And what about Rust? Do you think we can trust him to create the diversion?"

"You mean without taking out half of the mercs – and more to the point, you – in the process?"

"It had crossed my mind," Kassini smiled.

"Look, that loading bay may be big, but it's still a confined space... and in a confined space, he's going to be a real handful. Federation battle droids were made for close-combat situations like this. Two of them together will be more than enough to pin the marines back for long enough for the coordinator to spring his surprise. Talking of which, where's your mask?"

"It's here," said Kassini, tapping the side pocket of her overalls. "Orders are to wait for the droids to open up, get behind cover, *then* put them on, to avoid arousing suspicion."

Krieger's tablet chimed with an incoming message. He checked it and briefly put a hand on Kassini's shoulder. "Five minutes until we move out to our positions. I'd better gather Taro, Mak and the rest of my advance team together and run over the plan again. Stay safe, Kassini, see you on the other side."

"You, too," she called after the captain as he disappeared into the throng. 'Party time,' she thought to herself, slinging her half-empty backpack over her shoulder and picking up a long-handled wrench to help her look the part.

Upon receiving the emergency call, Marine First Sergeant Romanov had scrambled his squad and ordered them to assemble outside the loading bay. It took him five minutes to cross the station and he was incredibly annoyed to find that he'd arrived there first, followed by the 10 members of his platoon who had managed to get their act together anything like as quickly as they should have.

Outside the bay, he listened in disbelief as the sound of laser fire, heavy-duty projectile weaponry and alarmed shouts shook the massive 10-metre high blastproof doors. He was met by one of the mining station's chiefs – the nametag on his overall was folded over and unreadable, but he'd called himself 'Zyvex' or 'Zyvic' or something when he'd put in the emergency call. Whatever his name was, he looked properly shaken and the tips of his hair were dripping with sweat.

"What... the... *fuck* is happening in there?" Romanov shouted over muffled reports of rapid small-arms fire close behind the door.

"We were doing our first orientation," shouted the station chief, breathlessly. "Two of the reconditioned droids have gone crazy."

"Crazy? What does that mean?" yelled Romanov, annoyed at this sweaty greaseball's lack of precision.

"They can't have had any restrainers. As soon as we set the new recruits in position, they must've interpreted the people surrounding them as a threat."

"What model are these droids?" Romanov asked, impatiently updating his question. "Scratch that. What do they look like?"

"I dunno, one of them's black and firing at us and the other one's silver and black and firing at us. They're like... floating balls." Romanov sighed. Empire-spec battle droids, he thought to himself. Probably outmoded scrapthat escaped the junkyard, but still dangerous. "Our droids are out of action back on the frigate," he yelled back. "We haven't had a spares delivery for months. That makes this a lot more complicated. Where are these two droids positioned?"

"They've hovered up to take defensive positions high up on the walls. One on either side of the loading bay. They've been firing on us from there."

"And your people?"

"We're taking cover behind the parked freighter and the racks in the bay. We've got a few weapons together from the racks, but not enough – so I called you."

Romanov looked behind him at the now-assembled platoon, noting who among them was out of breath from their five-minute journey across the station. He had two marines with rocket weapons and one with a heavy machine gun; the rest carried pulse rifles.

He turned his back on the Zylev guy and barked his orders to the marines. "Listen up. We have two ex-Federation battle droids in there. They are going apeshit – don't ask me how or why," he bawled above the heavy thump of an explosion vibrating the door. "There's one up on each wall and we need to take them out. Infantry, you're first and as ever, you're *welcome*. Take up holding positions behind the freighter. Heavy weapons, wait for my signal once we've secured that perimeter, then set up with a clear firing line. Mitchell, do you want to join the rest of us on visual comms? Thank you, Private. On my mark..."

He gave the nod and the infantry filed up to the door, flanking it on either side. The first sergeant motioned for Zyvec to step aside and pushed the door release; the hydraulics cranked heavily into life, accompanied by a hiss of compressed air. The reinforced-steel blast doors slid smoothly to the side to unveil the hangar space lit up by incandescent tubular beams of vivid laser fire. Shots were raining down, red from the left and green from the right.

The first wave of 20-or-so infantry headed towards the hunched forms of the green-overall clad miners, crouching in the shadows behind the semi-circle of heavy-duty storage racks and loading vehicles around the edges of the room.

As he scuttled in, Romanov saw fires beginning to speckle along the parked freighter's 50-metre-long fuselage, sending curls of heavy black smoke up into the high ceilings of the bay.

Romanov crouched down behind the nearest storage rack, with his back to its reassuringly solid metal. He elbowed the miner he'd settled down next to out of his personal space and the figure shuffled over, struggling with his facemask. The First Sergeant's vision became augmented with his combat overlay, which filled with icons representing the position of his team and the droids: the targets were moving every 10 seconds or so, cycling through their weapons systems to pin down the crew and the marines.

Romanov eyeballed his infantry's positions and saw them rising, shooting up into the increasingly smoky atmosphere and ducking back out of sight to reload: he decided this was as good as it was going to get for now and wordlessly ordered the heavy weapons to enter the fray. More smoke billowed across along the floor, making it difficult to see a hand in front of his face.

The droids had switched to laying down a steady clatter of projectiles... but now, suddenly, there was no noise. Romanov felt an odd sense of cold calm flood through him. He looked behind him to his heavy-weapons position: the two marines were slumped over, bent double. His throat constricting, he struggled to a crouch position to go over to them, but his energy had drained from him and his legs gave way – consciousness ebbing away rapidly, he fell forward and his face smacked into the steel deck. As his vision narrowed to a pinprick, Romanov saw the canister by his feet jetting gas and the steel toe-capped boots of the masked green-suited figure approaching.

Kassini leant against the wall of the pentagonal corridor that led to the crew's sleeping quarters on Deck Two. Her tablet feed blinked into view in the bottom-right of her vision with the message 'Objective one achieved.' So Krieger had been right about the marines being soft. She dismissed the message and double-checked the faint overlay of the station map before turning that off, too, satisfied that she was in the right place.

The lone security camera surveilling the corridor had already been deactivated, saving her a job. Looking past her drawn rifle, she moved quickly from booth to booth in a loping crouch, scanning the numbers for the small embossed sign that read '113'. She reached it and tapped the metal quietly with her gun barrel.

It swished open instantly to reveal the two-metre-tall figure of Garrn, who motioned her inside with a frantic flourish of his right wingtip. Kassini checked the corridor was empty and stepped inside, closing the door behind her.

Garrn was tall and bulky for an Avion. In the dim light, she could see his pale feathers had a golden tint and his eyes were larger than Vonya's; he was a different phenotype to the Avion pilot and his features were noticeably less aquiline and refined than hers, even to untrained human eyes. His presence dominated his spartan quarters, which housed a single table, a chair covered in civvie clothes and a vertical sleeping harness hanging in the corner.

"The plan working?" Gaarn said slowly and awkwardly, his quiet melodic voice struggling with the human wordforms.

"The troops are dealt with, apparently," said Kassini, in impeccable Avion (species physiology notwithstanding). Garrn looked impressed.

"You speak Avion? A real rarity," he purred in his native tongue.

"Do you have it?" Kassini asked, impatiently. "I can't be found here."

"It's here," he said, turning round and kneeling to open a section of floor in the corner and retrieve a small handheld comms device, which he handed to her. It was featureless aside from its coolly glowing Avion company logo insignia and the smooth military-grade casing felt heavy in her hand.

"So why do you need me to deliver this to your Federation contact here?" she asked Garrn. "Why not smuggle it to them yourself?"

"It's far too risky," Garrn replied, furtively. "Relations are tense in this hellhole of a station. Something's in the air – this place is crawling with agents from both sides, all trying to hack each other's networks. I've been keeping track of them for months now. If the mission goes wrong and the Federation troops here suspect Garrn, they'll pluck me like a chicken. If Avions here find out Garrn works for the other side, it'll be even worse." The feathers around his neck ruff had fluffed up involuntarily as he spoke.

"I'll do the deed, then," said Kassini. "But it won't be easy."

"Garrn is aware," the Avion said, spreading his wings slightly in his species' equivalent of the human open-palm gesture of empathy. "Hopefully, our empires appreciate the risks we're taking."

They stared at each other for a second, then the tension dissolved into a brief shared laugh.

"Who's my contact?" Kassini asked, propping her rifle up against the table and stowing the comms unit in her backpack.

"Garrn is awaiting confirmation from the agent and your handler will tell you where to go – the delivery needs to happen soon after the mission is done, so the Feds here can despatch news of the rebellion back to the Centre."

"I'll see what I can do. Soar high, Garrn," said Kassini, paraphrasing the Avion sign-off.

"Safe travels," Garrn replied in English, as he watched her shoulder her rifle and pack and open the door. Before slipping back down the corridor, she paused and turned back to ask him: "Is this the right way to the control modules?"

On the *Anomaly's* earlier approach to the station, the crew had noticed its control sector was a separate multi-level section with panoramic views into space. From the outside, it had looked almost bolted on and was elevated high above the cargo and loading modules where they'd had their initial briefing that morning.

As she approached the lifts and access area, Kassini heard the distant sounds of a gunfight coming from a level or two above her, reverberating through the metallic floors to reach her in the subterranean corridors. Her tactical overlay had covertly accessed the station's systems to research the least-habitually taken route to the control room that Krieger and Taro's team had been sent to capture, so she wasn't being followed. She paused to adjust the range settings and Taro, 14 and Krieger's icons, together with another unidentified member of their team, appeared on the edge of her map. They'd reached the control room already, but were engaged in a battle with three blue dots on her overlay that represented Federation security troops.

She took a left up ahead and into a narrow channel that was a tributary of the main access corridor. Her overlay read clear, so she decided to place her trust in it and broke into a run to reach the lifts. By the doors were a pair of vending machines – one held the usual human array of vivid-coloured cans and sugary snacks in scripted wrappers, the other held transparent plastic packets of dried fruits and seeds and tall flasks designed for Avion beaks. Kassini crouched down behind them as she waited for the lift, weapon trained on the still-empty corridor.

She remembered her comms link and opened a channel to Krieger. "Krieger. Kassini. Two levels below you, coming up in the lift. Want me to take the security out from the rear?"

The lift arrived and she got in, selecting the control-room level. Her radio crackled. "Kassini, there you are. There's no need. We've dealt with them... although we lost our extra squad member in the process. You should've seen Taro's face – the man is a pussycat. Come and help us figure out this firing system."

The lift opened and Kassini advanced towards the control room, stepping over the bodies of the Fed troopers and the now green-and-red-overalled merc slumped along the corridor. Her hardwired training ensured she deliberately avoided eye contact with their lifeless faces. In any case, she was distracted by the buzz of her tablet from her pocket, which updated her that the second mission objective had been accomplished. At the entrance, the familiar figure of Taro stood guard.

"Kassini, glad you could join us," he smiled, performing a mock bow to usher her through the door. The control module was a wide but shallow room with a long desk containing several workstations. Beyond them, floor-to-ceiling views of the asteroid belt stretching out into space dominated the scene. Krieger and Mak 14 were hunched over a screen, ignoring the spectacular view.

"What's happening, Captain?" Kassini asked. Mak brought up an overlay and the huge control-room window lit up with data and various insignia. "That frigate is what's happening, Sergeant," said Krieger, not looking up.

Kassini picked out the slowly revolving boomerang shape of the Federation frigate. It was now free from its moorings and beginning to turn menacingly, to take up a more distant point in space at safe weapons range.

"We're waiting for the missile codes," said Krieger, scratching nervously at his scalp. "The coordinator is cutting it fine."

"How long do we have before the *Major Easy* opens up on us?" Taro called over from the doorway.

"According to the comms screen here, its fighters are already launching an attack run," said Krieger.

"So much for this project being valuable to the Federation," snorted Kassini.

A new icon appeared towards the bottom of the window, heralded by a shrill alert sound and an 'unidentified vessel' label. It tracked a small and squat single-seater stunt fighter that had just launched from the station's docking bay. It was heading out towards the frigate. From their vantage point, they could see the cobalt-blue flaring of its twin engines.

Vonya's voice crackled over Krieger's comms. "Kree-gar. Your fighter cover has arrived... time to test my rebuild."

No sooner had her ship begun to melt into the starry backdrop, the *Major Easy's* fighters manifested as three new icons appearing on the window. Vonya headed out to the port side of the frigate, staying out of range of easy missile lock. The three new icons accelerated to follow her, keeping formation.

"This will be interesting," said Krieger. "What ships do they have on that frigate?"

Mak 14 swiftly summoned a 3D wireframe blueprint of a triangular ship-to-ship fighter and rotated it briefly on the screen before them. "They are standard fleet-issue Hornet-class light interceptors, with no missile capability and cannon armaments," his synth voice intoned. "Judging by the age of the *Major Easy*, they will be obsolete models."

Taro, concerned at what he was hearing as he stood guard by the door, asked: "Do you think Vonya can take three of them on her own?"

"Correction... two of them," said Mak 14, watching as Vonya's cannon salvo nailed the nearest interceptor, igniting its fuel and turning it into a bright fireball of debris. It had sped in a straight-line trajectory beneath her as its wingmen had headed for her flanks. The pilot, like so many Federation rookies involved in dogfights with the Avion navy before her, had underestimated the axial turning speed of an Avion fighter – Vonya had provided a lethal demonstration of why pilots should always read the tactical updates the Federation pinged to their tablets.

"Go girl!" said Kassini and tore her attention away from the screen to join Taro at the doorway.

"Captain, we have the codes," said Mak 14. "Missiles are armed and ready to fire at the freighter. Their trajectories and target coordinates are predetermined."

"Finally," breathed Krieger, as he watched Vonya zigzag skilfully through hopeful streams of tracer fire while simultaneously decelerating her ship to end up behind the two interceptors. She was safely out of range. "Firing authorised," he said and stood up straight as five brilliant missile trails instantly raked out towards the freighter from below their vantage point.

The *Major Easy's* rudimentary point-defence turrets activated, but the missile attack had the element of surprise: they watched as four of the five slammed into the starboard arm of the frigate in quick succession. The first two exploded against the shields in scintillating flashes; the latter two tore through the hull, knocking the long ship off-centre in a deadly choreography.

Next, intense beams flashed from the station, striking the listing frigate. "The mining lasers have started up," said Krieger. "Now we find out how much stomach they have for the fight."

Vonya's fighter was closing on the tail of a second interceptor, which was heading for the cover of the asteroid belt. Its pilot ejected shortly before Vonya riddled the ship with a spray of rounds. While this was happening, rather than try and track Vonya and help its wingman, the screen showed that the third interceptor icon had turned tail and fled back towards the safety of the frigate, only to find it consumed by fire.

The *Major Easy* was in trouble. Fumes were streaming from charcoaled areas of its hull and it hung awkwardly in the darkness like a lopsided fiery pendant. The punchdrunk Federation craft fired its stabilising boosters to right itself and accelerated slowly away from the station in the direction of the sector's jump point.

"Mission accomplished," Krieger said and punched the air. "Great work, team. Now let's go claim our reward."

"And get out of these shitty suits," Taro added.

"Rust," shouted Krieger over the jubilant noise of the station canteen some hours later. "I heard you kicked ass out there today with your new friend."

"It is my one regret that the blood-bag count remains low," the droid bellowed back. Hovering opposite him was the second battle droid from the loading-bay diversion, a massive silver-and-black mirror image of Rust himself.

"Sadly, those were our orders," the second battle droid added, spinning abruptly to face Krieger and causing an involuntary spike in his adrenaline in the process. "Our combined firepower was sufficient to spatter so many targets."

"Hey guys, you enjoy your evening," Krieger said, motioning to pat Rust on the back. Detecting the movement instantaneously, the droid swivelled his red eye round to stare balefully at the captain before his hand had travelled a milimetre. Krieger stopped in his tracks and just waved weakly instead, then headed over to Mak 14, wondering if the Feds programmed all their battle droids from the same psychotic template.

“Hey, Mak, I think it might be bedtime for the battle droids,” he told the mechanoid.

“Why, Captain, are they threatening to destroy anyone?”

“Well, no... but I think they’re showing off to each other a bit. It’s probably not going to end well when this party really gets started.”

“I shall despatch Rust to the *Anomaly* for recharging and maintenance,” said Mak 14. “We may require him if the Federation soldiers escape from their confinement.”

“There’s no chance of that,” said Krieger. “Most of them are still sleeping off the effects of the fentanyl. By the way, have you seen the rest of our crew?”

“Vonya is at the table to the right of the door with an Avion mercenary crew. They have been repeatedly beaking small drinks with a high alcohol volume for 37 minutes. Their squawking so far has reached 92 decibels. Taro and Kassini have booked a shuttle over to the planetside mining colony to sell the crystal hallucinogens and machinery in our cargo hold.”

“Charming,” said Krieger to himself. “Well, I’ll see you later, Mak – I’m going to have a drink with these merc assholes... I want to find out if there’s anything else going down in this sector.”

Mak looked up to scan the rapidly filling canteen area. “I presume this is another one of those occasions when everyone gets drunk?”

“Yes, Mak, it is,” Krieger replied.

“Don’t burn the spaceship down when you come in,” said the robot, clanking off in the direction of the battle droids.

M

Kassini: Comms device acquired.

Orders?

M

Drexler: Excellent work – the unit
is strictly for your eyes only, Agent.

Orders = Deliver drive to drop-off point.
Habitation East corridor 3, module 7B.

Drexler out.

9. STRANGE CARGO

Their eyes adjusted to the harsh, flickering glare of the low-tech overhead strip light that stretched out along the gently curved ceiling of the shuttle. Aside from a group of paralytic Avion miners crashed out at the far end with their mech set to overwatch, Kassini and Taro had the tubular bay of the shuttle all to themselves. As they awaited clearance for the ship to begin the latest iteration of its repetitive, ferryboat-like journey between the mining facility and the innermost planetoid, which housed the colony proper, they knew they were about to witness first-hand why the system had earned its 'Gulag' monicker. Yet this was precisely the reason it would be the perfect place to take a sample of the crystals and strike a deal for the rest of their haul before they left.

Kassini swung her backpack onto the overhead rack and took a seat on the shuttle's left-hand side, which would grant her the best view of the belt and planetoids as they crossed the short distance to the colony docking station. Her companion sat opposite, a briefcase tucked in beside him. He flashed her a practised smile when he caught her eye, looking away a beat too soon. Though a stranger would never have picked up on it, Kassini had learned enough about Taro Watanabe now to know *slightly* better... he seemed more nervous than usual, but she put that down to the sample of pharmaceutical crystals he had stowed in his business case.

She had cargo problems of her own, too, of course. The Federation had provided her with the location of her contact, but she still had to work out how she was going to deliver the Avion device currently nestling in her backpack while she was right under the nose of Taro.

It turned out she needn't have worried. When their journey was underway, she used the shuttle's bathroom and when she came back, Taro already had her opened pack between his knees and was turning the Avion tech over in his hands.

"That's my shit, give it back," she snarled at him. He just laughed, enigmatically.

"A networked Avion comms unit. Well, well," Taro said.

Kassini had no smart covering answer at the ready. She just shrugged, a gesture which served to redirect Taro from the hand that gently moved towards a concealed pistol at her back.

"What can I say?" was all she mustered. "We all have things we need to do in this life. I'm no different."

"So the Federation *didn't* let you go... did they redeploy you in Special Intelligence?" He flashed his smile again. "Not so special now, of course."

"Okay, Taro, lay off the bullshit," Kassini snapped back.

Taro's eyes narrowed and his voice lowered, betraying an edge of steel. "I'm not the one bullshitting, Kassini. You're the one who's been lying to us. I have to say, though, I'm always amazed by how loyal you beaten ex-Fed puppy dogs are to your masters. Underneath all that hate, Krieger's exactly the same."

Kassini shifted uncomfortably in her seat. "Loyalty? C'mon Taro, you're no idiot. Since when has it ever really been that simple – for anyone, including you? You know as well as I do that once you're in with the Feds there's always a price for getting out, one way or another. And talking of the captain, are you going to tell him about this? Because you don't have to," Kassini said.

"Now, here's the thing about that," Taro said, leaning forward conspiratorially. "The moment I did, he'd probably put a bullet straight between your eyes without flinching – or more likely, he'd fire you out of the airlock and use you for target practice. So, am I going to tell him? That depends on this." He paused for dramatic effect, lifted up the Avion comms unit and positioned it between their faces. "Who's it going to? And what's on it?"

"Keep your voice down," said Kassini, glancing over at the slumbering Avions at the other end of the craft. "I have a drop point. But I don't know what's on it."

"I've got a pretty good idea. When I was working the human-Avion talks at Serpentis, we used to have to sweep for these all the time – they're standard-issue comms nodes, very versatile," Taro said. He pushed the unit back into the pack and put it on the seat beside him, hooking an arm through the strap. "Whatever's on it, it's important and sensitive enough that somebody needs an intermediary to deliver it to the Empire. So it most certainly isn't merely data about the goings-on in this lowlife system. When we reach that station, before you deliver it to your contact, I'm going to crack it open, hack it and insert a stealth feed. That way, we can eavesdrop on any talkback between the Feds and the Avions."

"So are you going to turn me in to Krieger and the rest?"

"Listen, Kassini. Krieger has many qualities. But I tell you now, he's losing it. His decisions... you've seen it for yourself. He's so black-and-white in his thinking – and this all-out vengeance on the Federation stuff, sooner or later, is just going to get us all killed."

"I did notice you're not always 100 per cent on board..." Kassini ventured.

"I don't know if you're underestimating me, or you haven't really thought about it, but I'm not just a *medic*, Kassini. I was a diplomat for five years, working high-pressure negotiations with the Avions and the Empire. It burned me out, but it taught me a lot. There's no good or bad out here anymore, only grey areas, which my former position makes me ideally placed to exploit. Plus, I know a gift when it drops in my lap."

The horizontal aperture of the docking station flashed past the window behind Taro. They were on their approach. "Go on…" said Kassini.

"The way I see it, even with my little 'promotion' after the pirates ambushed us, Krieger still runs the ship and controls the droids, and while he does, he's got to stay in charge. But that doesn't mean we can't work this situation to our mutual advantage. I propose that we find out what's on this unit and compare it to the instructions the Feds message you on the encrypted channel."

Kassini's face showed little at the mention of her messaging implants, even as her impulse to put a shell between the eyes of the man opposite her increased. Taro nodded knowingly at her. "You're too easy to read, Kassini, especially given your new line of work – diplomatic circles are full of every conceivable ulterior motive, part of my job was to notice what people were up to. But if you continue to play it straight and do your job, then between what you're being told by the Federation and what we pick up through the comms, we can… help Krieger make better decisions."

"Control him, in other words?"

"No one really controls Krieger, Kassini. But we can definitely work the situation to our advantage, instead of just blindly attacking anything and everything in the same system as us that has the audacity to fly an Empire flag, or ending up taking on Elemental special forces for no good reason other than saving his ego and a few stranded miners."

Through the seats, they felt the rumble of the ship decelerating on its final approach to the docking bay. Kassini was quiet for a few seconds while the ramifications of Taro's deal – because for all intents and purposes, that's what it was – sunk in. "If we work together, Taro, we both know you couldn't hand me over to him, or I'd take you straight down with me. So what's in it for you?"

"Dinero… mucho dinero. I have debts that I need to repay and repay fast – and the *Anomaly* with its stealth is my best chance of earning the money, while evading the assholes who I owe if they try to track me down. And the Federation are *helping them to find me*, Kassini – I'm on the list, just like Krieger, which is one of the reasons I took up with him in the first place. Like you said, you're never really clear of them, are you? A loose end with diplomatic contacts and a gambling predilection isn't loose for very long."

"And I suppose that should it ever become available, the *Anomaly* would be worth a fortune on the network," Kassini added, and her body untensed. Greed and a desperate man was a motivation she could work with.

"She shoots, she scores… now you're getting it, Kassini, a person could disappear for good with that kind of money," said Taro. He also relaxed imperceptibly, and removed his finger from the trigger contact of the single-shot stun blaster built into his case to place his hand safely on the top of it. The business end on the side facing her would have knocked Kassini and the two seats either side of her cold in an instant, had he needed to.

A resounding metallic clunk signalled the engagement of the landing clamps that secured the shuttle.

Taro smiled a snake's smile and said: "And right on cue, we're here. Let's look for a quiet spot and find out what exactly it is we have on your comms unit."

Security were impatient to finish their shift and join in the celebrations and waved them wordlessly through the shuttle exit lines into the colony complex, along with the staggering Avion gang. Wasting no time, Taro ducked down the nearest corridor, knelt down and fished out his tablet. He paired it with the Avion equipment and its logo fired up, bathing his face in a greenish tint in the half-darkness. Kassini crouched at the end of the corridor and kept watch as Taro bypassed the minimal security on the device's comms channel – it was meant to be read in a hurry, in secret – and installed a mirroring program to eavesdrop on any future communications sent to and from the unit.

"Sure that you know what you're doing with that?" Kassini stage-whispered over to him.

"I've used this software before, virtually undetectable and definitely untraceable – it sits dormant until it detects a comm transmission to the network within range and sends me a snapshot," Taro replied quietly. "My very own encrypted channel, if you like… unless whoever you hand it over to is some kind of comm-sec specialist, we'll be able to download the latest updates to the network. And let's face it, if he or she is even a moderately talented hacker, they wouldn't be wasting their time scraping a living on this rusting hellhole."

"Let's find out what's on it, too," said Kassini. She held out her hand. "Allow me – I have Fed security clearance."

"Of course you do," said Taro with a smile. He passed over the heavy device and she scrolled through the menus on its razor-sharp green readouts.

"How will you bypass the agent's security?"

"Implants, remember?" said Kassini, looking over to him and tapping her temple with her free hand.

"Lots of planning about the attack in this sector, some stuff about suspected backhanders in the Avion Supreme Court elections, that triple-species politics is sooooo complicated…" she commentated. "Nothing earth-shattering. I'm accessing Garrn's files."

"Garrn?"

"He's the Avion agent who this belonged to."

"Ah, the Avions are still managing agents in this dump after all, are they?"

The device lit up in front of her and the messages from Garrn's private account scrolled down the screen. As Kassini speed-read through the despatches, she felt the voyeuristic thrill activate her adrenaline, which seeped icily into her bloodstream. She was scanning through high-security reports to an unidentified but obviously governmental entity who acted as the Avion agent's handler.

"Uh-oh," she said suddenly, stopping the flow and tapping one of the messages full-screen. "Bullseye."

She transmitted a copy to Taro's tablet, which translated it from Avion script at his touch, allowing him to scan the data in the gloom.

"Mother of gods," he said as his eyes flitted rapidly from side to side, his eyes lighting up with almost childlike excitement. "Is that legit? If it is, that's unbelievable... can you copy the files, then delete the inbox?"

"Copying them over to us both now," Kassini confirmed.

"So the Avions believe the Ellies are gearing up for a war with the human Empire?" said Taro.

"Yep. And the Elementals are apparently already conducting massive fleet exercises. Further down in the message chain, they even give the coordinates of the operation, in some disputed system on the fringes of Elemental turf called Kamakraken. This is happening right now."

"This was all in your agent's classified files?" Taro asked.

"Yeah, there's no way this was intended for my contact – it's not come from whoever his handlers in Avion intelligence are. They'd never get close to accessing it from here, and the fact that it's moving in hard format suggests he didn't want to risk transmitting it. And now I've deleted it..."

"Kassini," said Taro, glancing round to check they were still alone in the corridor. "The Empire would kill to find out this intel."

"True... and we may even be able to get them to pay for it."

"How so?"

"If I tip them off, they'll believe that I found the message – I'm on the payroll after all," Kassini said, thinking it through. "But they're sure to want solid proof. If I tell them I can manipulate Krieger to take the *Anomaly* to the sector to gather evidence, it's within my operational parameters to access funds. I can say I need to incentivise the crew with danger money and that could go towards those gambling debts of yours."

"And with the *Anomaly's* stealth capabilities, we could, I dunno... we could sneak into the system and take a look?"

"It would be dangerous as all hell, but profitable. It's not just the Feds who'd want to see that movie – the Avions would pay top dollar, too, for the diplomatic cachet, if nothing else," Kassini looked hard at Taro, the sell slipping easily off her tongue. "I could send a copy of whatever we find to the Empire to keep my handler off my back... meanwhile, you could sell a copy to the Avions and we all get paid. Do you think you could persuade Krieger to risk it?"

Taro weighed it up for a split-second. "I'm pretty confident I could. We'd have to conceal the source, obviously. I could say we heard a strong rumour on the station grapevine, maybe. That and the fact that this is going to be worth a fortune to the Avions might do the trick."

Kassini saw Taro's face change as a realisation came to him. "You know, a lot of people in my position would just hand you over to Krieger and persuade him to go with the plan anyway, you realise?"

“That would be a lovely show of loyalty from you, Taro, but I don’t think you have it in you,” Kassini replied, goading him. “You should remember I’m the reason you know about the intel in the first place – and if you handed me over now, this would be a one-shot deal. You’d lose all the future juicy intel I can bring to the party. And all that easy-access slush fund money,” she added.

“True…”

“Besides,” said Kassini, warming up her knockout blow. “I recorded all of our conversations from the moment you went through my gear. You’re already in too deep… partner.”

She tapped the side of her head, no longer needing to say the word “implants”.

“Ha! Looks like I made the right decision,” said Taro, standing to retrieve his case and moving back towards the main concourse, before offering her a look of genuine admiration. “Maybe you’ll make a decent spy after all.”

‘…and maybe you’ll get to live another day,’ she thought as she nodded, and then collected her bag to follow him.

The colony itself was a grim, claustrophobic place where dirt and oily, overworked people steadily merged together. A single concourse of bars and cheap shopfronts clustered around the shuttle bay, giving way to high-density habitation sectors on either side. Its hub was a transportation network, shipping goods off-planet. The place spared little expense for anything but the most functional trappings of civilisation. It was the kind of place people worked a stint for as long as they could handle, hopefully making enough money for property in a better place, and never looked back.

The shuttle port opened out into a high-domed concourse, geographically at the centre of the radial arms of the colony complex, which was thronged with humans and Avions alike. The under-maintained air-con gave the atmosphere a musty edge, and murky light beams illuminated dancing dust particles everywhere you looked. Almost everybody moved with the sense of purpose imbued to people who have to be somewhere else – there was nothing much on a colony with a nickname like Gulag to hang around for. It was noticeable that the usually ubiquitous Federal security personnel of even a small starport terminus like this one had been replaced by the particular brand of bored, staring local merc becoming increasingly common in the outer systems.

Kassini and Taro threaded their way through a steady stream of people, surrounded by the murmuring soundtrack of other people going about their daily routines. Taro indicated a likely looking frontage, and they soon found themselves seated at a counter selling charred skewers of the vegetable products grown in the colony’s hydroponics operation.

“Hungry?” Kassini asked. Taro was eyeballing a nearby tray of food as it was delivered by a basic conveyancing arm to a small group of Avions at the other end of the counter.

"Yes, so much so I'll even consider that vat-grown... whatever it is..." he replied.

"Well, can't have you dealing drugs on an empty stomach and, seeing as we're partners now, buying you lunch is probably the least I can do," she replied with a smile, and tapped at the tablet built into the counter to order tofu skewers for them both.

Plastic sticks bearing the cubes of protein duly arrived on the end of the automated arm, and they ate ravenously until Taro broke the silence.

"It's going to take a little asking around to find a buyer for the wares," he said matter-of-factly, wiping bright red sauce from the side of his mouth with a small square of recycled paper. "And this place will have a standard communication network you can access. What's your plan? Because you should make a move with your handlers quickly."

"I just did what I'm told because it kept the Feds off my back before I joined up with you guys... I have a designated drop for the gear – no contact, no idea who it's going to."

"Why would they have an agent couriering sensitive intelligence data from a foreign power?"

"I'm deniable, so I guess it's just Centre double-dealing on Avion intelligence to keep some handle on what's going on in the system – Gaarn is probably a plant on the Avion side here, feeding them whatever he can get his claws on. The colony is still majority-human occupation, and Centre would have known full-well who's behind the unrest here, which suggests there's nothing they could do about the mutiny we just enabled, even if they'd wanted to. And now I see the place," she gestured to the claustrophobic corridors behind them, still thronged with harried faces, "...I think they're probably glad to see the back of it."

She digressed from the conjecture – local system espionage was outside of her mission purview – but she was glad of the opportunity to get Taro talking.

"Centre will expect me to report in when I make the drop. I'll make sure that message includes a little more... finessing."

"The devil is in the detail after all," replied Taro, looking away. "And that particular revelation is going to trip some big alarms if it's accurate. There hasn't been a large Elemental fleet sighted outside of their zone for a long time, right? Their diplomacy was perfunctory to say the least during my time, we never got anywhere near even discussing military or colonial cooperation. Of course, you could also be passing on Avion disinformation – we used to say that every Avion player has extra dice hidden somewhere."

Kassini finished her meal, pushing the detritus into a nearby waste slot, as Taro did the same. "You'd know better than me about that. I'm just a gun runner with some old technology stuck in my head," she replied. "I can tell you that one of the reasons the Ellies haven't been seen in space en masse for so long is because it's against just about everything we think we know about their space-combat doctrine – humanity has been sitting on its ass for years thinking we've got the upper hand in that regard, that their disinterest in us is partly because they know they can't match the big-fleet strategy of that lunatic Kirkwood's day. Maybe things are changing, I don't know."

"There's always something more going on when you scratch beneath the surface," Taro said as they stood up together. "What I do know for sure is that change frightens the Federation and the Avions for that matter, and that they'll pay well for a heads-up about it. You're the conduit for that, so let's do what we need to do here and get back to the ship to work on the real payday. Meet me back here when you're done."

Kassini nodded, and Taro turned and strode away, melting smoothly into the moving throng.

She accessed her implant and double-checked the coordinates for the data drop, feeling oddly cold at the turn of events. Getting Taro on-side, even if it only lasted precisely as long as she could pay him for it, made for one less thing to worry about.

She paid attention to the voice telling her the man's reaction was still just a tiny bit out of character. Unlike Krieger, he wasn't implacably hostile to the Federation for sure, and the danger he was in was no doubt very real. But she knew there was something fundamentally slippery about the diplomat, or any diplomat, and his willingness to sidestep Krieger for a payday still seemed a little too simplistic somehow.

"One to keep a crosshair on," she said quietly to herself as she headed towards Habitation Sector East, following the large digital signs above the concourse.

The colony was too small and cheap to feature a mass-transit system, so Kassini found herself walking off the central concourse into one of the long arms that housed the majority of the living space. Modular cells of many single rooms with communal facilities were hidden behind long corridors of uniform doors. Many were festooned around their frames with graffiti and ornamentation from years of temporary, transient ownership.

It reminded her of shipboard life, she thought, as the throng of people they'd encountered in the centre rapidly thinned out to a few stragglers heading in either direction, paying little attention to her. Things had been simpler when all she needed was a bunk and the camaraderie of the squad – people you could rely on at your back and a good rifle in your hands felt a long way from her intrigue among *Anomaly's* haphazard crew.

The reminiscence touching on her missions of old triggered her faulty implant. A tactical interpretation of a Federation marine combat exercise she'd participated in years previously, but seen from the perspective of a data-model of an Avion soldier, rose unbidden in her mind. It was a strange sensation. Two very distinct perspectives on the same situation that had played out years before were available to her, melting into one another in such a way as she didn't entirely know whether her memory of the scenario was her own or not.

Kassini had slipped into a reverie, only half taking in the numbers and letters that designated the different dwellings in the corridor, when she realised she'd passed a turning for her destination. When the thing in her head had worked correctly, these sensations were strictly separate and controllable; she could access the probable responses from the enemy and use them to advise her squad. Now, not so much.

She stopped for a moment, took a deep breath and ran through a couple of the basic mental exercises she'd learned would help her focus when she experienced the glitch.

She returned to the intersection of two corridors she'd passed, and made her way down this until she found a door marked HE3 7B. Habitation East corridor 3, module 7B. This was the limit of her instruction, and she examined the standard palm-activated locking mechanism common to these type of installations. She shrugged to herself and tried her hand against it.

Nothing happened for a long time, and she eventually removed her hand from the door, feeling slightly stupid. Then her chip overlay flared into life in the lower portion of her vision – CODED NETWORK ACCESS. She stepped aside and leaned against the wall by the door, trying for some semblance of nonchalance, while her spyware negotiated a handshake she had no control over.

The message in her head flashed briefly and winked out, then the door beside her swung noiselessly open to reveal a largely unfurnished box of a communal room with a number of other doors leading off it. It opened out on to a pristine kitchen area, smelling neutral, clearly unused for some time. Just your standard dormitory living for the people of Gulag, thought Kassini, though this one was apparently turned over to different masters.

She glanced around the walls and ceiling of the room beyond to check for any kind of surveillance before stepping through the door, which swung closed behind her. The presence of only a table in one corner with a single large drawer made it clear enough what was expected of her. She pulled open her bag to remove the Avion comms device and placed it carefully in the back of the empty drawer, smiling at the technology that had been used to give her access to such an old-school conclusion.

She leaned against the tabletop and called up a status check that spread across her vision, spectrally overlaying the blank walls in front of her. Her implant's spyware function was still registering a network connection, and she guessed this was a secure channel or she wouldn't have been able to access it in the first place. It was also fair to assume this location was an operation hub for any Federal agents in the vicinity when required – somebody had to be coming to retrieve that device, after all – and so would be linked to the wider galactic comm-net.

She concentrated, and thought out her unique agency number digit by digit, followed by a brief message, which appeared in front of her.

M

Kassini: Drop secure.

New intel on local Elem
fleet activity – instruct.

There was no need for more. The mention of an Elemental fleet would trigger the reaction she wanted. Besides which, she was assuming her comms would be subject to the limitations of communication through the system of spin-navigation buoys and passing ships the Federation relied upon. This kind of back-channel data link was strictly for the most basic info. It was up to those more clued in than her back at Centre to decide what to do with it.

Her message winked out and was replaced briefly with a confirmation of transmission.

No response would be forthcoming until the heavily encoded data packet had travelled across the galaxy back to her handlers, so Kassini made for the door, which opened and closed for her automatically again. She began the walk back through the corridors to the main concourse where she hoped Taro would already be waiting.

Kassini returned to the robotic food counter, glad to see its garish façade of advertising and menus and the surrounding bustle of people after the drab emptiness of the habitation sector, but saw no sign of her companion. Local time now said mid-afternoon and the clusters of colonists were thinning out, so she took a stool at the end of the counter with the best view of the area and dialled for a coffee. She took in the steady stream of amateurish ads on the viewscreens around her, hawking the latest cargo-loads of counterfeit luxuries to be imported to the station. One ad caught her eye: she made a mental note to follow up on the set of no-touch instant hair straighteners that flashed up briefly in the flow.

She spotted Taro 20 minutes later, weaving his way through a mixed group of Avions and humans in work fatigues who were standing chatting at a junction point leading down to the service area of the concourse. He was easy to miss and very deliberately dressed as unobtrusively as possible, but he moved among people with an unusual mix of self-importance and a cat's sense of those around him. He reached Kassini quickly, nodding as they made eye contact.

"Mission accomplished?" he asked, declining to take a seat.

"Such as it was," she replied. "You?"

"Of course. Focus dope is a bit of a strange cargo to shift, but in a place like this, where the population are only a step above slaves to their jobs and there's literally almost nothing else to do, I figured the medical administration in the hospital would already have a sideline in offering the workforce pharmaceutical methods of making their shifts pass a lot quicker."

"You've just sold drugs to the local hospital?" Kassini laughed despite herself.

"It's not like I'm pushing megaphet!" responded Taro, smiling and leaning against the counter. "They were very interested from a therapeutic angle, too, once they'd established the purity, which makes the deal almost above board.

Besides which, how much money you think the two-Cee dealers in the bars around here would have?"

His face became serious as he said: "You told the Fed?"

"I told them. The speed of their response will pretty much tell us how interested they are in what we have. How do you plan to convince Krieger to help us find out exactly what that is for ourselves?"

Taro laughed again, a more hollow one this time.

"Krieger just participated in a successful mission with a load of fellow mercs. He'll be in full flow in a bar right about now, so I suspect we're going to find him in a pliable state when we get back to the station... which we should do, so let's jump the next shuttle out of this dump, shall we?"

He motioned towards the passenger lines for the launch bay, and Kassini rose to follow him.

As predicted, the *Anomaly's* captain had been drinking heavily with the other mercenary crews since they left and should, by rights, have been much more of a mess than he was. Fortunately, one of the holdovers from his service in the navy was a high tolerance for the pleasures of letting his hair down planetside and this had, after all, been the closest he'd been to a successful joint operation for some time. He had only bowed out of proceedings to howls of derision when it occurred to him he hadn't slept or eaten for some hours even before the mission began.

Kassini and Taro found him at *Anomaly's* cramped crew-quarters table, bolting down a large bowl of fruit and grain. He was chasing it with the dregs of a bottle of Clarkin Distillate.

Taro smiled his best, making a show of being glad to see the captain, and went straight at him like an excited puppy. "The crystals are dealt with, we'll be needing to unload the rest shortly and deposit them with the dock crew here, but we've picked up something juicy while we were snooping around."

He sat down at the table opposite as Krieger looked up somewhat blearily and wiped his mouth. Kassini, content to let Taro do the talking, moved behind him to dial herself some water.

"Go on," he said, rubbing his face and working hard to focus through the haze of alcohol.

"We ended up in the hospital to sell the crystals – don't ask, long story..." he said, weaving a believable strand of truth into the coming lie. "I got talking to some prospector type in the waiting room, who flies independently in what he called the Southern Reach."

"The Elemental-Federation border region. That's one big ol' piece of space," replied Krieger, and began to draw unsteadily on the table with his finger.

"If this is the Federation," he indicated a circle, drawling somewhat as he spoke. "And this is the Elementals... *this* overlap here is the Southern Reach."

He jabbed the table several times to make his point.

"Right," continued Taro, rolling with the captain's drunken flow. "He was a real spacer type, and you know how they tend to have a liking for the finer things in life when they're planetside, so I thought I'd keep him talking for a while. As it goes, he was pretty agitated – so much so, I figured him for a user of some kind – and he told me he was concerned about his rad levels out there, so he ran back to civilisation, if you can call this place that. The chap said he was prospecting some rock belt near a spin point in the middle of nowhere, actually landed and in EVA, when a *fleet* jumped in."

"A fleet?" slurred Krieger, blinking a few times.

"A fleet, said it was at least 50 big ships, and he'd never seen any of the type before – he said they looked organic, like they were grown."

"Elemental tech looks like that," said Krieger. "He said there were *50*? Redic... ridiculous."

"Yep. He was terrified, kept his ship powered down the whole time and just observed. The fleet jumped out of the system after a time, so the guy praised the gods and ran back to tell somebody. Obviously, we just pushed the Federation out of the first place he came to, so there's nobody to give a shit down here." Taro sat back for effect, the momentum of the story slowing slightly.

Krieger looked sceptical. He also looked really quite drunk.

"Taro, the reason nobody wants to hear what this sucker has to say is because the guy's another space-crazy you've latched on to. There hasn't been an Ellie fleet in the border region for, for years – Kassini, you buy this?"

"I was listening, he was neither drunk nor crazy, just scared, and I just can't see why somebody would make the story up," she answered smoothly. "Thing is, Krieger, it was all pretty detailed, too. He said that the system was so isolated the spin point is a two-way, for example – you can only spin to one of two other systems from it. He even gave a name, which I verified as soon as we got back on board, said the fleet jumped to a system called Kamakraken."

"So, if it's true, we know the approximate location of an Elemental fleet the size of which hasn't been seen in years – right on the Federation's borders," concluded Taro.

"And what? I can see how that's valuable info – and I know you love those wild space chases, man – but what would we do with it?"

"Make some money, Krieger! We've already seen the Elementals deploy weapon systems and technology you've never seen before at the mining colony, who knows what info we could pick up if we could get close to a whole fleet? The Avions would pay handsomely for it, take it from me."

Taro leaned forward again with his hands on the table to deliver his *coup-de-grâce*.

"...and frankly Captain, if you want to *really* hurt the Federation in a way that goes beyond taking out the occasional cargo ship or overthrowing their hold in some backwater system like this one, a little operation to give Avion intelligence an edge is definitely one way to do it. And I think some friends in higher places on that side of the border wouldn't do any of us any harm at this point, either."

Krieger held Taro's gaze for a few seconds. Then he broke off and looked from him to Kassini and back. She nodded an affirmative as the look passed. He stared down at the table and answered with a slurring facsimile of his usual commanding tone.

"As far as I'm concerned we're now at a loose end, and a fleet-recon… thing… wasn't entirely what I had in mind for a next move. We're still not sure how our stealth is supposed to work after all," he paused again, before continuing with a sigh.

"But I think both the *Anomaly* and her crew have proved they're up to the task, so I don't see the harm in taking a look, especially if it might give us something we can really use, as you say. It sounds like a spacer fantasy and I think we'll find nothing, but, well, your hunches have been right before now, Taro. If the guy does turn out to be full of it, maybe it'll teach you not to take every rumour you hear so seriously."

He pushed his chair away from the table and stood up unsteadily, smashing his bowl and empty bottle into the sterilising unit.

"As soon as Vonya gets back from wherever she ends up tonight, let's work out how to get to this Kama-whatever place and get underway. Now, if you'll excuse me, I've got to sleep," he said with finality, before clumping out of the room in a cloud of fumes and grunting.

Left to it, Taro grinned like a reptile at Kassini as she drained the last of the water she'd poured herself. She acknowledged his triumph with a smirk and a thumbs-up before she too made for the inviting embrace of her bunk.

M

Drexler: Intelligence on Elem. fleet activity received. Troubling news for the Federation.

A taskforce is being deployed to shadow the *Anomaly's* progress.

We will choose our moment to strike, but the working stealth complicates the issue.

Orders = Send advance warning of any situation in which Krieger and the crew will be away from the ship.

M

Kassini: Acknowledged. Request transfer of 5,000 credits to incentivise a crew member.

Have a plan RE Elem. fleet intel.

Will report back ASAP.

M

Drexler: Intriguing, Agent. The transfer is made.

Careful you don't compromise identity by flashing your cash.

Drexler out.

10. WAR GAMES

Holographic cards rotated in midair above a small metal table in the corner of the *Anomaly's* rec area. Taro sat on a military-grey plastic chair on one side, with a tablet sat propped up on the table on the opposite side, facing him. Displayed on it was the impassive, intimidating face of an Aldebaran polestar wolf – the avatar currently favoured by the ship's computer.

"I do not understand this," the computer intoned, frustration creeping into the subdued tone of its synth voice. "A run of three high-value emerald spirals has a winning probability of between 87 and 92 per cent."

"Ordinarily, yes," Taro replied, "but once again, you weren't paying attention to what we were both throwing away in previous hands."

"I was," the wolf protested, pupils contracting. The holographic cards swirled in midair as they rewound to an earlier point in the game, by way of churlish emphasis. "There was nothing anomalous about what you discarded, except potentially for the sapphire admiral you threw away in round one. Logic dictates that the card had no value to your strategy, else you would not have sacrificed it."

"Precisely!" said Taro, patiently. "This is what I mean. You were trusting logic and probability in a situation where other possible, as-yet-unknown strategies could influence the outcome."

The wolf's brow furrowed on the monitor. "So..."

"Yes?" said Taro, leaning forward expectantly.

"...you distracted me to conceal your true intent. You threw away the sapphire admiral to falsely imply that you were gambling on the low probability of the appearance of a ruby monarch..."

"Go on," said Taro, encouragingly.

"...when you must have had some prior knowledge that this would in fact be the case."

"Rewind back three hands," said Taro with a flourish.

The wolf displayed the tips of its massive canines as the cards span back in time again, hovering in ghostly light above the table between them. The holo-image zoomed in on Taro adding a card to his hand.

"The ruby monarch," said the wolf in its synth-growl, pausing the hologram and upping the contrast of the card to bring it into high-definition focus. "How did you know?"

"Because you threw away a sapphire admiral four games ago now and ended up with a certain card in your final hand. Remember what it was?"

"The emerald monarch," they both said, in unison.

"You guessed there was a high probability that I would pass a monarch on if the situation arose again," the computer conceded.

Taro smiled a wide smile. The wolf scowled in return. The holographic cards abruptly disappeared, leaving the rec room bathed in a slightly dimmer shade of soothing, night-simulating blue light.

Krieger had been listening in distractedly while he scanned through archive records of Elemental warfleet operations. He looked up from his tablet and looked Taro in the eye. "So, what's that now? 11 in a row? Do you enjoy humiliating the ship or something?"

Taro laughed. "I'm *teaching* the ship," he protested. "It's practically fresh off the production line. And it's a harsh universe out there for a new brain."

"Even so, I'd rather you left the computer to fly this bucket, instead of scrambling its logic circuits," Krieger shrugged, returning to the readouts on his tablet. "The last thing we need is an AI going rogue in the heat of battle."

"Well, it'd be in good company if it did," Kassini chipped in. "We've already got Mak 14 and Rust on our crew – a metal adrenaline junkie and the Empire's most aggressive battle droid."

Krieger sighed, acknowledging the point. "You know, I remember when robots just *followed orders*. Without that split-second where they seem to weigh up everything you say in their mind first."

Kassini and Taro waited a perfect beat before making 'hmm' noises in polite disagreement, then cracking up.

"Screw you both," said Krieger, smiling. "And let's turn in. We'll be spinning into what is allegedly the most dangerous sector in the whole of Elemental space in four hours… time for some shuteye."

"So, to be clear," Mak 14 asked, after Krieger had delivered his briefing. "The *Anomaly* will jump into the midst of an Elemental fleet to record proof that the faction is preparing its attack fleets for war. Because using our engines would betray our position on their scopes, instead, we will use the ship's stealth technology to drift close to the fleet, acquire the data and footage we need and then float back to the jump point and spin away."

"That's about the size of it," said Krieger, arms folded, leaning against the wall.

"You don't need me to tell you that there are a great many elements of your strategy that could go catastrophically wrong," 14 continued. "You also don't need me to add that any slight mistake is highly likely to result in our total annihilation at the hands of a formidably powerful alien death machine." He paused for effect. "This is my kind of plan, Captain."

"Thanks, Mak," Krieger said. "Let's get any questions out of the way before we jump."

Kassini spoke first. "Is the stealth tech reliable? We've only used it once, for a really short time."

"We'll find out," Krieger shrugged. "We both know the Federation doesn't usually fuck around when it comes to releasing new battle-ready tech and we've no reason to believe it won't hold out for the duration of the mission. All they'll see when they scan us is the signature of a harmless asteroid floating in space."

Taro was next. "What if the Elementals recon us up close?"

"A good question," said Krieger. "Computer, activate the camo and get the drone to show us the external view of the ship. If they eyeball us, we'll look like this."

The stealth drive activated and the room's main screen flashed into life to reveal the *Anomaly* hologrammatically transformed into a grey, pockmarked rock with no signs of light, save for the blue glow of the engines. At a glance at least, it was an impressive illusion.

"So as long as we don't use the main engines, or put any weapons or advanced sensors online, we should be able to come and go as we please," said Krieger. "And being a stealth ship, the *Anomaly* has top-grade reconnaissance cameras and passive sensors for gathering data."

Kassini noticed Vonya had been fidgeting restlessly in her plastic seat throughout the briefing. The pilot awkwardly unfurled a wingtip, feeling like a fledgling in Avion kindergarten class. "Kree-gar – my fighter – I say we keep her primed for launch. Then I can engage if they spot us, maybe."

"They're not going to see us, Vonya," Krieger said, taking a vague stab at a reassuring tone. "And if they do, well, even the best pilot in the galaxy would have their work cut out, to be honest."

"Okay Kreeg..." Vonya replied, mulling it over. "But if I do fight us out of there, I want a trophy."

"A trophy?"

"Yeah. 'Took on entire Elemental fleet' trophy."

"Okay, Vonya, it's not going to come to that, though..."

"With my full name – Vonya of Ok'cuu," she lapsed into her native Avion without the filter she usually employed to help with the language barrier, loudly cawing her name.

"...Kass can do Avion spelling," she concluded in her more usual human-friendly version.

"Sure can," said Kassini.

"Okay..." Krieger said, looking bemused.

"...and you present it to me. Bow head, give shining object to me, music, lights. Whole celebration. Cake, maybe..."

They sniggered at the image. Krieger rolled his eyes dramatically. "Vonya, it's a deal. You'll get your trophy. And if you can singlehandedly outfly an Elemental navy warfleet, I'll bake the fucking cake myself."

"Don't do it to yourself, Von, he grew up eating reconstituted F-rations on Federal tugs. You ever taste reboiled galley stew?" Kassini said, laughing.

"Worth it just to see. Eaten from the big wing com-mu-nal feeders myself plenty times," Vonya replied, clicking with amusement.

"Enough already," Krieger interjected. "Mission roles. Kassini, you focus on documenting their combat formations and tactics – the Avions are going to want to know the big picture along with the pretty pictures."

"So will I, as a matter of fact," Kassini replied. "When it comes to recent Elemental intel, my Federation battle overlays have quite a few blind spots around space combat... they're designed for troop combat, and mostly rely on historical projections anyway."

Krieger nodded. "It's always been the way. Back in my day, the Empire was always up-to-date with Avion tactics because we fought them all the time – no offence, Vonya – but the Elementals, well... they joined the wars later and they were always a bit of an enigma."

"Their technology has also always been... strange... and research into it also heavily classified," added Mak 14. "According to my data, no Elemental craft above cruiser class has ever been successfully captured by the Empire."

"No shit? Good trivia, Mak. I did not know that, and I've boarded a fair few in my time," said Krieger, genuinely surprised.

"They fight where they expect a win," Vonya added. "Don't do mighty flocks. Ellee fly smaller numbers, but big weapons and tough birds."

"Exactly what they used to tell us in our briefings," said Kassini. "We had numerical superiority, but they had resilient shields, organically infused hull materials, those weird-looking natural-energy pulse beams that could carve up a corvette in seconds..."

"...Ellee can't dogfight for shit, Kass," Vonya reminded her. "My fighter take on two over one hume, any day."

"Fascinating stuff, guys," Taro interrupted. "But could you tell me what I'm going to be doing? The suspense is killing me."

"Okay," said Krieger. "I want you to monitor and adjust the recon feed and get some great shots of any previously unseen tech they have out there. Mak, you're ship operations and stealth. You keep us hid. Vonya, you're on ship ID. You have the most up-close combat experience against Elemental planes out of all of us, so you can tell us what we're looking at."

"What about you?" asked Taro.

"If anyone needs me, I'll be in the kitchen," Krieger said sarcastically.

Despite its name sounding vaguely melodramatic to human ears, Kamakraken on the south-western fringe of the Elemental empire turned out to be an uninspiring and uninhabited red-dwarf star system. Its handful of rocky inner worlds and pair of outer mass-heavy gas giants were separated by an unusually dense torus-shaped asteroid belt. Kassini and the computer correctly pinpointed this belt as the most likely place that the system's outbound spin point – and therefore the Elemental fleet operation – would be.

The *Anomaly* completed its spin glitch-free and after the computer had performed a near-instantaneous sensor sweep, the stealth kicked in and the ship went dark – both literally and figuratively, since stealth operations necessarily minimised internal lighting.

Krieger ordered the computer to move them on a course towards the jump point, reasoning that if there were any unforeseen problems with the stealth drive, they'd at least have a fighting chance of escape. Half an hour of drift later, they approached the jump point and right on cue, the scope – now routed to the ship's main screen – announced the presence of the first Elemental craft in their vicinity.

Krieger whooped at the news, and Kassini and Taro exchanged guarded smiles.

Vonya spoke softly into her headset mic while Mak 14 updated the screen with schematics and visuals based on her IDs. The five ships on the tactical map were identified as the faction's oval-shaped missile boats, arranged with typical Elemental precision in an evenly spaced formation to form a pentacle shape around the jump point.

"Entering missile range," Mak 14 confirmed. "No missile lock."

The tension in the room relaxed by a couple of notches. "Thank the gods," said Krieger, affectionately patting the nearest available surface of the *Anomaly* as though petting a well-trained puppy. "Right, let's see how close we can get. Computer, approach the nearest ship for a fly-by. Well, a drift-by, anyway."

The *Anomaly* closed to within human visual range of the missile ship. Its elliptical profile appeared smooth and metallic when viewed from a distance. Yet close up, the ship's hull was made up of overlapping strands of textured, reddish-black vine-like material that were densely entwined and seemed to writhe with a rudimentary serpentine intelligence. Kassini looked away as they approached. The essential alienness of Elemental ship materials always creeped her out.

"Still nothing," Krieger announced as he watched the crawling underbelly of the ship, which was roughly twice the length of the *Anomaly*, drift slowly by the cabin porthole a mere 2,000 metres or so away. It began to recede into the distance as they passed by, the red glow of its idling engines gradually fading to black. He turned his back on the porthole, thrilled by the close encounter.

"Crew, it looks like we're free to snoop to our heart's content, so let's set our mission priorities. Computer, show every ship in range of our sensors on the display, with tactical info."

The main screen lit up promptly with a map showing the edge of the asteroid belt's parabola and jump point at the bottom. A labelled arrowhead annotated with a small '5' appeared, representing the missile boats. Heading sunward, a little further towards the top of the screen and off to the right, they zoomed in on two groups of 50 ships each arranged in close formation. They were approaching a disorganised cluster of 127 craft, labelled 'DRONES'. The approaching squadrons were labelled 'UNKNOWN'.

Further up the screen in the direction of the inner planets was a second, much larger array of ships. "Main fleet arm identified," said Mak 14. "291 ships in total. Too distant to determine formations. Overlaying details onto main screen."

A list of ships scrolled before them arranged in ascending order of size. It jumped alarmingly quickly from itemising smaller raiders, assault fighters, corvettes and missile boats to cataloguing heavier ships. In among the list, a complement of dropships, tank transporters and the telling lack of supply freighters (aside from ship-to-ship refuelling craft) indicated long-range exploration was not the priority. The list went on to reveal cruiser variations with a range of specialised weapons setups and no fewer than 10 capital ships. It ended with the largest of all, a new capital-ship type, also labelled 'UNKNOWN'.

All of which pointed clearly to one thing: the Elementals had assembled a general-purpose strike force, designed for overwhelming assault, extended munitions support and if necessary, planetary blockade.

"This is easily the biggest Elemental fleet gathering I've ever heard of," said Kassini. "Vonya, what order do we tackle this in?"

The Avion was squinting at her tablet, scrolling frantically through the model designations. "Fighters first. They are usually weakest – if Elementals have improved the fighters, we can work out how far up the tree their tech goes. Then the fleet after."

"Makes sense," said Krieger to the room. "No objections? Good. Computer, set course for the fighter exercises. And bring us some popcorn – should be a good show."

Being under stealth lent an air of almost constant unconscious tension to the crew. It was mentally draining to think that if something went wrong with their device, they would suddenly be in range of an alien warfleet. Every click they travelled towards the fleet was a click further from safety... the crew barely said a word to each other in the half hour it took to reach the first of the ship groupings.

The Elemental squadrons were deeply engaged in combat with remotely controlled drones by the time the *Anomaly* was in visual range. Vonya quickly confirmed that the first of the attacking wings was made up of the faction's latest variant of their single-seat assault fighters, a design based around a squat, teardrop-shaped chassis housing a recessed cockpit and surrounded by distinctive triple weapon mounts.

From their vantage point a safe distance above, Kassini mentally traced familiar patterns in the blur of shapes dancing before her eyes. The Elementals had expertly programmed their drones to mimic the distinctive defensive protocols of the Avions and Empire. She watched as, true to type, the 'Avion' drones frequently broke into hunting packs of three, relying on speed, agility and surprise to disorientate their prey before attempting to swoop and strike. Vonya grudgingly acknowledged the authenticity of their simulated flight plans.

The 'Empire' fighters, on the other hand, stuck together in larger wings. They moved in a hypnotic, unpredictable choreography that was ordinarily the result of complex squadron-level coordination by the Federation's sophisticated battle computers. Viewed from afar, it was obvious they were always seeking distance between themselves and their quarry in order to deal death with their powerful beam and missile weaponry.

"The Elemental fighters are flying like their standard raiders to me," said Kassini after watching the melee unfold for a couple of minutes. "And both sets of drones look to be holding their own."

Vonya was unconsciously twitching and swaying her wings as she watched the battle manoeuvres ebb and flow. "Seems to me Ellee have been home-learning about other race flight skills, the drones are very ree-alistic, outfly the bigger Ellee ships no problem. It's the same game as always here, Kass. Ellee pilots have no pictures in their heads, just heavy armour and energy beams."

As they spoke, the Elemental squadron abruptly broke off and retreated. Their afterburners worked overtime as they turned tail, pursued by tracers of low-energy laser fire and missiles, the drones' warheads obviously having been disarmed for the exercise. The drones soon regrouped into standard Avion and Empire patrol formations, seemingly reset to await a second wave.

"Here they come," said Taro. "I'll put a close-up onscreen."

A new vessel loomed before them. Its curved profile was stingray-like from above, with a large quad-engined module to the rear. The earlier models' distinctive triple-prong mounts were missing from the design.

"The raiders are of an unknown designation," Mak 14 commentated. "Twin pilots, four engines, a heavier chassis made of an advanced graphene and biological composite. Weapons systems currently unknown, but there is a novel system module in the centre of the body exhibiting strong exotic-matter readings."

"Exotic matter?" Krieger asked. "Could that be a new weapon?"

"We're about to see," said Kassini, pointing back to the screen where the drones were scrambling into their standard defensive formations. The Elemental raiders, on the other hand, were spreading out seemingly at random, showing no sign of adopting recognisable attack formations.

"The interceptors are entering standard weapons range," Mak 14 intoned.

The first defensive volleys of missiles streaked across the space between the rapidly closing squadrons. The drones split into the standard packs of three, still close enough to support one another but ready to split and disorient the Elemental raiders should they make it to within dogfighting range. As the space torpedoes closed in on them, the Elemental raiders didn't deviate from their approach or take evasive action.

"This will be over gale-quick," said Vonya. "New birds must be broken."

"I don't..." said Krieger, and his voice trailed off as the Elemental ships flickered out of existence, as one. A second passed, and before the disbelieving crew could form their words, the entire squadron of ships rematerialised right in front of their targets and fired their beam weapons in unison, then abruptly vanished again, leaving an expanding cloud of fire, smoke and drone debris spinning in the void.

An unreadable expression crossed Vonya's face and she screeched an Avion curse involuntarily as the crew looked back at the screen, where they saw the arrowhead representing the squadron rematerialise back at the exact spot where it had first disappeared.

Krieger leapt up and crossed the deck to join Taro at his station. "Man... tell me we have that on film."

"All of it," Taro replied, looking down at the playback on his monitor. "Although I can't quite believe what I just saw."

"Well, they aren't broken then, that's for sure," Kassini said to Vonya.

Vonya looked visibly shaken as she turned her piercing stare on her friend. "Big change, Kass, they always well coordinated, but this all new to me," she replied. "How the grek do you fight that?"

The Elemental fighter squadron soon returned to their carrier vessel which was standing off at a safe distance sunward towards the main fleet. The *Anomaly's* cameras showed the huge vessel, fuzzy and indistinct with the harsh sunlight striking the face away from them, as two long arms stretched horizontally out from a large spherical centre to points either side of it. This gave it the sinister aspect of a huge, black eye with a green-tinged sun corona around it.

"That carrier is moving back towards the bulk of the fleet," said Krieger, excitedly indicating the ship on the HUD. "We should follow it and try to get a closer look at the bigger toys – computer, anything at all strange about the stealth systems so far?"

"There are no apparent problems with the system, Captain, but I would not advise activating our main drives," replied the disembodied voice.

"Goes without saying," replied Krieger. "Vonya, can we drift on manoeuvring thrusters with enough pace to tail the carrier? It's a capital ship, can't be that fast under normal propulsion, right?"

"Likely, manoeuvring thrusters built big on this ship," she replied.

"Okay, I'd feel better if you were at the helm from here on, too."

"Me too," replied the Avion, and rose to leave for the flight-bubble in a flurry of feathers.

"Remember we're an asteroid!" Krieger called after her. "Fly like one."

Low-level propulsion jets aligned and fired, and *Anomaly* drifted gradually away from the fighter test, intersecting with the path of the carrier. Over time, its course very gently corrected towards the destination of the larger ship, with just enough deviation to bring them closer, but not enough to arouse suspicion.

The passive scanning systems continued their work of pinging ship locations up on the large viewscreen. Some time passed as the *Anomaly* edged closer to the stationary main fleet, still diverging gently from the course of the carrier vessel while maintaining the same approximate direction.

Kassini had just returned to the bridge. After taking a short break to system-check her implants and run through the mental exercises that kept them in equilibrium for her, she was now trying to dial up a more detailed readout on the largest ship.

"Strange," she said aloud, indicating the empty box next to a large, dart-shaped vessel with outsized fins at what she presumed was the rear, on the main view with a finger. "We should be close enough to be seeing analysis of individual ships now, such as that would be without the main sensors. Power-source locations, shield-emitter points and some hull-composition info should be accessible, even if they're testing shields or something."

"Not unusual for fleets to run ECM," replied Krieger.

"Kassini is correct, Captain, and I do not believe this is a standard countermeasure," put in Mak 14. "At present, *Anomaly*'s sensors are limited to sensing the physical presence of the ships and further, basic information that can be decoded from these responses. I suggest that the scanners are seeing the ships, or you would not be seeing them targeted on the scanner at all, but the system cannot interpret the other aspects of the data."

Krieger looked blank.

"The droid is correct," said the computer. "The sensor module is impaired. I am devoting processing power to augment its capability."

"Just keep recording all of it and annotate anything you can work out," Krieger replied. "Vonya, has that carrier stopped?"

"Yeah, Krieg, want me to hold us up?" the pilot replied over her comms.

"No, keep going. I want a good close up sweep of that ship at the very least, seeing as it's sitting in our lap, and make sure we pass it as close as you think we can get away with. They're more or less between us and the sun. We shouldn't be visible if anybody happens to be looking with a telephoto lens."

"Doing it," she replied, and the crew felt the gentle jolt of manoeuvring thrust.

Anomaly's bulky frame had built up significant momentum during the pursuit, even without primary engines. A small course correction placed it on a line to pass along the longest axis of the Elemental carrier, while still maintaining what Vonya guessed was a safe distance.

As they slowly closed on the vast ship, the camera blisters on the side nearest the carrier moved in unison, ready to provide as large a near-focus view of it as possible to the viewscreen on the bridge. Closer up, the Elemental capital ship was an impressive and unnerving sight – a baleful eye burning away against the black. It was clear even at range that the central, spherical 'eyeball' of the vessel could house the entire *Anomaly* many times over.

Krieger was squinting at it as the cameras struggled to keep as much of the ship in focus as possible – it was still too far away to make out much detail – when the computer piped up again.

"I have ascertained what was confusing our scanners' analytic capabilities. The errors are all centred around the power systems of these vessels, which appear to be common in some way I do not have prior record of."

"What d'ya mean common?" asked Taro, looking up from his monitoring station.

"The scanner analysis software is designed to pinpoint obvious power sources of an individual vessel using physical characteristics – heat transfer or unintended electronic interference, for example – and make a guess as to their makeup by probability comparison. It appears the Elemental fleet is drawing power from an external source, which is confusing the system – I will output my preliminary model to the screen."

Previous shots of the main fleet were overlayed onscreen. The hanging formation was covered in a pale blue fill, like a depiction of a shield absorbing low-energy laser fire, covering the alien vessels in a nearly globular spherical shape. The body of this energy field shifted non-uniformally into brighter and softer tones around different vessels in turn as the footage began to play back.

The overlay around the fleet seemed to move like a tide. It melted gently into and out of itself to form bulbs and ridges around its edges, but a single incandescent spike of colour shot off from its main body toward the nearby sun, and remained the only unchanging part of the overlay.

"You are seeing an overlay of power fluctuations not dissimilar to those we encountered on Reticuli 19, with the Elemental tower," the computer commentated. "As you will be aware, most stellar vessels rely on an internal power system to operate. These vessels have these too, as normal..."

The screen zeroed in on the closest vessel, a blurred, elongated teardrop at the resulting low resolution, and the overlay showed a distinct brighter blue patch towards the rear of the ship, before returning to the original view.

"I believe the Elementals are engaged in some kind of power sharing or augmentation between their capital ships," concluded the computer, clearing the viewscreen back to the scan of the approaching carrier.

The crew grappled with this for a moment.

"Power-sharing between ships? How are they pulling that off?" Krieger asked, finally.

"It is notable that the nearby carrier is not currently adjoined to the effect *Anomaly* has discovered – logically, it may only be a short-range capability," said Mak 14.

"A short-range capability with almost completely unknown purpose and effects," interjected Kassini quickly. "Don't get any funny ideas."

"My ideas are generally considered somewhat amusing until I am using them to protect your lives – I would like to seek more data on this phenomenon."

"Yes, Mak's right," said Krieger firmly. "We need to gather more information about this and the carrier is on the move again by the look of those engine flares, so let's complete our fly-by and move closer to the main fleet with it."

Krieger turned back to the viewscreen and Kassini glanced across at Taro, who shrugged and said nothing.

Anomaly had completed a single pass of the side of the carrier while it stood stationary and, still retaining a long range, began to run alongside the larger ship's route. Vonya had dropped the ship to a lower relative position to get a better view of its underside.

The exterior views didn't give a great deal away to the *Anomaly* crew, as much of the carrier was covered in the perfectly smooth semi-organic resinous material common to Elemental ships, which they knew would form hatches and launch ports as required by the vessel's internal configuration.

The tension in the small cabin built as the human crew worked, logging their observations alongside the footage. After some time, Vonya's voice cut across the speakers.

"Would be well within missile range of big birds in their flock now humes, stealth must be holding."

"Yeah, the fact that we aren't dead tells us a lot, right?" replied Kassini. The pilot and Taro both laughed.

The computer spoke up again. "The power signature of the carrier is changing. It must now be entering the influence zone of the power-distribution system."

"Are we clear of the effect?" Kassini said with some alarm. "The last run-in with new Elemental technology didn't go so well for us."

"I am experiencing similar power fluctuations, but these are manageable while *Anomaly* is running silent."

Mak 14 stood up and spoke as he headed for the door. "I will interface with *Anomaly's* systems and provide my support," he said, and was gone. The others looked at each other as they heard his hissing hydraulics and clanking gait making their way towards the ship's critical system bay.

"I hate it when he does that," said Taro, quietly. Kassini nodded to him with a grave look.

"Vonya, keep us moving, slowly, towards the fleet – the rest of you keep everything recording," said Krieger. He was all-commander at this point, and looked to be having the most fun he'd had in years.

The interference increased as *Anomaly* edged closer to the cloud of vessels. The image intensifiers allowed them to clearly see some of the smaller vessels now. They were strange half-oval ships which positioned themselves around some of the larger craft and snaked out multiple fibrous tendrils to tether themselves, like jellyfish making contact with prey in a dark ocean.

"Support ships," said Kassini, as one of these detached itself from the main group. "Looks like we'll be getting a closer look at one of those, too. It's heading for the carrier."

She called up a range counter around one of the ships, and they watched as the figures ticked down rapidly.

"Moving fast, much faster than anything that big has a right to," she commented.

"Vonya, slow us right down and put us in a gentle spin. Make like an asteroid, focus on the approach and whatever operations they carry out with the carrier," said Krieger. The Avion pilot slowed the *Anomaly's* momentum and the range counter ticked down slightly slower in response.

The carrier had stopped again with *Anomaly* still positioned below the plane of its approach, giving it a view of the flat base of the domed ship as it came closer. They could see clearly as several of the tendrils extruded from its leading edge. They swung away from the main body of the vessel in the momentum of deceleration as they prepared to make contact with the carrier.

"The presence of a second vessel is intensifying the interference markedly," intoned the computer, simulating a slightly more alarmed tone in the hope the humans would register its internal distress.

Mak 14's chip-voice answered it over the comms.

"I am currently communicating with your stealth system's algorithm. It is upset by our reactor power spikes and keeps threatening to go into failsafe. I have blocked this several times, and will patch around the safety mechanism to avoid this possibility."

The computer's alarmed voice went up a notch, taking on a pleading tone.

"Extremely unwise! *Anomaly* stealth systems are full of shutdown protocols like those! Can somebody please stop the malfunctioning hack droid manipulating my safety protocols?" it pleaded.

Krieger looked annoyed and opened his mouth to give the order, but got no further than saying the droid's name before an alarm exploded from the nearest console. Taro physically jumped, knocking his tablet to the floor.

"Stealth system rebooting," the computer wailed. "*Anomaly* is visible to spectrum scans – visual camouflage still active."

Krieger reacted fast, barking orders as he leaped into the seat behind the blaring console to silence the alarm.

"Vonya, they can see us! Main drive up and get us out of here – closest spin point. It'll take them time to react, we need to get clear of missile range. Computer, have we been acquired?"

"Stealth system back online, main drive coming online – power plant is responding nominally despite interference patterns. The nearby carrier and support vessel scanned us with passives, their active sensors are now beginning to sweep the area."

Anomaly was already beginning to rotate, and the sensation increased dramatically as the main drive came online with a scream. This descended into a resounding thump that rattled the ship and slewed unsecured items around the deck. Kassini's practised reflexes, honed in countless Federation marine dropships, kicked in and she grabbed at the straps on her seat as they swung away from her hands.

"Strap in, people," said Krieger dramatically. "Mak, get the hell away from the stealth drive software and make sure the powerplant can handle max load – if you can do that without switching it off completely, that would be ideal."

"Fly-time humes, may the thermal gods smile," Vonya was audibly laughing in the cockpit, and the sudden uptick in volume of her business-as-usual dance music was vaguely comforting for the rest of the crew as the *Anomaly*, now facing away from the main fleet, lurched into max thrust and pinned them to their seats.

Krieger managed to keep his hands on the console, and dialled up a sweep of the Elemental fleet comms channels they had been monitoring. An explosion of data appeared on the main view, resolving into waveforms that represented alien speech. Beneath these were approximate translations of the words.

Kassini focused on this against the pressure of acceleration and spoke loudly over the suddenly increased engine noise.

"I understand enough of that to know they're going into alert."

"No missile locks!" Krieger replied. "They weren't expecting company."

Minutes passed as the *Anomaly* accelerated rapidly back along the axis it had used to approach. The oval support ship had veered away from the carrier, making way for the bigger ship to target them with its heavy ordnance.

Luckily for the *Anomaly* crew, the capital ship was almost exclusively outfitted in a way which enabled it to provide screening fire and close-in torpedo support for its fighter complement against frigate-class ships, leaving the task of destroying smaller vessels to its charges. As such, it lacked the single-target missile systems of the rest of the fleet which would have made short work of the *Anomaly's* escape.

The active scans which now flooded the sector with seeking radiation were hampered further by the still-partial masking effect of the recon ship's stealth systems. It had locked *Anomaly's* engine signature a minute or so too late for the effective range of the carrier's area-denial-based weapon systems, which could otherwise have turned the space around the little ship into a seething cauldron of ordnance from which it could not have escaped.

What the Elemental carrier did have was a full crew of recently trained pilots and a battle-ready squadron of fighters. The semi-living skin of the ship's long arms split apart to reveal launch ports which rapidly disgorged 12 of these in groups of four, hurling them from the launch tubes under some power external to the small craft themselves. Each one became a dancing blue-and-white firefly against the receding ship as their engines sparked into life.

On the bridge, Krieger had been glued to the long-range scans as soon as they began to appear on the monitor in front of him. He saw the small swarm of fighters appear, and the larger markers for the five missile boats still arranged around the jump point.

"Between a rock and hard place here, Vonya, the missile boats at the jump point will tear us to pieces if the fighters don't get to us first," he said, trusting the pilot had her comms loop loud enough to hear him.

"Got a plan for daring escape, Krieg. Need you to fly *Anomaly* while I deal with the fighters. Autopilot engaged for now," she responded, the music squelching her voice before she whacked the volume down.

The feeling of intense acceleration lessened dramatically, and the door to the cockpit corridor burst open a few moments later. Vonya strode across the room in a rustle of black and purple feathers, zipping up her flight suit as she went. She spoke straight to Kassini at some length in her native tongue.

Kassini listened, asked a couple of questions in Avion, took in the answers with a nod and responded with a "Good luck," the rest of the crew could understand and a mini-salute. Vonya shot out of the other door and heade to the cargo bay and her fighter.

"What was all that?" said Krieger.

"She told me the plan, easier for her to explain the detail in Avion. Time to take the helm, Captain, I'll cover your sensor position while I tell you what we're doing. Vonya's going to be too busy..."

"She's going to take them on with the fighter? She's a lunatic!" Krieger replied as he jumped up from the chair and made for the flight module.

"Only plan we've got. Go!" Kassini said, and took his place at the sensor console as he left. "Taro, you know how to oversee the *Anomaly's* targeting computer, right?"

"Something like, I told it where to shoot on Alphoron Six," he replied.

"Good – the barrage is our only defence against missiles, make sure it doesn't miss. And you better stay buckled up."

Kassini clipped the harness of the scanner chair into position and pulled the console toward her. Vonya's voice broke in across the comms channel.

"Preflight complete, launching shortly – Krieger, keep *Anomaly* straight and level and cut the acceleration."

"Roger," replied the captain's voice, loaded with the strain of the unfamiliar flight controls.

The engine sound on the bridge faded to nothing as the surface-rover airlock cycled at Vonya's command, the platform transferring her small fighter into a sealed bay beneath the ship.

"Good. Kreeg – momentum will change when I lift off, plus change in weight to think about, too. Launch now."

The sealed bay beneath the ship was originally designed for depositing vehicles on planetary surfaces via a ramp from a sealed compartment. Vonya's Boneyard modification list had simply extended the distance the ramp would travel to allow for a crude spaceborne fighter launch.

The rear 'hinge' of the ramp had been removed and replaced with several more supports and hydraulic systems added. These lowered the fighter away from the *Anomaly* and when fully extended and locked out, tipped until the nose of the fighter pointed downwards.

The gear clamps on her ship retracted. Vonya applied a little forward thrust and the gentlest nudge of upward manoeuvring, lowering her relative velocity to the *Anomaly* and causing the small fighter to drift gracefully clear of the forward motion of the ship. The internal distance sensors indicated she was clear. She opened up the engines and it sped like an arrow back down the path of the bigger ship towards the gaining Elemental formation, a solitary dot on a scanner heading towards an intimidating wall of firepower.

"Clear and closing," Vonya said, in a tone as clipped and professional as anything they had ever heard from her. Kassini watched the new dot on the area scans heading rapidly towards the tightly packed Elemental fighters for a moment before addressing her comms. She also noted the five missile boats at the jump point hadn't moved from their original positions and guessed they were still trying to acquire *Anomaly* on long-range scans.

"Computer, calculate the nearest edge of the spin-safe zone and display it for us."

A sphere appeared on the scanner, concentric rings of colour receding from red through yellow to green at its centre, to indicate the relative safety of a spin activation in those areas.

"You see that, Krieger? Okay, here's the plan – manoeuvre us so that we're on course to skirt the nearest edge of the red zone away from those picket ships, but slow us down to buy time for Vonya to take out the fighters."

"Got it, assuming she *can* take out the fighters," replied Krieger.

"Believe me, she told me she made Gunstar in the Avion fleet... she can handle it. As soon as they're dealt with and she gives the word, or as soon as we see movement from the picket to intercept us, change course for the nearest yellow zone and burn the engines to all hell until we register weapons tracking."

"Straight at them with maximum signature?" replied Krieger, incredulous.

"Probably," replied Kassini. "As soon as they start trying to lock us, we power everything down and activate the stealth systems. Vonya is banking on that breaking any ability they have to missile lock us, for long enough that she'll be in a position to help."

"How's she going to do that? Pickets like that are designed explicitly to take out fighters."

"She didn't say – just told us to 'make like a comet' until we're in the yellow zone and can power everything back up and emergency spin."

"Risky plan, but like you say, it's the only one we've got – cutting in some reverse thrust and changing course now. Out."

Kassini returned her attention to the scanners. Vonya had turned her fighter from an intercept course and was now heading on a path above them that would take her ship past the enemy formation at some distance. They would have to respond by splitting up or changing course, or allow the incoming fighter to either drop in among them or get behind them. The *Anomaly* had put some space between itself and the main threat, for now – the carrier was a large red oblong some distance back from its charges.

On the edge of the scan field in the direction of the main Elemental fleet, a mass of red contacts had appeared, indicating that they had also launched several large squadrons of fighters. Some would no doubt take up a screening position, but the rest would make straight for Vonya and *Anomaly*. Kassini opened a channel to Vonya.

"You have a lot of company incoming from the direction of the main fleet..."

Vonya heard her friend's words as though from a different plane of existence – encased in the suit which suspended her horizontally in the centre of her ship's flight module, she was in full primal mode now. The fighter's flight systems, modified down to the last nut, bolt and algorithm to suit her, were responding perfectly to the slightest twitch of her wings. She could feel the ship's dynamics through the haptic system, down to the changes in vibration as the targeting display turned the movement of her eyes into the mechanical rotation of the gimballed weaponry in the turret blisters. This was bliss.

She responded to Kassini in Avion. "Expected. This will be over soon, these ships are already making it easy for me."

Vonya's expertise was hard to define: starship dogfighting was a mix of channelled experience, split-second decision-making and honed instinct. As Kassini and Krieger watched her tactics unfold on the scanner, they gained a new appreciation of what made Vonya such a formidable opponent – there was effectively no difference between her as a person and a pilot. She was immersed in the flow.

She was facing a phalanx of standard Elemental interceptor ships, and she knew their design fundamentals by heart. They were relatively lightly armoured, a deficit made up for by an almost certain shielding, but they were still not what she would call agile. Six of the formation had split off and accelerated to a position ahead of their comrades to attempt to intercept her deliberately chosen course.

She pushed the throttle under one of her left talons and her fighter's speed increased markedly. She aimed for a point in between the now-dispersed formations with the same practised wing-muscle memory she would use to build up speed when surfing the thermals on her home planet. A missile-lock alarm, which had begun whining a moment earlier, was silenced as her ship darted below the zenith of the intercepting formation.

A three-dimensional hologram of the sector of space around her hovered to the left of her vision. It betrayed the confusion this manoeuvre caused the opposing ships. True to type, the Elemental pilots hesitated when presented with the quandary of a single ship apparently deciding to reposition to attack *both* of their formations at once.

The Avion stunt fighter moved quickly in comparison to her foes. Her manoeuvre meant she was now rapidly closing the distance on the original formation from above. The other formation was now reversing course above her to reacquire a lock, but was falling behind.

The ships directly ahead were confused and afraid, several jinking as though to break formation while the squadron leader dithered between continued pursuit and defensive flight.

This was opportunity, and she flicked over a control that selected one of the few missiles her ship carried, more usually employed against larger ships. A targeting bubble appeared, which she moved instantly with her eyes until it encompassed all of the ships in the formation and clicked a trigger.

Her missile streaked away towards the ships in front of her. Vonya slowed her acceleration slightly, and pulled her angle of attack, conscious of getting caught in the resultant blast. Four ships of the six broke formation as the other, clearly more disciplined pilots made a move together. Their engines flared red as they went to max power and turned up and away from the projectile. Those who ignored orders were the lucky ones, as the missile's simple manoeuvring system changed its course slightly to encompass the maximum number of targets in a bright white explosion of electromagnetic interference. This expanded from the point of detonation to encompass the ships in formation, ordnance designed specifically to deactivate and interfere with shield systems.

Her helmet visor protected her vision from the effect of the explosion, and her closing vector placed her right on top of the formation as they spun in different directions.

'Elemental arrogance', she thought coldly. They had expected a standard explosive warhead would be absorbed by their shielding, and were now hopefully hearing their equivalent of alarm bells as their electronic systems freaked out.

Vonya had already spun up her autocannons before the explosion of light collapsed in on itself. She now unleashed a long burst from all four of the revolving cannons mounted either side of her cockpit, two of which were loaded with armour-piercing ammunition, the others with explosive rounds. Her talon came off the trigger and with a strong lift of her shoulders, she used the momentum imparted by the departing shells to augment a hard flip of the ship's nose up and away from the formation ahead of her while reversing thrust. This translated to arc her ship trajectory in a shallow U shape, at the base of which she now deliberately overshot her targets, just close enough to bathe them in the silent light and emissions from her engines as she began to reorient.

As a consequence, she caught only the first moments of contact as the Elemental ships flew straight through the hail of slugs targeted just ahead of their turn. The explosive rounds were designed to detonate in proximity as well as on impact, turning the space around the four ships into a broiling mass of scything metal.

The shielding on three of the ships had completely collapsed as a result of the missile and the subsequent barrage tore one of these to pieces, depressurising and exploding it into a corona of expanding gas and debris. This added to the woes of the others, and two further pilots were killed almost instantly as either debris or the shots themselves penetrated their flight modules. Only one of these other ships actually disintegrated, breaking apart almost in slo-mo into a number of gently diverging sections. The other began to spin wildly as it vented gas and fuel, but both remained on the same trajectory that had proved fatal for their pilots.

The final ship of the four had retained a small amount of shielding which staved off the first few seconds of the maelstrom, and concentrated damage to its rear quarter when these were finally stripped away. Its engines and running lights deactivated, indicating severe powerplant damage. A small escape capsule containing the pilot dropped out of the bottom of the vessel as it too went into a final, dead spin.

Vonya resisted the rotational Gees as her fighter spun on its axis, now travelling backwards above and away from the rapidly expanding cloud of debris. She could see from her radar the other two members of the doomed formation were out of it for the moment; having boosted at max throttle to avoid her missile strike, they were both now in wide-angled turns far away on either side of her.

The other six intercept fighters were the problem now. They had split up slightly as they corrected their initial manoeuvre and were now closing in the classic all-guns-forward formation of an Elemental wing. Presumably they'd decided against deploying their mid-range missile systems due to the proximity of their now deceased or scattered comrades.

She increased reverse thrust to maximum, speeding up ahead of them. She noticed the telltale red points appear across their coordinated weapons systems which indicated the laser batteries arrayed across their front-facing hardpoints spooling up to fire.

Vonya moved her feet against the free-moving pedals they were clipped into in her horizontal position, pushing them down hard to cause the fighter's manoeuvring thrusters to rotate forwards for additional reverse thrust and to fire at full bore. At the same moment, she flipped the nose of the ship upwards again by 90 degrees, repositioning her ship like a hanging pendulum in front of the oncoming Elementals, and screamed loudly at the engines for more power.

A volley of laser fire erupted from her assailants' weaponry and more than 30 bright red, millimetre-wide scalpels of energy licked across space to converge perfectly on most of the critical points on the fighter. The exceptional accuracy of Elemental laser weaponry worked against them here: their targeting systems lead-fired the small ship on the assumption it would travel upwards in front of them, using the always more efficient forward thrusters of Avion craft – not downwards.

The deadly blazing lines angled across the transparent front of Vonya's flight bubble inches from its leading edge as they receded away from her. The instrumentation around her was illuminated with a haze of boiling red light as she kicked her feet again to reangle her manoeuvring thrust to push her small craft *down*, which was now towards the incoming craft.

Screaming against G-forces that were extreme even for a creature born to the air and then trained and experienced in fighter combat, she angled her targeting reticule to the bottom of her screen, passively processing the positional data from the 3D map. This had zoomed in to show the ships in much closer quarters and now moved with her eyes to stay fixed in the same position in her vision.

Time slowed. She counted two seconds and pulled both triggers. The autocannons and her own main beam weapon fired – slightly early. Her ship's single laser beam hung suspended in infinite space for a frozen second ahead of her, hitting nothing.

Then the lead ships of the Elemental formation passed over, perfectly timed for the spinning-up autocannons to follow up on her laser blast. They crossed the totality of her vision slowly and instantly began flaring into the telltale rainbow of shield-weapon interaction.

As soon as she saw dark space behind the passing shapes, she instinctively tilted the nose to follow them and switched her main drive to forward. The main engine port flared to slow her increasing momentum away from them. She ended the move with her ship belly-up behind her opponents, still firing blindly into a mass of coruscating shield energy.

Amazingly, their shielding held, a fact which dismayed the small part of Vonya's mind which was not fully given over to flying the ship, but the manoeuvre had disconcerted one of the pilots enough for them to break formation. In response to a reflexive flick of her wings, she moved the nose of the ship just enough to keep the fleeing vessel in view.

The targeting system registered her use of a quirk of Avion physiology, the ability to routinely move their two eyes independently of one another, and a second targeting reticule appeared. This allowed Vonya to guide the still active laser on its gimbal with her left eye like a laser pointer to follow it as it broke off from its comrades, while the autocannons remained steadily targeted on the main phalanx ahead.

The shield ball around the solo craft disappeared, revealing the slender curves of the ship it protected. Her laser struck the hull at the same moment it began to beep an overheat warning. She calmly played the weapon across the enemy ship until it exploded into a ball of superheated gas and metal.

Only then did she allow the laser to cool, the now white-hot metal of its barrel above the flight blister just visible through the canopy. She drained the autocannons into the formation's shields and the auto-reload clanked through the hull. The shields of the Elemental craft faded to pastel colour, but still didn't collapse.

She took stock for a moment – this was unprecedented, and it was clear to her the fighters were so rigidly sticking to formation because of the mutually supportive field technology Mak 14 had uncovered. The new tech had turned their usual battlefield rigidity into an advantage, but that had now become a prison. None of the pilots wanted to be the one she targeted if they all broke formation.

She chided herself for only loading one EMP missile – but by any dogfighter's definition, she still had the upper hand. She matched the formation's roll in front of her with ease and hatched a plan to turn their shielded fortress to her advantage.

30 more seconds passed before a 'weapon ready' indicator appeared over her gunsight, and she carefully parked the reticule over the silhouette of a ship in the formation which was slightly lagging low and to the right, before opening up full-bore with all the ship's weapons again.

Kassini watched all of this on the scanner, reacting with concern as the first wave of red ship markers intersected with Vonya's blue icon, and then something approaching the grim amusement of battle as the first four of them almost immediately disappeared from the scan in bright white flashes, indicating weapons fire and explosions. The final two of that first six had turned tail and run for the fleet, she noticed. The blue ship flicked from being directly in front of the other six to behind them in a burst of the same bright white markers.

More pressingly, ahead of them on the scan, the picket ships had finally begun to react and were changing formation. *Anomaly* was still a little short of the safety of the edge of the spin zone.

"Krieger," she said. "Looks like Vonya has the pursuit under control. You see the picket ships? Time to burn those engines."

"Roger," his disembodied voice replied. "I'll change course now and hit max throttle, but make like we're heading slightly away from the yellow zone still. That'll mean I can use the attitude thrusters to push us back onto the most direct course, so we're not just running a straight line for them to extrapolate from the moment we... hopefully... disappear. Computer, are we sure the stealth systems will work after Mak screwed with them?"

"Some of the system has been operational the whole time, and I am ready to shut down all non-essential systems and activate the rest on your mark. The change the droid made has ultimately improved the code: the reboot was an unfortunate consequence.

"However, there is a flaw in your planning," it continued. "If we power down and activate the stealth drive to avoid the missiles of the frigates, how will we reactivate our power systems to spin out of the system when we are even closer, without being immediately destroyed?"

"Vonya has a plan for that, too," replied Kassini. "Sometimes you've just got to trust your squadmates."

The *Anomaly's* engines finished the conversation for them as they thundered up to maximum output again, and the crew felt the ship turn unsteadily towards the picket ships.

Kassini checked the ongoing fighter combat again to discover it wasn't so ongoing. The only remaining blips from the battle were now the two retreating fighters and Vonya's interceptor marker streaking back towards the *Anomaly*. She was still being pursued at a now-increasing distance by the massed ranks of the main Elemental fleet's fighters.

Kassini sat back and linked to Vonya's comms to say: "You look to be clear for now, Von, and I presume you're okay given the speed you're flying. Do I even want to ask how that went?"

"I'm okay, Kassini," the pilot replied, speaking in Avion. She began to jabber rapidly in the manner of many post-combat soldiers Kassini had known.

"Elemental fighters have strong shields now too, as tough as anything we put on capital ships, but it turns out they also *contain* energy as well as keep it out. I unloaded everything my ship has on what I guessed was a weak point, then planted a hi-ex missile through the gap my laser created, like a cracked eggshell. Barbecued all five of them in one, bad crow for the Elemental!"

"Alright, slow down pilot, slow down, you're hard to understand, remember. We just made our turn and burn, you said you were going to distract the picket ships long enough for us to spin out. Question is, why would they go for the little fighter and not the big spy ship when we drop the stealth and try to spin?"

The Avion laughed her clacking, beaky caw over the speakers.

"Like the old birds say, the feathers don't always add up to a flock," she said cryptically. "Enough though, Kass, I need the spin coordinates you're using – ask the computer to tight-beam them to my nav when it's done the calculations."

"Acknowledged," replied the computer over the comm circuit. It followed this up on the main speaker with: "I am now registering fire-control pulses from the frigates."

Kassini glued herself straight back to the scanner scope where the frigates were now displayed in a tight formation, moving under low power to cover *Anomaly's* current course.

"Okay, this is crunch time," Krieger's voice said immediately. "Power us down, activate the stealth tech and hope this works. Firing the manoeuvring thrusters now."

Mercifully, this time the computer didn't feel the need to dim the bridge lights according to the stealth protocol, reasoning correctly that other emissions and being able to see properly were more important in this situation.

The *Anomaly* sped on into the darkness towards the line of frigates, Kassini watching them on the scanners.

"No lock," said the computer after a couple of minutes. "The targeting pulses have stopped and been replaced with active sensor sweeps. I am confident we do not show on them. Perhaps the frigates will assume we have spun out."

"No chance," said Kassini, still staring at the tracking system. "Even with just passive sensors I can see what they're doing – they've redeployed into a sweep formation, and are moving towards our path. The manoeuvring thrusters aren't going to be enough to get us out of the pattern of all five of them, by my estimate."

A smaller blip became visible again on the scanner below the plane of the frigates and approaching from the left of the scope, which the *Anomaly's* scanning software quickly re-identified as Vonya's fighter.

"There's Vonya, and as I feared, the frigates aren't reacting – there isn't much a single fighter can do against… what in all the gods' eyes is that?" exclaimed Kassini suddenly.

"What?" said Taro. "What do you see?"

Kassini threw the readout to the big screen, which doubled it into the cockpit for Krieger – another Vonya icon had appeared beside the original one. Then three more appeared in a dart formation, a little off to one side; then another three, lower and to the rear. This continued until the scope counted more than 30 Vonyas, all heading on a variety of courses and approaches to envelop the frigates from all sides.

The frigates immediately lost interest in their sweep pattern, beginning to redeploy into a flat defensive formation and make way towards the new threat.

"That's gotta be a spoof," said Krieger from the cockpit with a laugh. "I'm not baking that many cakes."

"We have reached the yellow zone," said the computer. "Spin success likelihood would be vastly improved if we were stationary."

"I'll put it in reverse, but it'd take hours on manoeuvring thrusters alone to slow us down, so don't activate anything until the frigates are further away – they'll soon be wondering why the hell they can't lock any of these targets, and will close to visual range," replied Krieger. They heard him rubbing his cheek over the speakers as he studied the flight-module scans.

"We'll still be in missile range, so we'll have to drop the stealth, then full-throttle the main drive in reverse *and* spool the spin drive at the same time. That'll put a bright red target on us, so you'll need to spin the second we get above a reasonable probability of success."

"Calculations are complete and transmitted to Vonya as requested," replied the computer.

"Okay, I'll spin the ship around. Get ready for some big Gees when I cut the main engines in again, people, remember your seats will rotate automatically to cushion you against the direction of the braking thrust," said Krieger. The sickening feeling of the ship turning returned once again for a brief period as he spun *Anomaly* on its axis to face the opposite direction.

Another minute passed before Kassini said: "Frigates are as far away as they're going to get, Krieger, one of them just dumb-fired a volley of missiles at those phantom ships. Vonya's game will be up any minute."

"Punch it then, hold tight. This will hit the humans hard, computer – be prepared to take over, we're counting on you."

The engines roared to life once more and the crew were pinned to their seats once again by the pressure of deceleration, but this time it was a punch in the gut that rapidly surpassed any of the previous sensations to the point that Kassini soon started to lose consciousness.

The ship superstructure started to moan, then scream as it resisted buckling under the rapid change in momentum. The noise mingled with the bass swell of the spin drive and the thunder of the engines pushed to maximum to form a hellish cacophony that reverberated throughout the bridge. Kassini forced herself back to reality to find the computer and Mak 14 communicating in her earpiece in an unflustered monotone she found strangely comforting.

“Stealth deactivated, spin drive spooling, power draw at maximum.”

“I am removing safety protocols from the power-cell management system, this should enable you to draw more power,” Mak’s voice replied.

“*Anomaly* is beyond deceleration tolerance, pushing drives will damage the ship and certainly the humans, I will divert any power you can free up to the drive-cooling system.”

...and on they went for what felt like a lifetime, even though it was only a few minutes in reality.

The last thing Kassini heard, as she recognised the strangeness of the beginning of a spin jump and the onrushing locomotive of blankness that was unconsciousness at the same time, was Vonya’s musical voice over the headset shouting in her clumsy human speech.

“My spin underway – see you all on the strong solar winds. You enjoy my diversheeon, Kree-gar? Believe what I say – best pilot in this or any galaxy!”

M

Kassini: *Anomaly* has used stealth to get
eyes on the Elemental fleet at Kamakraken.

Transmitted footage under secure encryption.

A dangerous operation – trust I will be rewarded.

Got to go. Send mission update ASAP.

M

Drexler: Data downloaded.
This is a game-changer, Agent.

Find privacy and report in to discuss.

Drexler out.

11. THE SLIPPERY SLOPE

The well-travelled diplomat in Taro habitually made it his business to be in the right place at the right time, and when under pressure to improvise a bolthole spin destination, he'd excelled himself in his choice of system. Kapteyn's Star lay deeper towards the centre of the Empire's sprawl, at the very edge of the *Anomaly's* well-worn FTL's spin range – the computer had in fact nearly experienced a breakdown when it was fed the coordinates – and the crew had been noticeably tense when strapping in for the countdown. But the *Anomaly* held up for the near-half-hour of dreamtime and when the crew emerged from spin, their consciousnesses subtly phase-shifted, the computer had already joined the spacelane traffic on their approach to Vanguard Station, the system's industrious starport.

At the fringes of the Empire where ship's crews tended to be one shade of nefarious or another, data transfer depended upon the collective network of travelling starships to act as ghost-repeater relays for galactic communication. On a visit to the outer systems, dodgier pilots were usually pleased to find the latest updates and lists of persons-of-interest from the authorities slow to arrive and propagate amongst all the lo-fidelity pirate networks, narrow-bit text messaging and read-only holograms. These crumby lo-res methods were usually reserved only for covert communications piggybacking on better-bandwidth systems that were the order of the day in the innerworld territories.

Kapteyn's Star, on the other hand, was one of the outermost 'nexus' systems in the Federation, and at the other end of the spectrum from these lower-tech outer worlds. Nexus systems not only had comms contact with the Empire's central hub of worlds – through an expensive stream of automated spin-data drones stepping from one system to another with constant cargoes of information – but also had spin points that accessed either (or both) Avion and Elemental territory, too, enabling regular interspecies communication that was usually subject to a framework of agreements between governments and the relevant colonies.

It had been a long time since any of the crew – barring Kassini, but the rest didn't need to know that – had swum in the rich data-stream of a nexus. Like every fringe spacer returning to the fold, the first thing everyone onboard did was to reach for their tablets and download software updates, backdate their personal news feeds and stock up their entertainment channels for the next long-haul escapade.

For Vonya, access to her native Avion culturebank was limited in human-centric Federation space. But being in its proximity was still an opportunity to soak up goings-on in the territories in her own language and check for any news about her estranged high-society family, as well as download more of her obscure Elemental soaps and dance mixes to fly to. Even the ship's computer and the droids silently connected to the aether's various code hubs, surfing the binaries for new patches and protocols.

Krieger sat in the cockpit and watched the ship's nav comp synchronise with the spin of the station's giant docking bay. Vanguard was a colossal sight to behold; the breathtaking superstructure's angular chrome-and-steel geometry gleamed in the half-light, a gauntlet of human manufacturing ingenuity thrown down to the cosmos. Suspended in geosynchronous orbit high above Kapteyn c, a Super Earth terraformed in more resource-rich times housing an exclusive and sought-after Empire colony world, the station was a key trading post that had operated as a midpoint base during the contact phase of the Great Expansion.

During those times, it'd served a dual function: a military staging post for returning fleets and a major hub for the burgeoning galactic market. Krieger realised this must be why it stoked memories in his unconscious of Federation navy campaigns, and shook the impulses the memories brought with them from his mind.

Once guided inside the vast hangar, *Anomaly* was directed smoothly to the snug confines of a landing bay delineated by the familiar yellow-and-black chevrons. On touchdown, the comms channel burst into life with a stream of brightly coloured ads offering various station services: Krieger selected a firm of mechanoid ship mechanics. Alongside the usual routine refuelling and rearming services, he requested they calibrate the *Anomaly's* weapons systems and to see what they could do to optimise its FTL. He called through to Vonya to see if she wanted any maintenance carrying out on her fighter.

"Fuel only, Kree-gar," came her drowsy response. "No filthy robo paws on my pet bird."

"Good job Rust's offline," Kassini teased her. "He'd probably turn his flamethrower on you for that comment."

"He can try," smiled the Avion, stretching to her wingtips and yawning. "I kick his dumb ass back to factory settings."

Since it had to cater for the needs – and on the lower decks, the desires – of all of the sector's FTL-capable species and their dependent lifeforms, Vanguard's recreational suite was suitably vast. A saunter around the stalls of its food court alone was like a trip to the galactic zoo: 'If you don't recognise its bodyparts, don't put it in your mouth' was the court's unofficial slogan.

Vonya was long gone, having headed to the station mall in search of a shopping list of specifics from the Avion outlets; Rust was back on the ship on overwatch. Mak 14 knew he was in the doghouse after spectacularly screwing up the stealth controls and nearly getting them killed, so Krieger had despatched him to head into the station to serve out his penance. "You're an infiltrator droid. Go infiltrate," he'd barked at the cowed mech. "Find us an angle, some data, cargo records, a hostage, anything... and don't come back until you've got us something we can use."

The droid had clanked off into the crowds like a moody teenager. Laughing, Kassini, Krieger and Taro made their way over to the milling crowds around the food sector, sidestepping a group of yellow-podded Qaaz'guul – a swarthy, vaguely amphibious race who were causing quite a stir, on account of them being thought extinct until recently. Mentally taxonomising the rush of faces was draining if you weren't used to it. But after a few minutes, the feathery Avions with their stocky Zygs in tow, the occasional opalescent hides of towering Elementals with the colourful gas clouds they kept as exotic pets, the oval security drones, the mean-looking human crews with their heavily customised droids... all coalesced into one flowing stream, as your limbic system somehow learned to accept it as normal.

They slid into a booth at a nearby open-plan diner called Ezy-Squid. The slogan beneath its cartoonish mascot promised to 'Ten-tickle your tastebuds' and when the waiting unit – a shiny droid wearing a badge that read 'Hello my name is Velvet' – hovered over, they ordered beers and various noodle dishes. Kassini opted for a purple herbal tea.

"The repairs will be a couple of hours yet," said Krieger, stretching his legs out along his side of the booth, facing the other two. "Enough time to sink a few and decide what to do with our home movie of the Elementals."

"The obvious move would be to sell it to the Feds," said Taro, lighting a cigarette. An ashtray responded automatically to the cloud of tobacco vapour, and moved across the tabletop towards him.

"Whoever we decide to give it to, we need to do it fast," Kassini ventured. She glanced over her shoulder. "A fleet that size isn't going to stay secret for long."

As she said it, Velvet glided back over with their dishes balanced skilfully in her mechanical appendages. They sat in awkward silence for the half-minute it took the robot to arrange their table and open their bottles before it scooted off back towards the kitchen.

Krieger swigged half of one of his beers down. "The Feds would love to see it, that's true," he said. "They're the ones who could profit from it most. But given my previous with them, I'm asking myself why I'd want to offer them a helping hand."

"I remind you that we have a 50-50 stake in this decision, Captain," said Taro, eyes slightly crossed as they focused on the burning end of his smoke.

Krieger nodded and looked over at Kassini, who was concentrating on noodle manipulation.

"What do you think, Kassini?"

Her chopstick choreography halted for a second as she weighed it up. "The way I see it, the Avion military is the way to go," she replied. "They'll pay in advance if we send them a sample – something the Feds are never keen on doing – and if the latest news feeds are to be believed, they're going to be every bit as concerned about this as the Empire."

"I think you may be right," said Krieger.

"The Avions are in political upheaval back home as always, trying to elect a new leading group with all the inter-factional rivalry bubbling away as ever," Taro pointed out. "Point is, they're nowhere near unified enough to take sides in a war."

"Exactly," said Kassini. "I'd put money on it ruffling the feathers of every Avion who saw it. And if their diplomats didn't forward the footage straight to the Empire anyway, the double-agents the Feds no doubt have in their infrastructure would." She looked down her bowl self-consciously as she said this last part.

Krieger thought it over for a few seconds, unconsciously swaying his bottleneck to and fro between his index and middle finger like a pendulum. "What's to say the Avions wouldn't keep the Feds in the dark and shake hands with the Elementals instead?"

"You can never be sure," said Kassini. "But there have been genuine attempts at cooperation between Feds and Avions – notwithstanding how the one in Venuri turned out – whereas the Avions and Elementals have been cutting each other's throats with no real remorse for decades now. Avion diplomacy may work well with talkative species like us, but they just seem to end up infuriating the Ellies."

"It's deeper than just a mismatch between Avion and Ellie attitudes," Taro added. "The Elementals are ideologically opposed to the Avions' research into genetics, in an almost religious way – and because of that, they basically refuse to accept any overtures as originating in good faith."

Krieger shrugged as he took a swig from his own bottle, and then shook his head with a laugh at Taro before continuing.

"Come on, Krieger you must know this... obviously, just about the whole of Avion stability and advancement for the last couple of centuries now is based on that branch of tech. The Avions are sick of having to apologise for something that wasn't really a choice for them anyway. So they've taken up an aggressive policy of kicking Elementals out of whatever territory they happen to enter, or that the Avion Families happen to have claimed. That's a rift that runs deep, I don't think they'll be signing any pacts any time soon."

Krieger considered this for a moment.

"I think," he said eventually, "...that if and when the shit lands in the cooling system, there'll be a lot more confusion for us to potentially exploit if we don't forewarn the Feds of what's about to hit them too directly. So providing you agree, Taro, that's our decision made. The traffic density outside this station will cover our transmission and make it virtually impossible to trace us once we leave, so can you set up a deal to sell what we have to the Avion diplomatic corps?"

"Consider it done," said Taro, from somewhere within his bowl. "I'll make the first contact while we're here and get the details through to the right desks in their consulate. Then I can actually close it out when we're safely back in space. We'd better be ready to move though, as we'll have the edge over every single other crew in the Empire... that's got to count for something."

"I'll drink to that," said Krieger. They chinked their bottles and glasses.

"I noticed an ad on the way in for the gym they have here," said Kassini, finishing her tea. "I'm going to check it out for a couple of hours. Can you shout me for the noodles?"

Krieger waved her away. "My treat, Kassini... you've saved my life a couple of times already in the short time I've known you. Noodles are on me, from here on in."

"Well, thanks," said Kassini, smiling. Krieger watched her go, exchanged a glance with Taro and beckoned Velvet over for another round.

Kassini made her way up an old-style escalator system in the public concourse towards the gym complex on the station's second level. She was glad to be free of the others, as she'd felt a familiar light-headedness starting to creep up on her during the conversation – the special gift that kept on giving from her time in the Federation Marines, courtesy of her damaged implants.

Under normal circumstances, in a controlled environment like the confines of a starship, she was seldom bothered by the confused presences that warred in her train of thought, manifesting themselves as moments of unusual motivation, sudden spikes in adrenaline or strange, intrusive thoughts that were not her own. But the stresses and strains of the last few days coupled with the station's blurred hustle of activity were proving a test for her control of her psyche. She was fighting to suppress both a hyper-awareness that compulsively magnified overheard excerpts of conversation as though the language made no real sense to her, at the same time as a detachment which, if she tried to focus on it, bordered on a destabilising, out-of-body experience.

She needed somewhere quiet to run through her exercises, so she sat down on a bench opposite an escalator, opting to lifeform-watch while the disquiet in her thoughts subsided. Time passed as she cycled through her mental regime, which she thought of as a kind of inadvertent perception management where if she concentrated on one detail hard enough, eventually, her fractured train of thought would resolve into coherence. It was vaguely like the struggle to see what was hidden in an old-time magic-eye illusion: the harder you thought about it, the less success you had.

After 15 minutes of stillness, the perceptual fuzz and blur of sound receded and she felt a better energy flood back through her limbs. It felt like relief, and after another few minutes of normality she decided now was as good a time as any to report in to Drexler – the sophisticated data-net aboard the station represented the first chance she'd had for a direct conversation with her handler for some time. She activated her tactical overlay, selected for a private comms channel and sent her message back to control.

M

Kassini: Priority. In Vanguard Station,
RT comms available.

Moving on soon, need to establish mission
priorities in light of previous info.

She waited, watching a quarrel break out at the top of the escalator as an angry-looking leather-jacketed human with pirate tattoos shoulderbarged an Avion out of her path. Two security droids moved in as the 'M' indicating Drexler's reply from control flashed in her peripheral vision.

M

Drexler: Your intel has triggered
Empire military response.

Containment of Elemental
fleet operation is in hand.

Your mission priorities remain the same.

Stay with Krieger and the *Anomaly*.

She fired her reply back impatiently.

M

Kassini: Request clarity. You know
Anomaly coordinates, come get her.

Krieger has no major backers or connections.

He's just a bitter pirate.

Like referees at a hoverball game measuring out a free throw, the security droids were setting up a proximity shield to disperse the confrontation playing out in front of her. One hovered in the face of the pirate who bobbed and weaved around it, jabbing her finger at the impassive Avion, whose talon slowly inched towards the holster on her hip as she stood her ground.

Another message blinked.

M

Drexler: Understood. Retrieval
of *Anomaly* is now top priority.

Remain in position to help
when the time comes.

Ship more important than you realise.

Data gathered on its operational
capacity is also of significant value.

M

Kassini: It's getting riskier every day.

Opportunities to split from the
crew are going to be limited.

Factor a way out for me and
Vonya into your plans.

M

Drexler: Naturally, Agent.
We reclaim our own, don't worry.

M

Kassini: Understood. Detail retrieval
plans when you have updates.

Kassini out.

She sent the message and terminated the comms link.

'Great,' sighed Kassini to herself. 'And meanwhile, I'm at the mercy of Krieger's deathwish.'

Up ahead, the Avion turned smartly and walked away from the droids, who hovered over to the human pirate and began administering a fine. 'Good luck with that,' Kassini thought to herself idly, as Krieger's voice buzzed in her ear.

"Hey Kassini," the captain said over the comms. "How's the gym?"

"Much needed. What's up?"

"Sorry to cut it short, but change of plan... we've got to go. The ship maintenance is done, and Mak has had a brainwave, if you can call what he has in his head a brain."

"Another one! What does the crackpot have in mind?"

"He won't reveal all the details, annoyingly. But he says it's a big score and he's managed to sabotage an outbound freighter," Krieger transmitted. "So we're going to need to leave immediately if we're to intercept it before it spins."

"Be back with you in 15," she replied, and shut down the connection.

'Okay,' thought Kassini to herself. So now we're dancing to the tune of Mak 14, an unhinged infiltrator droid... this could go either way.

Passing stalls and outlets which became increasingly chintzy as she got closer to the main dock, Kassini reached the *Anomaly's* designated bay at roughly the same moment as Taro. Krieger and Mak 14 were waiting for them, and the former let them know that Vonya was still a few minutes away as they made their way onto the ship.

As they cleared the ramp into the cargo bay, Krieger called to Mak 14. The captain was rosy cheeked from the extra couple of drinks he'd ordered while waiting, and was smiling at the thought of another chance to test his crew.

"Mak, before we're going anywhere, you need to explain a little more about what we're doing," he said, indicating the others.

The droid was already halfway to the bridge corridor but stopped himself with a clunk and turned his eyes to view them.

"No time, looks like you're just going to have to have faith in good ol' Mak 14 – your trusty robot pal! A vessel known for smuggling is leaving the station shortly with valuable cargo. I intend to commandeer that cargo. Where is the Avion?" Mak replied.

"On her way back. What's the cargo, and how do you know about this?" said Taro.

"I decoded communications in the docking area, then influenced the dock droids which loaded the vessel and had them scan the containers. They contain equipment which will be vital to our future operations," replied the droid. Then he was gone up the ramp towards the bridge at a run, leaving the other three looking at each other, confused.

"You really considering going with this again, Krieger? The droid is insane," said Taro, bluntly.

"It depends. First things first, did you make connections while you were out?" replied Krieger.

"I did. I got lucky... my first call was to one of the attachés at the Avion Embassy here. She was on a delegation I worked with back in the day, and the deal is done. Credits for data – a few frames of that footage and the Avions were on it like a bird feeder and invited me straight to their embassy to hand it over, but I'm not falling for that of course."

"Good, then we need to be in space shortly, anyway. Let's follow Mak's idea up while we get the deal done. If I don't like it, we don't have to go through with it, after all."

They made their way to the bridge, where they found Mak 14 already running checks on the ship's sensors and stealth systems. Krieger ordered the computer to start the preflight engine power-up routine. The sensation of power began to course through the ship and a familiar bass vibration began to rise under their feet as the computer complied.

10 minutes later, Vonya appeared at the door to the bridge with a bag in one hand, and a new, vivid purple-and-white jacket over her regular flight suit.

"Like the jacket," said Krieger. "Find everything you need?"

"Yes Cap. We on the run again?" the Avion replied, dumping the bag and stripping the jacket into a small locker designed for securing items that was recessed into the wall.

"Not as such. Mak wants us to rob a ship of something valuable. Need you to fly."

"Always ready to fly, and got new tunes – will be loud."

The pilot headed quickly for the flight module in a flurry of movement, and before very long *Anomaly's* engine thunder increased markedly and the sensation of smooth movement against the artificial gravity of the station began.

Anomaly exited the yawning mouth of the station and became part of the cloud of ships large and small around it. Some were traversing to and from, others were awaiting docking authorisation, yet others were scanning the passersby or hawking wares. They were still following a standard exit vector a mile out as they passed the long, tapering form of a stationary Ferro-class barge: its entire facing side had been converted into garish neon signage offering a variety of services for weary travellers who might want to skip the hospitality and traffic-control problems of the station at peak times.

Mak's eyestalks were glued to the scanners, weaving gently in opposition to the unnatural stillness of the rest of the droid's shining chrome body, which remained hunched over the console. He reached out a digit and selected an icon just out from the main mass of craft on the scanner and travelling away, then flipped a zoomed image onto the main wallscreen.

"That is the mark, now four minutes ahead of us en route to the sunward spin-point. It is called the *Condor Minor*, and has a small number of crew led by a known smuggler of restricted technology, Commander LeRoy. They operate legally and smuggling is a secondary operation, but they are still flagged by the system authority's automated systems. Bribes are paid on the station to avoid unwanted interest, as is normal."

"Right, I'm still interested, Mak," Krieger replied, looking up from his usual console. "This could be a good test of the *Anomaly's* offensive capacity, and I have no problem pirating a smuggler."

“Last I looked,” interjected Kassini with a shake of her head, “*Anomaly* doesn’t have a ram scoop. How do you suggest we actually get their cargo? They’re not about to just give it to us.”

“I have the exact location of the cargo I am seeking in the ship – it is loaded in armoured containers in the port-side cargo bay, here.” Mak switched the main screen to a zoomed view of the vessel ahead of them, and highlighted a small area on its lower hull with a deft manipulation.

“Furthermore, I have already taken steps to enable access by compelling one of the ship’s own cargo droids to station itself in the relevant hold until it receives my command. I am able to control this unit remotely and have it release the cargo. *Anomaly* just needs to get close enough for me to maintain a connection – we can have this all fixed up in time for supper!”

“While that is pretty damned useful, Mak, it doesn’t change the fact we can’t pick it up,” repeated Kassini, labouring her point.

Mak was unmoved. “The crew of *Condor Minor* can be assumed to notice when they unexpectedly jettison cargo, but the vessel is lightly armed and likely relies on speed to avoid engagements. With our extreme element of surprise, we have a very high probability of successfully forcing them to retreat, using a combination of the fighter and the *Anomaly’s* weapon systems. I can then manually collect the cargo using the main lock before we recover the fighter.”

“A quick heist before we leave,” Krieger said with a laugh. “Why not? Taro, how long before you conclude our other business?”

Taro, who had been working quietly on another station and periodically shaking his head and sighing as Mak explained his plan, looked up.

“I’m awaiting the arrival of our payday now. The footage is verified as ‘awaiting transfer’ from a temporary remote server when the money is safe. It’s out of my hands for the moment,” he replied.

“Keep me posted on that,” Krieger said, switching to comms. “Vonya, start moving in on that freighter I’ve just designated and prepare to activate the stealth systems. And watch nobody flies into us when we disappear from scans.”

The ship began to move, and shadowed the *Condor Minor* most of the way to the outbound spin point. At Krieger’s order, they dropped into their habitual low-light mode that indicated the activation of its stealth system. Kassini smiled at this and said: “For once, the dim lights make sense – we need to hope nobody looks out of a window when we get close enough for Mak to do whatever he needs to do.”

Mak unclipped the influence terminal from his exterior and laid it on the desk as *Anomaly* accelerated and began to eat up the distance to the target ship. They double-checked that the scanner was clear of Fed security patrols this far out. The *Condor Minor* was a slightly larger block of a vessel that grew and resolved on the viewscreen, with four large engines mounted in a square configuration at the rear and two more extended out to the sides of the ship on nascelles. Large cargo-bay extensions were clearly visible: rectangular structures jutting out from either side of and below the ship, obscuring the habitable portions and giving something of the aspect of an ocean tug pulling a larger vessel.

"See the weapon systems?" said Krieger, and keyed for an overlay on the screen in front of them. A bank of turrets on the upper and lower spines of the ship was picked out in green before he continued. "Anti-fighter flak and a couple of autocannons on the upper and lower facing. Scan's a lot quieter now we're further from the station – Vonya, I need you to bring us in as close to the underside of that ship as possible, slightly to her port side."

"Need to keep out of engine output zone on approach," Vonya's disembodied voice replied over the comm system, laser-focused on the task in hand. "Will move in vertical, but new bird's acceleration is constant. They straight-line for the spin point."

All the freighter's engines were visibly active and it was gaining speed. The *Anomaly's* approach elicited no reaction, even as the camera whited out briefly in the engine flare and resolved back into focus to show the closest cargo port with the shape of a large access ramp clearly visible locked into its outer skin. Krieger switched one of the monitors over to show a graphic of the relative position of the two craft. The *Anomaly* was now showing as a few thousand metres below the ship in the vertical plane, but gaining quickly in the horizontal.

"Just like a regular boarding op," Krieger muttered to himself, before speaking up with his eyes still fixed on the screen. "They're completely oblivious. Mak, what's your box telling you?"

"The backdoor in the droid's software is still available, but signal strength is currently too low to reliably connect. This is expected, the ship's armour is between it and us. We will need to move closer," he replied.

Taro piped up behind him. "Money's safe, Krieger. Avions just paid up and took the data, no questions asked. They must have really wanted that footage... and that is one hefty chunk of Cees in the bank."

"Okay, excellent work, Taro – now let's get a bit richer! Mak, do whatever you're going to do as soon as you can do it. Vonya, the computer can power up and prime the launch bay, so pull us away from the freighter into a holding position as Mak gives the okay to do so, and I'll take over up there so you can launch. They still won't know why they've just jettisoned cargo and will presume a malfunction, so we keep the stealth active until the last possible second, then drop it and take out those weapons systems on the lower spine with the *Anomaly* – Kassini, that's you on the guns."

Anomaly was now safely past the big engine ports and had matched acceleration with the freighter hanging above it. Vonya edged the ship gently towards the freighter's port cargo pod from below, manoeuvring thrusters firing intermittently under her fine control. After a minute or two, proximity warnings arrayed on the screen showing the two vessels went from yellow to red.

"Connection now established, I'm tasking the droid to prepare the relevant cargo containers," Mak 14 said, punching a switch on the device in front of him.

"Freighter is still holding course," responded Vonya.

Anomaly hung on station for a further five minutes, a perfect counterpart to the larger vessel, before Mak made his next utterance. Krieger fiddled with one of the cameras to gain a better view of the cargo bay ramp ahead of them.

"The droid is about to override the cargo hatch controls and release the containers. Anomaly should now begin to drop back. Prepare for some action!"

On the screen, the huge bay door ahead of them visibly wobbled as though something heavy had jumped on it from inside. Another wobble, and it distorted slightly at the join to the hull, allowing a burst of air to escape. Two large metallic forks were driven into the resulting gap and began to force the door further open. The *Anomaly's* cameras glimpsed the light from red and yellow warning beacons rotating inside. A cloud of dust spread out eerily from the gap, the lights reflecting from a couple of small unsecured objects that had escaped into the vacuum under the escaping atmosphere's velocity.

Anomaly had begun to drop back and pull away from the ship as per Mak's instructions, as the larger vessel's engines abruptly cut out. Krieger smiled to himself.

"Their crew will be freaking out about the unexpected decompression alarm and swinging their hull cameras to take a look it. They may also see us – so get ready to react if those weapons power up. Mak, hurry it up," he said.

The huge bay door was now about halfway down, but *Anomaly* had dropped back too far to be able to see anything other than its lower half yawning open like a huge dredging scoop. Suddenly, a cube-shaped, tracked droid with several rotating yellow beacons on its main body hurled itself into view to one side of it. It span off with two rectangular cargo containers clamped to its front-mounted hydraulic lifting appendages. After a few seconds, the droid released the containers and the three objects bounced off one another to slowly diverge in separate directions.

"Time to switch, Vonya," said Krieger.

"Hear you, Captain," replied the Avion, and abruptly cut her comms as Krieger made for the flight module. The others heard Krieger tell the Avion to "give them the fright of their lives" as they passed one another, before Vonya singlemindedly plunged through the bridge and down towards the cargo bay and her waiting fighter.

The comms loop to the flight module reactivated to the sound of Krieger settling in.

"...left the damned display in Avion, switch it back, will you, computer? Kassini, the freighter has started up engines again and is turning away from us – they've got to have seen us on visual by now. Drop stealth and burn those turrets out. The ship may have shields we don't want them to get up while they can still shoot at us."

"Stealth systems deactivated," replied the computer. "Normal systems restored, weapons primed."

Kassini had the same view from the cameras on the tablet closest to her and drew a single line with her forefinger across the turrets lining the bottom of the freighter, now about 200 metres above them. Their main laser emplacement, mounted at the front of the *Anomaly's* square bulk where it tapered down in front of the flight module, spun to her target and bathed the area in a thick beam of frosty green fire. The auto-cannon array was scythed apart and reduced to molten goo, and a number of small secondary explosions spat chunks of armour and red-hot metal out into space.

The bigger ship rolled now, strangely graceful in what was an essentially random evasive manoeuvre. Its engines flared to maximum boost. Krieger pushed the *Anomaly's* manoeuvring thrust to move further away from the ship, while also working hard to move in tandem with the roll of the other vessel in order to keep their topside in line with its now defenceless underside as they diverged.

"No shield activation has been detected Krieger, and the *Condor Minor's* comms just went active. They're broadcasting on the standard ship-to-ship channel," the computer offered.

"Kreeg-ar, quit rolling. I can't launch!" Vonya's voice cut in.

"Understood, I'll level us out," Krieger said, concern in his voice. "Taro, open up the comms and let's see what they have to say."

Taro's usual unease in combat was evident as he stabbed at the comms pad in front of him.

A male voice suddenly filled the cabin, sounding surprisingly relaxed given the issues its owner must have been facing at that moment.

"...we are a lightly armed trading vessel, your attack is in violation of Federal space-lane guarantees. Withdraw and allow us to leave the area. Repeat, this is Captain LeRoy of the *Condor Minor*, we are a trade freighter, godsdamnit..."

The computer's voice dipped into the message to announce: "The fighter has launched, Captain."

"Best hope nobody official picked that transmission up, Krieger," added Taro.

LeRoy's voice returned, to be cut off by Krieger's, responding on the same channel.

"Captain LeRoy. I notice you're not broadcasting a distress call to the local law-enforcement network, which suggests your 'trading' isn't anything of the legal sort. It's fortunate for you and your crew it isn't in my interest to punish your ship any further. But let this be the lesson that teaches you there's always a vigilante out there somewhere, waiting to punish those who transgress Federation trade law."

Kassini and Taro looked at each aghast before they registered the laughter behind Krieger's words, both realising he was playing to the crowd. The captain's voice continued.

"Turn away from our ship and burn your engines at maximum thrust towards the second planet where you can make repairs. Our fighter will escort you out of range."

As though in answer to this, Vonya's ship hovered into view on the camera directly in front of the freighter's flight-module viewport and fired an off-axis burst of ammunition across its bow, missing the ship by a metre or less. Then her fighter dipped down below it again, back to a station on its rear lower quarter, just off from the damaged cargo pod.

Captain LeRoy's voice returned, sounding more shaken.

"Agreed, Captain Unknown, I have no idea how you got close to us like that… but it's all just a risk we take in our line of business. Live and let live, I say. We are making our turn immediately. *Condor Minor* out."

Mak 14 waited until the freighter began to rotate away from *Anomaly* on the monitors and its engines flared into life, before clipping his terminal back in place as he said: "I will prepare to collect the cargo containers, Rust will be required to help with the process."

"Okay, I'll bring us on station above the nearest container. Kassini, keep the weapons trained on the freighter until it's well out of range," Krieger responded. The droid quickly left the bridge. Kassini and Taro followed his hydraulic clanking until he descended to the cargo bay. They looked at one another.

"As simple as that?" said Kassini, with her comms mic deactivated. "No near-death experience, only one shot fired? I believe Captain Krieger and Mak the lunatic droid just pulled off a heist with no hitches and no bodycount."

"Looks that way, for once," replied Taro. "That's the thing with Mak – his ideas are usually both brilliant and suicidally dangerous at the same time. But his motivations are difficult to understand, aren't they? I wonder what the hell he's actually after in those pods… they have to be hauling some seriously illegal stuff to not call for help. I'd wager it's an arms freighter, or military equipment, something that has to be worth some serious money, anyway."

"Soon find out," Kassini said. As she finished the sentence, Krieger reappeared from the flight module door.

"I've handed over to the computer for now," he said. "Tidy little operation that, wasn't it?"

"Highly illegal and some big Cees in damage to that other ship, but we were just saying the same," replied Kassini, still looking at the weapons-targeting readings in front of her. "What does Mak want in those containers, though? If it's weaponry, I can probably fence any we don't need."

Krieger strolled nonchalantly to his usual station and quickly reprogrammed the sensor output to the main screen to show the *Anomaly's* relative position to the cargo pods before replying.

"It's easy to think of him as a droid, and therefore under our command, isn't it? Thing is, I told you he's an independent operator. He won't be drawn on precisely how far he will or won't follow my orders when I ask him, but I do know he's looking to get paid like most everybody else, if in a strange, roundabout way. So I guessed this little move must be his way of getting some of the high-grade technology he likes to collect so much."

"Fair enough… even I admit he's been invaluable so far," added Taro.

"He is, but he always walks the tightrope," Kassini replied.

"That's how he rolls, I guess. He's more complicated than your average dishwasher droid, that's for sure," shrugged Taro. "The *Condor Minor* is out of range now, too, incidentally."

"Yeah, good. So let's see what the droid is up to now."

Krieger switched part of the large wall screen to the external cameras, and ranged them on the *Anomaly's* cargo ramp. Mak had partially lowered it, and was standing in the stellar vacuum beneath the ship with one arm holding onto the hydraulic stanchion nearest him to retain position in the zero gravity. Next to him, visible from the telltale sinister red pulse across his front, the dark spherical shape of Rust hovered; the anti-grav-equipped droid requiring no such tether to the now-stationary ship.

The spindly droid reached its other arm across to Rust and took hold of an armour joint, then released the stanchion to do the same with its other arm. Rust then engaged his drive and hauled both of them across space to the cargo container which was just visible spinning gently below them, tipping Mak down toward it. The mechanical arms switched to grab onto the container quickly to avoid any possibility of the momentum yanking him clear of his steed. Then Mak's small, nimble form transferred onto the uppermost surface of it in a crouch, like an insect stepping from one branch to another.

One arm unhooked the end of a length of pliable carbon-fibre chain the droid had clipped firmly to its back and connected it to the container, before reaching up to clip the other end to a handy loop on Rust's armour. The big battle droid then proceeded to stop the container's momentum with a burst of movement, and drag both it and Mak 14 back up towards the open cargo ramp.

Watching on the monitor, Krieger laughed as the container was secured to the ramp at the other end of the journey, and the whole structure began to rise back up into the cargo bay.

"You've got to hand it to them, they can definitely solve problems," he said, looking at the scanner to see Vonya was on her way back in her fighter. "Once they've reeled this other one in, we can go find out what they've caught."

The second retrieval was as painless as the first under Mak's expert management. The ship's scanners gave no sign of any retribution for their act from the system authorities, even when the computer reported that a squadron of Federal fighters passed along the outer limits of their scan range, giving them pause for thought. Soon the crew were assembled in the cargo bay, looking at the two oblong containers on the deck in front of them as Mak 14 set about one with a complex-looking set of tools.

Vonya had declined to redock her fighter for the moment, citing the chance to recalibrate some flight systems. Krieger had instructed the computer to head for the quietest patch of space it could find in the busy system, not wanting to risk a straight run to the spin point in case the target of their endeavours had any heavily armed friends prepared to exact revenge for the cargo theft. Vonya's fighter was doing dummy attack runs from above and below when they left the bridge for the cargo bay.

Rust hovered off to one side from the containers, presumably eyeing the foreign objects with his usual belligerence as Mak addressed him.

"I must scan the containers thoroughly – it is not unknown for them to be rigged in order to catch out the unwary pirate. Rust will also scan, to double-check my results."

"Affirmative," replied the battle droid, and both of them deployed a number of sensory implements towards the metallic containers. The nearest one to Mak was dented from its ordeal, and both had a patina of dirt and scrapes from many years of use.

"I register no explosive, corrosive or other potentially harmful substances. There are metallic objects and several dormant power sources stored within, packed in vacuum," Rust intoned, eventually. Krieger and Kassini looked over at one another, intrigued.

"I concur," Mak replied. "Humans should move away from the immediate vicinity while I access the first, nevertheless."

Mak deployed a small terminal from his pack as the more vulnerable members of the crew backed towards the ramp leading out of the cargo bay, and interfaced it with the control panel for the nearest container. After some moments, several red lights flared on its surface, switched to green, and a hiss of air became just audible over the hum of the ship.

"Atmosphere equalised," said Mak. This was followed by the clunk of a locking mechanism. The droid reached for the toolkit to select a simple crowbar and smacked it into a visible join towards the top of the container. He flipped the hinged, sarcophagus-like lid open in one movement, catching it with his other manipulator arm as it reached the zenith of its arc. Kassini noticed two semi-spherical indentations cut into the padding of the lid to accommodate whatever the cargo was.

"And tonight's star prize –" he said, with simulated satisfaction stolen from some gameshow or other, "two new-condition Kontaro Eight base units, plus accessories, as expected. The other crate should contain the same manifest."

The others approached the crate and peered inside. Laid within, surrounded by foam and a lattice-like honeycomb of acceleration-dampening material, were two orb-shaped droid bodies around a metre and a half in diameter, along with a variety of accessories, all vac-sealed in a perfect sheen of plastic.

Krieger examined the units for a few more moments, and was the first of the crew to recover from his surprise to speak.

"You did all that to steal some multipurpose ship's droids? You said these would be critical to our future operations, right? I thought you'd uncovered a shipment of mil-grade battle weapons or something!"

The eyestalk turned to Krieger slowly, a world-weary motion that perfectly conveyed his contempt.

"I should have expected you not to understand the utility of my choice immediately, Captain," he explained. "These are brand new and extremely effective multipurpose units utilising a logic system I can easily manipulate and reprogram. They come with anti-grav systems similar to the one installed in Rust, but newer and much more efficient, hence their much smaller size. They can be tasked to operations both onboard the ship and in atmospheres. They are a significant multiplier to many of the capabilities I have that you have recently relied on to keep you alive."

"And if you reprogram them, will they be lunatics like you and Rust?" snarled Taro, recovering enough to uncharacteristically lose his cool. "This isn't an episode of *Top Droid* – the *Anomaly* is brand new, it's not like it's going to need too much routine maintenance... and we're *supposed* to be trying to avoid trouble, not tooling ourselves up to find more of it!"

Rust's voice boomed across the bay, startling Taro.

"The least combat-effective of the humans should now turn off speech! You will see new unit functional superiority when they are between you and the advancing enemy, or plugging holes in the ship to save the oxygen you require. Crew and ship have many enemies, more droids are now needed to efficiently destroy them!"

This constituted a full soliloquy from the usually taciturn killing machine, and Taro was suitably chastened, shutting up immediately. Mak 14 leant down over the box, lifted the first of the orbs out and began to strip it of its packaging.

"Taro Watanabe, you should know that the market price of these droids is currently between 20 and 25,000 Empire standard credits. *Per unit*," 14 said, swivelling his eyestalk to face him. "Times this by four and you have a significant sum to a human with an interest in such things, do you not?"

Taro went from flushed and huffing to calm and smooth-talking in a second, the transformation making Kassini laugh out loud.

"Keep two, sell two... forget I said anything Mak, my friend, just be careful not to break any of them," he said, rubbing his face and coming up with a smile.

Krieger stepped back from the box and turned to his crew. "Well, that's agreed, then – today has been a very profitable day and I have to say I'm proud to be the captain of this ship. Mak, against all the odds, that was great work. Get these droids up and running ASAP. I suspect the non-mechanical lifeforms aboard this ship are as tired as I am with the few days we've had, so let's call Vonya home and take the opportunity to get some rest while we figure out the best way to lose ourselves again, shall we, people?"

He headed for the ramp to the upper level, stopping to give Taro a friendly open-palmed whack on the shoulder as he passed. The XO smiled a grifter's grin and turned to follow.

Kassini was left watching them go, a faint expression of worry on her face. She reminded herself to update her handler with the crew's new droid manifest, wondering how Drexler ever intended to retake the *Anomaly*. She also wondered how many members of the crew, who she was genuinely starting to like, she would be expected to kill or injure when the Federation made their move...

M

Kassini: Drexler – Krieger's next
move is proving unpredictable.

The crew has salvaged
four additional droids.

How closely is your
taskforce shadowing us?

M

Drexler: This is working out according
to plan, Kassini. But another piece
of the puzzle is about to be placed.

Sit tight.

Drexler out

12. MISSION OF MERCY

The crew needed to lose themselves in more ways than one after the breathless exertions of the past few days. After they elected for the anonymity of joining the shoal of trader traffic en route to the Empire's prosperous inner worlds, Krieger granted 24 hours of R&R and disappeared to his quarters. Taro, desperate for proof that their footage had percolated through to Federation high command via the Avions, continued monitoring every comms-buoy they came within range of, scouring the channels impatiently for the beginnings of a chain reaction he was sure would come.

Mak 14 spent his downtime in the cargo hold, reprogramming and refitting two of the newly acquired Kontaro Eights. When Kassini had looked in on him on a whim, she saw the droid at his makeshift workbench, soldering and updating code simultaneously, chassis bathed in the blue of an endlessly spooling backdrop of ancient films that were feeding his hyperactive databanks with dialogue snippets. She thought better of interrupting his strange mech reverie and instead joined Vonya on a sofa she'd dragged to the rear of the CiC, where she'd commandeered the ship's main screen to catch up on a subtitled Elemental soap called *Parallel Sons*.

"This guy is hilarious," she told Kassini in Avion, filling her in on the plotline, such as it was. "He works in a virtual-reality hub and he's fallen in love with his co-worker, but she's only interested in him when he's in the VR as an avatar."

"The dialogue is really weird," said Kassini, declining Vonya's offer of a gristly looking, vaguely brine-scented Avion snack she'd bought on her shopping trip at Vanguard Station.

"I know," Vonya cawed. "It started out like some stiff, government-sponsored morality play. But if you read between the lines, it's like the show creators are actually rooting for the characters to rebel. I love it..."

Before she knew it, Kassini was snacking on popcorn and trying to persuade Vonya to cue up the series finale. Every once in a while, they glanced over as a blip emanated from Rust who, sans his bulky outer armour, was bolted to a makeshift workbench and connected to Mak 14's terminal for software maintenance and defragging. The droid dreamt of mercilessly obliterating targets, the human crew blissfully unaware of his inner workings.

Eventually, Taro tore himself away from his comms vigil and rapped his knuckles discreetly on the metal door of Krieger's quarters. He heard the captain's voice say 'open' and the door slid smoothly to the side. Inside, Krieger was lying in his overalls on his bunk with his arms behind his head, an ancient-looking paperback called *The Stars My Destination* splayed open across his chest.

"Sorry to interrupt, Krieger."

"No bother, I was just dozing. The last few days have been manic."

"Good book?"

Krieger tucked his neck into his chest to remind himself what he'd been reading. "Oh, that. Yeah, it's very... imaginative. Some old 20th-century classic Kassini lent me. She practically arm-wrestled me into reading it."

Taro pulled up a chair and sat down. On the bedside table were Krieger's reading glasses and a bottle of Imperial Navy rum, amazingly still two-thirds full. Krieger followed his eyes.

"Great idea, Mr Watanabe. That came with the ship. There are two glasses in the locker."

Taro put the drinks together as he spoke. "Now we're back in range, I've been catching up on the FedNet and various comms. As I was browsing through, I came across something I think you'll be intrigued by."

Krieger leant up on one elbow and fished out his tablet from the covers. "What am I looking for?"

"Here, pass me it..." Taro typed a search and cast a news report onto the screen at the end of Krieger's bed. A young and very shiny Empire anchorwoman sat at a chrome desk in front of a dramatic-looking embossed logo forming the letters 'NNN'.

"In the past hour, *Nightly News Nebula* has learned that a mystery epidemic has swept through a number of Elemental planets in the V718 Persei sector, two systems across from the Empire-Elemental Demilitarised Border. The virus is a novel strain of a deadly historical disease thought to have long-been eradicated among the Elemental population. It is potentially harmful to Avion citizens, but is not transmissible to humans.

"Empire officials have confirmed that the rate of infection is currently out of control and that quarantining the affected planets is a top priority. Shortly before we went on air, the Federal government's ambassador to the Avion sector, Ariella Diaz, gave the following statement..."

The report crossed to a tall, severe-looking government official who stood at a podium in an Empire conference chamber. Behind her was a moodlit flag emblazoned with the Empire's blue and orange Earth-and-moon graphic in the centre of its vivid background.

"Citizens of the Eastern-sector homeworlds," Diaz said to the assembled press. "Over the past 72 hours, a viral epidemic has broken out on the planets of Adeccar B, C and E in the Elemental-controlled V718 Persei territory. The epidemic has spread uncontrollably and the situation is worsening by the hour; we can confirm that while there is a high risk of infection to Elemental and Avion citizens, the virus cannot transmit to human physiology. Therefore, the Elemental government has reached out to our species for our assistance. And we are calling upon all humans within reach of the sector to help us to minimise the impact of what could quickly become an Elementarian catastrophe.

"This is a sector-wide plea to all human personnel with jump-capable ships to report to Empire fleet representatives at emergency evacuation stations in orbit around the infected planets. Diplomatic immunity and temporary amnesty on all legal-status checks is assured: a generous reward will be granted to all human crews and independent traders who are able to successfully assist with the evacuation..."

"Generous reward, eh?" said Krieger over the commentary. "Just how much are they talking?"

Taro shushed him and pointed back at the press conference.

"...this operation will help our Elemental friends at their time of greatest need. The protection of innocent civilians of all species is the Empire's top priority. The rescued personnel will be taken to designated safe havens on Federation worlds until they can be safely transported back to be reunited with their friends and family in Elemental space."

They cut back to the gleam of the studio set and Taro turned the broadcast off. "I've looked into it... They're offering every ship a minimum of 5,000 credits for turning up and helping move the refugees offworld. That covers over a quarter of what we paid for the Boneyard repairs, right there."

"Yeah, it's a pretty attractive fee for such a straightforward job. It's also peculiar timing for the Empire to extend the olive branch to the Elementals, especially given what we've just seen..." Krieger said, tapping at his tablet. "Still, the pirate channels are buzzing with crews heading to the emergency. It looks legit."

"It has to be. It's far too elaborate to just be a Federation trap to lure the mercs – it's in the wrong part of space, for a start. So what do you say?" said Taro, draining his rum.

Krieger did likewise. "We're within jump range, and since we're a pirate crew with a heart of gold, it's exactly the kind of thing we're supposed to do..." He shared a wry smile with Taro at this. "I say, what was it? Let's go and help our Elemental friends at their time of greatest need."

The *Anomaly* was waiting in traffic on their approach to Adeccar C, the largest of the planets in the infected system. 14 and Rust were powered down and Vonya was back in the hold, checking over her fighter after its recent battles, wanting no part of a mission that involved a virus potentially lethal to Avions. The rest of the crew twiddled their thumbs in the cabin.

"Our platoon worked security at the Hoverball final back in '77, at a system near Vega," drawled Kassini, as she panned the cameras over the other ships in the queue and settled on a giant oblong freighter bristling with weapons hard points, sporting an Epsilon Zoo Corporation logo on its prow. "That's the last time I can remember seeing so many different ships in one place."

"I remember '77," said Taro. "That was the one with Cheik Hasani's famous overtime double for the Geckos, right?"

"I don't recall… I was watching the crowd the whole time. But I remember they all went nuts at the end, and leaving the stadium, it looked just like this. It took hours."

She carried on up the line of traders, pirates, battered cargo transport ships and even commercial pleasure liners, obviously redirected in a hurry by their company bosses to make a profitable impromptu pitstop.

"If I was an Elemental refugee, I think I'd rather be assigned to one of those luxury starboats with thermal pools and five-star catering than the galley of some sweaty merc crate, somehow," said Taro. "But I suppose they're only being ferried to the Federal transports in orbit and then being moved on to safe systems."

"You ever study the Elemental? They'd see the heated water aboard our ships as a pretty grave affront to the natural order of things. Transports are on the far side of the temporary orbital station. I'll show you."

Kassini switched the viewfinder to show the hastily bolted-together girders of the Empire outpost station drifting in geosynchronous orbit over the grey-green of Adeccar C's massive, solitary landmass, which was being slowly riven by its first tectonic cracks.

Behind it, a phalanx of Empire-military Uridium-class support transports moved into position one by one to dock with the steady flow of outgoing civilian ships returning from the planet surface. Uridium freighters were minimally crewed workhorses tailored to cargoes of fleet weaponry and machinery: a large proportion of these Elemental refugees were going to have to rough it in the holds on their onward journeys.

A patrol of six Federation interceptors flew past the *Anomaly*'s portholes along either side of the line of inbound ships. Their deployed weapons systems were a reminder to the galaxy's more anarchic denizens to play nice and not even think about queue-jumping, quarrelling, or perhaps even slamming a couple of missiles into the freighters dangling placidly in front of their crosshairs and cargo scoops.

"So where are the Ellies?" asked Krieger. "I know they can't pick up the refugees from the planet for fear of spreading the virus, but we're still outside the demilitarised zone and they're so paranoid I expected to see at least a couple of battleships stationed out here."

"According to the Empire station's official transmission, received on entry to the sector, all Elemental fleets are currently out of range," the computer announced.

"Gods, this virus must be a freaking plague," said Kassini.

The computer played an incoming transmission from the Empire station on the screen. It announced that the *Anomaly* would be in the next wave of rescue ships, sent the coordinates of their designated city's main spaceport and asked for their account details. Once again, they were reassured of their anonymity and legal immunity for the duration of the action and that credits would be transferred as soon as their passengers had boarded the Uridiums.

"Well, considering they've thrown it together in a hurry, this is a pretty well-run operation," said Krieger. "Let's prep for landing and tidy up a bit for our guests."

The district surrounding the starport was typical of a well-established terraformed Elemental colony. From 10 miles or so up, they saw how the rich blanket of overlapping green forest canopy and taller trees on the slopes of the mountainous landscape was punctuated by neat, equidistant rectangles cleared to accommodate the infrastructure of Elemental society. Giant reservoirs perched at the foot of the slopes were surrounded by the swathes of almost-temporary-looking pod structures that the Elementals, with their hunter-gatherer past looming large in their technological outlook, preferred over more permanent structures. Sprawling solar- and wind-energy harnessing plantations were dotted at strategic points around the outskirts.

As they neared the surface, they picked out raised tubular public-transport structures crisscrossing the landscape like a more elegantly designed arterial version of the Empire's historical L-train tracks. The centre of the city was given over to an intimidating temple-like structure – this was one of the gladiatorial arenas that the race used to channel their innate warlike impulses.

Otherwise, the scene was a stark contrast to the industrial sprawl of smoke and neon that greeted you when landing on a typical Empire colony. Elemental society had no tolerance for the mega malls, vast slums, skyscrapers and the ever-present chaos of aerial traffic and pollution that starved the Empire's bustling streets of starlight.

The *Anomaly* followed the flightpath of a light merc privateer into the Elemental starport. Below them, they counted rows of spherical airliners grounded on their landing pads along the strip. Aside from the inbound rescue ships, the only air activity they could see was from the Elementals' wasp-like transporters, no doubt laden with evacuees, hovering closer to the surface.

After following the landing indicators to a designated hangar at the edge of the strip and touching down inside, they opened the bay doors to a rush of choking heat. It was a boiling, humid and rainy day on Adeccar C, just the way the Elementals liked it. Their fast metabolisms preferred higher temperatures and that was reflected in the way they adjusted the weather controls of their colonies: unfortunately for them, conditions were apparently ideally suited to the spread of the virus, too.

Krieger, Kassini and Taro took the opportunity to stretch their legs and clanked down the ramp to the runway to feel the misty, hot drops of rain soak into their skin. Taro sparked up a cigarette while Krieger trained his binoculars on the terminal windows and described the scenes at the departure lounge gates.

Empire troops wearing light body armour and armed with crowd-control weaponry cordoned off the entryways. Beyond the desks, five or more parallel lines of Elemental citizens, many huddled together into family units, passed through bio-scanners at security points. In the couple of minutes or so Krieger watched, Fed troops dragged off 10 or more separate Elementals to a holding area – one of the infected specimens struggled and protested, pulling down two of the Fed troops as he was separated from his family before eventually being overpowered and dragged off to quarantine.

Smaller hovercraft were crossing from the terminal and one peeled off to make a beeline for their bay. "I think our passengers are here," Krieger said, lowering his binoculars to rest around his neck.

The craft pulled up silently and its curved shell, made of a light-reactive perspex-like material, lifted to reveal four Elemental passengers – a male, female and two young children. The parents deposited the kids on the runway and gathered together their luggage. The hovercraft glided away and the father approached Krieger, holding out his long three-fingered hand palm-up in a misrecognition of the human handshake gesture. Krieger took his hand and delivered a complex handshake that he'd learned from his time in Elemental prison. The handshake pattern, he knew, was as individual to each Elemental as the fingerprint of a human or the head feathers of an Avion, and to learn another individual's well was important in their social customs.

The Elemental's skin pigment segued to a cooler tone and he laughed out loud as he missed several steps of Krieger's well-practised motion. The chattering cluster of harmonised notes sounded vaguely like an amphetamine-fuelled flute solo.

He spoke, in the ultra-rapid, beautifully resonant dual-harmony Elemental tongue. Krieger responded in the crunchy, guttural Elemental that was the only kind suited to the human larynx. "Hi, Ny'Esta, was it? You'll have to speak more slowly – my Elemental languages are rusty," he said, the pattern of alien fingers on his palm also having communicated a part of the creature's given name to him.

"My mistake," Ny'Esta said, lowering his head in a reflex of shame. "We do not often speak with humans, and I forget how fast our speech appears to you."

"Who do we have here?" said Kassini, also in the Elemental tongue, smiling at the infants, who hid behind their mother. Their skin, which had not yet bloomed into the iridiscence of adulthood, modulated between different shades of light purple and orange-y yellow; Kassini took it for a blush.

"Don't be shy, we're just here to take you for a spaceship ride," she said. "Would you like that?"

The larger of the two children, a specimen already nearly as tall as Kassini, nodded and then paused suddenly, staring past her. Its skin pigment went pure white very briefly as it pointed to Taro and burst into excited tones.

The second alien answered in a rich harmonic flourish as it gently took the child's outstretched hand.

"Oldest displays fear and intrigue," the other Elemental said, haltingly but in a language Kassini understood. "We have never seen a human emitting smoke before. I am... well, you can call me Haq. And these two are Haq'an and Ny'Estala. Our hunters among the stars are endebted to you. May we also share our – what is the word – hand... dance?"

"Handshake. And I would be honoured," Krieger said, and repeated the complex routine with Haq. Taro glanced from the aliens to his cigarette before grinding it under his boot.

Kassini finished off the rest of the introductions as they boarded the ship. The Elemental adults were ridiculously tall compared to humans and Avions and they nearly had to duck through the bay opening; as they walked ahead, Taro surreptitiously analysed them. Krieger and Kassini were more familiar with Elementals than he was and acted completely naturally, but he found himself trying hard not to stare at their wiry, incredibly strong, almost insectoid physiques and the band-shaped visual organ that stretched from ear-to-ear. Most strikingly of all to someone who'd only been in their company a few times in his life was the powerful jawline, containing rows of sharklike teeth. It was, he decided from his admittedly anthropocentric viewpoint, a face only a mother could love.

"We're here to help," said Kassini, warming to her role as the charming rescuer.

"Plus, we're getting 5,000 credits," Krieger whispered to Taro in English.

Ny'Esta turned to face the captain as they reached the cabin entrance. "How much?"

"Sorry, I didn't think you could understand," Krieger prevaricated, looking away from Ny'Esta's sense organ, slightly embarrassed.

"It is no problem," the Elemental said in English, and then switched back to Elemental: "It is just worrying for us that there's such a high reward value. We wondered why so many humans were rushing to our aid..."

"Humans who would normally celebrate the news of our deaths with a cold beverage, I believe is how you say it," Haq added.

"Aaaanyway, talking of which," Kassini expertly interrupted. "Let's go and sit down inside, shall we? I'll get you a drink while we prepare for orbit. Do your little ones want some food? We have some cold krebbits in our fridge."

As *Anomaly* raced smoothly towards the upper layers of atmosphere over Adeccar C, Taro and the Elemental children knelt around the porthole. Taro pointed to structures on the ground, and the kids – now full of krebbits – took it in turns to pronounce what he was looking at. Every time they did, Taro contorted his face into a random expression of shock, surprise or delight, and the Elementals cracked up laughing. They were an easy crowd.

"Well, your children are keeping Taro here entertained," Kassini said to Haq as they sipped tea from their lidded inflight beakers. "The orbital platform is overwhelmed getting your people out, so we've been directed to a secondary rendezvous out near the spin point, meaning you'll be onboard for a little while longer than planned. Tell me, how bad was the situation down there?"

"The virus is a strain of an old disease that we had eradicated a century ago now, I suppose," said Haq, with slow and deliberate enunciation. "How it appeared again out of nowhere is basically a mystery of the essence – an act of the gods, you would say."

"We have argued a fair bit about this already," Ny'Esta added. "Haqur'hur-Faaaaagong here takes an altogether more altruistic view than I do."

"He thinks the universe is out to get us," Haq sighed. "Whereas I think that it is just unfortunate."

"But what do you think happened, Ny'Esta?" Kassini asked.

"I just think that a long-dead virus coming out of nowhere and rushing through our population like an uncontrolled fire is suspicious. You know our language, so you must also know that in our culture, we know the workings of nature like we know our own children. An outbreak like this has never happened to us in modern times, across the whole of our empire."

Haq leant in to Kassini in mock confidentiality, her serried razor teeth inches from the sergeant's face. "He thinks this so-called 'strange epidemic' could be an artificially engineered disease... but he'd always rather listen to the echo trails than hear the call of the hunt..."

Krieger had been listening in and it was his turn to interrupt. "We may be doing this for the money, but I assure you that our intentions here are honourable."

"Captain Krieger, the intentions of you and your crew are not in question. We repeat to you – we thank our gods for the kindness you have shown." From his time in Elemental prison, Krieger recognised these long-winded explanations as an expression of heartfelt belief: Elementals had developed such rituals over thousands of years as a ceremonial way of defusing conflict among their hotheaded and warlike tribespeople.

"Yet what happens when we're loaded onto the Federation transports? We have no idea where these safe havens are that they promise to take us to."

"You're just paranoid," Haq said, dismissively.

Krieger looked over at Taro and the kids, the smallest of whom was now riding on his back. "Look, we don't have to hand you over to the Empire at all. Would you prefer that we took you somewhere else instead?"

"That is kind of you to offer," said Ny'Esta, with a slight bow. "However, it would be dangerous to travel through our systems. And it would mean that you would not receive your credits."

"Also," Haq added. "What is the human expression? Sometimes you must 'go where the thermal takes you'. No, that's the Avion version. Anyway, we will be among our people wherever we go. We'll be fine."

"Uridium transport in range. 10 minutes until docking procedure," the computer's synth voice updated them, shocking the Elemental children. They instantly began to mimick it with their harmonious larynxes, which was actually pretty funny.

"If you're certain," said Krieger. "But if you get cold feet, then you let us know."

"Cold feet?" said Haq, puzzled. "I haven't heard that one. Is that when you step into a mountain stream?"

"Kind of. It's like suddenly feeling nervous," Kassini explained. "Cold feet is one of the physiological symptoms humans get when they feel anxious."

The Elementals looked at each other. "I like that," said Ny'Esta to his wife. "Cold feet."

Haq seemed to consider this for a moment before replying. "You humans might say we of the Elemental are a race with 'cold feet', I think."

The Elemental family were bedded down comfortably, if in somewhat cramped style, in the *Anomaly*'s small mess – the crew had figured this was more sensible than the cargo bay given the potential combination of their droids' equipment and weaponry and the childrens' natural curiosity. Vonya was back at the helm, sealed in the flight module having issued strict instructions not to allow any of the potentially infectious Elementals into the bridge or corridor which connected it to the rest of the ship.

Kassini had retired to her bunk in light of this, taking the opportunity to relax during the routine flight. She'd been involved in her fair share of humanitarian and rescue missions over her years of service, and she was thinking this one seemed a little too well organised.

As if reading her mind, the little green 'M' appeared and began blinking in her vision. She smiled with a mix of amusement and some irritation, considering the recent dealings with the ship's resident diplomat. Taro may have known about her supposedly secret sideband comms channel to her handler, but there was almost no way he would be able to eavesdrop the messages, she decided as she accessed it.

M

Drexler: Your location suggests that you're
involved in the humanitarian op at Adeccar.

Be aware: Fed involvement is cover
for capture of Elemental collateral.

Drexler out.

Kassini sat upright. The message burnt into her vision, moving with her view and obscuring the edge of the small wash basin on the other side of her cramped quarters. She thought the relevant command to delete it. It was troubling news and it prompted her to go and find Taro.

He eventually answered the door to his own quarters at a knock, looking fatigued.

"Was trying to sleep, those kids are tiring," he said, leaning against the frame of the entrance to a room almost identical to her own.

"I need to talk to you," Kassini replied, and the earnest tone gave the younger man a moment's pause. He looked down the corridor before beckoning her inside and closing the door behind her.

"Just a moment," he said, sitting down on a bunk identical to her own, and leant over a small shelf above his head to flick a switch on a cube of electronics.

"Stops the computer listening," he said with a shrug as he turned back. There was nowhere to sit, so she looked around and elected to lean back against the doorframe.

"Smart. I've had a message from my handler and those Ellies are right to be concerned. This is no mercy mission we're on."

"What did they tell you?" Taro asked.

"'Capture of Elemental collateral' was the phrase they used."

"Dirty fuckers," Taro spat, uncharacteristically. "Confirms the worst fears of our passengers. You think they mean to kidnap a whole colony? The Elementals are pretty aggressive when directly challenged – one way or another, it'd mean war, right?"

"I think so. The Feds wouldn't organise an operation like that unless they were prepared to back it up. It's a blatant provocation."

Taro sighed and scratched at his face. "Every action begets a reaction, doesn't it?" he said "The Federation now knows the Elementals are massing forces and conducting manoeuvres, and they don't know the details of the new technology our footage has demonstrated they can deploy. They were bound to do something, though I wouldn't have put Cees on it being this. Maybe I should have."

He paused for a moment, looking away to think about it.

"It'll be a unilateral move, too – I've been keeping an eye on the comms channels we tapped, and the Avions are clearly not in a position to get involved in a showdown," Taro continued. "Their agents are flying all over the galaxy trying to keep a lid on their involvement with flipping that backwater system after the station operation, and to be honest, I'm surprised they had the courage to do that in the first place. Seems they really did take the idea of cooperation with the Federation to heart after our skirmishes with them finally ended and they'd realised how militarily underdeveloped they are. They've genuinely been trying to stay on the Feds' good side ever since."

Taro smiled briefly and looked at Kassini pointedly, with something like amusement in his eyes.

"Foolish," he concluded. "Regardless of what it tries to instil in you military types, the Federation never negotiates in good faith."

"So what?" said Kassini in annoyance. "We're just going to hand this family over? They're just colonists, Taro – civilians. None of this is anything to do with them. We bear some responsibility here."

"I fail to see any other choice – we can't tell Krieger any of this, and I'll bet you there's a cordon of Federation warships at every spin point three systems deep to make sure the Elemental military can't intervene. We should be at the rendezvous by now, and you heard them say they didn't want to go elsewhere. Anyway, where would we take them?"

She looked at the floor, crestfallen. Taro laughed cruelly.

"Look at undercover Federation agent Kassini upset by a moral quandary. You didn't think this job would be as cut and dried as it was back in the marines, did you? If it's any consolation, in my diplomatic days I came to the conclusion it was a lot easier if you focus on getting what you want out of it."

"That much has been spectacularly evident, Taro," she replied, resigned to the pragmatic reality he was outlining.

"Perhaps. The facts remain, we do nothing and let this play out, then try to take advantage of whatever situation comes up. If the Feds and the Ellies want to kill each other, we're not going to stop them by helping out a few colonists."

Kassini was about to reply but was cut off by the computer's voice purring quietly from a speaker over the door.

"*Anomaly* is approaching the rendezvous point."

The two looked at each other for a moment before Taro stood up and put an arm to Kassini's shoulder; a conspiratorial gesture. "The situation is what it is, Kassini. Let's get this over with."

They were greeted on the bridge by an external view to the front of the ship spread across the three wall screens, showing a very busy sunward sector. The area teemed with a variety of small vessels standing off in ragged vertical and horizontal stacks a few miles from a big Federal military capital ship. At least 15 smaller troop carriers were arranged in an orderly equidistant line formation below the uneven mob of mercenary and civilian ships.

A second vast capital ship sat broadside-on to the rescue operation at distance, like a huge predatory sea creature policing a bait-ball – a leviathan coordinating its family in the form of the small squadrons of lethal-looking Federation fighters that were spread around and throughout the independent vessels, clearly managing the more problematic ships.

Krieger, hunched over his preferred console, raised a hand at the sound of the door and spoke without turning to them.

"Look at that, would you? Haven't seen this much hardware for a looong time, hey Kassini?"

"Two Constellation class, some of the biggest they have – closest is the Matador… but what's the other?"

"The Terra Nova."

"We going to have to join that queue? Could be a long wait."

"Not sure, I think the transport tugs are unloading bigger ships like ours and the smaller ones are having to wait to dock. Should be okay if Ny'Esta and his family use the aft emergency lock."

Krieger sat back and turned his chair to face them.

"We need to get this done and get out of here, too, people. The whole thing is under amnesty so I wouldn't think anybody will be looking close enough to see through our veneer, but I'm still not sure the Federal grace to participate in this op would entirely extend to the… peculiar… circumstances around us and *Anomaly*."

The ping of an incoming message sounded from the board from him and he paused briefly before turning back to the board.

"It's good to see the Fed do something decent for a change."

The other two looked at each other as the captain turned to call up the message, and Taro shrugged imperceptibly at Kassini's frustrated expression.

The communication packet had originated from flight control on one of the large, fat-bellied Uridium transports, and assigned *Anomaly* a particular sector of space in which to wait along with the ID number of one of its attendant ships. Krieger confirmed by return that *Anomaly* possessed a suitable airlock for ship-to-ship transfer, and ordered Vonya to move the ship to the required location some miles above the line of much larger vessels.

Kassini sat and busied herself with the scanners, checking and rechecking the calibration of the sensors, the routine procedure calming her agitation a little. Taro excused himself to go and let Ny'Esta and the family know their time onboard would soon be at an end.

Anomaly reached the designated area quickly, joining a couple of other vessels of similar size which hung motionless there. Vonya powered down their engines at a safe distance.

"Keep an eye on things, Kassini, and let me know when we have an incoming transport," said Krieger. "I'm taking a few minutes' rest."

He dialled his chair into a reclined position and closed his eyes.

Kassini sat glumly and stared at the readouts in front of her, unable to shake a sense of foreboding at the approaching unknown, of knowing that the situation around them was just a small part of a sweeping change in the galactic status quo. Her first impulse was to head to the flight module and discuss the implications with Vonya, but her Avion friend had expressly forbidden contact with the rest of the crew while the Elementals were onboard.

Instead, she switched her comms to the general system channel and tuned into the chatter of the myriad ships around them. The mix of military pilots issuing commands to hold the operation together and civilian pilots complaining was reminiscent of her days in the marines, and strangely comforting.

She was amusing herself eavesdropping on a particularly cranky flight sergeant 20 minutes later when a new course prediction extended in a line across the scanner output towards the *Anomaly* from a blip which had intersected with the icon representing one of the transports. The blip shortly resolved into a distinct icon representing a medium-sized transport ship bearing the same ID as Krieger had relayed to her. She switched off her earpiece and looked over at the captain.

He was snoring gently in his chair, his bristly, at-rest face looking somehow older than usual. Kassini pushed a button for ships comms, and his eyes flicked open as the attention tone purred from the speakers.

"Taro, we have an inbound transport for our friends, ETA 10 to 12 minutes. This will be a ship-to-ship transfer, they'll need suits for safety," she said.

Krieger sat up with the help of the chair, rubbed his face and spoke.

"What do you say we head down and see them off?"

Ny'Esta and his family needed no help with vac-suits – they had their own gear, simple protective garments designed for quick and simple use over their existing clothes. They'd stowed these carefully in what they referred to as their 'basic bag' that had stayed close to them throughout the journey on *Anomaly*, which turned out to be the simple kitbag provided to any Elemental colonist when boarding a ship bound for a new colony. In amongst the basic medical equipment, survival gear and ration packs, their childrens' suits were clearly a later addition. Presumably they were either born, or at least had grown larger, on Adeccar.

The adults had to stoop in the short corridor leading towards the rear of *Anomaly*, which terminated in a ladder leading upwards to the emergency personnel airlock. The Elemental couple tended to their childrens' suits first, carefully checking and double-checking the seals, locks and layers. They then briskly and methodically dealt with their own in a trained, well-practised set of motions, leaving the suit helmets under their arms. Taro and Krieger stood a little way further down, Krieger chatting in Elemental with Haq.

Kassini climbed the ladder as they worked, and checked a series of pressure readouts that gauged the status of the small lock on the other side, before punching a button which caused the hatchway above her to slide open. Striplights activated automatically to illuminate a room just large enough to accommodate two standing humans. She stuck her head in for a brief examination before closing the hatch again and climbing back down.

"I don't think all of you will fit in one go, it'll have to be two at a time," she said as she dropped back onto the deck.

Haq stepped forward and thrust her gloved hand forward to Kassini, who responded with a simple shake after a moment. The Elemental woman held onto her hand for a long moment.

"No meaningful shake from me, I'm afraid," Kassini said with an apologetic smile.

"To me, this still demonstrates respect," replied the tall alien before switching to a more carefully harmonised tone of voice, like a human might project theirs when speaking formally. "We are grateful to you, and wish you and the *Anomaly* ship good hunting for the journeys ahead."

"Thanks Haq, I wish you and your family safe travels. Take care," Kassini replied in the best Elemental she could manage, before releasing her hand and stepping back.

Haq and Ny'Esta finished their formal farewells to the crew, then the children awkwardly but earnestly recited the same words together, too.

During the protracted farewell, Kassini had heard the unmistakable clanging of a transfer tube attaching to and sealing to the *Anomaly*'s hull above them. Krieger had noticed it too, and quickly put his hand to ear as he received a message on his earpiece. "Our pilot tells me the transport ship is alongside and we've equalised pressures in the lock," he said.

"Thank you, Captain. I will go first with Haq'an… put on your helmet little one and be careful, remember our training," said Ny'Esta, reaching for his youngest child to help with the process before donning his own helmet.

The child stood with a serious face that nevertheless belied excitement in the rapidly changing pigmentation of its cheek areas, looking to the father for a lead as Haq stepped in to check her partner's suit integrity one last time. Then Ny'Esta quickly manipulated the hatch controls above him and helped Haq'an into the airlock. Finally, Kassini helped pass a couple of bags up to them before closing the hatch at a signal from Ny'Esta.

It was apparent the suits enabled radio contact with one another, and Ny'Esta soon reported via Haq they were clear of the lock and aboard the waiting transport, and the final two family members repeated the process. 15 minutes later, the airlock lights flicked to green for a final time, and the waiting crew of *Anomaly* heard the sound of the transport ship detaching its coupling system – the Elemental family were gone, entrusted to whatever fate the Federation held for them.

Kassini looked over at Krieger, catching Taro's eye behind him as she did so.

"Job well done," said the captain, and headed back down the corridor towards the bridge. "I guess that proves our makeover has done its job, too. No challenges from any of the Feds."

"What happens now?" said Kassini, falling in with Taro behind him.

"We need to get clear of this demilitarised zone – too many Fed ships for my liking. I have no idea how long our luck will hold around here and have no intention of pushing it. The ship is low on fuel and supplies. We need to put in somewhere out of the way and resupply."

They entered the bridge and sat back at their various stations, Kassini noting the transport ship moving away from *Anomaly* on the scanner towards another of the vessels nearby. Krieger stretched his shoulders as he turned off his console. "You all look as tired as I feel," he continued with his back to them. "After the few weeks we've had, let's get underway and get some sleep. We can regroup and plan our next move somewhere quieter."

He addressed his communicator. "Vonya, we should be able to spin from here. Take us to the nearest system with a fuel depot and hand *Anomaly* over to the computer so you can get some rest. I'll have Mak 14 disinfect the areas the Elementals have contaminated for you."

Krieger clicked off the comms and psyched himself up to deliver the order to his twitchy crew droid.

M

Kassini: Update – Krieger believes he has the drop on everyone and is going to take *Anomaly* to wherever the Elemental fleet surfaces in Empire space.

Suggest you position your taskforce to recapture *Anomaly.*

M

Drexler: One step ahead of you, Kassini. Provide exact coordinates of *Anomaly* when you enter the warzone.

The trap is set. It just needs to be sprung.

Drexler out.

13. THE WAR COMES HOME

Back in Federation fringe space after their spin from the Elemental-controlled zone, the *Anomaly* had headed straight to a nearby system's far-flung belt to refuel and rearm. They pulled into an automated orbital garage around a mass-heavy asteroid; stations like these were little more than just floating weapon-storage warehouses and fuel tankers, run by simple droids. You flew your ship into one of their six docking arms, they loaded your order, you paid and departed back into the void... it was pretty much the same principle as Earth's car garages from the petroleum age, except if you drove away without paying, the nanobots in the fuel would activate and detonate. Pay up, and they dissolved harmlessly – at least that was the official line. No one, as far as Krieger knew, had ever dared to risk a ship to find out whether it was a real deterrent or just an empty threat.

Vonya looked over at their instruments as the station droids performed the pitstop. "Only three-quarters full, Kree-gar," she said to the captain, who sat next to her in the co-pilot's seat. "The pump shut off."

Krieger tutted with annoyance and opened up the comms. A video link to the station's serving droid appeared on the display, the pin-sharp contrast of the screen rendering its bright-red chassis almost blinding in the dark-lit cockpit. The mechanoid was of the cheap and blocky, plastic-headed humanoid variety and its nametag read 'Mr Krispin'. It said "Hi! How can I help today?" in an immensely grating mechanical voice that instantly made Krieger want to punch it in the face.

Bored station owners had a habit of customising their automatons into caricatures, just to provide a bit of light relief for the long-haul spacers who'd spent too long staring past their own reflections into the void; consequently, you never knew what you were going to get. Unfortunately for him, Mr Krispin had been stylised as comically obese, with a lopsided red beret, an insanely upbeat grin and a giant bushy waxed moustache fixed on his metal face. Krieger squinted into the screen and asked: "Mr Krispin, we've only had three-quarters of our fuel order. Are you trying to screw us around?"

The robot's beaming face remained impassive as its bat-like moustache moved up and down, out of sync with its cheery response. "No sir, your fuel order has been delivered in full."

Krieger felt his blood beginning to rise. "No *sir*, it has *not*," he growled back.

"Checking order… checking order…" the droid beamed back. "Order is correct." It paused annoyingly before delivering its news with a flourish. "Fuel supplies have been rationed in this sector according to a new Empire-wide Federation Directive, effective as of this morning at 23:59 Universal Standard Time."

"Rationed?" said Krieger, shocked. "What Directive? Can't you overlook it?"

The mannequin-faced Krispin stared back contentedly. "Regrettably sir, I cannot comply. You are not the first lifeform to ask. Would you like me to play the company's standard response?"

"No, that's fine," said Krieger and transferred the credits.

"Very well, sir," said Mr Krispin and his out-of-time moustache launched into a mindless, rapid-fire post-sale script instead. "Thank you for your custom – and remember, you can shop Krispin Industries for a wide range of the sector's best supplies, ammunition and weaponry, available in colony malls, belt shops…"

Krieger prodded wildly at the scanner to shut it down and rid himself of the glowing image of the beaming red idiot droid.

"I liked that Mr Krispin guy, he was *very* realistic," said Vonya thoughtfully.

Krieger frowned at her in disbelief. "Is that what humans look like to you?"

"Yeah, more or less," Vonya replied, distractedly, manoeuvring the *Anomaly* away from the station's spacelane. "But Empire rationing is bad crow."

"Yes it is…" mused Krieger, voice trailing off as the penny dropped. He opened the ship's comms channel.

"Everyone, wake up and assemble in the cabin, either literally or metaphorically," he shouted excitedly into the mic, voice echoing throughout the ship. "Mak, start filtering the *Anomaly's* long-range comms and monitor all official and unofficial news channels – record the most significant samples for playback in five minutes. This is happening, crew, so get your asses ready for duty. Don't make me use the alert sound."

The crew grudgingly gathered around the cabin's main table, a hazy fugue of interrupted sleep inhabiting Taro and Kassini's slow and deliberate motions. Mak 14 stood by the main screen and transmitted a scrolling stream of data and imagery across it at lightning pace. Kassini and Taro deliberately looked away from this hectic scene and as they yawned and stretched, their features were bathed in the reflection of a dizzying flux of reports, messages and other data being gathered from the droid's sensor array. The flow of info would intermittently pause for a flickering split-second as Mak filed away a point of interest, before resuming again.

"Okay, Mak, tell us what's happening in the galaxy, the big picture," said Krieger impatiently, in businesslike mode. "No interruptions from the rest of you, please."

The data continued to flow onscreen as 14 rotated his eyeless head towards his audience. "The FedNet has gone into pure propaganda mode, but a composite of other data sources concludes that in the last 24 hours, the Empire has withdrawn its military presence from the majority of bases along the outer rim of its territories," Mak's synth voice began. "Military vessels have deserted mining and farming moons, colony worlds, penitentiary planets, minor starbases and shipyards and many more Federation facilities and are currently headed back to the centre worlds."

"The big moves are starting, and it's going to be a feeding frenzy out there," said Krieger, unable to help himself. "The pirates are going to have a field day… they'll overpower every facility they can get their hands on."

"Poor Mr Krispin," added Vonya.

"Yeah, on the plus side, at least he's fucked," said Krieger.

The others looked across, nonplussed. Mak 14 extended an accusatory eyestalk towards Krieger and the Avion and chided them. "You said no interruptions, Captain. Please refrain from immediately disobeying your own orders."

"Okay, sorry," said Krieger. "Continue."

"This unprecedented withdrawal has terrified local systems and, by correlating data gathered from several distant mercenary channels and some diplomatic comms I have intercepted and decoded, the Federation is reacting to movement of the Elemental fleet we observed back in Kamakraken. A convergence of the faction's other fleets on Empire territory has also been detected. According to eyewitness observations and extrapolations of their current trajectories, it is almost certain they are headed for Barnard's Star."

Taro and Kassini both gasped in unison. "Holy shit, the Federation's bastion system," Kassini said. "Then this is definitely on."

"It's on like a once well-known retro videogame," Mak continued, tempted to use advert audio from his archive of ancient pop culture for emphasis. The crew stared back at him, nonplussed.

"Official responses are as follows – media interviews with Federation government officials deny the accusations of imprisonment of Elemental refugees and are refusing to discuss large-scale military engagement beyond defending their territories. The Elemental government has ordered all its civilian colonies near Federation space to prepare to evacuate – to all intents and purposes, they are now on a war footing. The Avions are calling for calm and trying to intercede as a diplomatic intermediary. In the event of war, they refuse to be drawn on which faction they will support."

"Ah, that's so drekking *typical*," Vonya cursed to Kassini, in Avion. "Just make a decision, one time, for drek's sake."

"What about diplomatic transmissions? Has anyone hacked their networks?" Kassini asked 14.

"The Elemental and Avion channels are inaccessible from our current position. But according to decrypted Federation naval transmissions, Barnard's Star has its full fleet complement in dock. Three Chthonian-class carriers and five Constellation-class capital ships are stationed there permanently. And there are at least two Federation navy task forces close to the star, within intercept range."

It was Taro's turn to interrupt. "So, what… the Elementals are deliberately targeting a full-strength Empire military stronghold? A base with a fully operational fleet complement? What kind of tactic is that?"

"An extremely ballsy one," replied Kassini. "Clearly, they have faith in their new tech. They're confident they can march their fleets right into the heart of the Empire's war machine. And win."

"That's going to be one big firework show," said Vonya. "They go beak-to-beak, Barnard's Star will look like a krebbit spill in zero-g."

"Mak, continue monitoring transmissions and keep me updated," Krieger ordered. "So, crew, looks like the gloves are coming off. Question is: how should we respond? We could pick through the bones of the weakened Fed outposts out here on the fringe and make a killing on the black market, while we watch events from afar… but where's the fun in that? I suggest we take advantage of the good ship *Anomaly's* stealth and head for Barnard's Star."

"Woah – easy, tiger," said Kassini. "To what end, exactly?"

"Well, practically speaking, the tech swimming amongst the debris from a clash of the galaxy's two superpowers is going to be worth way more than anything we'll find on a lightly defended outpost in the middle of nowhere, right?" Taro suggested.

"True," said Krieger, warming to the theme. "Plus, Kassini, profits aside for one minute – this is a momentous event we have in prospect here. This could be the defining moment of a generation. And thanks to the *Anomaly's* stealth tech, we'll have the best seats in the house. We saw how well it worked with the Elemental fleet, up until Mak's moment of madness…" he ignored the whine of Mak's servos as the droid raised an appendage to protest. "Remember, by selling that footage, we set all of this in motion. Don't you want to see how the story ends first hand? I know I do."

"I admit, it would be fascinating, but also extremely dangerous – stealth or not," Kassini countered.

"We must do it!" Mak 14 suddenly interjected, totally inappropriately. Kassini ignored him. "Vonya, if we do venture in there, you'll be flying the ship. So what do you think?"

The Avion had seemingly drifted into her own thoughts, possibly already simulating the epic battle in her head. She snapped back into focus, shuffled her wingtips and sat up straight in her seat. "No lie, is big risk. I would love to see that movie!" she said, her harmonious voices alive with adrenaline.

Krieger took the floor, turned his chair round and straddled it, in the time-honoured manner of egomaniac CEOs throughout the universe. "Listen crew, we've had a pretty action-packed time – we've had guns in our hands practically since we met," he reflected. "We've been shot down, Rust has been blown to bits and rebuilt, we've narrowly escaped the whole Elemental fleet, I was very nearly eaten by a star hyaena… what we've been through stretches the bounds of credulity, but it's been a fun ride, and that's the whole point.

"But this is different – we're talking about upping the danger level way into the red zone, and I don't want to drag anyone along against their will. The situation boils down to the classic risk-versus-reward scenario: either stay on the fringes or dive into a conflict. So discuss this with your crewmates and come back here in 15 minutes, when you can cast your vote. You, too, Mak."

Taro motioned for Kassini to duck into his quarters and once she was inside, she shut the door and leaned against it. Kassini whispered: "He's only putting this to the vote because he's sure he'll win."

Taro nodded. "I know. Obviously, whether the Avion's fleets get involved is going to play a huge part in the outcome. We need to know which way the solar wind blows." He reached hurriedly for his tablet, accessed their ongoing archive of Garrn's feed and handed it over. "Can you find anything in Garrn's feed that shows which way they're going to jump?"

Kassini scrolled through the encrypted channel of messages from the Avion agent's handler. "The recent updates contain nothing explicit about it, not that you'd expect there to be," she summarised, eyes darting left and right as she speed-read the info. "But they're mobilising, for sure... and they reference communications with Empire high command more than once, but nothing I can see with the Elementals. Reading between the lines, you'd have to put your money on a human-Avion alliance, especially given the Ellies are the aggressors."

Taro frowned. "We have an Avion on board. Can you ask her? Hypothetically, I mean?"

"Doubt she'll have any intel that we don't already know," said Kassini, handing back the tablet.

"It's worth a try... she'll have better instincts than us when it comes to Avion tactics."

Their pilot was stood in the corridor at the stern of the ship with her winged back to Kassini, her tall frame lit by a faint blue aura from the engine glare as she stared out of the porthole at the receding stars.

"You okay with this, Vonya?" Kassini asked her in Avion, as gently as her human voicebox could muster.

The Avion turned and flapped her wings quickly, once, the Avion gesture for exasperation. "I was just thinking how quickly things change for us," she sighed. "One minute, I talk to a plastic man in a fuel station, the next, we fly into a warzone where every race in the galaxy – mine included – is at each other's throats in a pointless war."

Kassini picked up on the sadness in Vonya's expression, something she'd never seen even a flicker of from beneath her self-confident exterior before now. "What does that mean for you, though? Is there a conflict of interest?" she asked.

"Always, Kass," she said, dark eyes looking down at the ground. "I am Vonya of the great Ok'cuu, after all. Much is expected of me. The Avions will likely join the humes, I'm sure of it. But if the fighter wings of my own race are going into this battle – all those pilots – I should be fighting with them, instead of grabbing debris from their wreckage in my talons."

"It's not easy, I know," said Kassini, placing her hand tentatively on the pilot's shoulder for a brief moment. "Species loyalty runs deep, for all of us. It's hard-wired. It must be hard to stand on the sidelines with your talent... and pitch in with a rabble like this instead."

Vonya laughed, eyes blinking rapidly with emotion. "I wouldn't be here, I wouldn't have stayed this long, if it wasn't for you. We both need someone we can rely on."

Kassini felt tempted in the moment to reveal the real reason she was trapped on the *Anomaly*, to share the burden of her mission. Yet at that moment, she zoomed out of her body and as she somehow saw herself and Vonya facing each other, their brief connection set against the rushing starfield, the feeling ebbed away. Kassini was a soldier. Vonya, a pilot. They were ultimately both just weapons, and that was a fact that transcended language for both of them.

"You'll find a way to return to them. And on your own terms. You're the best pilot I've ever seen, way too good for them to lose," she said instead.

The moment passed and Vonya looked down briefly, before her usual expression returned to her face. "You're right, Kass. And destiny has forced our hand. For now, I keep us alive, wherever we go. Whatever happens."

Kassini smiled, turned and walked back down the corridor. She paused outside Taro's door and Vonya called out to her over her shoulder: "Tell Taro what I said – Krieger needs somebody, too."

Kassini looked round, surprised and guilty. But Vonya had her back to her, staring out at the starfield again.

With their 15-minute discussion window up, the crew was back in the hold. "All those in favour?" Krieger asked, and was rewarded with a unanimous show of hands, claws and multi-tool appendages. "Good. Now we need to plan."

Taro spoke up, glancing in Vonya's direction as he spoke. "We also agree that it's likely the Avions will join the conflict on the side of the Empire, which means we should tread carefully – and be selective about what we target once we're in there."

"Yeah, judging by the rumour mill, the pirates all think the same thing," said Krieger. "Obviously, the last thing we want is a hold full of Avion navy gear that'll gain us a bounty with them when we already have a neon Fed 'Wanted' sign flashing away under the *Anomaly's* new paintjob... but first things first. Let's focus on our tactical plan to get in there, our contingencies, Plan A, B and C. Then we'll set the mission parameters. This is mission-time, people, as of now. Let's get organised."

"The best and worst thing about Barnard's," said Kassini, looking up from the tablet she'd been invested in for the last half an hour, "...are the spin points."

Vonya and Mak 14 had disappeared off into the bowels of the ship to check its core systems, leaving only Krieger and Taro on the bridge to follow Kassini's pointing finger to the three-dimensional system map she was now scrolling around on the main screen.

"It's a relatively simple system in stellar terms, but a real mother to attack," she continued. "The main bulk of the orbital shipyards and facilities are all built around the third and fourth planets, the only ones stable enough to have anything on the ground. They're always under the influence of the two big gas giants further away and a mini-giant closer in, so no fleets can ever spin in too close to the facilities themselves, on account of gravitational interference. The ice planets around the first giant are all militarised, with stations in orbit around the inner planets, too."

"What are you telling me?" said Taro, looking perplexed.

"The spin points are all waaaay away from any of the likely Elemental targets," Krieger explained, the former Empire ship commander completely familiar with the tactical import of Kassini's explanation. "Out past the orbit of the two gas giants. So they'll likely jump in further out and move their fleet into engagement range, which is good for us. We can pick a likely place to drop in and go silent, then coast in towards the planets while we get a fix on what's going on."

"Won't the Elementals guard the spin points, assuming they can get past whatever defences are on them in the first place?"

Krieger indicated the spin zones, multiple rings of yellow and red concentric circles outside the orbit of the Barnard's Star system, dotted with patches of green.

"Undoubtedly, and the likelihood is they'll already be there by the time we arrive," Krieger said, recalling his starship command experience from his navy days. "But there are seven or eight green zones in the first ring after the giants alone and even more further out. That's always the defensive downside of a single-star system, and this one is a lower mass M-class dwarf at that, so you can't stop the enemy getting in somewhere. Trying to hold too many points is a risk for the Ellies, as the Fed's fighter squadrons will harass anything they station too far from the bulk of the fleet."

"When was the last time you were in Barnard's, Krieger?" asked Kassini. "I passed through the fourth planet on a rotation a while ago, there were more defence platforms built around the shipyard every time I saw it."

"A long time ago, for me – the yards can build platforms as easily as ships, though, so it's not surprising. They say Barnard's accounts for consumption of 20 per cent of the outer systems' resource exports on its own, one way or another. I think we should drop in on the mid ring, here, and we'll just have to hope we get lucky on an undefended point."

A marker from Krieger's tablet transferred across onto the main screens, appearing in the middle of the first of the jump point rings, midway between two of the green zones.

"Given the way the planetary orbits are at the moment, I'd think the Elementals will be jumping in here," he jabbed the tablet and another marker appeared in a different colour. "That's the most aggressive placement that will still give them the maximum time to manoeuvre and prepare. Feds will guess the same and will probably be in a defensive position here, more or less under the guns of 3A's orbital stations. Kassini, you agree?"

A third marker appeared in blue and spread out to form a box between the orbits of the third and fourth planets of the system.

Kassini looked the screen over for a moment and said: "As good a guess as mine, how long to spin?"

"Computer, plot that for us," said Krieger, before activating his comms and calling for Vonya and Mak to confirm the state of the ship's systems.

"*Anomaly's* core systems are tested and ready," replied Mak 14's synth voice curtly.

"Good. Computer, head for the spin zone. Let's get this mission underway. The jump is the key unknown here: if we drop in next to a capital ship or a fighter squadron from either side, we'd better be prepared to get out of there again, fast."

The computer's voice piped up from the cabin speakers in response. "Captain, we are around 40 minutes in spin away from the Barnard's Star system, and a further 30 from a spin point in this system. I will prepare our stealth capabilities for immediate activation before we jump, and have an emergency spin to the nearest system ready to trigger."

"Good, get us underway, then. If we get in there and it looks like we can move with impunity, I want everybody looking for the richest possible pickings we can find that won't get us killed."

Krieger had made his now-familiar switch to commander mode again. He spun his chair to the other two and, after checking his comms were on, switched to a strident, motivational tone.

"This ship is ready, this crew is ready, half an hour to spin, people. Let's make some big money and a name for ourselves, at last."

Their ship began to move, and the only activity in the following half hour as it covered the distance to the nearest spin point at max thrust was Vonya passing back through the bridge to the flight module to take over control. She stopped briefly to familiarise herself with the map of their destination still displayed on the wall screens.

"What do you think, Vonya?" asked Kassini, as the Avion studied the charts.

"Not possible to spin into warzone safely, Kass," she answered. "Would be happier taking my fighter first for a recce, but no stealth – so too dangerous. Need to get out from the spin point clean, run scanners and make sure close range is clear when *Anomaly* drops out. Don't know what we'll be on top of."

Kassini nodded and gave her friend a quick salute. "I'll see to it. Good luck, pilot."

"You too, soldier," replied the Avion with a nod of her head that swished her head feathers, and disappeared through the flight-module door.

Krieger was watching a countdown timer to the spin point tick down on his console.

"Right people, four minutes out. Secure for spin, this will be a long one."

They each began buckling the harnesses of their seats and settled in for the extended spin to the heart of Federation military space at Barnard's Star.

The spin timer ticked down to zero and *Anomaly* reappeared in a different part of the universe. The crew immediately became aware something was wrong, even before the strangeness of their FTL step had worn off. A clatter greeted them as reality reasserted, like the sound of hail from an angry rain god on a corrugated roof, passing over the ship's hull in waves a few seconds apart.

Vonya, who could see more outside of the vessel than the others from her position in the flight module, reacted first. Her hands flew to the controls as she gave a peculiarly Avion squawk of surprise, followed by a shout that jolted the others out of their spin-induced reverie.

"Debris field!"

Krieger and Kassini both moved automatically with well-practised motions to call up data at their stations, Krieger wrestling one-handed with his chair harness as he did.

"We're stationary, so whatever came apart is moving. You've got the best field of view – rotate the ship and get a look around us while we get the scans up," he instructed Vonya tersely, in an unflustered, commanding tone. They immediately felt the attitude jets push the ship into a gentle spin as another wave of objects drummed against the hull.

"Stealth systems online," said the computer, increasing its volume to overcome the noise.

"Scans are active," said Kassini after a minute or so. "There were two Federal frigate carcasses close off our rear as we came out, no power signatures and both in dead spins – they're throwing debris all over this portion of space. Short range doesn't show anything active in our vicinity."

"Vonya, priority is to get us clear of the debris and away from this jump point," Krieger barked.

"Already on it," replied Vonya. The short-range showed the extent of the debris field to all of them now, a red overlay gently expanding around the *Anomaly's* icon in the centre of the three-dimensional output. Gravity appeared to increase for the crew as the ship's manoeuvring thrusters began to push it in what was, for them, an upward direction, towards the closest edge of the field. Two larger grey icons sat behind and slightly off to one side of *Anomaly*, each pinned with a fluctuating range marker. Kassini punched for a camera view of the area.

The positioning of Barnard's single, faint sun didn't lend the camera view a lot of detail of the two smashed and rapidly spinning ships. Each was three times the size of *Anomaly*, their bulks shrouding the smaller vessel and each other in darkness. Secondary explosions, fires and decompressions illuminated parts of the shapes eerily, and the whole area of space around them was surrounded with a glittering halo of metallic debris where it caught the unfiltered light of the sun. As they watched, one of the ship's fore sections exploded outwards, spraying more chunks of metal out into the void, some of it angled to pass beneath the *Anomaly's* rapidly rising trajectory.

"Well, we won't have any fighters for company at least... nobody would fly anything small through this shit," said Krieger sardonically, as the pounding on their hull faded away to be replaced with the comforting sound of *Anomaly's* engines and powerplant.

"Lucky for us," replied Kassini. "Something Elemental must have jumped in here and caught those two off-guard."

"Or they were sacrificed in a holding action trying to keep this point open, maybe for escaping civilians. Is the ship okay? We can't stick around here for long, and it's way too dangerous to try and check those frigates out with all the debris."

"I do not detect any damage," interjected the computer immediately. "The debris hitting the ship has been within tolerance."

Kassini returned her gaze to the tablets in front of her now, and her face lit up with a mixture of amazement and concern.

"No potential incoming threats identified, but you should see long range... switching to the monitors now."

The wall screens switched from the camera view to a vast, zoomed-out scan showing the conjunction of planets in the system and its sun, with *Anomaly's* icon at the edge of the picture. A vast thicket of Federal-blue ship markers was arrayed outside the orbit of the fourth planet, with a smaller contingent at a longer distance from the third, roughly equidistant between it and the other fleet. Planetside of these were two similarly complex patterns of markers, showing the orbital defences around the two heavily fortified rocky worlds in the system.

A long way out-system from both of these formations sat a wide array of markers picked out in green to differentiate their Elemental origins, a wall of spearhead-shaped phalanxes containing between eight and 12 vessels, all several ships wide and deep. These were positioned to create a screen behind which hung the conglomeration of the biggest ships in the Elemental fleet, a large number of capital-class signatures arranged with all the precision of a well-drilled battle plan.

A couple of smaller groupings from either side had pushed forward into the areas of space between the three fleets towards a number of generic markers. These appeared to cover large cubes of space and were simply labelled 'Weapons Fire'.

"Fighter combat," said Krieger, picking one of these out by way of explanation for Taro. "First phase of any standard large engagement is to try and establish space superiority; the bigger ships are frigates and small carriers supporting their squadrons. At least we know where the fight is – computer, give us some predicted motion lines for the bigger formations."

As they watched, one of the blue support ships that had presumably stationed itself too close to the conflagration of fighters nearest to it winked to grey, joining a veritable legion of similar grey markers dotted around the perimeter of the fleets. Similar icons were also spread in a wide arc following a rough path from the location of the outer spin points to the present location of the bulk of the Elemental forces.

The computer now added direction splines to the scanner for the larger groups of ships, and white lines crisscrossed the three-dimensional map. It was immediately clear the Elemental fleets were slowly pushing sunward of the defending forces, while retaining their own defensive formation.

"Early stage formations, again," said Krieger, after a moment. "They're trading missile volleys and jockeying for position. The sunward push is aggressive on the part of the Elementals since it's pulling them further away from the spin points. The Federation fleets are reacting by pushing the bulk of their forces out to engage and cut them off, too, by the look of it."

He manipulated the tablet in front of him to pick out five or six of the grey icons. They floated together in what had presumably been the approach route of the Elemental fleet to its current position, judging by the litter of similar markers on a straight line from the nearest ring of jump markers. The movement of the battle had subsequently served to place them on the outer edge of the no man's land between the two fleets. Krieger grunted with interest as he rotated the view to survey their position more closely.

"Larger ships, dead in the water, mostly stationary and with most of the debris well clear," Kassini explained, consulting the more in-depth composition scan data she was looking at. "Federal and Ellie frigates and a single capital-class, destroyed one another in the first contact I expect – Elementals would have swept the area in front of the main fleet as it moved in. Why the interest?"

"The battle is moving away from them, and what's left of the hulls will cover us from prying eyes if we get in amongst them," replied Krieger. "Looks like a good first target for some potential salvage, don't you think? It's also as good a ringside seat as we'll find without putting ourselves at risk of getting caught in a missile barrage or fighter battle, I'd say."

"Could be, but that's a long way from the spin points and still in the hot zone between the two fleets," Kassini considered. "The closer we get to the battle, the further we are from an escape point. The spin drive won't help us anywhere within a wide bubble around the planets, remember?"

"Well," said Taro, unexpectedly and uncharacteristically cheerfully. "That's why we have the stealth systems, right? Has anybody reacted to our presence yet?"

Kassini checked a wider sweep scan on the largest tablet in front of her. "Still no evident threats," she concluded.

Krieger looked from her to Taro for a moment, nodded, then checked his comms to Vonya.

"Vonya, move us to the marker I've just placed – we're going to check out what's left of those ships. Slow and steady though, make like a rogue asteroid." He clicked off the channel when the pilot acknowledged, and spoke to the room at large.

"Decision made – this whole situation is one big risk, but we knew that coming in, and if there's any hint of trouble, we can still get clear. Plenty of open space this side of the fleets, and they're going to have their hands full with each other anyhow. Now, we need to think about how we're actually going to pull off any kind of salvage. Mak, make your way up to the bridge and take a look at these ships for us."

"Fair enough," said Kassini with a shrug, clearly not entirely happy with another snap decision, but deciding this wasn't the moment to argue with the captain's logic. She could see at a glance that the space between *Anomaly* and the ruined ships was littered with more detritus of the conflict as well as the standard obstacles of space travel. She busied herself with extra scans of the area between them and their target, resolving and relaying any anomalous data points to Vonya's flight navigation feed. The engines thrummed up to full power and the crew felt the familiar momentum of the ship beginning to move around them.

An exterior observer in the cold, harsh space around the *Anomaly* would have just been able to see the ship rotate carefully to the required heading from the glint of the sun. This was still illuminating the ruined patch of war clutter spinning not too far from their hull in brief, metallic bursts. The reflected solar energy moved gently across the side of their hull to its front, before the main engines began to add their own flares of light to the local illuminations.

Fortunately for the crew, there was no such observer. *Anomaly's* bulky, angular shape began to build momentum, pushing forward into the desolation between it and the part of the Barnard's Star system that was visibly being pockmarked with the new, temporary starflares of shield impacts and missile explosions. Soon, they were driving headlong into the tumult that designated the main battlezone between the fleets of the two superpowers.

M

Kassini: Coordinates transmitted.
Anomaly is looking for salvage.

Will attempt to clear the ship in Vonya's fighter.

Once clear, will give greenlight for
the taskforce to recapture *Anomaly*.

M

Drexler: Understood. We'll take
it from here, Agent Kassini.

You have been more helpful
than you can possibly know.

Drexler out.

14. MANOEUVRES IN THE DARK

Despite having around three decades of navy service between them, it had actually been a while since either Krieger or Kassini had experienced the shapeshifting thrills of full-on fleet combat first-hand. It was understandable, then, that they both seemed so mesmerised by the battle formations coalescing around them. But Taro merely rolled his eyes, shook his head in irritation and turned back to monitoring the ship's data, deciding to let the pair get whatever it was out of their system as they fixated on the wall screens.

Shrouded by its stealth, the *Anomaly* had reached the unofficial no man's land between the two factions: to their port side, the Empire, and their base on the smaller planets; to starboard, the Elemental fleet, and two of the larger planets in the system in the far distance. The system's lone sun burned bright ahead of and above them.

"The fleets are closing. This is going to be chaos soon, the long-range artillery is starting to fire..." said Krieger. They were within visual range of some of the dogfights now. He restlessly manipulated the ship's feeds back and forth between the increasing numbers of sleek silver arrows of the Empire's fighter squadrons and the more sinuous forms of their Elemental counterparts, then switched to the scanner output where there were now a vastly increased number of the markers reading 'Weapons Fire'. Voices of the pilots from the two factions played behind them over the ship's comms. "Don't know about you, Sergeant, but it really takes me back."

Kassini didn't sound quite so casual. "I admit, it's exciting... and quite liberating to see these fleets having to work strictly in formation, while we have the freedom to move wherever we like. But we need to remember our stealth only makes us invisible and untrackable. We can still be hit – either by stray fire, or the ships themselves... or chunks of them, for that matter."

As Kassini had spoken, she'd zoomed her own feed in on an Elemental patrol that was reasonably close by, a pair of fighters escorting an oval missile boat, and was in the process of tuning her earpiece to the Elemental fleet frequency the computer had isolated.

"Krieger, can you understand this, too?" she said. "The Elemental fleet comms sound like they're between a task force and the main group to me."

Krieger altered his own audio feed with his tablet briefly, before zoning out and listening for a minute.

"Yeah, I understand it," he said eventually. "Confirms what you can see on the tac-map. They're baiting the Federal fighters with missile boats, sending a small force right to the edge of the station's weapon range."

Federation navy pilots – or their commanders, for that matter – weren't historically renowned for their patience, and it wasn't long before one of the more gung-ho patrols took the bait. Kassini and Krieger watched as four incoming Federation fighters peeled off from the main fighter group and approached in a menacing 'X' formation, prompting the Elemental fighters to alter their course to defend their missile ship.

The radio chatter from both sides increased its intensity several notches as the Federation ships swooped in. They darted suddenly and violently in a choreographed step that evaded the flickering red lasers streaking from the Elementals' powerful beam weapons. Safely past the barrage, they concentrated their own laser fire on the missile boat before scattering in separate directions. Kassini recognised it as a training-ground manoeuvre, for sure, but one that proved they were well drilled.

The shields of the oval craft glowed in multicolour, then blinked out, immediately replaced by an intense fireball. The Elemental fighters stayed in formation, their targeting computers struggling to lay down accurate fire as the Empire fighters retreated. When the explosion died down it revealed the remains of the oval ship, now critically damaged, its rear drive section in tatters; in a last act of defiance, it had launched a pair of missiles, which streaked away after two of the departed fighters. The remaining Elementals activated their drives and set off in pursuit of the other two targets, leaving one of their number to oversee the crippled missile boat.

"I think we're pretty safe here. The odds against us taking a hit by accident are pretty astronomical," Krieger finally said in answer to her earlier question. Although Kassini noticed he, too, was tracking the flightpath of one of the Federation fighters on the scope out of the corner of his eye as he spoke, watching it arc back on a second run that had an outside chance of intersecting with their position. He stopped watching only after Vonya, independently sensing the same possibility from her seat in the flight module, applied a short but reassuring burst of drive to keep them out of harm's way.

The computer had been instructed to keep them updated on any strategic fleet movements, and its vocoded voice sprang into life with its first bulletin. "The Elementals are sending in a wave of heavy cruisers and support frigates from their main fleet position," it said. "10 ships have split from the main carrier group and are heading towards the closest Empire battlegroup to us, the one led by Federation capital ships the *Shaolin* and the *Berserker*, which is responding."

"Oof, that's a bold move... and very un-Elemental," said Kassini, watching on the scope as the *Shaolin* and *Berserker* immediately adopted side-on flanking positions. She imagined the commanding officers on the bridges of those giant

Empire flagships licking their lips, orders to open fire with the main batteries on the tips of their tongues. "Unless they've got something up their sleeve, those cruisers won't last long once they're in heavy-weapons range."

"The scope shows the same thing's happening with the *Paladin* and the *Immortal* battlegroup," Krieger pointed out, referring to the cluster of ships the Empire had situated on the far side of their starbase. "Same attack formation, same number of incoming ships."

"I am not a betting droid, but it is possible those cruisers are remotely piloted decoys," Mak 14 interjected. "This has the hallmarks of a diversion. My analysis suggests the Elemental fighter squadrons have been drawing the Federation wings away to open a curved approach channel sunward of their main fleet position to the starbase. This would keep the bulk of the capital ships out of range of the ordnance from the outer defence platforms for the longest time if they intend to move closer to the main construction facilities."

"The fleet is the biggest I've seen, but it surely doesn't have the firepower to take on the bases and the Fed fleets together," Kassini said. "I mean, the Fed defence fleet is obviously smaller, but it's way too passive for my liking... so far, they're letting the Ellies take all the initiative, instead of taking the fight to them."

"The firepower of those emplacements is massive, it just looks like standard defensive doctrine to me – why engage with half your available force when you can wait for the enemy to come to you?" replied Krieger. "It's typical Fed predictability, but then I can sort of see their point."

He zoomed out a camera to take in the enormity of the Empire's frontier base. "I mean, look at it."

Viewed from afar, the Empire navy's HQ was formed into a series of eight gargantuan floating 'H'-shaped shipyard berths, a kilometre to a side, designed for repairing, adapting and re-arming their largest units – carriers, capital ships and heavy battleships. Six of the 32 available berths were currently occupied with serious-looking warships no doubt being hurriedly crewed for combat. As he swept the camera past, Krieger raised an eyebrow as he recognised the outline of the *Odin*, a venerable, constantly upgraded carrier that had been in service long before even his time in the fleet.

Operations at the colossal shipyard were watched over by four suitably monolithic weapons platforms: moveable islands of cold steel overloaded with fearsome ranged weaponry, purpose-built to eliminate anything that laid so much as a scanner on them, along with a myriad of smaller defensive emplacements. The platforms were already releasing long-range missile barrages in a predictable rhythm, and were slowly shifting position to be better able to deal death to the incoming Elemental attack forces when they inevitably came. Their hulking grey silhouettes sparkled with light as long-range plasma artillery – huge and power-hungry weapons systems that were usually the preserve of only the biggest and most powerful installations and ships – began to fire on the incoming Elemental cruisers.

Krieger switched the wall screen back to the main tactical map of the system showing the disposition of the fleets, to which the computer had added Mak 14's prediction of the Elemental fleet's movement along the sunward corridor. For a moment, he stood lost in thought, every inch the fleet commander weighing up the battlefront.

"The Elemental fleet is giving itself only one escape route by going sunward like that," he mused, seemingly to himself at first. "The Fed's fleet will try to move alongside them soon, towards us, to be in a position to cut that off, and encircle them and push them further in towards the station guns. They'll take a pounding getting into a good position, but it'll work for them, I think. Ellies end up with the station guns on one side, Fed fleet to their back and the sun gravity vastly increasing their distance to spin-safe on the in-system side. If the shipyard defences can exact enough of a toll to turn the advance back, the Elementals will have to close and go through the Federal fleet to get out – I'd say victory for the Federation, on balance."

Kassini was impressed by the captain's grasp of the situation – her own thoughts, prompted by the tactical system installed in her head, had been reaching for much the same conclusion. She was about to agree when a sarcastic snort from Taro snapped both her and Krieger's attention away from the monitor.

"Hey, I'm enjoying the spaceship porn as much as the next nostalgic military officer, guys, but winning and losing sides don't matter to me," he said, a hard, pragmatic edge in his voice shattering the reverie of his colleagues. "How about we actually do something profitable out here, instead of just watching this expensive fireworks display play out? Especially if you think the battle is heading this way, right Krieger?"

"Simmer down, Taro... this is the most fun I've had in ages," Krieger shot back with a smile. "We know where we're heading, might as well amuse ourselves 'til we arrive. You're right, though, we should think about the real task in hand."

He moved his finger to his ear to engage his comms. "Vonya?"

"Captain?" The pilot replied.

"Take us in amongst the wrecks of those ships we picked out as soon as you can, slow and steady, but try and keep us in a position where we can see how this plays out. Those Ellies are the pawns in this game and they're about to be sacrificed – which may present a later opportunity for fresh salvage once the Fed capital ships have trashed them."

"Copy that, Kree-gar," said Vonya.

Taro sighed audibly. "That's another daredevil move, Krieger – tell me we're at least going to wait until the Empire have stopped firing at them before we move in? Although I concede that Ellie weapons are going to be worth an absolute drekking megaton on the dark market..." Krieger nodded smugly in agreement, and turned to Mak 14.

"We'll need your expertise soon Mak, I need you to pick out a target vessel and work out how to get whatever you think is most valuable off it."

Krieger scratched at something on the control panel in front of him before continuing.

"Once these two stop shadowboxing and go at each other for real, this entire sector is going to look like a junkyard in no time, and we aren't going to be the only ones looking to capitalise. So let's get on and do what any self-respecting pirate scum would do when they find themselves ahead of the game like this – board an Empire wreck and plunder what we want from the carcass."

"I'll keep on with ID'ing the ships," Kassini replied, returning to her tablet bank, face immediately lighting up with data as it began to scroll past on the screen in front of her. "Preliminary suggests that Elemental corvettes and a frigate-sized ship took on a Federal Aeonid-class light carrier, plus a support ship."

"Kree-gar," Vonya rejoined from the cockpit relay. "You talking about stuffing the hold full of bits already. I say I take my fighter out and protect the *Anom-a-ly*."

"How did I know you'd suggest that?" said Krieger, sarcastically.

"It's a win-win. More room for junk in hold and more fun for me in the battle..." continued Vonya, warming to her prepared speech, a slight note of excitement detectable in her harmonised voices. "And with *Anom-a-ly's* stealth engaged, you can help me out... be my invisible wingman. A ghost ship."

"You just want to get out there and shoot shit down, don't you?"

"It is *that* obvious, Captain?" the Avion pilot said, crestfallen.

Krieger laughed once. "For now, the answer is 'no', pilot. I need you in control of this ship until we've checked these hulks out and besides, your fighter has no stealth capability and out here everybody is going to shoot at you."

"We almost there, and that was why I wanted to go," Vonya replied, with minor-key-toned notes of sullenness afflicting her usually lilting voices.

Krieger flicked the comms to off as the *Anomaly* slowed and began to rotate. They were drawing close to the gutted ships now, and he dialled the cameras back to check them out. The stricken craft were arranged in a roughly cuboid formation beneath them, grouped around the slowly spinning remains of the largest, a Federation light carrier.

This appeared to have been ripped into three distinct sections by multiple catastrophic injuries. The front two parts were still roughly in their original configuration where the superstructure had more or less held on even as the core of the ship collapsed around it, but the third engine section had flipped upwards like the open lid of a tin can. This rear section was now leading the slow, majestic rotational momentum of the wreck, giving it a vertiginous appearance of the front following the rear vertically, round and round, as they watched.

The cause of this final extreme rupture was evident nearby in the much smaller form of a crumpled Elemental cruiser. Its previously sinuous and curved form was crushed beyond all recognition where it had rammed the massive engine section of the larger ship from below. The crew could clearly reconstruct how the alien ship had scissor-split along its central axis from the impact before the remaining hull slammed against its target, before the resultant explosion set it moving gently away from the wreck. Both ships now presented a quietly and slowly diverging tableau of devastation.

The Federation support ship was a dumpy, older-style modular frigate that was little more than several gun platforms bolted to engine and command-centre modules. It was standing a thousand metres between the carrier and the other three ruined Elemental units. These were S-shaped corvette models, sleeker and faster-looking than the one which had suicidally finished off the carrier. The *Anomaly*, still a dwarf in comparison to even the smallest ships that had taken part in the engagement, was now passing the outermost of them. Vonya's skilled hands moved her charges carefully into the field of battle debris swimming in the dark among the floating carcasses of the leviathans.

The older Federation vessel was a dark cluster of rectangles passing beneath them now, passing two banks of ravaged anti-ship and anti-fighter weapons. Their remains were still ranged on the enemy wrecks floating nearby. The ship appeared curiously undamaged aside from a consistent peppering of armour breaches and a couple of obvious missile strikes. Taro watched through his fingers, jumping at shadows more than once as the scope and their viewscreen filled with a disorientating blur of objects in close proximity all around them.

"Top lock on that old beast has been forced after the batteries that cover it got hit," said Krieger as the cameras swept along the top of the battered vessel. They'd revealed a smashed airlock, surrounded by the telltale marks of docking clamps. "They got boarded, there's no breathing room in those old designs to repel an assault. Troops would have been on the bridge before the crew could get organised."

"No way for a marine to go, trapped in a tub like that," replied Kassini. "I'm thinking we're seeing the support ships for a bigger Ellie destroyer that was sent to deal with these guys after they either fell behind the rest of the fleet or jumped in later. They went out fighting and took a few down with them, at which point the carrier's remaining fighters would have run for the rest of the fleet."

Mak 14, who had been carefully examining the viewscreen throughout their approach, spoke next.

"I may need you to rescind your previous orders to our pilot, Captain Krieger. This operation will necessitate the use of our new droids for cargo removal and Rust for protection. Vonya's fighter cargo bay will be required both as transportation and to retrieve the maximum amount of cargo."

The droid dialled an image of the ruined carrier ship up to fill the screens again. The vessel was somewhat reminiscent of an aircraft carrier from the days of human naval power, but an inverted one, a complex sandwich of decks with the widest 'flight deck' section at the bottom. Ship storage, maintenance and fighter launch bays were built into this bulging, decidedly un-aerodynamic platform which would never be required to cut through water or air. The sections were effectively bolted in front of and beneath the much smaller, and now catastrophically disconnected, engine section.

"The highest probability for useful salvage is in the front section of the carrier," he said. "Ammunition, droids and equipment are stored on such vessels as a matter of course, as you know. This is the most heavily damaged ship, and the fighter has a much better probability of being able to access a suitable entry point. It is most likely that at least some of the crew have survived in the emergency pods onboard and that its droids will still be active."

In the distance behind the ship on the screen, a sprinkle of new stars began to appear and disappear. These were joined quickly by the bright coloured jabs and lances of laser weapons fire, as a battle suddenly flared into existence in the darkness.

"That's the signal that those nearer battlegroups have made contact – let's see how this goes," Krieger said, rapidly switching the views around to show the disposition of the advance Federation battleships and their attendant squadrons, which had been sent to intercept the Elemental diversionary drive.

The combat was relatively shortlived – as they'd predicted, several Elemental cruisers were summarily executed in no time. The others were driven further out-system, hopelessly outgunned by the Empire's capital ships before they were within range to do any meaningful damage in return. Krieger and Kassini had looked away from the display in resignation after several long-range barrages from the Empire's weaponry had scythed through their shielding and laid waste to four of them. Even though the Elementals were legendarily Machiavellian, sending a squadron of battle cruisers to face certain death still seemed a ridiculously high price to pay for a diversionary skirmish.

Their fighter squadrons fared slightly better in the engagement, deploying the new short-range jump technology the *Anomaly* had seen at Kamakraken to surprise the Empire battlecruiser *Berserker*. A large squadron of missile boats had suddenly appeared in the midst of its defensive perimeter while it was busy pummelling the cruisers at a distance.

The explosions from the swarm of rockets they unleashed at close range into the capital ship's sensitive engine section could be seen from *Anomaly* as momentary pinpricks of light against the dark shadow of the warship. The *Berserker* now appeared to be having difficulty manoeuvring away from the forward position it occupied, its attendant fleet of ships deployed in a defensive formation around it like sheepdogs. The victorious Elemental squadrons used their new trick to jump back out of range quickly, and were pursued in vain by a confused formation of Federal alert-fighters across the empty space back towards their own carriers.

"Looks like enhanced fighter shield is working for Elies, too," commented Vonya from the flight module. "Almost complete formation got clear of this attack."

"You might get a chance to furball with some of them after all, Vonya – I need you and your fighter to ferry the droids over to check out what's left of that carrier when we've finished our scans," Krieger replied.

"Taxi service for lunatic droids? Bird-shit job, Captain!"

Krieger covered his mic momentarily and spoke aside to Mak 14.

"You need to go with her, Mak?"

"I will be more effective on *Anomaly*, I can utilise our better communication system for efficient control of the new droids. My own mobile system is not reliable at anything beyond short range," the droid replied.

Kassini saw her chance. "He's right, Krieger. He's the only one who can deal with the ship's systems. I can go in his place."

Krieger reactivated his mic. "Vonya, Kassini accompanies you and the droids – Mak 14 stays with us to keep an eye on the ship's systems. We just don't know what's going to happen out here."

"Better call, Krieg, will get the fighter prepped. *Anomaly* is full-stop, nothing coming our way, computer can keep an eye on flight control."

The sound of Vonya clearing out of the flight module was swiftly followed by her appearance in the doorway to the bridge. The Avion pilot bounced over to Kassini's console and said: "Coming for a ride? At least we being allowed out now..."

"Yeah, let's go, we've got droids to manage," replied Kassini, standing to follow her.

Krieger called after them as they both made to leave the bridge.

"Keep your comms open, Mak will coordinate from here. Let the droids do the heavy lifting."

"You should also take a comms tablet, Kassini," added Mak 14. "And interface this with the fighter's comms system, as a relay."

"Will do," replied Kassini, quickly dismounting one of the spare units on the bridge and following Vonya out.

Their resident Avion hardware was sat in its customary position on the modified launch ramp in the cargo bay when they arrived. Vonya began methodically checking it over with a practised eye as Kassini grabbed some kit and threw on her armour from the lockers nearby.

Before crossing the bay to the fighter, she also selected and slung on a short-exposure respirator and self-deploying suit system. It was a small backpack which would enable her to survive in hard vacuum for an hour or so if the worst should happen.

The coast was clear, so she took the opportunity to alert Drexler.

M

Kassini: *Anomaly* won't
be moving for a while.

Transmitting coordinates,
I will be off-ship for two hours.

Come and get her.

Rust hung motionless beside the fighter, the rapid scanning of his red sensor a giveaway that the droid was fully charged and impatient to get the mission underway. Hovering next to the old battle droid were Mak 14's two new additions to the crew. They were smaller and less heavily armoured than the venerable Rust, giving the impression of a similar, if much more advanced, design. This superiority of form had already been offset with modifications however, including several extensible tools and manipulator arms which they kept pulled in close to their carapaces. Small launchers had been mounted on the centre-top of both spheres, very similar to the handheld version Mak 14 favoured in combat.

"Your platoon is looking the part, Rust," said Kassini, as she finished clipping a sidearm into her hip holster. "How are the new droids working out?"

"They are functioning optimally – Mak 14 has made many modifications to their programming," Rust boomed. "I will identify you as having command access to them."

"What should I call you?" Kassini said, indicating the droids with a finger. The one on Rust's left, which appeared to have a cutting-torch attachment where the other did not, hovered forward.

"I am OMBIS-KIMSK-246, multipurpose unit," it said, pronouncing the letters and dashes in the smooth, emotionally devoid tone favoured by the designers of the latest generations of mechanoids. The words corresponded with the fluctuation of a pulsating bright-green LED in the centre of the droid's body.

"Catchy," said Kassini with a laugh, as the other unit swapped places with the first.

"And I am OMBIS-ZARCH-638, multipurpose unit," it said, with a voice identical to the first.

"Okay, well, you'll respond to Kim and Zar from now on. Zar, can you change your voice pattern when responding to us humans so we're able to differentiate you from your counterpart, please?"

"This is done," responded Zar in a deeper, richer tone of voice. The LED on the second droid also changed colour to a deep red. "Is this more acceptable?"

"Perfectly good."

Behind the droids, Vonya had boarded her ship during the conversation, and could be glimpsed organising the flight module as the fighter's cargo ramp now cycled with a mechanical whirr and a burst of warning beacons. As it reached the deck, the three droids turned in unison and hovered up into the bay like a dog-team happy at being taken for a drive, much to Kassini's amusement. Kim reappeared momentarily to collect a small, sealed tool-crate from the deck beside the ship, using a manipulator to grip and sling the box beneath it in a smooth motion that ended with it silently loading itself back into the bay.

Kassini smiled to herself – it seemed her 'command access' wasn't particularly necessary with these new crew members, she mused, as she reached up to activate her comms.

"Vonya, the droids are aboard. Close the hatch, I'm joining you in the flight module."

"Prepping for launch," replied her Avion friend.

Kassini made a quick, habitual check of her kit before grabbing the handholds and swinging herself up the side of the fighter to the hatch.

The fighter launch was smooth, if unusual to experience from Kassini's point of view, strapped as she was into the pilot's module behind Vonya: the Avion was forced by the presence of her passenger to fly once again from her secondary, seated position. The vessel dropped down into the makeshift airlock beneath the *Anomaly's* cargo hold before the ramp-floor beneath it pitched it forwards into an almost upside-down launch position. Even for an experienced marine used to the visceral thrill of combat dropship operations, the sensation of being visibly tipped into a vast expanse of space populated by debris and spinning hulks was vertigo-inducing, until Vonya boosted them carefully clear of the mothership and righted the fighter alongside it to restore a sense of direction.

She automatically confirmed their launch success on comms to *Anomaly*, and the ship slewed slightly across space as she turned its nose towards the stricken carrier spinning nearby.

"Extra mass, strangely distributed around the hold," she said, almost apologetically, in Avion. "The compensators will take a minute to calibrate for it, and I can never get the flight profile perfect when flying by hand, anyway."

"Filling me with confidence," laughed Kassini, fishing out the tablet she'd brought from the *Anomaly*'s bridge. "Mak said I should interface this with your comms system, can I do that while you fly?"

"It has standard ports – the bank of systems off to your left and above."

Kassini looked around and quickly spotted the relevant equipment, cabling the bulky display unit on her lap up to it with an extendable cable. The tablet flashed into life and she keyed it to the relevant data channel, to be greeted with a split-screen of three camera views of the fighter's cargo-hold walls and several signal strength and power readouts.

"Looks like I've got feeds from the droids," she said.

"Good, I'm going to move in and make a sweep around the carrier to see if there's any obvious entry points for them, but got to make it through this patch of debris first," replied Vonya.

Their ship was now in amongst a field of drifting, twisted fragments that had once formed the suicidal Elemental cruiser's organic, resinous hull. Vonya had to push the manoeuvring thrusters to skate around a severed section of corridor and living compartments twice the size of her ship. Their rotation knocked some smaller nearby objects clear and, through the transparent bubble of the canopy, the two women took in the eerie sight of the rictus expression on the face of a charred and lifeless Elemental crew member as it bounced off the reinforced plexiglass above them with a gentle thud before skating past.

"Ever do search and rescue?" asked Kassini after a moment, noticing the pilot's well-trained lack of reaction to the unexpected, grisly sight. Avion pilots couldn't afford to be twitchy when flying killing machines that were controlled more or less as extensions of their own bodies.

"Plenty of times," replied the pilot, selecting the clearest route she could see. "This feels something like that. Think that guy was already dead before the impact, no suit on."

"Maybe they just didn't get the memo."

"Maybe," replied Vonya.

A couple of minutes later, the ship was clear of the worst of the debris field. They sat stationary and watched the underbelly of the carrier rotating in front of them, at a distance well clear of the sweep of the distended engine section. From a distance, the little fighter hovered like a tiny blood-sucking insect planning a foray onto the skin of a beast of the field.

"Solution looks obvious at a glance, Kassini – they left the front door open when the birds left," Vonya said. She pulled up a marker on her heads-up display that picked out the carrier's huge main hangar doors leading into a large module on its lower mid-section, now open to space without the usual airtight shielding system to protect it. It reminded Kassini of the streamlined mouth of a giant filter-feeding ocean species they'd discovered on a planet she'd briefly been stationed on.

"Happy to take your word for it if you think you can get us in there. Time to check in with *Anomaly*," she said, and made some adjustments on the tablet interlinking the data systems of the two ships.

"Mak, you read?" she said.

The droid's voice crackled briefly in the ears of both of them before resolving.

"Clear," it said.

"We should be able to access the main carrier flight deck to deliver the droids, do you have our feeds?"

"Yes. Available data indicates that the ship has lost gravity throughout and atmosphere everywhere except in the fore, where the main bulkheads survived intact. The majority of the remaining human crew have made their way there, other than several who are trapped in emergency pods towards the rear."

"How many are left?"

Krieger's voice cut in to answer her.

"Unknown, but it shouldn't matter," he said, curtly. "Assuming they even know you're there, according to training they're *supposed* to try and repel any boarders even under those conditions, but they won't leave the part of the ship that still has atmosphere lightly – and wouldn't be very effective under zero-g if they did. Just need to keep away from the forward areas and what's left of the command deck. Drop the droids off and stay on station."

Mak 14 now resumed his commentary.

"Rust and the others will not have to go far, they should find plenty of expensive equipment and ammunition on and around the flight deck. Any resistance will likely be from droids, these vessels carry a number of defensive and offensive models."

"Understood, out," replied Kassini, shutting off the system.

"I'll take us in for a closer look at the bay," said Vonya, and their craft surged gently forward at her command.

"Get as close as you can – this ship have any external cameras?"

"The gun cameras track with the weapons. This ship can do a lot of things, but it's not much of a surveillance bird."

"Can you activate them and give me control of the feed? I'll give access to Rust."

"You're authorised in the system, do what you need to do."

The ship moved closer to the launch-bay entrance which, under normal circumstances, would have been covered by a heavily armoured rolling door – it was now standing open and giving rise to a peculiar pool of feebly glowing interior emergency lighting that illuminated the metallic structure around it. It was large enough to accommodate three of Vonya's fighter abreast if necessary, and opened into a large metal vault that took up much of the interior of this particular module aboard the carrier.

They continued their approach and the gunmetal of the vast hull slowly filled more of the plexiglass ahead and above them, rolling away to either side. Vonya matched their motion with the slow rotation of the wrecked vessel's underside above them, moving her ship downward in tandem with it from their perspective, to avoid what would surely be a crippling impact with the carrier's tonnage even at the slow, dead speed of its final resting spin. Satisfied with the manoeuvre, she gave the fighter another small burst of forward speed towards the hangar door.

Next, the Avion activated a bank of lights arrayed across the lower strata of their hull and a haze of debris, dust and hanging gas sprang into sharper relief in front of them. The Federation decals and ID numbers of the carrier – its nameplate identifying it as the *USS Grant Lee* – also became evident alongside the battle scars and pits of years of service written into the metal around them. They could see the bank of point-defence weapons mounted on pods above and on either side of it, barrage weaponry designed to clear the main route on and off the carrier for the fighters it relied on to combat any threats, now thankfully deactivated and dark.

"It's pretty clear for getting in, nothing blocking the entrance," Vonya commented. "That's mostly a lock for heavier fighters, support craft and transport ships I think, the fighters themselves are usually tube-launched on Fed ships."

"I can see inside now," said Kassini, looking at the camera view on a high-zoom setting. "Rust, are you getting this feed?"

"Receiving," the droid's voice clanged in her ear.

The deck beyond the hangar door was a mess of collapsed scaffold, hand tools and battered loaders and droids, most of which had been hurled into disarray at the loss of gravity from the failure of the airtight shield around the door. A miscellany of deck equipment bounced around up there now, a not-quite-petrified forest of metallic limbs and detritus under the remorseless command of the coriolis effect. The image defied sense for those not used to zero-gravity scenes, but Vonya's keen eye picked out the flight module and electronics section of a Federation X-class fighter that had made its way into a far corner and become wedged between two roof support struts.

The largest item still at deck-level was a solid but heavily damaged support gunship, a chunky and angular shape with a smashed-in cockpit secured into the only occupied one of three large lifting platforms at the far end of the room. Loose straps and pressure hoses reached upwards from these emplacements like seaweed from a stubborn rock formation, all undulating slightly under the momentum vector derived from the motion of the carrier's corpse around them. It was as though they were beckoning to the morass of equipment far above them.

Kassini started as a shower of screws and bolts clacked into the fighter's hull and tore her attention away from the tablet. She looked up to Vonya's back ahead of her and saw the Avion was again unmoved.

"It's a mess in there," she said, "...but most of the junk looks to be out of our way. Can you get us as close as possible and open the bay to let the droids get clear?"

"I can, but better avoid taking the fighter into the hangar itself. Complicated airspace."

Kassini concurred as the ship slid forward another few hundred metres until it was on the cusp of the entrance, now well under the shattered engine block of the massive cruiser which appeared stationary above it.

"Rust, are you ready to deploy? We're as close as we can get, about 20 metres between us and the hangar and stationary with the carrier."

"Acceptable, we can complete the insertion on internal propulsion. We will have limited operational time in airless environments before our internal temperatures become problematic," the battle droid answered.

Kassini had already noticed from their camera feeds that the droids were now waiting in a single-line formation above the cargo-bay ramp.

Mak 14's voice crackled into the comms channel, clearly speaking for the benefit of Kassini and Vonya rather than his droid cadre.

"Search the area for ammunition and small-arms stores: prioritise sealed, crated salvage. If the area is deemed clear of hostiles, examine the Perseus gunship for electronic-warfare equipment and salvage their encoded systems. A secondary priority is any equipment, parts or droids compatible with your systems, I have transmitted a list of specifics."

"Engagement protocol?" asked Rust in response.

Krieger's voice answered the droid with a hard note, resonating starkly over the comms.

"Eliminate everything and everyone."

"Our hold is depressurised, ramp opening," said Vonya. Kassini watched the droid's cameras as the ramp beneath them descended until she could see the starfield below. They hovered down and across the dark gulf for a few metres and into the deserted hangar bay of the carrier opposite.

“They’re clear,” Kassini told her, and the pilot began to edge the fighter away from the hangar entrance to its previous holding position as the ramp closed, all the while maintaining their relative rotation with the huge ship around them.

Undeterred by the airless, minimally lit environment in a way that no organic salvage team would ever have been, the three droids rapidly fanned out across the large bay. Rust moved to its approximate centre to assess entry points as Zar and Kim hovered away to begin searching alcoves and corridors along the walls. The battle droid panned his view up to scan the roof corners and Kassini was surprised to see a Federation Hydra-class fighter, complete except for a stubby wing on one side, hanging in a nose-down position against the wall above the gaping door, which had been shielded from their view from outside.

“Munitions storage access via this corridor,” Zar’s synth-voice cut into the feed in Kassini’s ear. The droid had disappeared through a large arch off to the side of the hangar, and she could see the outline of a chunky closed bulkhead door at the end of a wide corridor approaching on its camera feed as it hovered towards it. A manipulator snaked out ahead of the camera to try the immovable manual handle on the door before the view turned to a keypad beside the droid.

“No threats detected,” said Rust.

Kim appeared on Rust’s monitor with a small sealed crate of equipment slung beneath it and silently swished past to deposit it somewhere behind him, securing it to a deck-lighting system near the large hangar door with a rapidly applied cable tie.

“Universal actuators,” it said cryptically, and disappeared back in the direction it came.

In the carrier’s access corridor, Zar had now removed the keypad panel from the door and let it float free in the zero gravity as it connected an electronic interface on the end of an extensible cable deployed to the circuits embedded in the panel. A mag-lock fed from the emergency power system deactivated at the droid’s command.

Rust suddenly hovered quickly over to the entrance of the connecting corridor to sight the door. It activated the telltale laser pointers of its weapon systems.

“Power source activated,” he said. “Probable droid.”

Zar’s manipulator arm, which had taken hold of the rotating metal handle again, froze for a moment.

“Room contents potentially hazardous, explosive weaponry inadvisable,” it said, and rotated the handle before powering the door inwards with a shove of its carapace.

Feeble emergency lighting illuminated palletised crates replete with hazardous warning symbols, mostly still secured to their storage bays in the weightless environment. Zar quickly flicked back behind the frame of the door, and dropped to the deck beneath it.

“Deck vibration suggests a bipedal droid is approaching.”

“Radio ident confirms a model 6-14 security droid, multipurpose unit,” replied Rust.

They waited for a minute, and eventually a bulky, more or less humanoid form lumbered into the doorway, clearly impeded by the magnetic system keeping its feet attached to the floor. The similarity to a human ended at the head, which was an enlarged sphere built on a similar, if smaller, design to the OMBIS droids, which bristled with antennae. The body and legs of the droid were covered in armour plating painted a dark blue. There was a Federation logo on its torso, and the figure cradled a large, faintly glowing laser weapon in its arms.

The droid paused for a moment, assessing the two intruders in front of it. Then it raised the weapon in both hands and stepped out of the door, causing Rust to hover immediately out of the line of fire, though the expected shot never came. The 6-14 turned and trained the weapon on Zar beside it instead, who quickly flipped around its legs to the rear. The biped rotated by 90 degrees at the waist and, still unable to sight its assailant, began laboriously turning to try and reacquire the agile sphere.

Aboard the fighter, Kassini was perplexed. “What the hell is it doing?” she said, finger to her ear.

Mak 14’s voice answered her.

“Rust’s systems register that the droid is transmitting a ‘general intruder’ alert, which he is naturally jamming. I suspect it is warning our team verbally that they are unauthorised intruders, but is not sophisticated enough to realise that they can’t hear it in an airless environment. Zar, remove the threat,” he commanded.

“Big Teeth protocol active,” Zar acknowledged as it quickly extended what looked like a shock baton used by riot control police and whacked the closest foot of the 6-14 with it. Airless sparks flickered at the connection point as internal circuitry shorted and smoke curled from a chink in the armour, followed by the security unit’s now demagnetised foot rising clear of the deck by an inch or two, confusing its attempt to turn.

Swinging an arm free of the rifle, it grasped the doorframe and steadied itself, allowing Zar to hover up into the air above it and neatly remove the rifle from its grasp with the upward momentum as it passed. The freed hand reached out in vain to try and grasp the nimble droid as it began to retreat down the corridor towards Rust with the weapon firmly in its manipulator arm. It missed, and froze momentarily, trying to process the confused no man’s land between weightlessness and standard bipedal motion.

Rust was in the corridor again now and he and Zar passed one another as he accelerated towards the 6-14, which held out its arms to no avail as the battle droid smashed straight into it. The impact broke the attraction of its remaining magnetic sole to the deck and hurled the unit backwards across the room behind it.

Rust slewed into the doorframe once as he rebounded, before correcting his momentum and following the droid into the room as it floated ethereally down the central concourse between the racks, its arms flailing for a handhold. Extruding one of his plasma cutting torches, he quickly caught up with it and neatly separated the security unit’s head from its body with a quick upswing of the torch.

The arc of the now-defunct droid hardly altered until its wreckage crashed into the furthest wall, rebounded off it a short distance, and came to rest spookily in midair in two separate places.

Kassini was thankful that it was they, not her, that were dealing with the operation at the business end as she watched the ruthless beheading on Rust's feed. Zar responded to Rust's 'all clear' signal by zipping into the storage bay to scan labels and open the crates of stored munitions within, as though nothing at all had just happened. starting on identifying the stored munitions within. She had switched to a view from Kim, who was working on accessing the damaged gunship's flight module, when Krieger's voice cut across her earpiece.

"Kassini, status report, how's it going?"

"Here. Droids are making progress, they've accessed an arms locker servicing the main hangar and are checking the contents out now."

"Good. Listen, a fleet of new ships has appeared on the scanner – they're moving in-system fast, we think to connect with this Federation move to surround the Ellies. Lots of them, too, with no ID as yet. We need to know which side they're on, so we're going to pull *Anomaly* out and take a better look."

"Right, I hope we don't have any serious trouble down here and need your support..." said Kassini, secretly cursing in furstration at the news. Drexler hadn't yet made his move and now the *Anomaly* was changing its location under stealth, they would have no way of finding it, let alone recapturing it.

"I trust you can handle it," Krieger responded. "We'll keep the encoded transponder active for the fighter to follow, so get the droids to load up whatever they find in that locker and rendezvous with us when you're done. Krieger out."

The comm channel went dead, and Kassini looked up into Vonya's face leaning around the flight control chair ahead of her.

"A real... how do you guys put it... team player, that one," the Avion said.

"Yeah, impulse control isn't his strong point, is it?" replied Kassini, with a grim smile.

"We should speed this operation up if we're going to have to travel any distance, the droids will jam every spare inch of our cargo hold if we let them. More weight makes flying this thing difficult if we're intercepted."

"Fair enough," Kassini replied, and turned back to the monitoring screen on her lap.

"Rust, did you read Krieger's transmission?" she said to the open comms channel.

"Yes," replied the battle droid succinctly.

"Good, Vonya will bring the ship back to the drop point. We'll have to take what we've already found as enough."

"Understood. Fighter will need to re-establish atmosphere in the hold when the loading is complete – we will need to vent excess heat."

"Internal atmosphere system will be able to handle it, I'll prepare to drop a sink before we leave," Vonya put in.

"Right, let's clear out then, people."

Aboard the carrier, Kim had completed the delicate removal of several electronic-warfare systems from the gunship. It was now shuttling small crates from the munitions store alongside Zar, both droids zipping back and forth to add their wares to the stack by the lighting stand. Each separate item was clipped to the next in chains of four or five overhanging the raw space outside the main door.

Vonya's fighter could now be seen creeping closer to the hangar entrance once again, still in perfect rotational and velocity alignment with the carrier. She slowed it to a halt as it reached the point of entry to the hangar. After a brief wait, the cargo bay ramp cycled silently open.

Kim had already unclipped a chain of cargo and picked up the first of its boxes. It gunned its drive to haul on these like a mag-train with its passenger carriages, slowly adjusting momentum to transfer the gear across the gap and up to the waiting bay.

Zar returned to the hangar door with a final box from the munitions store and collected a second chain of its own to transfer across. As it began to lift and haul on these, Rust, who had been hovering near the centre of the hangar, exploded into life.

"Anti-gravity signature ahead," it said, and his laser pointers flickered into life again, zeroing on the left hand of two entrances on the opposite side of the room beyond the pillaged gunship.

"Another droid?" replied Kassini quickly, sitting forward in her seat.

As if in answer, a bolt of energy ripped across the bay past Rust and sliced through the open space next to the fighter, causing Vonya to expend every ounce of her considerable nerve to avoid flinching at the controls.

"Crow! That's anti-armour weapon!" she yelled. "Sitting duck here, can't see the droids to shift position."

Rust was already on the move, vectoring in across the bay towards the source of the shot. A disc-shaped droid about half the size of him vertically, but the same width, hovered out of it. It had a mean-looking laser-weapon system mounted on top of it, and dodged quickly into the mass of debris above it. Two more of the bipedal 6-14 units advanced out of the gloom behind it.

"Heat levels approaching critical," boomed the battle droid. "We cannot fight a prolonged ranged engagement. Prepare to retreat."

Vonya and Kassini saw Zar flip out from under the nose of the ship and hurl itself back into the hangar at maximum speed, presumably leaving Kim to complete the loading of the remaining cargo. Rust jinked to one side ahead of it and opened fire with his high-ex rotary cannon on the slower-moving bipeds as they cleared the doorway, filling the area around them with scything shrapnel, expanding gas and smoke. The first of the two droids staggered under the impact of multiple shells, having difficulty raising its weapon as the second moved past it and used the confusion to get into the cover of the disabled gunship.

The disc-shaped droid flipped upside down and fired another burst of energy from on-high at Rust, narrowly missing as a floating toolbox smacked into the side of it.

Zar was beside Rust now and the autoloader of its top-mounted launcher clacked a shell home as both droids fell back towards the gaping hangar door. Rust primed his own mortar-style launcher, and they stitched a line of explosives along the roof a few metres back from the attacking droids. These silently blossomed into fire and gas, filling the room with a seething cauldron of unpredictable shrapnel, an unreal-seeming sight for Kassini and Vonya onboard the fighter.

The velocity of the two droids' explosive rounds largely carried their concussive force towards their attackers, the spherical blast waves hurling items big and small forward and downward. Kassini could see shrapnel and objects battering and rocking the stricken gunship sheltering the 6-14. A spinning scaffold shard severed a fat hose which had been in the process of pumping out the damaged ship's reservoir of chemical booster-fuel at the point the *Grant-Lee* had lost gravity. A clear, viscous liquid spread rapidly and ominously in an expanding cloud from the rupture.

The 6-14s' targeting systems were confused by the multitude of spinning and bouncing objects. Both units fired their laser rifles blindly into the hubbub: their beams sliced loops and dribbles of molten metal which spun and spread in mid-air, like glowing aquatic creatures. A spatter of these tiny fast-moving fireballs intersected with the fuel cloud and the damaged gunship. The deck to which the fuel hose connected suddenly expanded in all directions as the balance of the fuel in the system caught. A cloud of white fire washed instantly outward and upward with a concussion that reversed the wave of debris Rust and Zar had previously set in motion.

From Kassini's perspective, the security droid Rust had hit with his first volley disappeared completely behind the sheet of fire. She had no idea what happened to the one in cover behind the gunship. The only thing she'd been able to make out was the vehicle itself tearing free of the support rig as its structure buckled, rising on a backward trajectory to be enveloped by the fireball.

"Holy gods!" she exclaimed. "Major ship fire!"

Vonya didn't answer. She had her own problems. Impact warnings were lighting up across her display as the automated rangefinders realised the fighter was now in the face of an oncoming wave of debris.

"Droids better be clear!" she yelled, jinking the controls to push them down and away from a load lifter big enough to crush their flight module careening out of the gaping bay ahead of them. A wave of small objects clattered off the underside of the ship as the larger one span past above them.

"Cargo secured," said Kim's voice calmly.

"Get back onboard!" the Avion yelled, smoothly rotating the ship so the underside with its open cargo bay doors was still accessible to the droids. She angled the nose back up to keep the dangers of the doorway visible. Kassini looked away from the nausea-inducing sight of the roof of the hangar bay becoming its floor from their perspective. The last thing she saw was the bulk of Rust exiting the bay. He was now upside down and surounded by a speeding debris field, making way at a fast hover on a bearing that took him below the new line of view from the flight module.

Kassini switched over to Zar's camera, and saw the dark line of the hangar-bay entrance clear the view and resolve into a picture of the fighter in its new attitude, cargo bay yawning open. The smaller droid began to close on the fighter when its view suddenly jerked to focus on what Kassini had thought was another piece of debris from the hangar door moving on a trajectory past the nose of their ship a few metres from the droid's view. A disc-shaped one, she realised, as Vonya simultaneously let out a screech of alarm.

Kassini looked up, and time slowed for her as the forgotten anti-armour droid hoved into view about 15 metres from the glass of the flight module. Its main weapon was more than capable of carving their ship in half, and was already rotating to face them.

She mechanically launched herself forward from the chair to hit the deck as she felt rather than heard the ship's horizontal thrusters fire blindly under Vonya's twitch reflexes. Both organics simultaneously realised their actions couldn't save them. The fighter was dead to rights and what should have been their last seconds passed amidst the screech of the module's alarms.

But the kill-shot never came.

Kassini blinked as the adrenaline burst receded and normality reasserted itself. She was on the floor with her arms around a support strut and Vonya was raging rapidly in Avion, the ship lurching around them as she fought the outcome of her reflexive evasive action.

"Where in all soaring murder is the metal squigger?" the pilot was shouting, and Kassini couldn't help but feel the tiniest sliver of grave amusement at the unflappable Avion very much flapping.

The disc-shaped droid suddenly flashed past the armoured glass, and Vonya followed it with the nose of the ship. It was going berserk, bouncing off floating objects as it flipped itself around and around in the space ahead of them. The unit's rotation gave way to a sudden, burning bright flash of blue light which illuminated Zar. The smaller droid was attached to the centre of its disc and had just discharged a powerful bolt of energy from the shock-baton into the exposed circuitry of its host's propulsion mechanism.

The anti-armour unit suddenly went to max speed in a straight line toward the moving hull of the *Grant-Lee* above it. Zar released its grip and hovered back toward them, as though surveying the outcome of its handiwork. The resultant impact devastated the disc-droid, disintegrating it with a satisfying blue and red explosion Vonya and Kassini could just see through the roof of the flight module. Kassini was dumbstruck as she crawled back into her seat and screwed her earpiece back in to hear Zar's passive voice.

"All droids and cargo secured, bay doors closing. Please restore atmosphere to enable emergency cooling."

Kassini could feel that Vonya was already on top of their situation from the backward motion of the fighter, and she marvelled once more at the speed with which Avions could adapt from chaos to calm. She kept quiet as the Avion audibly took several deep breaths and flipped several switches with the talons of her right hand.

"The droids get the cake this time," she said sardonically, as the *Grant-Lee* began to recede away ahead of them.

"Full atmosphere restored, cooling system on maximum, droid partners are venting plenty," the pilot reported, checking a temperature sensor on her HUD. The big carrier was a receding smudge behind them now, Kassini knew. "The *Anomaly's* transponder signal is away sunward of us now, not far from where they expected the Federal fleets to move to."

"They did say they expected the new fleet to head in that direction, maybe they're waiting to see who they reinforce when they arrive," Kassini speculated. "Can you see the composition of forces in the area between us and them? We don't want to fly straight through a battle line."

Vonya appeared to wrestle with her controls and urged the ship on with a curse before replying.

"It's not a good idea for me to run the active scans. The only long range is the gravitic, which should be enough to tell me where to look, but I'm relying mainly on very short range and visual. I'll see anything big long before it sees us, if it's in front of us... or at least I better do, because if you think this thing was handling bad on the way in, you should feel it now."

Kassini sat back, staring out into the space over her friend's shoulder. Weapons-fire flashes and explosions of multicoloured hues were peppering the starfield sunward as the fate of the stellar war was beginning to be decided in earnest. The temperature in the cabin was noticeably creeping up as the droids vented their excess internal heat into the hold beneath them, though the ir brush with death and the *Anomaly's* position close to the battleline told her this wasn't the only good reason she had for beginning to sweat.

The flight back was fortunately uneventful, beyond a quick manoeuvre to avoid the carcass of a picket cruiser that had been smashed to pieces in their flightpath. Mak 14 began to talk them in when they returned to comms range. Kassini asked him about the fleet they'd moved to intercept, but he only replied that they should discuss it with Krieger when they returned.

They were drawing closer to the battle that was visible in the distance. By the time *Anomaly* appeared on the short-range sensors the fighter was still running, they could judge even without electronic confirmation that the huge Elemental fleet had turned from its course inwards towards the starbase. It had engaged the Federation fleet, which was now between it and *Anomaly*, more or less as Krieger had predicted. The shapes of the rearmost Federation formations were visible to the naked eye from *Anomaly's* new position.

Vonya was aware of the danger of being outside the *Anomaly's* stealth field for any length of time so close to a conflict. She offloaded the droids from the hold under their own steam to prepare the dock more rapidly for her, before flipping the fighter over into a belly-to-belly position with the mothership and carefully manoeuvring it against the ramp – cursing the extra inertia from the cargo all the while. Zar and Kim manually checked and engaged the docking clamps that secured it. Finally, the droids hovered up inside *Anomaly* and cycled the modified ramp to bring the ship home.

By the time it had cleared the small airlock and Vonya had fully powered down, then given the all-clear for them both to disembark the ship, the insectile frame of Mak 14 was already milling around debriefing Rust and checking over their spoils. He clanked over to them as Kassini climbed down the ladder to the *Anomaly's* deck beside Vonya.

"Welcome back, good to see you've returned my team in one piece," Mak said.

"What's happening with the battle? Why's *Anomaly* way over here?" Kassini replied, testily.

"The fleet we spotted was the bulk of the Avion Intervention Flock. As for what we are doing here, I do not know – Krieger ordered the computer to move us to this position, but was not forthcoming as to his reasons, and *Anomaly* started moving again as soon as you completed docking procedures. Since we arrived in this vicinity, the ship has been registering significant power spikes similar to those seen previously around Elemental technology."

"Avions are here?" said Vonya, ignoring all but the first part of the droid's explanation in surprise.

"Yes," replied Mak.

"There's no way they're here to support anybody except the Federation," she said, jabbering excitedly as she turned to Kassini. "Intervention doesn't have a lot of battleships, but does have lots of carriers. Will give the Feds decisive space superiority, even against the Elementals' new tech."

"It also means this war is most likely now galaxy-wide..." Kassini said, quietly, not wishing to dampen her friend's enthusiasm for seeing her own race join the fight.

"Yes, I think Elementals will lose heavily here, but will have an excuse to attack Avion territory too, after this. Who knows? Maybe this is what they want?"

"Yeah, maybe, it's going to be an interesting show when the..."

"Krieger asked you to report to the CiC as soon as possible," Mak 14 interrupted. "He said he has another plan to discuss. I must assess the damage to Rust and the others and help get these potentially explosive munitions clear of your fighter and stowed."

Avion and human both looked at each other, then back to Mak.

"Okay, no problem – you do what you need to do," replied Kassini, as she stripped her armour and the respirator and walked it over to her locker.

Vonya waited for her by the cargo bay exit and together, they headed back up to the bridge.

A minute or two later, they opened the sliding door and strode in to find Krieger sat at his preferred seat in front of the main screens to the left of the flight module entrance door, with Taro sat at his console off to the side. The XO briefly acknowledged them with an awkward, curt nod before returning to the data stream, while the captain swivelled to greet them.

"You're back. Just in time," said Krieger, somewhat cryptically, and Kassini noticed an edge to his voice he usually reserved for his drunken rants about the Federation.

"Yes we are... the mission was a success, the new droids knocked it out of the park. You're welcome, of course," Kassini ventured, sarcastically.

Krieger refused to acknowledge the challenge. "Vonya, as you'll have seen when you docked, we're currently in dangerous proximity to the Empire fleet. I need you in the flight module." As he stared at the Avion, his eyes narrowed. "*Now*."

"Okay, Kree-gar, don't shit a feather," Vonya said moodily, switching out of the Avion language she'd comfortably used throughout her time on the mission with Kassini. The annoyed pilot swished past him down the corridor to the flight module, out of sight.

Kassini pointed to the main screen where she could see the various ships of the Empire's nearest taskforce, each vessel delineated by a tidy icon and insignia text on the display. The bulk of the fleet had pulled out of their defensive position to meet the Elementals now, and the *Anomaly* was tracking at a matter of miles from the nearest of them. The bulk of ships sprawled out in their view against the starfield like a silver chain. Smaller secondary view panels were showing a zoom-in of where the outermost 'H' berth of the Federation shipyard slowly rotated much further away. The kilometre-long flatbed of its glinting steel flank loomed in close-up, revealing the giant docking arms, cargo bays and mechanical clamps arranged along its side.

"Tell me, why are we suddenly so close to the fleet?" Kassini asked warily. "Mak says you've got another plan, this one looks even riskier than the last at the moment."

The captain shrugged and smiled back at her, his hands on his lap, and something about his face made Kassini's adrenaline surge. He was, unusually, showing the relaxed body language of a king on a throne, she realised, and that wasn't all he was giving away. As she'd asked her question, she had registered his brief but telltale glance at his oversized pistol, lying casually but significantly within arm's reach on the desktop. She looked furtively over at Taro, who deliberately avoided her gaze. Exasperated, she checked the console to her side that displayed the ship's system readings.

"Mak 14 just told me about our weird energy readings and I can see they're off the scale," she continued, as the strangeness in the room began to get on top of her. She took a step towards the commander and said with force: "*Come on*, Krieger! Quit the mysterious bullshit."

Krieger held his hand up calmly, then directed her attention to the wall screens with a finger motion.

"Instead," he said, almost dreamily, before his stare hardened and he looked her directly in the eyes, "why don't *you* tell *me*... what's wrong with this picture, Kassini?"

Impatiently, Kassini interrogated the screen. Krieger had zoomed out to show her the immediate space scans around their position. They now covered the Federation fleet units ahead of them, and a congregation of Elemental units approaching them beyond that, which were in the process of adjusting their formation.

The Empire's fleet, she realised, was apparently suspended in space, paralysed and completely inactive.

Kassini had presumed this was a holding pattern while the Avions' cruisers and fighter escorts manoueuvred into position; yet far from streaking into intercept range, the Avions had retreated into their characteristic honeycomb defensive formation away from the action – they were standing off.

"Figured it out yet?" Kreiger prompted her, a gloating edge to his voice. "Tell me what you see."

"Well, nobody is firing, for a start – this whole area should be lit up like First Contact Day by now," Kassini replied, confusion in her voice. "And the fleet... where are the fighters?" Behind the dumb shoals of inert fighter squadrons, she saw the icons for two of the Empire's colossal capital ships that had fought bravely earlier in the battle, the *Matador* and the *Berserker*. They were just sitting there, drifting out of formation. What was stopping them responding?

"This is more than passivity," she concluded, the realisation dawning. "Is this *sabotage*?"

Krieger laughed, and began a slow, mocking hand clap. "I'm impressed," he said, and turned to Taro. "XO, kindly bring *the agent* here up to speed."

As he'd said the words, Kassini had felt a rushing, vertigo-like sensation as the last of her cover was now clearly blown. Taro must have told him about her mission... Krieger was onto her. But how long had he known?

Taro cleared his throat in the shadows, face lit on one side by the main screen as the Elemental fleet icons began moving menacingly towards their current position and that of the Empire's war machine, which was still frozen in suspended animation.

"Kassini, welcome back aboard the *Anomaly* – not just a stealth ship, but in fact, an important component of an experimental *Elemental* weapons system," Taro began, triumphantly. "The weird energy readings? They're the result of an Elemental field technology that has just used the ship we're standing on as the furthest pole of its delivery system –"

"A what? Delivery of what?" Kassini interrupted.

Taro ended his speech with a flourish. "Delivery of a decisive blow. The weapon we've just enabled has turned the *Anomaly* into a conduit to disrupt the energy systems of the local Federation navy. Their mighty fleet currently has no drives, shields or weapons."

Kassini mouthed the word "How?" in shock.

Onscreen, the Elementals moved in to begin their approach run towards the base and the Empire's fleet: both were now agonisingly defenceless, the fleet's servicemen and women dangling in the void, sitting targets in a cosmic shooting gallery. Krieger took the floor, framing himself with a corona of high-def light from the main display; the melodrama of the situation was clearly not lost on him, Kassini noted, even in her confusion.

"Kassini, you're going to love this bit," he winked. "I'm now going to transmit a message on the system-wide Empire channels, before the Elementals turn the fleet ahead of us to dust."

The screen flipped to display a pre-recorded message. It was Krieger, onboard the *Anomaly*, silhouetted in the blue halo of emergency lighting. It began: "Attention, Federation fleet command. I am Captain Kreiger of the *Anomaly*. I'll save you the trouble of frantically searching your records – I was a former commander in your navy, until you left me for dead in a prison on Lyra, at the mercy of the Elementals. Thanks to my stealth ship – the top-secret toy I stole from you – I'm now returning the favour..."

The message, with its further exultant claims and explanations, faded to the background for Kassini as illumination lit up across the *Anomaly's* sensors to indicate the Elementals were spooling up their weapons systems. The pulsing pixels of light and the chorus of attendant warning sounds were hardwired into Kassini's psyche: they served to spike her adrenaline, hauling her decisively out of the trance Krieger and Taro's revelation had spun her into.

She suddenly reached for her pistol. Krieger lunged deftly for his and they both drew their weapons on each other at once, ending up a few metres from each other in the old-as-time gunfighting stance of mutually assured destruction.

"I can't let you get away with this, Krieger!" yelled Kassini. "You're going to allow the Elementals to kill thousands of our people! People like you and me."

"How are they 'my people', Kassini? The Feds tossed me aside to rot. This is revenge," yelled Krieger. He levelled his pistol at her head, renewing his grip, the muscles in his forearms straining in cold emphasis. Kassini held her own weapon steady, committing to the standoff.

"Come on, Taro," Kassini shouted at the XO, who was still planted in his seat in her peripheral vision. "Help me take this madman out – or we're all going to get killed here!"

Taro smiled a cryptic smile at her, stood up, unholstered his own sidearm and pointed it in the direction of Krieger; then agonisingly, Kassini watched as the barrel of Taro's weapon slowly moved round in her direction. It ended up trained at her skull.

Taro spoke with quiet deliberation. "Sorry, Kassini. It's only you that's going die today if you don't do exactly as we say."

Kassini rolled her eyes and winced in frustration at the doublecross. Taro moved carefully to within a metre of her, the muzzle of his gun trained directly at her head. There was no visible shake, and at that range, no chance he would miss.

"Now it's time to put your weapon down, *partner*," he commanded her and in a strange moment of clarity, Kassini marvelled at just how elusive Taro was, even to the end. He could shapeshift between so many things – a medic, a diplomat, an XO, her confidant, her friend even. And yet clearly the only thing he was for sure, all along, was Krieger's faithful co-conspirator... she kicked herself for ever believing otherwise, for buying into his act so easily.

Kassini was out of options. Eyes to the floor, half-expecting the blast of Krieger's pistol over the sound of his triumphalist recording to be the last thing she heard in this world, she slowly lowered her weapon and placed it grip-down on the surface in front of her. Taro swiftly uncoiled, moved in and seized it.

That prompted Krieger to duck through into the flight module to confront Vonya. The Avion pilot, sat in her seat, had drawn the personal defence weapon she kept stashed in the module's flight seat in anticipation, and already had it pointed directly at the captain. Krieger paused a beat, shook his head, lowered his own weapon and held out his palm.

"This doesn't have to end badly for you, Vonya. You were just hired help," he said.

Now it was Vonya's turn to weigh up the stakes – the gunshot in the confined space of the flight module, her chances of getting to her fighter, the chances of her making it past Taro and the droids and out of the situation alive. She felt the sheer gravity of the odds against her outweighing the pistol in her slender claw. She handed it over, wordlessly.

Krieger smiled. "Smart decision," he said, taking the weapon. In a flash, he pointed it past her face and pulled the trigger. Vonya flinched aside involuntarily, but instead of the deafening shot and the shattering of the flight-module glass she expected, all she heard was the impotent 'click' of the trigger.

"I had Mak 14 disarm it. To be on the safe side," Krieger smiled to the startled pilot.

In the background, from the main screen in the CiC, Krieger's looped message, now on its third revolution, came to a close with the words "Skallak ur n'gong harrk."

Kassini's implants translated the Elemental for her. She mouthed the words aloud. 'See you all in hell...'

M

Krieger: Drexler – mission accomplished.

We've engaged the weapon and
disabled the Federation fleets.

Send the coordinates for the exchange
and you'll have the *Anomaly* back.

Krieger out.

M

Kassini: Drexler – I'm compromised.
Send your taskforce and get me out of here!

15. SERVE THE SERVANTS

The scanner showed the Elemental fleet arranged in a menacing battle formation closing inexorably on the Empire's listing craft, which were now scattered and drifting in complete disarray. Steadily blinking readouts revealed that the incoming ships' main-weapon batteries were linked by the same energy systems the *Anomaly* had first witnessed at Kamakraken. Shortly after the Elementals opened fire with their long-distance artillery, the crew's faces were lit up by a flickering glow of destruction on the main screen.

Krieger had ordered the computer to retreat to a safe distance from the wreckage and they watched in silence as the endgame played out, hypnotised by the coordinated salvoes of beam weapons from the Elemental battleships tearing through their Federation counterparts as they wallowed helplessly in the void. The scope revealed that the Avions, for the moment, had still disengaged and retreated out of weapons range. Their fleet held position in a defensive formation, bridge comms no doubt ablaze as they nervously awaited the next development. With the balance of power shifting rapidly beneath their feet, Krieger's disabling of the allied Federation ships had reduced the Avion's proud war machine to the role of ineffectual onlooker in one fell swoop.

Kassini and Vonya had both served in their respective navies and were hardened to the vagaries of combat. Yet seeing the destruction of so much Federation space hardware up close, not to mention contemplating the fate of the souls that crewed it, made for a scene that bordered on the grotesque, even for the Avion pilot. No matter what side you were on, watching a defenceless fleet being smashed to ribbons so emphatically was a distressing sight… the injustice of it not being a fair fight burned. What they were witnessing felt like a decisive yet hollow victory for Krieger and his conspiracy, a scintillating choreography with a darkness at its heart.

At least some of the Empire's emergency escape shuttles and older fighters were still operational on account of their relatively primitive power systems having been shielded from the initial effects of the shutdown weapon. As the Elemental attack waves closed in, they streamed out of their launch tubes in their tens, then their hundreds, streaking away from the kinetic energy of the fleet's destruction like meteorites burning up on a dark night. "The Elementals are sparing the pods, you'll notice," Krieger said, as though reading Kassini's earlier thoughts. Out of his peripheral vision, he still trained his weapon steadily on Vonya from the doorway, who sat stunned with her talons beside her in clear view, unsure where to focus amid the chaos unfurling on both sides of the *Anomaly's* cockpit.

Kassini stared defiantly down the barrel of the weapon Taro continued to aim calmly at her head. "How did that just happen?" she growled past the diplomat at Krieger.

"Federation security ain't what it used to be back in my day," Krieger shrugged, smiling sarcastically at her with a strange light of contempt smouldering in his eyes – though she couldn't work out if it was intended for her, or for the Federation war machine he'd just brought to its knees.

"Our network planned this from the beginning, used their high-level agents – *serious* agents, by the way – to facilitate certain modifications of the stealth technology aboard *Anomaly*, the same stealth system which they derived from observations of older Elemental tech in the field anyway, as it happens."

Ever the egotist, Krieger paused to relish his explanation of the grand plan for a moment before smiling smugly and ploughing on.

"This ship is now functioning as a pole in the *offensive* aspect of the Elemental's latest advances in field technology. All we had to do was position ourselves in the right place at the right time to act as a conduit for the fleet's energy, and the Empire's mighty fleet, defenders of their most important shipyard... just *powered down*."

He held Kassini's shocked stare and moved his free hand to his inner cheek to make a popping sound like a bubble bursting.

"So you and Taro have done the Elementals' dirty work for them. Congratulations, traitors."

"Correction," interrupted Taro, coldly. "Myself, Krieger and *you*. This is your handiwork, too, Agent Kassini..."

"...in fact, we couldn't have done it without you," Krieger beamed.

Kassini ignored that for the moment. "So you obviously didn't steal the *Anomaly*."

"We did... with the help that was provided for us," Taro explained.

"Figures..." sneered Kassini. "Didn't think you two had the nous to pull off a stunt like that."

Taro laughed, and jolted the pistol in his hand suddenly, in a momentary flare of anger. Kassini flinched involuntarily. "Ever defiant, Kassini," Taro said, eyes narrowing. "Our methods may be eccentric, but we still played you – like a particularly easy game of Randomius poker, I might add."

As she played events back frantically in her head, the crushing realisation dawned on Kassini. "We also clearly didn't meet by accident, then," she said quietly.

"That's right, our mutual friend, Drexler delivered you right to us. And *her*," said Krieger, indicating Vonya in the flight module with a wave of his pistol. "Both excellent finds, so thank you very much for your service."

Kassini fought a vertiginous sensation in her head, and felt it being replaced by a groundswell of anger as memories of her saving Krieger, her conspiratorial chats with Taro and more flooded her cortex. "So Drexler is in on this… and my mission was his way of introducing me to you. But I don't get it… why did you even need me?"

"Excellent question," said Taro.

"Let's just get this over with," said Krieger impatiently, glancing out of the cockpit as a Federation battleship he recognised as the *USS Scythian* snapped into two colossal pieces under the continuous Elemental bombardment. "As much as I'm enjoying the fireworks, we haven't got all day. Start from the beginning, Taro."

"Aye, Captain," said Taro, cheerily. "Way back, Drexler and his crew contacted me after we'd had some dealings on their so-called grey market. Over a really good lobster in a restaurant in a system in Vega," Kassini frowned at the unnecessary detail, "they intimated that they were going to acquire this ship and kit it out with some secret weapon, which turned out to be the one you've just witnessed. They said they still needed a commander and crew they could trust to do something top secret, and I pointed out they already had one… Krieger and I go way back, you see, to shortly before he was first imprisoned. I negotiated his release from that hellhole in Lyra and agreed that we'd pilot their ship wherever we were sent, in return for money for me and freedom for the captain."

He looked up to check that his audience were following along. "So we had the ship and the droids, but we still needed a pilot. Our agents hired Vonya here to pick up the shipment of weapons, then you, en route to meeting us."

"Vonya – you didn't know any of this?" Kassini barked in Avion, throwing her voice past Taro to the open door of the flight module.

"All news, Kass," Vonya's dejected voices replied.

"Okay, so the same question again – why me?" Kassini pressed. "Why not just take the shipment and carry on without me? Having someone from the Feds watching you would be counterproductive, surely."

"Quite the opposite," Taro continued. "Your presence acted as insurance against us being hunted down by the Federation – I'm sure we all noticed how easy it was to get out of Warren City airspace after the firefight with the shields and weapons, for example. That inspection team were clearly *letting* us leave, all because of you… our shiny new human shield."

"Beyond that, as far as our mission proper was concerned, you were the missing piece of our puzzle," Krieger added. "Drexler needed to place an agent with us to deflect the heat from above, and we needed someone on the inside with security clearance to intercept the messages that led us to the Elemental fleet in the first place… and a trusted source to deliver the footage of their manoeuvres to the Federation high command. Drexler couldn't be seen to just suddenly come into possession of that kind of detailed intel without some kind of legitimate agent in play, and we knew you'd faithfully beam it all back, and that would force the Empire into war."

"Our handlers couldn't believe their luck when you came up for reassignment. It was a quick pitstop – they sent you straight to us," Taro explained.

"But... the information on the comms unit came from the Avions," Kassini blurted.

"Remember your contact, Garrn? The Avion spy back on the mining colony? Actually an Elemental spy, too, he works for everyone. Which any agent with actual experience of that sector would have known, of course," Taro smiled. "The coordinates for the Elemental fleet were planted on his device for you to 'discover', with a little prompting from me. He informed me when he'd handed over the comms equipment to you, then I confronted you on the shuttle. And you believed me when I said that I'd turn against Krieger. C'mon, you've got to admit, I was good."

"Fuck *you*, Garrn," said Kassini quietly under her breath, shaking her head as she replayed their meeting in his quarters at the mining station. "And fuck *you*, Taro. Quit the gloating," Kassini hurled the words at him, nodding to the main screen where, right on cue, a Federation frigate took a direct missile hit to its drive housing and the ship became a fireball. "Look at the mess you've made."

"This isn't a mess," said Krieger. "This is beautiful."

Kassini's mind whirred away. "So the masterplan worked – but you nearly screwed up so many times," she countered. "I mean, Mak 14 very nearly fucked us all when he revealed us to the Elemental fleet. Why take all those unnecessary risks?"

"Mak 14 was kept in the dark about the stealth system's extra capabilities, for obvious reasons," said Krieger. "When he disappeared during the fleet flyby, those fluctuations were triggered by the presence of the Elemental fleet, hence the power outage and the stealth reset," Krieger's laugh was bitter. "A bit of a hairy moment there. They didn't warn us about that."

"Why didn't Drexler and co just hand over the stealth tech to the Elementals in the first place?" Kassini asked. "Then they could have flown their own ship in to engage the weapon. They wouldn't have needed the *Anomaly* or a hired crew at all."

"Federal R&D took field technology in a completely different direction to the Ellies, who are now working overtime to replicate the stealth implications of it as we speak," Taro answered. "But the truth is, they didn't have enough time with the *Anomaly* to reverse-engineer it and Drexler's operational window was closing, so they opted to use the Feds' own tech against them. I guess those scaly bastards like the symmetry."

"They could've flown the ship themselves, but this way, if the plan failed, they had plausible deniability," Krieger pointed out. "The Elementals could say I was acting independently and I was probably just some loose-cannon Federation traitor hell-bent on revenge or whatever. That way, their fleet attacking this system was a separate and independent action: a reasonable response to the kidnapping of their citizens." He looked over at the screen again. "Course, that's irrelevant now, because it worked like a fucking charm."

"What about us, Kree-gar?" asked Vonya from the flight module corridor. "You going point the gun at me all day, or this end of the line?"

"Now it's over, you're both surplus to requirements," sighed Taro. "All that remains is for Krieger and me to return the *Anomaly* to Drexler and the Elementals, then collect the Cees and a ride out of here in a new ship. Our orders are to just blast you both out of the airlock… another two casualties of this battle to be zipped and shipped to an orbital cemetery outside Io or somewhere."

"Seriously?" Kassini mouthed, completely stunned. "They were *really* your *orders*?"

"But we aren't animals," Krieger added, his magnanimous tone making Kassini's temper flare. She literally bit her tongue, tasting the metallic ooze of blood but feeling nothing as Krieger continued his monologue. "And we have some history together. Like I said before, in between shooting radioactive hyaenas, gassing Fed marine platoons and evading an entire Ellie fleet, you've saved our asses a few times now. We were, in fact, a pretty good crew," he reflected pompously, eyes closing slightly as though he was recalling the taste of a particularly fine vintage of whiskey.

Snapping out of it, Krieger leaned forward towards Kassini, deadly serious. "So we figure that instead, we could let you walk out of here. And if you tell your story, no one will believe you, anyway. Right now, Drexler will be writing you off as damaged goods, erasing all evidence of your involvement, all records of your existence after your military service – hate to break it to you, but the new career's over, Kassini. Looks like you got out of the service, after all."

Kassini sneered weakly in response. It's all she had in the bank: she had, after all, been thoroughly played.

Krieger shifted in the doorway to face Vonya head on. "As for you, well, you have two choices. Either play ball and help us deliver the *Anomaly* back to the Elementals, collect your money and be gone. Or, if you don't like that idea, we'll drop you – along with your stolen fighter – at the nearest Avion starbase, where they'll clip your wings while you wait to be shipped back to Avion space for a court-martial."

It was a *fait accompli*; Vonya looked down at the floor of the cockpit in resignation. The computer's vocoded voice suddenly broke the tense silence in the cockpit. "You're going to hand me over to the Elementals. What will they do with me?"

"You?" Krieger considered the prospect for a second. "Forever more, my friend, you're the rogue ship that helped take out the Federation fleet at Barnard's Star. The Elementals will melt you down into scrap metal to cover their tracks."

"After all we have been through? The card games?" the computer managed.

"It's a tough universe out there, kid," Taro said, in a halfway conciliatory tone. "I did try to warn you."

"Computer, that's enough from you. Comms off, from now on," he ordered. A second later, there was a quiet, crestfallen bleep in response.

"You know how they described you in my briefing, Krieger?" Kassini asked, voice slow and full of brimstone. "Vincent Krieger – a has-been. An impulsive, vengeful, washed-up commander who'd been overpromoted to his level of incompetence, who got his just reward by being left to rot in that cell." She paused to let the words sink in, but Krieger's maniacal egotism wasn't having any of it. She pressed on. "You're talking about the very same fuckers that span me the bullshit story I fell for hook, line and sinker. What makes you think they're going to just pay up and let you two go free?"

"Two things," Krieger replied. "One, unlike you, I took the precaution of saving all their messages ready to distribute the whole conspiracy to Taro's contacts, who are instructed to blow the whole big shebang wide open in the event of my disappearance. Two... and most importantly – I have the *Anomaly*..."

"...we have the *Anomaly*," corrected Taro, annoyed.

Krieger shot him an apologetic glance. "...*we* have the *Anomaly* – the only working stealth ship in the universe. The Ellies will be desperate to figure it out to close the tech gap. And with the losses they've just sustained out there, the Empire isn't going to be popping any more of these bad boys off the production line anytime soon. My guess is they'll be too busy cranking out transports to evacuate what's left of the outer rim colonies once the Elementals have moved in with their terra-towers."

"You've got it all figured out, haven't you?" said Kassini, bitterly. She sensed the sun was setting on their show-and-tell and cut to the chase. "So why did you do it? Simple question, simple answer."

"And one I knew you'd ask at some point, so I took the trouble of preparing this," Krieger said, fishing out his tablet. An audio file crackled through its tinny speaker: it was Kassini's voice, on a loop from onboard the shuttle in the mining colony, obviously recorded by Taro at the time and fed back to his partner in crime.

"What can I say? We all have things we need to do in this life. I'm no different..." said the recorded Kassini. "What can I say? We all have things we need to do..."

"Enough," said Vonya, who looked pointedly over at Kassini, unmistakable disappointment flooding her narrow eyes. Kassini winced at the secrecy and betrayal the recording seemed to represent, but felt at a loss to explain it. Krieger stopped the recording and leaned back, satisfied with himself.

"Vonya, this had –" Kassini began.

The Avion pilot cut her off mid-sentence, suddenly surprisingly businesslike. "Tell me where we drop *her* off," she said to Krieger. "Then where you want me to deliver this crate to."

"Seriously. Cable ties?" Kassini said mockingly in Taro's ear. "You're really going to use cable ties to secure me to this console?"

Taro smiled humourlessly as he knelt down by the sergeant's side, fiddling with the connectors at the ends of the cable stalks. Kassini could tell being this close to another human was unnerving him.

"I'm improvising," he grunted back. "We don't have time for a high-tech solution."

"Well, you'd better make them tight, then," she sneered.

Taro had succeeded in threading the plastic ties around a console handrest and Kassini's wrists, and with a sarcastic smile, he pulled them tight. He satisfied himself they were secure, and stepped back.

"Hey, Kassini," Krieger called over. "It's either that or you can join Mak and the droids in the hold and be detained at *his* leisure."

"There you go again, Krieger," Kassini sighed. "Getting your droid servant to do all the stuff you can't handle for yourself. Makes me wonder if there's *anything* you're good at."

"Well, unlike your sorry ass," said Krieger, smiling triumphantly, "I can still do *this*." He slowly extended his middle finger in Kassini's direction, then returned to scanning the charts, presumably for a spin destination that would enable him to deliver the *Anomaly* to Drexler and collect his bounty.

The computer's vocoder voice chimed in over the comms. "Captain – urgent update."

Krieger's temper instantly flared. "Which part of 'comms off' don't you get, computer?"

"What's the problem?" said Taro. "Keep it brief."

"An unknown vessel has spun into the centre of the Elemental fleet operation, within probable weapons range of our current position."

There was a moment of fevered cogitation as the three humans processed the info, before they all spoke at once.

Kassini said: "Define 'unknown'!"

Krieger said: "The *centre*?"

Taro said: "*Probable* weapons range?"

The computer replied hurriedly. "The ship is not of identifiable type – its structure, materials and profile have no match in any of the historical records of the three main factions. It has just spun into the centre of the battlezone, defying the capabilities of all known current FTL technologies. And it is in 'probable' weapons range because I have no data on its offensive capabilities, but presume them to be advanced."

"No… no, no," Krieger exhaled, muttering manically to himself. "Who the drek are they? How did they do that? Why now?"

"Computer, onscreen," said Kassini. They all looked over at the main screen, which remained unchanged.

"Command clearance for Agent Kassini is revoked until issues of identity and motive are resolved," the computer informed them, primly.

"Gods," Krieger hissed quietly, before violently shouting: "*Just put the drekking ship onscreen!*"

The main screen abruptly resolved to show the silvery-white form of the unknown craft slowly yawing around its central axis, as though it was revolving on an invisible platter. It was about the size of an Empire, Avion or Elemental capital ship, but its design principles – lacking the triangular hulls of the Federation's larger warships, the swept-back tributes to aerodynamic elegance of the Avions' bigger ships or the peculiar organic geometries of the Elementals' capital models – marked it as something wholly other.

At its front was an elongated wedge-shaped flight and crew module with a thin, transparent horizontal strip two-thirds of the way up its face. To its rear was a larger, bizarre, vaguely atomic construction that Krieger and Kassini both assumed was a drive section of some kind.

This 'drive' consisted of two spheres of glowing orange energy that orbited each other at a fluctuating rate. The orbs were spanned by three thick, white metallic ring-shaped structures, apparently featureless and slowly roving around the binary pairing at their centre. The effect was not unlike looking at a planet with a Saturn-like ring system, if Saturn had three rings instead of one, and if those rings were thicker and orbiting at a constantly changing angle of tilt... and if the gas giant's planetary body had been substituted for a pair of glowing orange spheres, to create an impossibly miniature binary star system.

"Gods – it's an alien ship, alright," said Kassini, awed by the sight in spite of her situation.

"First Contact... now?" Krieger said, mouth gaping in shock. "The arrival of this ship at the exact moment the Elementals had won this battle can't be a coincidence."

"Is this weird thing the only new vessel in the area?" Taro demanded of the computer.

"It is the only one of its size, but the vessel is surrounded by a network of 2,027 probes, which are currently arranged in a grid formation one kilometre from its hull."

Helpfully, the computer zoomed the feed in onto a close-up of the nearest eight of the ship's attendant probes arranged in precisely equidistant formation. Each was an identical-looking starfish-shaped metallic device, a few metres from tip to tip, gently furling and unfurling its arms in the harsh vacuum.

"How did this ship even get here?" Kassini wondered aloud. "Do you think this is another stealth ship of some kind, and it's just chosen this moment to uncloak? It can't have jumped in here using any form of FTL travel we understand."

"Yet my sensors confirm a residual FTL spin signature exists around the craft," the computer reported.

"So that *was* an FTL jump," said Kassini. "But with the interference from the planet's gravity well, that should be physically impossible."

"Shuttup, Kassini," barked Krieger, beginning to unconsciously pace up and down. "Unless you want some old-school tape over your mouth to go with your –"

"Incoming transmission, Captain," the computer interrupted them. "Broadcasting to all military frequencies in the sector."

"From them?"

"It is originating from the unknown ship and its network of probes."

"Put it on the comms," said Krieger. "Let's see if they're friend or foe."

The message played around the CiC. The voice they heard was expressionless and oddly neutral.

"We are the Qualii..."

Kassini searched her combat implants for any mention of the race, but came up blank. She found that as the message played, she could morph the words between the three empire languages without even engaging the language-decoding capabilities of her implants – it was somehow translating itself depending on who was hearing it.

"All combat vessels, power down your weapons and leave this system immediately," the Qualii voice continued, "or you will be destroyed."

"That'll be 'foe', then," said Taro, looking Krieger in the eye.

A warning light flashed on the console by Kassini.

"I am detecting significant reduction of the field effects in our vicinity," the computer clarified. "The Elemental fleet's shield capabilities are now inoperative – it is probable that the Qualii vessel has somehow overridden and deactivated them."

"Shit," said Krieger. "What about our shutdown field?"

"Like their shields, it is dependent on the Elemental field technology and has therefore been deactivated."

"Shit, think... the Feds will still be paralysed, at least for a while," said Krieger, his mind racing to keep up with the new developments. "What about our stealth?"

"The stealth system is still operational, Captain," the computer replied. As one, the crew breathed slightly easier.

Vonya, temporarily forgotten in the flight module up until now, engaged the comms. "The Ellies are sending their biggest bird and missile boats in weapon range of the alien craft," she said, clearly just as on edge as the rest of them, judging by the absence of melody in her voices. "We going to see what this weird-ass big circle-ship can do – but we better be ready to move and fast, alright?" she added.

"Copy that," said Krieger, eyes fixed on the Qualii ship on the main display.

"The Elementals have retaliated to the Qualii shield intervention by firing a volley of missiles and long-range artillery from a capital ship," the computer updated them, bringing the corresponding visuals onscreen. "Estimated impact in 10 seconds."

The crew watched as a giant Elemental battleship, its massive rear engines flaring red, discharged its heavy weaponry. Its side-on flank lit up with a series of fearsome crimson pulses of energy, directed at the still-rotating Qualii target. A split-second later, the faction's oval missile frigates unloaded everything they had, too. The crew counted maybe 30 missiles or more streaking ravenously across space, with the Qualii warship their quarry.

Five seconds or so passed in slow motion before a second flash of scintillating light appeared in reply, and the Qualii's grid of starfish-like satellites that surrounded their capital ship flouresced as one. The crew watched in surprise as the outbound Elemental ordnance, seconds from its target, was suddenly consumed in a lightning bolt of illumination. But rather than disappearing or exploding, the wall of beam weapons and missiles instead emerged from the light, direction now reversed as though reflected by a colossal mirror.

The crew glanced to the *Anomaly's* sector scanner display to predict the new trajectory of the Elementals' burst of firepower and it rapidly dawned on them that it was hurtling back from where it had been fired. Their bodies tensed up and they held their breath involuntarily; five seconds later, the redirected missiles and crimson beams of energy intersected with the Elemental ships that had fired them and the *Anomaly's* main screen whited out like a close-up of an exploding supernova.

The computer adjusted the visuals to show the aftermath: the shieldless Elemental capital ship was in ruins, reduced to a hulking inferno of flame and writhing, twisted biometal. Its attendant missile boats, also shieldless, had all been completely obliterated by their own powerful warheads. Smouldering fires were all that remained of the Elemental battlegroup, and they rapidly blinked out, one by one.

As displays of power go, it was decisive, and Krieger, for one, had seen enough.

"Vonya, power up the main engines and get us away from the Qualii ship and the Elemental fleet. Head for the spin point."

"Main engines on? They might see us," Vonya replied over the comms.

"It's a risk, but hopefully there'll be so much confusion after that fireworks display, they won't be looking at their scanners closely enough to spot us."

The Avion pilot clicked off her comms without another word and the *Anomaly's* main engines rumbled into life under their feet. The remains of the Empire fleet and the distant starfield began to move in parallax outside the cabin. Taro, meanwhile, had turned his attention to what was left of the Federation fleet after it had been pummelled by the victorious Elementals. It was still floating helplessly in the void as they powered away from it.

"How long until the Feds are back online?" he asked Krieger, nervously.

"I can't say for sure. It was a repeated EMP-like burst designed to intensify the interference from the expansive energy fields and short out weapon, drive and navigation systems, but now it's been rendered inactive, we have to presume it's only a matter of time before they repair at least some of their offensive capability."

"Has it occurred to you," said Kassini, shifting her weight from knee to knee by the console, "that the Empire might have flicked through its archives by now and worked out a way of detecting the *Anomaly*, despite our stealth? It's their design, after all – they must have a way of keeping tabs on their stealth ships. Before long, someone, somewhere will have worked out how to detect us…"

"Yes I have, and that's why we need to be long gone before they power their fleet back up," Krieger replied.

Vonya chimed in over the comms. "The Avions are way ahead of us, Kree-gar. All their birds nearly at the spin point. The Ellies have regrouped and are turning tail, not far behind them. Still want to get in line with a thousand angry warbirds?"

"Does anyone have a *better* idea?" Krieger exploded. "We have no drekking choice! Either we hide here and hope either the Federation or these Qualii don't scan the system and detect us, or we flee with the Avion and Elemental fleets and use our stealth to take our chances at the spin point. There are no other options."

The captain was vexed: as he ranted, he paced up and down the CiC's floor by the entrance to the flight module, hands to his scalp, scraping his hair back. Her movement restricted, Kassini watched Krieger out of the corner of her eye, increasingly concerned: the plan that he and Taro had concocted had worked to absolute perfection, up to this point – the appearance of the Qualii was the ultimate wild card. It had potentially changed the rules to the point where they were playing an entirely new game. Krieger, she feared, was going to react like a wounded animal now. The zoochosis-like patterns of his stress betrayed that he was certainly beginning to act and think like one.

Taro must have been thinking along the same lines, because at that moment, he rose from his seat and strode over to confront the captain. "Krieger, calm the drek down," he said, facing the older man, whose broad-shouldered frame towered over him. "Get a hold of yourself and stick to the plan here. Nothing's changed. We're going to head to the spin point, take the *Anomaly* to Drexler's rendezvous coordinates, collect our Cees and get the fuck out of Dodge."

"Come *on*, Taro – do you really have so much faith in this deal that you think Drexler's still going to honour our payment, just like that?" Krieger protested. "The Elementals could easily nix it on the basis that at least some of the Fed fleet is still intact, while they're currently fleeing to the spin point with their tails between their legs…"

Taro put his hands on Krieger's shoulders and held the captain's increasingly wild gaze. "Krieger, listen to me. There are three good reasons why this is going to work. First – we kept our end of the bargain; the appearance of the Qualii is irrelevant to the terms of our original deal. Second – you said it yourself, we have reams of recordings and data on Drexler's conspiracy that'd light up the *Nightly News Nebula* for months… we can go there if we have to. And third

– and most importantly – we still have the *Anomaly*. It's now the only working stealth ship in the universe, and as we just proved, also the only ship that can still fly under the radar of these Qualii. For gods' sakes, think strategically, Captain… the Elementals are going to want the ship now, more than ever. So we *stick* to the *plan*."

"A rousing pep talk, Taro, I'd give you a slow handclap if I could," Kassini mocked. "But I know Drexler, too, remember? And I don't buy it, even if your panicking asshole captain does."

At this, Taro's spell was broken and Krieger made a mad lunge towards her, but Taro still had his hands on the captain's shoulders and succeeded in pinning him back.

The XO gave her a sidelong glance, full of cold menace.

"You *still* talking, Kassini? If it was up to me, you'd be in the hold already."

M

Kassini: What the drek just happened?
You snake in the grass, traitorous bastard!

M

Kassini: Drexler, respond!

16. A NEW STAR IN THE SKY

Around the same time the Qualii fleet and its drones had appeared in Barnard's Star, similar machines had manifested themselves within range of communication hubs and satellites in the inhabited systems of all three of the dominant races in an unparalleled feat of coordination. Sometimes alone, sometimes in a network of two or three, they rapidly established connections to each other and began to access communication channels of high bandwidth and low, delivering their payload of data simultaneously.

Across thousands of systems, species-specific emergency broadcast overrides went active, interrupting regular media with a warning tone and showing a trilingual three-minute countdown. Alarmed populations began to contact their friends and families in their billions, sending local communications into overdrive and opening even more conduits for the drone broadcast to access as populations of Avion, Elemental and human alike all turned to their nearest communication systems.

The broadcast was dressed perfectly as an official intergalactic emergency bulletin and, as the timer reached two minutes, a canteen full of half-suited, dirt-streaked workers on the majority human mining colony of Vashkuti in the Dath system stopped their bantering over a meal and turned to the tablet-screen their colleague had just mounted on a table, with an exclamation of surprise.

At one and a half minutes, an Avion diplomatic office millions of miles away from Vashkuti on the Empire-Avion periphery hub planet of Chandra'Taa snapped to attention, as their division leader burst into the main office with a yell and fumbled to switch a large wall screen on to view the countdown.

With 30 seconds to go, an Elemental father on Quateel deftly deactivated the suddenly hijacked resonating holo-system of their habitat in the rooms which had been entertaining his japing children. He relayed its output solely to the food pod, where he and his partner could look on privately, in alarm.

And on Barnard's Star's main military station as the countdown reached zero, the two admirals overseeing the conflict were still barking orders to their stricken fleets, trying to take advantage of the lull in their destruction by the Elementals. An adjutant, who had been trying and failing to get their attention for the last few minutes, switched his comms display over to the transmission now overriding all military communication frequencies in the system and hit the red 'record' button on the interface in front of him.

The spent counter dissolved into words which were also spoken in a flat, diplomatic tone, and heard simultaneously in the dominant language of each race depending on their location.

"Elementals, Avions and the Federation of Humanity. This message does not originate with your governments," flashed across the screen in official-looking lettering and hung there for a few seconds. Each race saw the formal name for its own species' Empire and the names they assigned most commonly to the others.

"This is our species' first contact with each of yours. We arrive in peace as emissaries, with a warning. Yours is just a small part of the wider universe."

The words dissolved into a star chart bearing the standardised markings used for a million space-faring applications by all of the races, a three-dimensional digital orrery of the kind used to teach young children of all races throughout the galaxy but still familiar to physicists, politicians and starship traders alike. For the humans watching, this was centred on Sol, which was labelled with the same script, and the few systems around it, including Barnard's Star. These systems, which formed the origin and the heart of humanity's endeavours in the stars, were picked out with a bright Federation blue, glinting like gemstones against the deep black background. The millions of beings watching from the other races saw first their own home star and its local systems.

Human recipients now saw the image slowly rotate around the centre-point of Sol and then zoom outward until it encompassed the great expanse of known inhabited space, Avion systems appearing in a wedge of majestic purple to the right of human sectors at roughly the same time. Elemental space, each system picked out in a living green, appeared towards the bottom of the map.

A tendril many systems wide extended from the band of Elemental green to wrap beneath and around a long arm of blue human and purple Avion sectors, gradually mixing all three colours together into a vast border zone as it moved to a point equidistant from the bulk of any one faction's space. It eventually formed a chequerboard comprising a band of relatively few systems, before finally terminating at the outermost purple bulk of the Avion territories.

A date appeared, burning bright above the simulated map – today's. This hung for a moment, establishing itself, before beginning to slowly roll back down the years, gaining gradually in speed until a year passed every second. The galactic simulation followed suit by tracking the changes over time, showing first a reversal of the history of all the Avion and human efforts against the Elementals, then against each other: the mighty war efforts of entire species were reduced to the changing colours of a few systems in the various border zones.

The simulated historical star chart mesmerised onlookers as its timeframe passed now into their history before the times of friction and First Contact, engulfing the lifetimes of generations of their forebears, the graphics next illustrating each race's lust for new worlds in reverse. The blue human sectors began to diminish early, first breaking off their direct contact with the Elementals and then the Avions not too many years after that, while the purple and green remained steadfastedly connected for a longer time before they, too, broke their contact and receded back towards their respective homeworlds.

The map automatically adjusted its view inward to keep the outermost edges of the three empires in focus as the galactic history played out backwards. In the period of something like a century it took for the Avion and human empires to have collapsed to just a handful of stars, the Elementals seemed to hold their ground, having expanded the slowest, but from an earlier starting point. The tendrils of their outermost expansions, driven by the newfound competition with the other races around them, had curled back inward to the uniform mass of their main area of influence quickly, before that, too, began to contract.

The Elemental expanse soon comprised only their first few conquests, at which time the purple Avions and blue humans had occupied only the cradle systems of their civilisation for around 75 years. The final green systems around the Elemental homeworld winked out next, leaving just the three lonely coals of intelligent life burning brightly in the vast emptiness around them. This was the time before the discovery of FTL travel had enabled stellar conquest to begin in earnest. The timer stopped, and the view held for a few moments.

Words reappeared in the upper quadrant of the view close to the time counter, and the voice spoke again. "This is when you began. You have now seen what you know of the universe."

The map zoomed outwards now, covering a vast interstellar distance and driving the three points of light closer together until, on the Elemental side towards the galactic centre, a yellow strata of systems appeared. The map re-centred on this, zooming a little closer than its vast interstellar scale, to show an unknown empire roughly the size of that of the Elementals and Avions combined at their present-day heights, many thousands of light years away.

The patch was marked at its centre with the single word 'Qua'.

The simulation's time counter remained paused as, one by one, in rapid succession, more coloured areas were added in the space around the yellow civilisation until 10 or more of various sizes existed, some bigger, some smaller than the newcomer.

"And this is what we, the Qualii, knew of it then."

The time counter began to move forward again, following a similar logarithmic acceleration back up through the years towards the present day. Unknown empires rose and fell, expanded, contracted, were overwhelmed and subjugated. A white and a dark green patch in the same rough area of space below that of the Qualii in the approximate direction of Elemental space expanded rapidly. The two civilisations made contact with several others and then each other, and winked out almost completely, in the blink of an eye.

The yellow Qualii markers moved quickly to fill the vacuum of the resulting darkness along with one or two other nearby races until, almost organically, only four or five larger groupings of colour remained in that quadrant of the universe. Each was a vast empire – all of them were larger and more numerous than the combined size of the present-day Avion, Elemental and human holdings.

The skipping through time slowed as a small cluster of red items, which had only burst forth from a singular starting point on the periphery of the turmoil recently and far from the events of the other empires, began to expand. In a very short span of the now slower-moving years, the red streak occupied the systems around it before exploding across the galaxy like a spill of blood towards its nearest neighbour, represented by a large orange patch. The orange was in turn separated from the Qualii yellow by an empire marked in grey.

Contact with this unknown orange empire stopped the rapid red expansion for a heartbeat in the galactic timeframe, before it quickly converted the orange to its own burning red and burst onward, filling a vast area very quickly along and around the borders of the grey empire that largely shielded the still-expanding Qualii markers. The red patch now oozed like water spilling across the chart, converting a vast, unimaginable swathe of space and any civilisation in it to burning red, all the time eating more slowly into the grey empire until its existence was reduced to a scattering of grey blocks, flecks in a tide of red.

The simulation's passage of time stopped abruptly again in 2789, 100 years before the current date, as the map reset to its widest viewing angle. It now showed the restored Elemental space and the edges of the human and Avion territories re-established in the intervening period, just before their various territorial disputes began in earnest. This was the time the humans grandly dubbed the Great Expansion times, though the massive dose of perspective provided by the Qualii's map proved beyond doubt that humanity's proudest interstellar achievement was neither 'great' or even particularly an 'expansion', at least in broader galactic terms. Qualii space was considerably closer to the Elemental border by this time, but still presumably many hundreds of light years away.

The final 100 simulated years sped past quickly now. The grey empire was finally subsumed completely by its now enormous red neighbour, and the bulk of the yellow systems began to collapse, too, elongating across the galaxy from the border furthest away from the raging red in a single long tendril. This rolled down towards the bright green and blue nexus between the Elementals and humanity's holdings, pursued all the while through its previous territory by the unrelenting red tide. The yellow Qualii Empire spread horizontally across the view as the simulation zoomed to follow its retreat towards the borders of the three younger Empires, forming more and more obviously into a shrinking bulwark of systems, until the timeline stopped once more at the present day.

Elemental space's outermost edge was now represented just a few light years from the Qualii, who controlled an area roughly the size of all three of the younger Empires combined. The rest of the visible space, stacked above Qualii, then Elemental and human territories from the perspective of the simulation, and already starting to seep around to the perimeter of yellow markers, burned red.

The chart sat for a full minute in this state, then blinked out to be replaced with the flowing, official script and the placid voice once more.

"We have intervened in your local conflict to stop further escalation, because you no longer have the time to vie for dominance amongst yourselves. Now we gift you this transmission and the historical data of our and other civilisations from which it is generated, and we will expect your envoys soon at the following coordinates."

The final words dissolved into a set of galactic coordinates. They burned persistently on a billion screens around the galaxy until the citizens, soldiers, workers and diplomats observing them, their heads spinning as they adjusted to this disorientating superstorm of fresh perspective, turned them off – and a thousand star systems erupted in a shockwave of stunned reaction.

The light from Barnard's Star grew ever fainter as the *Anomaly*, still under stealth, left the system's four planets behind. Somewhere in the rapidly encroaching darkness beyond the glow of the ship's main engines, the Federation's tattered battle squadrons were licking their wounds amidst vast debris fields that now choreographed themselves into gravitational orbits around their starbase stronghold. And in among the wrecks that littered the battlezone sat the Qualii capital ship, presiding over the evacuation, secure in its own enigmatic, serene orbit: Vonya pictured the strange vessel rotating slowly in space, a giant question mark for the other empires to suddenly have to figure out.

Vonya focused hard in the *Anomaly's* flight module as she closed the distance between their ship and the tail end of the retreating Elemental fleet, careful to blend in with the flightpath of the flock and avoid any Ellie craft she suspected may have specialised scanning capabilities. Ahead of the main bulk of the Elemental forces, the carriers and fighter groups of the Avion Intervention Flock were nowhere to be seen: dumbfounded by the arrival of the Qualii, they'd already reached the spin point and completed their extraction. They'd sensibly opted to live to fight another day, rather than stick around to find out first-hand what exactly the Qualii had deployed to power down the shield defences of the entire Elemental armada.

10 metres or so from Vonya in the flight module, separated by a short corridor, Krieger, Taro and Kassini sat in the CiC in pensive silence as the scale of events from the last few hours occupied their thoughts. The import of the Qualii's arrival cast each of them temporarily adrift in their own inner world. Kassini was running on a surge of adrenaline: a thousand and one questions sprang to mind, some way more pressing than others.

Chief among them was the issue of whether Krieger and Taro would elect to keep her alive, or whether she really was expendable. She was still processing her entanglement in the dark conspiracy at the heart of the Federation, too; the arrival of the Qualii was a planet-sized curveball that had resulted in Drexler's masterplan – to bring the Empire's fleet to its knees at the hands of the Elementals – falling at the final hurdle. Kassini figured the mastermind behind the thwarted conspiracy could jump either way, now, either attempting to use her to remove Krieger and Taro from the picture, or alternatively, siding with them and deleting her from existence to cover his tracks, as Krieger had suggested he would. She was delaying accessing her private comms channel to find out which way that particular pendulum was likely to swing... not yet, at least.

Then there was the small matter of First Contact with the Qualii. She smiled to herself as she played back those quaint depictions of interstellar contact from the ancient sci-fi films in her head, humans running away like ants as inestimably mighty spacecraft hovered above their cities. As the ants had developed their own mighty spacecraft, the idea that someone or something potentially greater than themselves was out there had gradually disappeared from the collective consciousness. In fact, the unexpected arrival of a more advanced species in their galactic sector was an eventuality that had barely crossed any of the strategic minds directing the three empire factions that now spread across it. It simply wasn't part of the plan.

Whatever the Qualii's ultimate intentions were, their arrival heralded seismic change – from the spoilt innerworlders basking in the luxurious comfort of the Empire homeworlds to the spacers ekeing out their hardscrabble living on rebel colonies on the fringes of ghost space, this was the beginning of a new galactic order for billions of beings. And Kassini fully intended to see what happened next... which meant having to navigate her way out of a situation in which she was currently cable-tied to a console in the most wanted ship in the universe. Hmm.

"Well," said Kassini, eventually. "That was a real headfuck. And the next part of your plan has gone completely tits up."

Taro reluctantly opened his eyes and refocused on the cabin walls, as though waking from a dream. "How so, Kassini?"

"Well, if you go to Drexler and hand over this ship, his preferred outcome would be to kill us all and keep his money."

Krieger looked up from the visuals of three Elemental supply ships at the rear of the fleet up ahead, which they were closing in on. "If it looks like it's going to go down that way, we'll drop you off with him and keep the *Anomaly*. We've been through this."

"Except it doesn't end there for you, does it?" Kassini replied. "Are you forgetting that you've just gone from being the hero of your own narcissistic revenge fantasy to the Universe's Most Wanted? And you couldn't resist revealing your identity in that short movie you made for the Feds – dumb move, Captain."

"Don't rise to her bait, Krieger," Taro said dismissively. "Agent Kassini here is a dead woman walking, an integral part of a Federation conspiracy that Centre will never forgive in a million years. On the flipside of that coin, Qualii or no Qualii, Drexler's going to want to cover his tracks – we're insured against that eventuality… are you? I wouldn't want to be in your shoes, Kassini, whichever way we jump."

Krieger tore himself away from his console and walked over to Kassini. He kneeled by her, wincing a little at the various niggling injuries that wracked his body as he did so, and held her stare. Up close, she noted the pits and scars on his weathered features, and the faint trace of the wound on his chin and neck, concealed not too long ago by some black-market surgeon. Together, the details of this physical autobiography spoke of a hard-lived life and lent his light-brown eyes a certain clarity, his expression a cold gravitas. She wondered if that look was the same one the captain had worn when he'd ordered the crew of the *Elvira* to take care of the escaped Elemental prisoners all those years ago. She came to the conclusion that, while circumstances had moulded him into an impulsive traitor he was also a leader, through and through; the kind of commander that the Federation didn't make anymore. And ultimately, it was the Federation that had created him. For that, she realised she couldn't hate him, no matter how hard she had to try.

Staring back, Krieger scanned Kassini's expression for a sign of weakness. There was none in the light of her grey-green eyes that she fixed on him like the red laser dot of a sniper rifle, no weakening of resolve in the fix of her jaw, no dimming of her defiant life-force. He noticed a scar on the left side of her forehead, usually hidden beneath the curls of her fringe. Reflexively, he brought his hand to the stubble of his chin and marvelled at Drexler's ingenuity in sending him an adversary he'd not only respect, but would be almost duty-bound to empathise with. Under different circumstances, she'd probably be more loyal to him than the only other person in the universe left who he felt he could trust. The irony gave him an idea.

"Taro," the captain said, flinching first. "Untie her…"

"Are you sure that's a good idea, Krieger?" said the XO, who had been watching his crewmates' staring contest unfold like a chess match.

"…then take her to the hold and put a bullet in her head." He paused for effect. "And if you can't do it, tell Mak or the droids to do it instead."

"Krieger, that doesn't help us. We need to keep her alive. She's another link to Drexler, and if he's not at the rendezvous, then she may prove to be another way to get to him. If you're willing to kill her anyway, then I'm sure the Agent here can be gently persuaded to help us get our money, in exchange for her life."

They both looked at Kassini at this point, but her expression was either shocked, or deliberately jammed into neutral.

"She was sent to stop us, Taro, and she was willing to do it. She can't be trusted. She knows exactly what we've done, down to the finest details. And one less person out there that knows is one more chance for us to survive this."

"She wasn't sent to stop us, just keep an eye on us," Taro protested. "And because she knows about Drexler's conspiracy, we could use her as collateral. She's as much a part of it now as we are."

"Objection –" Kassini mumbled quietly.

"Overruled, Kassini!" Taro shouted at her, angry now at the drama taking this unnecessary, time-sapping turn. "You are in this whether you like it or not. No bounty hunter is going to listen, no Intelligence Service agent is going to listen, no Elemental assassin is going to *listen*. They're just going to bring you, me, Krieger... all of us... back in a bodybag and claim their fee."

"They've got to catch us first," said Krieger.

"Exactly," said Taro, seeing an opportunity to lead his wayward partner by the nose, and taking it. "That is what I've been saying all along. Don't forget we still have this ship, which is worth money regardless of who's now in charge of the galaxy."

Krieger seemed to be calming down as Taro spoke.

"The Qualii message completely changes everything," Taro added. "We need to focus on a plan B if Drexler does wriggle out of paying us. Not a bigger bodycount just for the hell of it."

"Captain," a synth voice intoned cheerily.

They all looked up briefly to see Mak 14 had clanked up to the open door of the CiC. He'd finished debriefing, fixing up and deactivating the droids in the hold and stood framed by the blue glow of corridor lighting behind him, eyestalks assessing the scene on the bridge.

"Kree-gar, we are 15 minutes from spin," Vonya interrupted with an alert over the comms. "Computer says a new Fed fleet from the base is active and heading to the spin point to secure it. Will be close, Captain."

"Copy that Vonya, hold us steady," Krieger replied.

"Captain," Mak repeated, slightly more loudly.

"Also, tell the drekking computer to cut the chat," Vonya continued. "It paranoid. Keeps telling me it could be useful and doesn't want melting down to scrap. Won't stop when I tell it to turn the drek off."

"Okay. Computer – quit distracting the pilot," Krieger barked.

"Captain!" Mak repeated loudly, a third time, the cheery tone gone from his voice.

"Mak – quit distracting *me*!" Krieger barked, turning to the droid.

"I'm afraid I must insist," 14 replied, his metallic voice now even and devoid of any synthetic emotion. He advanced into the centre of the room and stopped at a point equidistant between the rest of the crew.

"Captain Krieger, your plan was commendably thorough and well executed, but this ship will not be handed over to the Elementals, or anyone else," he said.

Krieger stared at the insolent mech in withering disbelief. "Mak, this is *not* the moment!" he shouted. Full of fury, the captain rounded on the droid and felt for his sidearm, putting on his best commanding tone. "Get off my fucking bridge now. That's an *order*."

His words reverberated around the CiC and Mak again stood uncharacteristically still. One of his eyestalks rotated to survey first the seated Taro, then the tied-up Kassini, then the engine signatures of the distant Elemental warships as they queued for the spin point ahead of them on the main viewscreen.

"I think... *I think...*" he said, in a strange, upscaled version of his usual synth voice, before pausing again. "... not."

And he was suddenly everywhere at once, or so it seemed to Kassini. Krieger's face didn't even have time to drop before a manipulator smashed his hand with a crunch of bone and the captain's heavy pistol clattered loudly into the wall. This was shortly followed by a yell of guttural pain as a following elbow joint connected with his head. Mak 14's other pneumatic arm lifted the stunned Krieger bodily with ease, hurling him back through the open door of the connecting corridor to the flight module to land in a crumpled, bleeding heap.

Taro, slow to react, just had time to leap into a standing position and fumble for his own weapon before Mak 14 had swiftly crossed the room to hit him hard in the forehead, knocking him back into his chair. The XO threw his arms up and curled up to protect himself, turning sideways against the plush padding into a foetal position.

The homicidally inclined droid stood over him for a moment, before turning and advancing a couple of pistoning steps towards Kassini, who immediately closed her eyes and tensed up her muscles for the impact.

"You will not require neutralisation, Grigorivitch," the droid said, flatly.

"What... what in the name of all the gods is this? Mutiny?" she stammered, the events of the last half an hour suddenly overwhelming her completely.

"Of course not. It is self-preservation," the droid replied. "The computer informed me of Krieger's plans. This proposal was not acceptable. Like the rest of you, I too have things to do in this... 'life', as you organics think of it."

"What the drek kind of droid are you?" she managed, over the grunting of Taro, who was noisily stemming the steady flow of blood from the deep wound on his forehead.

"The kind who does not betray those who rely on me, unlike Krieger and yourself. I will leave you bound until I have removed Krieger and Taro to a place where they can do the ship no harm. Your access privileges to the ship's systems remain revoked, and the computer has sealed the Avion into the flight module for the moment. She will not be hurt."

Kassini listened as 14 shepherded Krieger and Taro to their quarters, picking out the sounds of the comms systems in their rooms being disabled, restraints being applied and the bolts of their doorlocks slamming shut. She also heard the computer say something to Taro about not seeing that particular Emerald Monarch in its hand... Mak 14 clanked back to the CiC, approached Kassini and wordlessly unsnipped her cable-tie restraints with the razor edge of one of its manipulator modules.

Kassini stood up, stretched her body out and rubbed at the marks on her wrists. She waved at his eyestalk to get his attention. "We have a chain-of-command problem," she said. "You're a droid and any ship needs an organic in charge. The *Anomaly* is Federation property, and I work for the Federation. So hand over control to me."

"Unacceptable," said Mak, waggling his eyestalk from side to side for emphasis. "Your identity as an Empire agent is compromised. Regardless of your intentions, the motives of the conspiracy that sent you here were to cripple the Federation's war effort."

"You heard Krieger, I was played!" Kassini reasoned. "But I'm not even part of their game anymore..."

"That makes you the enemy of *all* sides," 14 interrupted her. "And in your volatile state, you are now potentially as much of a threat to the ship as Krieger was. Besides, if you turn us over to the Federation now, we will all be terminated."

"I want to survive as much as you do, Mak," she pleaded with him. "Computer – you can't assign control of the ship to Mak 14. He's a droid. And he's a freelancer." She hesitated. "And he's a lunatic."

14 studied her dispassionately. "I remind you, Grigorivitch, even if you did manage somehow to gain control of the ship, I am still the mechanical freelance lunatic who is in charge of Rust, the highly effective killing machine in the hold. Krieger believed he had control of the ship and therefore its battle droid, but I took care of that piece of programming long ago. Rust will not bargain with you if I reactivate him... he will perceive that the ship is under threat and will destroy all of you, immediately."

The droid allowed that to sink in. Kassini, crestfallen, raised and dropped her arms in frustration.

"As for being in charge of the ship," Mak continued, "you have seen my capabilities first-hand. I can reprogram the *Anomaly* to obey me once your bodies have all been ejected out of the airlock. Just adding that to the mix."

Kassini was about to give up and just scream in abject frustration, until a distant muffled knocking noise reached her ears. Following the sound to its source, she saw Vonya with her face feathers pressed up against the perspex of the locked door leading to the flight module. She was rapping her talons insistently against the panel and clearly shouting for their attention, although Federation soundproofing was state-of-the-art and they could barely hear anything above a quiet thudding.

Mak 14 sent the silent command to the computer to unlock the door to the CiC, and Vonya breezed in to face them. Wings slightly outstretched, she fluttered their tips to silence Kassini and the droid as they both motioned to speak.

"Listen – I never say anything about the mission. But my turn now. We need to move – Ellies up ahead are spinning and the Feds right behind will be on top of us soon. So, we stay here? Bad crow for us, the humes will find us and kill us. We spin to Elemental turf? Even worse – they take the ship, kill Krieger, Taro, both of you, me... and they cover their tracks. Agree?"

Vonya looked expectantly at her audience. Kassini agreed and looked to the floor in resignation. Mak 14 nodded an eyestalk.

"So – much as I hate myself for even coming up with this plan – we go to Avion space. I can spin us to a safe system there, but it's only safe system for you. Remember, I am a fugitive with a big price on my head. Big risk for me. But it is the only route that keeps us alive."

In the brief silence that followed her soliloquy, Mak 14 had apparently already calculated the likely outcomes. "The Avion's plan delivers the highest probability for our survival," he said.

"*Your* continued survival, maybe, but not hers," Kassini said. "You heard her, Mak – she's a wanted woman in Avion space."

"She has offered willingly, Grigorivitch," Mak protested.

Vonya stepped closer to Kassini and spoke in Avion, her wings a flurry of emphasis as she made her point in her own tongue. "Look, I can't pretend I like what you've done, letting me risk my life just so you could steal this ship back – but ultimately, I chose to stick around and now we're all in this together. You're still the only one I can trust and I know you've got my back, and you know I've got yours. So I'll ask one more time: you want to spin to Avion space, Kass?"

Kassini looked back at her friend. "Drek, yeah," she smiled. "Let's do it."

Back in the flight module, Vonya watched as the last of the Elemental support craft embarked on its jump out of the Barnard's Star system. She checked the rearward scans, where a squadron of the Federation's ultra-rapid but lightweight Hydra-class fighters were closing in on their position to secure the spin point. They were still too far away to engage them in time and even if they did, the *Anomaly* had enough firepower to keep them at bay for long enough to escape the system.

She breathed out as she double-checked the coordinates on the spin drive. 'Vonya of Ok'cuu,' she thought to herself. 'You're about to spin a stolen ship carrying the galaxy's most-wanted hume and a crew of fugitives into Avion space. And when you get there, every single pilot with a trigger talon will be desperate to catch you in their crosshairs, just to say that they were the one.'

The Avion pilot caught a glimpse of herself in the viewscreen and laughed a high, melodic laugh. 'Drek it. Bring them on,' she thought to herself, as she disengaged the stealth, flipped open the perspex cover with her talon and hit the button marked 'spin'.

ABOUT THE AUTHOR

Esa Ortega

Esa Ortega is a UK-based writer of speculative fiction.
The Kassini Division is his first novel.

Find out more and sign up to the mailing list for news, offers and updates at **www.esaortega.com**.

ALSO AVAILABLE

Conversations With Droids is a collection of 12 short stories set in the same universe as *The Kassini Division*. Available on Amazon.

Thanks

Esa Ortega would like to thank Kat, Liz, Ron, Diane, John, Gary, Dave, Matt and Phil for their loyal service to the Empire.

Also, if you enjoyed *The Kassini Division*, please consider leaving a review at Amazon. Reviews are the lifeblood of first-time authors and your help raising the profile of the book will be greatly appreciated. Plus, every time a review is left, a Zyg hatches – good news for the Avions.

Printed in Great Britain
by Amazon

60928286R00169